I0563644

THE LAST CAMPOUT

THE LAST
CAMPOUT

⸺&⸺

A Story by: Ron McNaight
Edited by: Dillon Patrick McNaight

ISBN: 0692871195
ISBN 13: 9780692871195
Moonshine Publishing, Deer Park, WA

CHAPTER 1

—ꝏꝏ—

"YELLOW DOG, THIS IS SILENT Stalker. What's your position, over?"

"Yellow dog here, I've got the southern exposure in sight, the area is secure, over."

"Ten-four yellow dog, I'm moving in."

Private Ryan moves swiftly and silently into position. He spy's his target. Yellow dog is carefully watching the southern exposure, with ears perked and tail wagging as the target looks unsuspecting in the mirror, pulling the razor across his face and tapping the foamy substance into the basin below. The moment of truth has arrived. Private Ryan MUST succeed with his mission. The whole free world is counting on him! The southern exposure is within range. Ryan carefully twists his cotton weapon to a tight spiral and wets the end with his saliva. He slowly peeks around the corner of the bathroom door, and with every ounce of strength in his twelve-year-old body, he slings his weapon toward the unsuspecting boxers, and at just the precise moment, he snaps the makeshift whip. CRACK!

"OUCH!" yells John. "YOU LITTLE BRAT!"

"BULLSEYE!" yells Ryan as he runs for the living room laughing hysterically with yellow dog close behind him. John grabs the can of shaving lotion and chases after him.

"Come back here you little shit!" yells John as he races behind him through the house.

"Brett help, dad's trying to get me!" yells Ryan. But Brett can't be bothered. He's too busy primping with hopes of running into Cindy today, the girl down the street. John finally corners Ryan in the kitchen with the help of yellow dog holding a leg down by the cuff of his pants. He puts the shaving cream can inside Ryan's shorts and presses the button. Ryan lets out a blood-curdling scream. Now Brett just HAS to come and see what's happening. Brett and John laughingly give each other high fives as Ryan stands and looks at the mountain of shave cream in his shorts.

"Oh man, now I gotta take another shower!"

"No time," says John, "you can take a shower later at Grandma's, I have to get to work. And by the way, you left a welt on my butt you little brat. That hurt!"

Ryan laughs, "That was a good one, wasn't it?"

"Don't worry. Your day is coming. Now hurry and get cleaned up, we gotta get going."

The date is September 3rd, 1999, the Friday before Labor Day weekend. Another school year is about to start. John McDuffy is a single father, thirty-eight years old with two sons, Brett and Ryan, who are the light of his life. Brett is fourteen and Ryan is twelve. John is about six feet two inches tall, two hundred and twenty pounds and very solid. He has long raven hair pulled back in a ponytail and sky blue eyes. Brett has blond hair and green eyes like his mother and is very popular with the girls. Ryan has red hair and brown eyes, and is the most mischievous of the two.

After dropping the boys off at his moms so she can cook breakfast for them, John races to work. He's barely there five minutes, without even a cup of coffee in his hand yet, when he hears...

"John line one," across the intercom.

"This is John."

"John, this is Bill," shouts a voice from the other end of the line.

"Ya Bill," says John, "what can I do for ya?"

"Well, you start by telling me where the hell my water pump is!"

"It should be showing up today by UPS," explains John.

"Well, UPS just left and it ain't here!"

"Oh great," says John. "I'll have to make a phone call and find out where it's at, and I'll call ya back."

"How fucking long is THAT gonna take?" barks Bill.

"I don't know, but I'll call you just as soon as I find out something."

"You know, this piece of shit skidder you guys sold me has been nothing but a pain in my side. I'm about ready to drive it right up somebody's ass! But then again, I can't do that cause the fucker's always broke down. Now I'm gonna miss more work because YOU incompetent assholes can't seem to get me the parts I need! I can't function without my skidder!"

"I know Bill."

"If that pump doesn't show up today, you guy's better get me a loaner till I can get this one fixed!"

"I don't have a skidder I can loan you Bill."

"Then take a new one off the lot!"

"I can't do that Bill."

"Well, then you sure as hell better think of something, cause if I have to sit on my ass this weekend, somebody's gonna pay!"

"I know Bill, I'll find out what happened, and I'll call ya."

"Ok, goodbye!"

"Goodbye, Bill." John hangs up the phone and mutters under his breath… "Screw you, asshole!"

John McDuffy is the parts manager for R&R Equipment Inc., a large farm equipment supplier in Great Falls, Montana. Great Falls is a busy farm and ranch community located smack dab in the middle of Montana. John has been doing this now for about 15 years, and he's not bad at his job. Nothing irritates him more than when somebody drops the ball on one of his orders. He can understand why Bill is pissed, but he still hates the asshole. Bill is a logger from Ovando, a little town about 100 miles west of Great Falls. He bought a used skidder from R&R last year, and it's given him nothing but trouble. Of course, John and everyone else in the parts department knows that if Bill weren't so hard on his equipment, it wouldn't break down so much. John would love to tell him that but then…the customer is always right.

"John, line one! And three is still holding!" bellows Sue, the receptionist.

"Sue?" says John. "How am I supposed to answer two calls at once?"

"Ya got two ears, don't ya?!"

"Hilarious! Could you take a message on one please?"

"I don't have time to take messages for you guys too! Besides, he said he wants to hold." Sue is an irritable old bitty who answers the phone and does secretarial duties for the equipment sales department. She doesn't think she should have to answer phones for the parts department too, but out of town customers will use the toll-free equipment line to call the parts department. She thinks she has too much to do already…poor baby. John picks up line three…

"This is John."

"This is Bill!"

"Hi Bill, I haven't had a chance to track down the pump yet."

"Never mind, it just showed up!"

"Great!" says John.

"It's the wrong fucking one!"

"What!?"

"You heard me! This one looks like it's for a D9!"

"Oh no!"

"Oh yes! Now I can't work this weekend! You assholes are gonna get billed for my lost time!"

John thinks to himself, 'It's Labor Day weekend, why doesn't the cranky old bastard spend the time with his family.'

"I'll get to the bottom of it Bill, and I'll get you the right pump! You have my word on it!"

"Now THAT'S comforting!" Bill smirks.

"I'll find the right one and get it to you Saturday delivery. If I can't, I'll call you back. Otherwise, you'll see it tomorrow!"

"I better!"

"Goodbye, Bill." CLICK. Bill hangs up without saying goodbye. John notices line one is still holding.

"This is John."

"John, this is Roger at Caterpillar."

"Yes, Roger."

"I think we shipped your customer the wrong pump yesterday."

"No shit! I just got off the phone with him, and my ear is still ringing."

"I'm sorry John. We had a mix-up in the shipping department, and your customer got a pump for a D9."

"I know!"

"We'll get the right one shipped out today for Saturday delivery."

"Thanks Roger, have a good holiday."

"You too John, goodbye."

'Whew!' John thinks to himself...'That's over.' Normally it's pretty dead the day before a holiday weekend so John let his two counter salesmen have the day off so they could spend a four-day weekend with their families. But today it's been busier than hell for some reason. John can't wait for the day to be over because he and his two boys are going camping for three days. They all love to camp, and John just bought new mountain bikes for them. He got one for himself last year, and rides it a lot. The boys had outgrown their old bikes, so he splurged and bought them new ones last night. They can't wait to get up to the mountains and ride them. John had decided to drive up to Granite Butte, a beautiful area southeast of Lincoln, Mt., and camp there for three days. From there, they can ride their bikes on the Continental Divide trail between Granite Butte and Stemple Pass.

He's heard that it is breath-taking up there, so he wants to see for himself.

"John, line one," bellows Sue, "I think it's your ex."

'Great!' John thinks. 'That's all I need.'

"This is John."

"Hi," says Laura, his ex-wife.

"Hi," replies John, "what's happenin?"

"Oh, I was just wondering if you got all the boy's school supplies bought yet?"

"Yup, did that Wednesday."

"How about school clothes?"

"No, I ran out of money. Besides, they said they didn't need any."

"Of course they're gonna say that," barks Laura, "they wanted to make sure they got their new bikes! I would think you would be wise to their schemes by now!"

"So, they do need clothes?" John asks in very innocent tone.

"Duh!" screams Laura. John is holding the phone away from his ear now. "I think you need to take those bikes back and buy some school clothes! I sure as hell can't afford them!"

John thinks to himself… 'She and her husband have two paychecks coming in, not to mention the $800.00/month he pays her for child support, and they can't afford school clothes, but he can? What a crock.' John and Laura usually get along pretty well, that is until it comes to money. That is the one thing they always seem to argue about. It's what caused their divorce, and it's the wedge driven between them now.

"Tell you what," says John, trying to hold back his temper, "after they start school and see what the kids are wearing, we'll go shopping, ok?"

"Ok," agrees Laura.

"I don't want to take the bikes back cause trail riding is something we really enjoy."

"I know," says Laura, now in a calmer voice. "Where are you guy's going this weekend?"

"Over by Lincoln."

"Ted's stomping grounds?"

"Ya," chuckles John, "maybe we'll come across a booby-trap."

"You guys be careful!" snaps Laura. "There could still be some stuff lying around!"

"We won't be anywhere close to where he lived," explains John, referring of course to the Unabomber, Ted Kaczynski, "so don't worry."

"Ok, well be careful anyways, and bring the boy's back early Monday so they can take their showers and get a good night's sleep."

"I will," assures John. "Bye."

"John, would you come into my office when you got a chance?" bellows Ed Johnson, the office manager, and John's boss.

"Ok, Ed."

John wonders what HE could want. Ed is a stuffy old guy. John doesn't particularly like him, but he does respect him. He's been running R&R Equipment for about 20 years now, and he has managed to turn it from a one room sales office to multi-million-dollar business spreading out over two acres of ground on the outskirts of Great Falls. People come from all over Montana and Canada to buy equipment and parts.

"You wanted to see me, Ed?" John asks as he lightly taps on Ed's door.

"Yes sir, have a seat." Ed is always so formal. "John... is everything ok?" asks Ed.

"What do you mean?"

"Well, for one thing, your sales are down considerably this month compared to last year. Got any idea why?"

"People aren't buying as much?" replies John.

No shit!" smirks Ed. "But why aren't the people buying as much John?" responds Ed in a condescending tone.

"Because they don't have any money?" John can see that Ed is starting to lose his patients. "No, seriously Ed, I think that people are just being conservative because of the war in the Middle East.

"I've wondered the same thing myself."

"I think a lot of customers are just waiting to see what happens over there before they sink a lot of money into their broken equipment."

"Well, you could be right," agrees Ed. "Another thing is I've been getting a lot of complaints about the parts dept."

"Let me guess," says John. "Bill Perkins?"

He one," replies Ed.

"Well, Bill's biggest complaint is, and I quote...'that piece of shit skidder' you sold him."

"I didn't call you in here to talk about equipment sales John. Bill says you can't seem to get him the right parts."

"There's been a rash of miss-shipments lately," John says sheepishly. "What can I say, Ed, mistakes happen."

"I've also received some complaints from Sue." Ed and Sue are pretty close.

"What's her problem?!"

"She doesn't understand why you gave both your counter salesmen the day off, and frankly, I've been wondering the same thing myself. The day before a holiday weekend? What could you be thinking?"

"It's usually slow the day before a holiday weekend, and I knew they both had big plans with their family, so I told them I could handle it."

"Well, apparently, you can't. Sue is tired of taking messages for you."

"Well then get the parts department its own 1-800 line!" snaps John.

"How is that going to help when you can't answer it? I'm looking into that, but in the meantime, you need to tell your customers to stop using the 1-800 line for parts orders. That line is meant for equipment sales."

'That's an excellent idea,' John thinks. 'That outta really help part sales.'

"And another thing, before you decide to give two people the day off at the same time, you need to get my approval, understand?"

"Yes, sir."

"Parts! Lines three and four are holding! Parts line THREE AND FOUR!" bellows Sue.

"Well, duty calls," says John as he quickly jumps up from the hot seat and heads for the door before Ed can bitch about anything else.

'Sometimes I really hate my job,' John thinks, 'I can't wait till five o'clock!' Lines three and four were going to have to wait because there was a customer in the parts department, and customers at the counter come before ones on the phone. It was one of John's golden rules. Sue was screaming now over the intercom. John has visions of Sue walking around with a phone cord trailing from under her dress. Finally, his customer was taken care of, and he could answer line three.

"This is John."

"Hey, dad." It was Brett.

"Hey Bud, can I call ya back? I'm slammed here."

"Ok."

Time for line four. "This is John."

"John, this Roger at Caterpillar."

"Yes, Roger."

"Bad news."

"I don't want to hear it."

"Well, I'm sorry, but apparently, there isn't any Saturday delivery service available tomorrow because of the holiday. Tuesday is the best I can do."

"Great!" John sighs. "Oh well, he's gonna bitch no matter what I do. Just do the best you can Roger."

"Ok, John. And again, I'm sorry for the mix-up. Got big plans for the weekend?"

"Ya, me and the boys are going camping and mountain biking on the Continental Divide at about seven thousand feet."

"Sounds awesome! Well, have a great time."

"I will. See ya, Roger." John hangs up the phone and thinks about calling Bill. It didn't take too long to decide 'screw it.' He's had his ass chewed enough today. He'll deal with Bill on Tuesday. Got to call the boy's back. Ryan answers…

"Hello?"

"What's happenin?" says John.

"Hey, dad! We were just wondering what kind of clothes to pack?"

"It's probably gonna be kind of hot and windy up there so pack for warm weather, but take a light jacket and sweats. I think your rain ponchos are already in the trailer."

"Ok, when ya gonna be home?"

"Hopefully right after five. I think instead of cooking when we get up there we'll just grab a burger on the way out of town. I didn't get lunch today and I'm starved."

"Cool!" says Ryan.

"I didn't think you'd complain."

"Should we start packing the trailer?"

"No, I'll do that. You guys just make sure you have all of your personal stuff ready to go."

"Ok," says Ryan. John can tell by the tone of his voice that he's excited.

"Did Brett need to talk to me?"

"No, he was just wondering what to pack."

"Ok, I'll see you guys after work."

"Bye dad."

"Bye."

John bought an old twenty-foot camp trailer last year and fixed it up. It's old, but everything works. Ol' Green pulls it pretty easily too. Ol' Green is a 1972 Chevy, ¾ ton 4x4 pickup with a 454cu. in. v8 that John rebuilt himself. It's a good old truck and John has it running like a top. But that's not his favorite ride. His baby is 'Chelly.' Chelly is a 1970 Chevy Chevelle SS 454 built to the nuts. It's also equipped with a 4-speed tranny and a posi rear end. It'll smoke just about anything in town. John has a break from the phones for a moment, so he's working on his camping checklist. Let's see…food, clothes, ax, shovel, water tank, check propane… 'Ring, Ring.' "Oh well, so much for that." John mutters.

"This is John."

"Johnnie ol' boy." It's Kevin, one of John's countermen.

"What are you doing?" laughs John.

"Well, I'm sitting out here in the middle of Flathead Lake and my son Justin just pulled in a 7-pound rainbow."

"No shit?"

"No shit! It took him about 30 minutes to get it in."

"That's great!"

"Hold on. He has something to tell ya."

"Ok."

"John?"

"Congratulations Justin!"

"Thanks! What I wanted to say is thank you for letting my dad have today off. The fishing has been great!"

"You're welcome bud."

"Bye."

Kevin gets back on the phone. "Has it been busy?"

"It's been a little busy but nothing I can't handle."

"Well, thanks for the day off, we've been having a blast!"

"No problem, have fun and I'll see you Tuesday."

"Bye Johnny."

As John hangs up the phone, he thinks… 'I sure have some great guys working for me.' Kevin has been with him about two years now, and his other counterman, Chuck, has been with him about five. They both work hard, and they deserved today off.

It's almost five o'clock, and there wasn't one call that John wasn't able to get too. He's made it through the day, and he's getting anxious to get out of there and go home. 'Ring, ring.'

"This is John."

"Dad?"

"Ya Brett."

"Grandma just brought us home, and we were loading our bikes in the back of Ol' Green, and I noticed there's a big puddle of oil in the driveway."

"GREAT!"

CHAPTER 2

JOHN RUSHED STRAIGHT HOME AFTER having a couple of quick beers with a customer and closing the shop at five o'clock. He can't for the life of him think of where that oil leak could be. That's all he needs, truck trouble! He remembers using the truck last night to pick up the boy's bikes at Johnson's Wheels'n'Stuff, and it seemed to be ok then. He did rap it up pretty good though when they pulled up next to a car full of teenage girls. Ol' Green is a pretty sharp truck, and Brett wanted to show off for the girls, so John revved it up pretty good and laid rubber when he took off from the light. Maybe he pushed it too hard and broke something or blew a gasket. GREAT! Just what he needs. He tries to think of his options if there IS something wrong with Green. He sure as hell can't use Chelly. Maybe he could borrow the parts truck from work! YA! If he has to, he'll borrow it. That'll piss Ed off! But like John always says... 'It's better to be pissed off than pissed on.' John pulls into the driveway, and the boy's come running out to meet him.

"Hey, dad!"

"Hi, guys!"

"Can we go to Burger King dad?" gasps Ryan.

"No! I want to go to McDonalds," gripes Brett.

"Do you guys ever agree on anything?"

"Well, Ryan always wants to go to Burger King."

"Well you always want to go to McDonalds," complains Ryan.

"We aren't going anywhere till I figure out what's wrong with Green," yells John. He looks under the truck and sees only a small drop of oil about the size of a quarter. He looks at Brett and say's... "So, where's this puddle of oil you were talking about?"

"Right there," says Brett.

"That little drop is a puddle of oil?" John says with a great amount of relief in his voice.

"Well I know how picky you are about your rigs, so I thought it might be something serious." Brett had that look on his face like he just screwed up and dad is disappointed in him.

John just smiled and said, "No it's not a big deal bud, and I appreciate you keeping your eyes open for any little problems you might see."

Ryan is poking around the exhaust pipes and suddenly announces, "Dad, the inside of your tailpipes is awfully black. Is that normal?"

"Yes bud, it's normal. But I appreciate your help too! Now, let's quit screwing around and get the trailer packed so we can get the heck out of dodge!"

"Yes!" exclaims Brett.

"I'm hungry dad, can we eat first?" asks Ryan.

"No! Let's eat on the way out of town say's Brett."

"Do you guys ever agree on anything?" asks John.

"Ya," says Ryan.

"What?"

"We agree that you're a big DOUGHHEAD!"

"That's it!" shouts John, and the chase was on. John runs after the boys across the lawn and finally catches them as he picks both of them up over his head. Then he eases them to the ground and tickles them just like when they were little. Ryan still likes to be tickled, but Brett can only tolerate it for so long. Guess he's just getting too old for that crap. They wrestle on the grass for a while until John runs out of steam and says… "Alright, alright, better get started packing, or it'll be dark before we get there."

Brett jumps up and says, "I'm all packed!"

"Me too!" says Ryan.

"Well I'm not!" says John, so you guys just stay out of my way and it'll go a lot faster." John had a system at packing for a camping trip. He always made a checklist and went through it methodically. He rarely forgets anything that way. If the boys tried to help, they would just screw up his system and possibly cause him to forget something. THAT would irritate him, for he's a bit of a perfectionist. So on to the checklist! Ax, shovel, bucket, fill the water tank, check propane...

"Dad?"

"Ya."

"Are you sure we can't help with something?"

John looks at the boy's sitting on the couch. He can't help but notice the sad look on their faces. Then it hits him. He's treating them like babies. 'Way to go John,' he thinks.

"Ok Ryan, you fill the water tank. Brett, here's the food list. You load the ice chests."

"Ok dad!" and off they go like a bullet.

"Now that's better," John thinks. His stomach is really starting to growl now. He'd better get busy packing his clothes and the rest of the gear and hit the road.

'Boy, is it hot out,' John's thinking, 'I hope Ol' Green doesn't have any trouble getting over Rogers Pass.' The temperature is about 95 degrees. That kind of heat can be hard on an engine. But John shakes it off and remembers what good shape Green is in.

"Ryan, how's the water tank coming?"

"Just about done dad!"

"Brett?"

"Just about done!"

"Well, that's just about everything. Time to hook the trailer up to the truck and test the lights.

"Dad, phone. It's mom," yells Ryan.

"Hello."

"Hi, I just wanted to remind you to bring my check when you bring the boys back Monday night."

"Don't worry."

"I don't suppose you could afford a little extra this time?"

"No."

"Why?"

"Can we discuss this some other time? I'm kind of in a hurry."

"Ok, but we WILL talk about it!"

"Ok, bye." 'Bitch,' thinks John, 'always asking for money.'

"Ok guys, time to make the final checks and hit the road. Got all your clothes?"

"Check!" answer the boys.

"Water?"

"Check!"

"Food?"

"Check!"

"Let's hit it!"

"Yaaay!"

"Ok, where are we gonna eat?"

"McDonalds!"

"Burgerking!"

"How 'bout we flip for it."

"Ok."

John pulls out a coin and hands it to Ryan since he's the closest to him. He flips it as Brett calls it.

"Looks like it's McDonalds," John says quietly, waiting for the wave of whining to come from Ryan.

"Ok," says Ryan.

"Whoa! No whining?"

"I don't care where we eat. I'm just hungry."

"Ok then, let's go!"

So off they go! John, Brett, Ryan, and Bufford, their three-year-old golden lab. First to McDonalds, then to the mountains. John cranks the CD player up. Born to be Wild is playing and all three are jamming to the tunes. It's a beautiful evening. About 7pm and it's already cooling off. Life is GOOD! They've got about a two-hour drive ahead of them through some of the most beautiful scenic country in the world. John was born and raised in Montana, and he wouldn't live anywhere else no matter what the pay. He believes that God took an extra day to make Montana just to get it right. He loves the fact that his boys are growing up in not only a beautiful land, but a safe one. They're just getting to the edge of town now, and John is finally starting to relax. The food is all eaten, the boys are strapped in, Green is running good, and he can't think of anything they might have forgotten.

"So, are you guy's looking forward to school starting?"

"Ya, kinda," says Ryan. He's going to be in the 7th grade this year and he's a little nervous about it.

"I can't wait!" says Brett. 'Mr. Popular.' He's going to be a freshman in high school. John remembers when he was that age, and the summer was almost over. What a drag! He hated school. He couldn't wait to graduate so he could start working for a living, which is precisely what he did right out of high school. He began working construction and has basically been building his life ever since with his back and two strong hands.

"How many girlfriends ya gonna have this year Brett?"

"A few," says Brett proudly.

"How 'bout you, Ryan?"

"I don't know." Ryan is about halfway between hating girls and tolerating them.

"Well don't get in too big of a hurry bud, you got your whole life ahead of you."

"Oh… I won't, I just want to get good grades so I can get into college."

John thinks, 'My God! What did I do to deserve such good boys?' The three are all silent now, thinking about the future ahead, even Bufford.

John pulls into a rest area to grab some refreshments from the cooler and let everyone stretch and relieve themselves. They're making pretty good time so what the hell. Everyone jumps out to relieve themselves in the restroom or a nearby tree, including the dog.

"What do you guys want to drink?"

It was unanimous.

"Dew!"

John decided a cold beer sounds good on a hot day. He gives the boys their Mountain Dews and cracks open his beer.

"DAD!"

"I know, I know. I'm only gonna have one."

He always tries to be a good example for the boys, but sometimes he breaks the rules. He finishes his beer, puts the empty in the bed of Ol' Green since they saved the empties, and hit the road. Before you know it they're in the pines and about a thousand feet higher. John notices there is a semi-tractor and trailer up ahead and knows the pass is coming up. He needs to get around him so he doesn't have to go up it at 20mph. Ryan has nodded off to sleep, and so has Bufford. Brett has his disc-man on, and he's got his head tipped back with his eyes closed. There's nothing to do now but concentrate on the road and dream about the campfire tonight. John sees a flat spot in the road coming up, so he drops down a gear and hits the gas. Ol' Green flies around the semi like it was standing still. He works his way up the mountain pass, and the boys are still out of it. Seems to be a lot of traffic on the road, but then it is Labor Day weekend. Up ahead some deer are standing by the road. Better slow down until he knows what they're gonna do. They decide at the last minute to cross the road. John lets off the gas and gears down. He decides to wake the boy's up.

"Hey, you guys look."

"Oh cool, deer," say's Ryan.

Bufford growls.

"Shut up dummy," chuckles John.

"Is this where you hunt dad?" asks Ryan.

"No, not here."

"Where then?"

"Everywhere the game has been three days before," Brett smiles.

Ryan asks, "Why?"

"Never mind. Go back to sleep."

Ryan and Bufford nod off again and Brett goes back to his music. The top of the pass is just ahead. Then it's downhill through a steep gorge for a stretch and open road after that. They should be in camp in about a half hour. Suddenly Ol' Green starts to buck!

"What the hell?" says John. The engine cuts out, then surges ahead again. "OH GREAT!"

CHAPTER 3

─────❦─────

"Hɪ Bᴏʙʙʏ, ɪᴛ's Aᴍʏ."

"Hey Amy, what's up?"

"Well, I'm on my way to Great Falls for the weekend. You gonna be around?"

"Ya, but why the hell are you coming to Great Falls? There's a lot more shit to do in Missoula than here!"

"I know, but my parents got plans to go to the lake. You know how that goes."

"Well, at least you get to do something. I gotta work all weekend."

"Bummer!"

"Ya, but maybe we can get together tonight. Chad and Josh are in town, and we're planning on getting trashed tonight. Wanna come?"

"I don't' know yet, I'm supposed to meet up with Keri tonight. I'll call you when I find out what she wants to do, ok?"

"Ok, I'll catch ya later then. Bye."

"Bye, bye."

Amy pushes end on her cell phone and proceeds to call Keri. Amy is nineteen years old and the pride and joy of Ron and Kathy Wader, who own Wader's Coffee Shop in Great Falls. She has finished her freshman year at the University of Montana in Missoula, about 160 miles west of Great Falls where she is earning outstanding grades. She will be starting school again soon, so Ron and Kathy want to spoil her this Labor Day weekend. Amy could use the break too, for she's been working forty hours a week at the restaurant where she is employed. Not to mention partying just about every night. She's taking business courses in hopes of someday taking over the family business. The family cabin is on Holter Lake, nestled in the mountains south of Great Falls, and that cool water will be a welcome sight on this hot weekend.

Keri finally answers her phone.

"Keri?"

"Oh my God Amy, where are you at?!"

"I'm on my way to Great Falls."

"Oh my God, really?"

"Ya, I got the weekend off, and my parents want to go to the lake this weekend. You gonna go?"

"I can go on Sunday or Monday, but I have to work Saturday."

"Bummer, what are you doin tonight?"

"Nothin."

"Well, I guess Bobby, Chad and Josh are going out tonight. You wanna go?"

"SURE! Chad is CUTE!"

"Isn't he a stud! But not as cute as Bobby of course."

"Of course."

"Ok, well I'll call ya when I get into town then."

"Ok. Where we goin, do ya know?"

"I don't know. Probably bar hoppin if I know those guys."

"Ok, well call me."

"I will, bye, bye."

"Bye."

"Shit!" Amy mutters as she reaches down to the passenger side floorboard of her 1991 Toyota. She dropped her cell phone and as luck would have it, it fell as far away as possible. A horn blares at her as her car drifts over the center line. She pops her head up and realizes she is a good foot over the center line. She jerks the wheel to the right and yells "Up Yours" to the passing motorist as she salutes him with one finger. She is definitely not the most careful driver in Montana, and tends to show some road rage now and then. She's never been in a serious accident or received any traffic tickets, but her car looks like it's been through a war. The outside hasn't been washed in months, and the inside looks like a child's closet. All her clothes, dirty and clean, are piled in the back seat. She plans on sweet talking her mother into doing her laundry this weekend. She decides to start putting on her makeup now since Great Falls is just on the other side of the pass.

John looks down at the gas gauge. Empty! He hits the switch under the seat and kicks in the other gas tank. Ol' Green says thank you as he surges forward again.

"No wonder it was bucking" John thinks. He drops down a gear for the long descent ahead.

Amy is fumbling around the floor looking for her makeup case. Her little car is all over the road.

John looks in the rear-view mirrors as he rounds a curve and notices the semi he passed a while back is right behind him. He looks forward again as another sharp curve is coming up. This canyon always makes him nervous. The road cuts through the mountain with a rocky hillside on the right and a deep gorge on the left.

Amy can't seem to find her makeup case on the floor so she searches the back seat as her car jumps all over the road.

John looks over at the boys. Ryan and Bufford are asleep, and Brett has his head tipped back with his eyes closed listening to his CDs on his Discman. He smiles and looks ahead again, and...

"OH SHIT!"

There is a little red car in his lane right in front of him! The boys are startled by John's outburst and both open their eyes.

"CRAP!" yells Brett.

"Dad look out!" yells Ryan.

John pushes on the horn and remembers it doesn't work. The car is still in his lane right in front of him. He must make a decision fast! What to do, what to do. Should he take the ditch on the right and totally destroy the truck and trailer on the rocks, or should he take a chance there aren't any cars behind this one around the curve and jump into the left lane to go around it. What to do, what to do…

He decides at the last second to jump into the left lane.

Amy looks up and sees that she is in the left lane with vehicles in front of her and screams. She sees John and the boy's terrified faces as they go by on her right. She also sees the semi in front of her, blaring its air horns. She is terrified herself and not thinking clearly. She jerks the wheel to the right as to get back into the right lane, and smacks right into John's camper trailer. Her car flips over on its roof and skids down the road.

John feels the impact and yells, "HOLD ON!"

The blow pushed the trailer off the edge of the road. It is tipping over and pulling Ol' Green with it.

Amy's car is still sliding on its roof. She is unconscious and blood is gushing from her head. The semi driver sees the car sliding towards him and locks up the breaks, jackknifing the trailer. He can't stop in time, and the tractor skids over the little car, crushing Amy inside.

John is trying to keep Ol' Green on the road as the trailer ball hitch breaks loose, but the safety chains hold true. John wishes he wouldn't have made them so stout. He fears the trailer is going to pull them down with it. Then, the unthinkable happens! Ol' Green is drug over the edge and tips over. The safety chains finally break free and the trailer tumbles down the hill, shattering it to pieces. As the truck tips over, the boys are screaming. Bufford is yelping and John is screaming, "HOLD ON!" He's glad the boys have their seat belts on, and wishes he would have remembered to put his on. The truck rolls over again and again, picking up speed with every turn. John and Bufford are being thrown around inside like rag dolls. The gorge is about a thousand feet deep, and they aren't even half way to the bottom. The screaming has stopped now as everyone has been knocked out. John and Bufford are thrown through the opening that used to be the windshield. They are both badly broken up inside and bleeding. The truck rolls over the top of John and breaks his leg, but luckily, he is wedged between a couple of big rocks, so it doesn't crush him completely as it rolls down the cliff with the boys still trapped inside. Over and over and over it rolls. Towards the bottom of the gorge is a twenty foot drop off with a dry creek bed at the bottom. The truck rolls over the edge, and for a brief moment, there is silence as it falls through the air. Suddenly, the silence is broken. SMASH! It lands on its side in the dry creek bed. Now there is silence again, an eerie silence of the worst kind. No screaming, no yelping, no sound of life at all. The semi driver is already on the radio calling for help. He checks to see if Amy is alive, but is quite sure she is dead as her body is almost completely bent in half backwards. Other vehicles are coming onto the scene now. One traveler walked up to Amy's car and looked inside, and immediately started vomiting. Once the truck driver saw this, he started keeping people back from the scene for he is a seasoned veteran driver who has witnessed many accidents of this magnitude. Traffic is backed up for miles from the wreckage. Some of the travelers want to go down the ravine and check for survivors, but it is too steep to attempt without ropes or something. Soon, a highway patrolman arrives on the scene and helps to back the cars up so the truck can back up off Amy's car and park so that traffic can get by. All the travelers look in horror as they drive by. Paramedics arrive from Great Falls and quickly survey the scene. Once doing so, they rig up their repelling equipment and start down the ravine. They're going to have to wait for more equipment to arrive before they can get all the way to the bottom, but at least they can get part way down. As they work their way down, they come upon Bufford.

"I found their dog," one of them radios to the others at the top.

"Is it alive?"

"Negative."

"10-4, keep looking."

One of them notices a boot sticking out from behind a big rock and works his way over to it.

"I got one," he radios to the others. "He's alive!"

Johns body is badly broken and bloody, but at least he's alive. They start working on him immediately. They quickly bandage his head wounds to try and slow down the bleeding. Next, they apply an air splint to his broken leg. Another paramedic is working his way down with a backboard to transport him back up to the top. John is not exactly a small man, so it's going to take all the strength they can muster up to get him to the road. An ambulance is now arriving from Great Falls. Perfect timing. The paramedics finally get John to the road, panting and sweating.

"He's alive, but pretty busted up," one yells to the ambulance attendant.

"Any more?" he asks.

"We don't know yet. We can't get to the bottom until more equipment arrives. This man was about half way down."

"Well, we'll get him to town and dispatch another ambulance."

"10-4," says the paramedic.

They strap John inside and rush him to Great Falls.

"He's badly in need of blood" the technician says to the driver. "I hope he makes it."

⸺∞⸺

CHAPTER 4

"Ok, we got a live one! Report is that it's a middle-aged male, Caucasian, multiple lacerations around the head and upper torso. Several broken ribs and a compound fracture of the left femur. He's lost a lot of blood, so that's the first priority. Ok people, let's roll. The ambulance is here!"

It's a busy night at Great Falls Medical Center in Great Falls. The holiday weekend has barely started, and already accident victims are pouring in. The ambulance pulls up to the emergency room doors as the EMTs quickly rush John inside. He still has a pulse, but it's fading. The emergency room staff roll him inside and start prepping him for the operating room. He has a nasty bump on the back of his head, and a deep gash right at the hairline. He also has several cuts on his face from the broken glass. Approximately four ribs on his left side are broken, and a large bone in his left leg. John was cursing himself for not having his seatbelt on before the accident unfolded, but in fact, the only reason he survived the accident is because he wasn't buckled in. The doctor on duty enters the operating room and checks John's vitals. He seems to be stabilizing, but he's still not out of the woods. The doctor orders several units of blood as they prepare him for x-ray's. It is a good thing that John is NOT conscious, because they would probably have to use restraints on him. An EMT enters the O.R. and whispers something in the doctor's ear. The doc gets a sad look on his face as he pats the EMT on the back and thanks him. He then informs the rest of the crew that there were two teenage boys in the vehicle with the patient, and they are both dead. If the patient regains consciousness, he might become violent when he realizes what happened.

"If he asks about his boy's, you don't know anything! UNDERSTAND?!"

"Yes doctor," replies the attendees.

"I don't want to drop a bomb like that on him until he is fully stabilized. Does anyone know if he has been identified?"

"Yes doctor," exclaims one of the prep nurses. "His name is John McDuffy, and the office is trying to locate a next of kin now."

"Good! He needs to have a family member around when he finds out his boys didn't make it."

"There was also a young female in another vehicle and a family dog that were killed in the accident."

"So, this man is the only survivor?"

"No. Apparently, there was a truck driver involved. He was not injured."

"I hate holiday weekends!" growls the doctor. The ex-rays come back, and sure enough, there are four broken ribs. They also show some internal hemorrhaging in the chest cavity. John is in bad shape, but the doctor believes he will pull through ok.

"He seems to be a strong, healthy man. He will need to be watched closely until he regains consciousness."

"Yes doctor," replies the attendant.

John spends several hours in the operating room getting patched back together before he is finally stable and moved to the recovery room. The compound fracture of his left femur is repaired and cast, with his ribs taped and his head bandaged. Monitors are attached to measure his vitals.

"Where is my son?! They told me my son is here! Where is he?!"

"Calm down ma'am! Who is your son?"

"John McDuffy! They said he was in an accident! Where is he?!"

"Please, please try to calm down ma'am! I'll go find out where your son is. Please have a seat and I'll come back for you, ok?"

"Ok, but hurry! Please!!"

"I will ma'am."

Kathleen McDuffy is seventy years old, and John is her youngest of two sons. Her husband has passed away, and her oldest son died in 1998 of cancer, so the thought of losing her youngest too is just too terrible to think about. Horrible thoughts are racing through her head as she waits in the emergency room. The hospital staff is trying their best to calm her down, but she won't rest until she sees that he is ok.

Finally, the attendant comes back and says, "Please come with me Mrs. McDuffy."

Kathleen follows close behind as another attendant holds her arm. They lead her into the room where John is, and she breaks down when she sees him.

"Is he going to be alright?!" she cries.

"Yes ma'am. We believe he is going to pull through just fine. He is still unconscious, but the medication seems to be working well and he is stabilizing."

Just then, the resident Chaplin walks in the room and introduces himself as he tries to console her the best that he can. Now it hits Kathleen.

"The boys?!"

This is the part of the Chaplin's job that he hates more than anything. The sadness of the news he is about to reveal spreads across his face like a flood. Kathleen realizes what the answer is without him saying a word. The Chaplin quickly grabs her as he sees she is getting weak in the knees, and carefully helps her to a chair. Now she is sobbing uncontrollably. Her heart is breaking into little pieces. She cannot believe her grandsons are gone. Just this afternoon she was hugging them kissing their smiling faces, and telling them to have a good time this weekend. Now they're gone, and she'll never see them again. The pain is just too much. The Chaplin holds her hands and offers a prayer. She bows her head and prays with him.

Once finished, she looks up at the Chaplin with tear filled eyes, "Does John know?"

"No Kathleen, he hasn't regained consciousness yet."

"It's going to kill him you know. He loves those boys more than life itself. I don't know how he's going to handle it."

"I know Kathleen. There is a tough road ahead for both of you, but with God by your sides, you CAN get through this. God loves you both, and knows the pain you are feeling. He felt the same pain when he had to give up his own son for us. Let him help you through this terrible time." The Chaplin's words seemed to be of some comfort to Kathleen, being the God-fearing woman that she is.

"Thank you, Father." Just then she realizes she has a phone call to make. Laura!

"Oh my Lord, how am I going to tell Laura?"

The Chaplin suggests that he give Kathleen a ride over to Laura's, and help her through this difficult task. Kathleen decides that maybe it would be better to go over to Laura's folks and tell them first. She has always gotten along really well with Betty and Bill, and maybe they would be of more comfort to Laura when they break the news. The Chaplin agrees with this plan, so he tells the hospital staff where they are going and they head out the door. He gives them his cell phone number in case there is any change with John, and out the door they go. On the way over to Betty and Bill's, Kathleen tells the Chaplin all about John and the boy's.

"I lost my husband in 1981, and my oldest son in 1998, and John has always taken good care of me ever since. He is such a good son and father." Just saying the word 'father' starts her crying again. She went on to say how John got the boys every weekend during the school year, and all summer long since the divorce.

"They loved to go camping, every weekend if they could. I even got to go along a couple of times. We just had a ball." Kathleen starts to weep again. She still can't believe the boys are gone. But she's going to have to try to pull herself together because Betty and Bill's house is just around the corner. They pull up in the driveway. The lights come on, and Betty and Bill step outside as if they know something is terribly wrong. Kathleen steps out of the car and looks up at them standing on their porch, holding each other tightly, bracing themselves for some bad news.

Kathleen breaks down and yells, "John and the boys have been in a terrible accident and the boys have been killed!"

Betty and Bill race to Kathleen and they all embrace.

Bill asks, "My God! What happened?" The Chaplin can see that Kathleen can't speak, so he introduces himself and explains.

"John and the boys were on their way camping up towards Lincoln when they got into an accident just on the other side of Rogers pass. John was thrown from the truck, but the boys were strapped inside."

"That big dummy never wore his seatbelt," says Bill as his eyes welled up with tears.

Betty cries, "Does Laura know?"

Kathleen looks at her with tear filled eyes, and Betty knows the answer.

She looks at Bill and says, "Honey, will you grab my purse?"

Bill goes in the house and grabs Betty's purse and it's off to Laura's.

As they pull up the drive, they notice that Carl's rig is gone. Probably just as well, for Carl, Laura's husband, never did like John, and it will be easier to break the news to Laura without him around. They tap on the door. They notice the television is pretty loud, so they tap louder. KNOCK, KNOCK, KNOCK! Finally, Laura comes to the door smiling at first. Then the smile slowly goes away as she looks at the grim faces outside her door. She invites everyone in as she turns down the TV. Before she has a chance to sit down, Betty hugs her and squeezes her tight.

"MOM! WHATS WRONG?!"

"It's the boy's honey."

"WHAT?!"

"Sit down baby," says Bill.

"WILL SOMEBODY TELL ME WHAT THE HELL IS GOING ON?" screams Laura.

"Baby, there has been a terrible accident, and the boys didn't make it."

Laura's face quickly turn's white. She says nothing, and just stares blankly at her dad. Then, she turns and looks at her mom, then Kathleen, then the Chaplin. As she looks from face to face in her living room, hers gradually turns redder, and redder.

"And John?" she says.

"He was thrown from the truck and is in the hospital. He's pretty busted up, but they think he'll be ok," explains the Chaplin.

"My boys are dead, and that son of a bitch is alive?!" screams Laura.

Bill rushes over and grabs her because he knows his daughter. Right now she's crazy with anger, and would tear the place apart if she could, but if he holds her tight and keeps telling her that he loves her, then pretty soon her rage will change to tears, and she will cry in his arms the rest of the night. Kathleen is hurt deeply by her outburst, but does her best to maintain her composure. She knows Laura is just angry and didn't mean what she said. She has always been a bit of a hothead. The Chaplin reaches out to hold her. Just then, his cell phone rings.

He goes to another room to answer it. After a few moments, he comes back. He bends down to Kathleen's ear and quietly says, "John has regained consciousness."

CHAPTER 5

⎯⎯ ∞ ⎯⎯

"WHERE AM I!? WHAT HAPPENED?" John asks the nurse who is attending to him.

"It's ok Mr. McDuffy, you've been in a bad accident, but you're going to be ok. The doctor will be in soon to see you, but you must lie still. You're pretty banged up."

John is sure she's right about that because his head is splitting, his chest is on fire, and his leg is throbbing. He regained consciousness about thirty minutes ago, and the nurses removed the breathing tubes so he could breathe on his own. His breathing is labored, but he is maintaining a good rhythm. The doctor finally makes it in to see him.

"How ya feeling John?"

"Like shit!" moans John.

"Well I'm not surprised. You've been through a very bad accident. You've got some broken ribs. That's why it's hard to breathe. Your left leg is broken too in case you're wondering why it hurts. You've suffered a pretty nasty concussion too. What do you remember about the accident John?"

"Nothing."

"Well, try not to think too hard on it for now. Just try to get some rest and let your body heal, ok?"

"Ok."

John closed his eyes and drifted off to sleep. The medication he is on is strong so it's hard for him to keep his eyes open. The doctor is not too worried just yet about the fact that John said he didn't remember anything. It's a normal effect of such a trauma to lose your memory temporally. Actually, it's a blessing right now because as soon as he does remember, he's going to be asking about his boys. Kathleen and the Chaplin enter the hospital now and meet up with the doctor in the hall.

"How is he doc?" asks the Chaplin.

"He's resting. He regained consciousness and his vitals are good. His breathing is labored, but at least he is breathing on his own. He is on some pretty heavy medication and seems to be resting comfortably."

"Does he remember the accident?" asks Kathleen.

"No, not yet, but I'm not concerned about that. It's a normal thing to happen. If he continues to have no memory of the accident several days from now, then we'll start some tests. The best thing for him now is to get lots of rest and let his body heal. I wouldn't try to force him to remember the accident. The more he heals, the more his memory will start to come back."

"Thank you doctor."

Kathleen goes over and sits down beside John. She tries to think about how she is going to break the news to him about the boys. She thinks about the mean thing that Laura said, and prays that God forgives her. Heaven only knows how she would react in Laura's shoes. Laura has always been a good mom to the boys, but she has resented John since the divorce. How she must truly hate him now. John is fidgeting. His eyebrows are moving up and down. His breathing is racing. He must be having thoughts of the accident. Kathleen is trying to decide what to do. Should she wake him, or let him sleep. She reaches out to hold his hand. This seems to ease his mind as he drifts off to sleep again. She hears some commotion out in the hallway. Laura and her folks enter the room. All three look like they've been sobbing, and Laura can hardly walk.

"Hi Kathleen, how is he?" asks Bill.

"Well, he's regained consciousness, but I haven't had a chance talk to him. The doctor says he doesn't remember the accident yet."

"We've just been to identify the boys." Laura can't stand up any more, she must sit down and weep.

"Kathleen," says Laura, "I'm so, so sorry for the things I said. I was just angry. I know John could never deliberately hurt the boys. He loved them as much as I did."

Kathleen goes to Laura and gives her a big hug.

"I know sweetheart!" cries Kathleen. "We all say things sometimes that we don't mean. We just have to find a way to get through this somehow."

Kathleen and Laura cry hard as they rock each other back and forth. They are both suffering a pain that can only be described by someone who has been through such loss. Kathleen has been through the loss of loved ones before, but this is Laura's first.

"How am I going to face tomorrow and the days to come? I can't imagine life without my boys," cry's Laura.

Just then, John starts to move around a bit and moan from the pain. All eyes look towards him as he begins to open his. Kathleen goes to him and puts her face close to his and gently touches his forehead.

"Mom?"

"Yes honey, it's me."

"Where am I?"

"You're in the hospital dear."

"What happened?"

Kathleen gulps with the thought of telling her son what happened and the results. She tries to hold back the tears for her son's sake.

"You were in a terrible accident sweetheart, and you were hurt pretty bad."

Laura and her folks work their way over to the bedside as John looks up at their despairing faces.

"Laura?"

"Yes John."

"Where are the boys?"

Laura can't take this. She buries her face in her dad's chest. Everyone starts to cry as they look at John's innocent, unknowing face.

Kathleen holds his hand tightly and says, "Sweetheart, I've got some very bad news."

John looks into her eyes and wonders what she could mean. He remembers a little bit about the accident now, the truck tipping over, and the boys screaming. His mind is racing as details are starting to come back to him. He remembers being thrown around in the cab of the truck as it rolled over and over. Then it hits him!

'Oh my God! The boys!' he thinks to himself as Kathleen looks down at him, trying to find the right words.

Suddenly, John says, "Are the boy's ok? Where are they?"

"Honey," says Kathleen softly, "the boys didn't make it. They were killed in the accident." Kathleen is sobbing uncontrollably now. This is one of the hardest things she's ever had to do. John is just stunned. He doesn't believe what he just heard. He looks around the room at everyone. Now they are all crying.

"NO!" says John, I don't believe you! I want to see my boys now!"

John starts to get up even though the pain is tremendous. Bill rushes over to hold him down.

"Johnny, Johnny," says Bill, "you have to lie down! You're too busted up to walk."

Kathleen is franticly pushing the nurse button by his bed.

"Well then take me to them! They can't be dead! You guys are wrong! I want to see them! PLEASE!"

A nurse enters the room now and rushes over to John and pushes down on his shoulders.

"You aren't going anywhere mister," she says. "You just lie down and take it easy."

"But I have to see my boys!" yells John.

His head is splitting, and his chest and left leg are throbbing, but the only pain he feels right now is in his heart. This can't be true. What they are telling him? Brett and Ryan HAVE to be ok. They just can't come to him, so he must get to them. The nurse looks around and realizes what's going on. John is in denial. There is no way he is going to accept the fact that his boys are gone. Kathleen comes to him and looks him in the eyes again. This time he sees in her eyes that she is telling the truth. His heart is racing now. His breathing is fast and broken. The nurse calls for the doctor. John is shaking all over now. His eyes are watering.

"They can't be dead!" says John. "We have to get camp set up! We've got a lot of riding to do! They can't be dead!"

This is even too much for the nurse to keep her composure. Her eyes are watering too.

"Honey, I know this is hard to accept," says Kathleen softly, "but there is nothing you can do. God has taken them to be by his side. Our hearts are breaking, but we have to accept it."

"NOOOOOO!!!!" yells John. "God can't have them yet! They're mine! Those boys belong to me and Laura! God is just gonna have to wait! We've got to get camp set up!"

Kathleen and Laura are both holding John tightly now. They knew he would react this way. He has always been a stubborn man and he usually gets his way. But this time he's not going to get his way.

"John, stop it!" snaps Laura. "You can't change it! The boys are gone, and you can't change it! I don't want to believe it either, but it is true! They're gone!"

Laura has always had the ability to control John. Five-foot-four-inches tall and all of 110 pounds, she could stand up to him better than any man could. That is what attracted him to her in the first place. When they first started dating, all she had to do is raise an eyebrow, and he would melt.

"Now lie down before you hurt yourself some more!" Laura says in a scolding voice.

John obeys her demands and lies back down. He looks into her sobbing eyes not as his ex-wife, but as the mother of his children. He sees the pain on her face, and realizes she is hurting just a badly as he is. Laura looks in his eyes and knows that he is ready to break down. She remembers this look from when his father died. It took a long time for him to accept his death, but once he was ready, Laura held him tightly while he wept until there were no more tears. That time has come again. Laura puts her arms around his neck and holds his head gently to her breast.

John cries softly and says, "Noooo. Please tell me our boys are ok!"

"I wish I could Johnny."

John is crying harder now. His big heart is breaking in two.

"I'm sorry! I'm sooo sorry Laura."

"It's not your fault Johnny. There's nothing you could have done. It was an accident."

"But I should have taken the ditch instead of trying to go around that idiot."

"Well, there's nothing you can do about it now, so stop blaming yourself. We just have to get through this somehow."

Laura rocks John back and forth, trying to console him the best she can. She wonders what he meant by taking the ditch instead of going around that idiot. Was he trying to pass someone? Did someone slam on the breaks in front of him? What caused the accident? So many questions are going through her mind, but now is not the time to ask them.

"I want my boy's baaaack!" cry's John. "Please God! Tell me this didn't happen. Take me instead! Just bring my boy's back!"

Laura keeps rocking him as the doctor enters the room and adds a sedative to John's I.V. He slowly drifts off to sleep and everyone leaves the room to let him rest.

As they stand in the hall talking, a highway patrolman walks up and says, "Is this John McDuffy's room?"

The doctor say's "Yes, may I help you?"

"Yes, I need to ask Mr. McDuffy some questions about the accident."

"Well, now is not a good time. I just gave him a sedative. He's resting."

"Will you notify our office the minute he is available for questioning?"

"Sure. Is there a problem officer?"

"Well, apparently, there were some empty beer cans found on the scene. We need to test Mr. McDuffy's blood/alcohol level."

CHAPTER 6

———∞∞∞———

"Blood/alcohol level!" barks Laura. "Are you saying he had been drinking?"

"We don't know ma'am. Like I said, there were some empty beer cans found on the scene. We don't even know if they belonged to Mr. McDuffy, it's just a routine procedure. Every accident has to be investigated."

"I'll have a nurse draw some blood right away," says the doctor.

Laura is thinking terrible thoughts right now. If she finds out that John had been drinking, she'll snap. She knows that he drinks, but she can't believe that he would actually drink and drive when the boys are with him.

"If he had been drinking, I would have smelled it on him!" says Kathleen to the officer. "I know my son! He would never be that irresponsible!"

"Yes ma'am, it's just routine," says the officer.

"The beer cans were probably left over from the last camping trip. John saves aluminum. He throws the cans in the back of the truck until there is enough to bag up."

"Yes ma'am, that's good to know, if you can think of anything else that will help the investigation please contact our office."

"I will," says Kathleen.

"We better take Laura home Kathleen," says Bill. "Are you gonna stay awhile?"

"Yes. You guys go ahead. I want to be here when John wakes up. He's pretty upset, and I'm afraid he might try to get up again."

"Well, you try to get some rest too," says Betty.

"Oh, I will, don't worry. I sleep in a chair all the time at home. I'll be fine."

Bill and Betty hold Laura's arms as they escort her out to the parking lot. She is so distraught that she can hardly walk. Kathleen watches as they leave. It's just about 3am, and Kathleen is beat. She asks the nurse for a blanket and pillow as she settles in the arm chair in the room, and closes her eyes. It doesn't take long at all and she's snoring. She dreams of Brett and Ryan when they were little. The way they used to bicker over the silliest things. The way their eyes would light up on Christmas morning. Christmas will never be the same now. She dreams about one year when the boys were real little, and John dressed up like Santa on Christmas eve and snuck around the house late at night after the boys had gone to bed, spreading the presents around the tree. Kathleen was asleep on the couch as Laura got up and snuck into their room to wake them. She made sure they set out some milk and cookies for Santa, and put some lights around the outside of the house so he would be sure to stop. After waking them, she told them Santa was in the living room, and they had to be real quiet or else he would hear them and disappear. The look on their eyes when they peered around the corner and saw Santa was worth more than anything money could buy.

"BRETT!!! Hold on bud! I'm coming!"

John was having a nightmare. Kathleen hurries to wake him. He wakes up again not knowing where he was at and just stares at Kathleen.

"It's ok hon, it's me. You were having a bad dream."

John's breathing is fast and his heart is racing. Kathleen decides to call the nurse.

"Where am I?"

"You're in the hospital dear. Remember? You were in a bad accident."

John starts to remember now. Brett and Ryan are dead. He slowly looks around the empty room.

"Where is everybody?"

"Laura and her folks went home to get some rest dear. You should go back to sleep too. It's late, and you've been through a lot."

"I dreamed Brett was stuck under the truck and was screaming for me, but my legs wouldn't move. I could see Ryan next to him, but he was quiet. No matter how much I tried, I couldn't move. Brett was screaming and crying HELP! DAD, PLEASE HELP! It was horrible! I couldn't help him."

"I know dear. You had a bad dream."

"But I couldn't do anything! I was helpless!"

"I know, but it was just a dream. It's over now. You're awake."

"I don't want to be awake! I want to go back to sleep and be with my boys! I have to help them! They need me!"

"I know sweetheart! But they can't be with you now. You have to accept that. You loved your boys, and they loved you very much! But a terrible accident has taken them from you and it WASN'T YOUR FAULT!!! You did everything you could to prevent it, but it was God's decision! Not yours! It was their time, and there was nothing you could do about it!"

"But I don't want it to be their time!"

John begins to weep again and Kathleen holds him as tightly as she can. The pain the two of them are feeling right now is enough to destroy entire nations. Neither of them know how they are going to face the rest of their lives. The nurse finally comes in and asks if everything is alright.

"It's ok," says Kathleen, "he just had a bad dream."

"When can I go home?" asks John.

"I don't know, that's up to the doctor. Don't be in such a hurry Johnny, your body has to heal up first."

"Well, it can heal at home. I hate hospitals!"

"Don't worry Mr. McDuffy, we'll send you home just as soon as the doctor says it's ok," explains the nurse.

"GOOD!"

John lies back down and thinks for a minute.

"Did they catch that idiot that ran me off the road?"

Kathleen just looks at him for a moment. Then she realizes that he has no idea the other driver was killed. She wonders what to say.

"John." She pauses, and says, "The other driver was killed."

"GOOD!" growls John. "That stupid son of a bitch deserved to die. He was right in my lane. My boys would still be alive if it weren't for him!"

"It was a girl."

"What?"

"The other driver. It was a college girl from Missoula. She was coming home for the weekend. Her folks own Wadder's Coffee Shop."

John thinks for a moment...

"She still shouldn't have been in my lane. She wasn't even watching the road. I should have just hit her!"

"Well, it's over now, and you need to get some rest."

"I know, so do you. Why don't you go on home mom, and get some sleep? I'll be fine."

"Are you sure?'

"Ya, go on."

"Ok, but I'll be back in a few hours to check on you."

"Ok."

"Good night sweetheart."

"Goodnight."

Kathleen leaves the room as John just lays there thinking. He still can't believe that in a wink of an eye, his boys are dead, and his life is changed forever. If only he could do it over. He would just run over that little car. The boys might get banged up a bit, but at least they would be alive. How is he going to live without them? They were his life. Everything he did was for them. God, why!? He rolls over on his side the best he can, and cries himself to sleep. The next afternoon he wakes up after having bad dreams all night as Kathleen dozes in the chair.

"Mom?"

"Yes dear," says Kathleen sleepily.

"Did Bufford make it?"

"No dear, he didn't."

John just stares out the window and thinks about when he brought Bufford home. The boys were so excited to have a puppy. They wouldn't leave him alone for a second. The minute the puppy would try to sleep, Ryan would wake him up. The poor thing couldn't get any sleep until Ryan was asleep. As Bufford grew, everywhere the boys went, he went too. He was a great companion for them, and a good protector. Nobody messed with them when he was around.

"Did anything survive the accident?" asks John.

"You did!"

"No, I mean was anything salvageable?"

"I don't know honey. They're still picking up the pieces."

"Sooo… how were the boys killed?"

"I don't know the details."

John could see that was not a good question to ask his mom. Her eyes were starting to water.

"I'm sorry. I shouldn't have asked you that."

"It's ok. Kathleen gulps. I think they said that they were trapped inside and they were just crushed. Laura had to identify the bodies and it upset her pretty bad."

"Dammit! Why couldn't they just wait for me to do it!? Now she has to live with that sight for the rest of her life."

"Well, then you would have to live with it."

"Better me than her. I was the one responsible, not her."

"Don't talk like that!" snaps Kathleen. "It was an accident!"

John is quiet before he says, "I bet Laura really hates me now."

"Well, it didn't help when the officer told us that they needed to do a blood/alcohol test on you."

"What?"

"Yes, apparently, they found some beer cans."

"Those were probably the ones in the back of my truck."

"That's what I told them."

"But, I did have a beer at the rest area, and a couple after work, but that's all, three beers."

"Well that's what I told them, and that you saved aluminum cans in the truck bed, and three beers shouldn't be over the limit," says Kathleen with a hint of worry in her voice.

"That's right. I would have to drink at least a six-pack. But you know me, I wouldn't do that if I had the boys with me."

"I know dear. But they don't know that."

"Great! So, they probably think I caused the accident!"

"They're doing a full investigation, so don't worry. I'm sure they'll see that it wasn't your fault."

"Ya, I guess you're right. I'm just being paranoid. Has the doc said when I can go home?"

"I haven't seen him yet today, but I'm sure he'll be stopping in some time to check on you. He seems like a nice man."

"Ya. I bet he'll be real NICE when he makes out the bill."

"I don't care! At least you're alive!"

"I'm sorry. I just hate doctors and hospitals. I always have."

"Good morning!"

"Speak of the devil. We were just wondering when you were gonna stop in."

"Well, you're at the top of my list. How are ya feeling John?"

"Not bad doc. Can I go home now?"

"Whoa, whoa, slow down boy. You haven't even been here twenty-four hours. Let's check out these wounds." The doctor gives John the once over and smiles. "Well, if you keep healing at this rate, you should be able to go home in a few days."

"Great!"

"I'll check in on you this evening."

"Thanks doc."

"How did you sleep dear?" asks Kathleen.

"Lousy. I couldn't stop thinking about Brett and Ryan. I suppose I'm gonna have to make funeral arrangements pretty soon."

"I've already taken care of everything."

"What?!"

"Well, I knew you would be in no shape to do it, and I've become an old pro at it, so all you and Laura have to do is sign the papers. That is if you guys agree on everything I did."

John is amazed. God really broke the mold after He made this woman. With all the pain in her heart she still managed to keep a stiff upper lip and make all the funeral arrangements.

"You didn't have to do that."

"I know, but it's best to get these things done as soon as possible, and get on with your lives. I wasn't sure how long you were going to be in the hospital, and Laura is in no shape to do it. Besides, I couldn't sleep, so I had to do something."

"So, when is the funeral?"

"The date hasn't been set yet because I wasn't sure how long you were going to be in here. When do you think would be a good day?"

"I don't care. All the days are going to be the same from now on."

"Mr. McDuffy?" asks an official looking man in a suit from the doorway.

"Yes?"

"I'm detective Bartlett," as he shows his badge. "I'd like to ask you a few questions about the accident."

John gulps as he replies, "Ok."

"Ma'am, I'm afraid I'm going to have to ask you to leave the room please."

"Why? He's my son."

"Yes ma'am, but I need to speak to Mt. McDuffy alone."

"It's ok mom. You go home and get some rest."

"Ok, I'll call ya later."

"Ok. Bye."

"Mr. McDuffy, I need to ask you some questions about the day of the accident."

"Ok."

"First of all, had you had a bad day at work Friday?"

"No, not really, just busy. Why?"

"Just routine questioning sir."

"Oh."

"Had you been drinking before the accident occurred?"

CHAPTER 7

———⟨∞⟩———

JOHN WAS AFRAID OF THIS line of questioning. They're going to try and pin this accident on him.

"Ya, if you call three beers drinking."

"So, you had consumed alcohol before the accident?"

"Yes, two beers after work, and one at a rest area on the way up there."

Twelve ounce cans?"

"Yes."

"Can you explain all the empty beer cans found on the scene?"

"Yes. They were probably from the back of my truck. I always throw the empties in there. Then, when there gets to be quite a few, I smash them and bag them up for recycling."

"And how long have you been accumulating them?"

"I think those have been in there for about two months."

"What do you remember from the accident?"

"I remember a little red car coming around the curve and being in my lane. I had to make a decision on whether to take the ditch, or go around on the left. I took a chance and tried to go around it, but it hit my trailer and tipped it over the edge of the road. I should have taken the ditch. My boys would probably still be alive then."

"I'm sorry about your boys, I only have a couple more questions. Were you on any medication before the accident?"

"No."

"Do you wear glasses?"

"No."

"I think that will be all for now Mr. McDuffy. We'll probably be in touch again. When do you get to go home?"

"In a few days, I hope."

"Is your address still 355 Hawthorn Road?"

"Yes."

"Thank you for your time, we'll be in touch."

John watched as the detective left the room. 'Those guys really got some nerve,' thinks John. He just lost his two sons. Can't this shit wait? He starts thinking about the accident again. The boys' screams keep echoing in his head. Why did this have to happen? Things were going pretty well. He just bought a new house, the boys were doing good in school, life was good. Now his life is over. How can he go on without Brett and Ryan? He thinks about suicide for a moment, but thinks again.

There is no way he could do that to his mother. With everything she has been through, and now this?! Losing him too would surely destroy her. He's just going to have to get through this somehow and get on with his life. He thinks about the funeral and how he's going to face everybody. He knows deep inside that they're going to blame him for this. But that's ok, if it'll make them feel better, than so be it. They're opinion doesn't really matter to him anyway. The only people he really cares about are his mother and his sons. Now they are gone. John lays his head down on the pillow and starts to cry again. The pain in his heart is the worst he's ever felt. He cries himself to sleep and dreams about camping trips of past. He dreams of one weekend when he and the boys and his brother Pat went camping in the Bob Marshall Wilderness in northcentral Montana. Bufford was along and they all had a great time. He remembers the campfire when Pat was telling the boys a ghost story...

"The hunter had been lost in the woods for several hours now. He was beginning to get that feeling in his stomach that told him he was in big trouble. It was starting to get dark and he had no idea which way the truck was. His body was drenched from sweating. The temperature was dropping rapidly. He began to shiver out of control. His eyes were playing tricks on him. 'WHAT'S THAT?' He thinks he sees a bear. He knows there are grizzlies in these parts so he reaches for his rifle and realizes it's not there! He must have left it at the last spot he stopped to rest. He must find it! He looks again at the shadow that looked like a bear and decides it's in fact not a bear, so he turns to start backtracking to find his rifle. It's getting harder and harder to see his tracks as the sky is getting darker and darker from the cloud cover. He wishes he wouldn't have left his backpack in the truck. It held his flashlight and matches and other survival gear. Now it's so dark that he can't even see his hand in front of his face. He hears a branch snap. Now he's really scared. What could it be?"

Brett and Ryan are poised and excited as John sneaks around behind them.

"He is praying that it isn't a grizzly. He remembers a story about a mauling in these mountains a couple of years ago, where a hiker was ripped to pieces by a huge male grizzly. He was torn up so bad that it took weeks to identify him. He listens again. SNAP! There it is again. He decides to yell, 'GO AWAY!' Now he hears a steady walking through the snow. Crunch…Crunch… Crunch!!! Then he hears a deep growl. What should he do? He can't run because his legs won't move. He wouldn't be able to see where he was going anyway. Crunch…Crunch…Crunch!!! It's getting closer and closer. He thinks he sees something now. He's so scared he can't stop shaking. His heart is racing and sweat is pouring out of his body. What IS it? Whatever it is it's big!

John is right behind the boys now.

"Then he finally realizes what it is. It's a BIG, 2000-pound slobbering, smelly...

John jumps up and grabs the boys and yells, "COW!"

The boys jump out of their skin and Pat rolls around on the ground laughing.

"DAD!" yells Ryan. "That's not funny!"

"Sure it is," says John, "you should have seen your faces."

"You didn't scare me," says Brett.

"Ya right! Then why are you shaking?"

"I'm cold."

"Whatever."

John grabs the boys and wrestles them to the ground laughing and tickling. Pat decides to get in on the fun too and yells, "DOG PILE!" as he jumps on top of John, Brett, and Ryan. Bufford even decides to join in as he grabs John's pant leg and gives it a good thrashing. That was one of the best weekends he can remember.

"John? John?" says the doctor as he moves John's arm. John opens his eyes.

"Hey doc."

"Sorry to wake you John, but I need to have a look at these wounds."

"That's ok."

The doctor gives him the once over and says, "Well, I'd like to keep you here a while longer, but you should be able to go home Monday morning."

"GREAT!"

"Do you have someone at home that can help you around?"

"My mom can."

"She's a strong woman, your mom."

"Yes, she is."

"Have you had a bowel movement yet?"

"Ya, just a little while ago."

"Any blood?"

"No, why?"

"We just want to make sure there isn't any internal bleeding."

"Oh."

"Well, I'll see about getting you some crutches then, and I'll see you in the morning."

"Thanks doc."

'Great,' John thinks. He gets to go home Monday. Good ridden to this stinking hospital.

"Hi honey," says Kathleen as she enters the room.

"Hi!"

"Boy, you sound chipper!"

"The doc just told me I can go home Monday."

"Oh, that's wonderful."

"I'm probably gonna need some help for a while though."

"I already planned on it. I canceled all my appointments for the next two weeks so I can take care of you."

"I should be back to work in a week."

"Don't push it! You don't want to reinjure yourself."

"I won't."

"How does Thursday sound for the service? That's the soonest the funeral home can do it."

"That's fine."

"I talked to Laura, and she wants to get it over with as soon as possible."

"Ya, I guess that's best."

"Are you going to be ok?"

"Ya. It's going to be hard, but I'll get through it."

"The accident was in the newspaper today. I'm so mad I could just spit!"

"Why?"

"They just had to mention that it's being investigated, and that alcohol might be a factor."

"That's our local paper for ya. They gotta make the story nice and juicy."

"You know that everyone's going to think that you were drunk."

"But I wasn't. That's all that counts."

"I know, but it just makes me mad!"

"Don't worry mom, everything will be fine. You go home and get a good night's sleep now. You're gonna need your strength to help this old cripple get around."

"Ok, I'll be back in the morning. You sleep well dear."

"Goodnight."

John lays his head down and tries to sleep, but all he can think about is the funeral. To see the boys laying in their caskets is not a sight he's looking forward to. He decides to try and think of happier days and drifts off to sleep. Sunday passes like molasses in summertime as John waits in anticipation of Monday, and going home.

"Good morning John," says the nurse from the Monday morning shift. "Looks like you're going home this morning."

"Ya, I can't wait."

"Well, we have to clean you up some, so I'm going to give you a bath.

"Like hell you are!"

"Don't worry John," smiles the nurse, "I've given lots of guys baths."

"Not THIS guy!"

"Are you going to give me trouble?"

"Not as long as you don't try to undress me!"

"Don't worry, I'll turn my back while you wash your privates."

"Well...ok then. But I'm not going to enjoy this!"

John grumbles as he gets his bath. Afterwards, the doctor comes in with his crutches, followed by Kathleen.

"Morning John."

"Hi doc. You're just in time. Tell these damn nurses to leave me alone!"

"Calm down big fella, she's just doing her job. Now, let's have a look here." The doctor gives John the once over. "Well, let's see if you can master crutches. Have you ever walked with crutches before?"

"No." The doctor helps John stand up and adjusts the crutches to fit. John takes a couple of steps and says, "No problem. I can handle this."

"Are you sure dear?" asks Kathleen. "We could get you a walker."

"No way! These will do just fine."

"I'll send the orderlies in to help you get dressed, and I'll get you checked out. I'll make an appointment for you to see me at my office in a week."

"Ok doc. Thanks!"

"You're welcome, John."

"I'll wait for you at the front desk hon," says Kathleen.

"Ok mom."

Finally, he gets to go home. It's gonna be nice to sleep in his own bed again. The orderlies help him get dressed and wheel him to the front door. Kathleen is there with his crutches. The car is waiting outside. John feels a lot of pain as he tries to position himself in the seat.

"Are you ok dear?"

"Ya, just get me home and I'll be fine."

They start the drive for home. John can feel every little bump. It's a beautiful day. Blue sky, sunshine, about 80-degrees. John is being quiet. He thinks he should be up in the mountains with Brett and Ryan right now.

"Did they give you any special diet?" asks Kathleen.

"No, but I better take it easy for a while. I don't think I could handle indigestion right now."

"I thought we'd have a cheese casserole tonight."

"Sounds good."

As they pull into John's driveway, they notice a big red ribbon tied around the tree in his front yard.

"What the hell is that doing there?" asks John.

"I don't know. It wasn't there this morning. I wonder who did that?"

"Isn't that the signature of MADD?" which stands for mothers against drunk drivers.

"Oh, that's right, it is. Well, I'm going to give them a piece of my mind!"

Kathleen helps John into the house and then goes back outside to tear that ribbon off the tree. The first thing John notices when he enters the house is all the pictures of Brett and Ryan. He does his best to hold his composure. Then he notices that there are several messages on his answering machine. He hits the play button, and the first one says, "You should have been the one to die you, drunken BASTARD! I hope you have a miserable fucking life!"

CHAPTER 8

———— ⛬ ————

"Boy, those people are gonna hear it from me! There is no reason for that."

"Don't worry about it mom, it doesn't bother me."

"Well, it bothers me!"

John thinks to himself, 'he really picked the wrong woman to mess with. They're going to get a taste of that Irish temper.'

"I think I'm going to lay down for a while. I'll be fine if you've got errands to run."

"Well, I do need to get some groceries. Do you need anything?"

"I probably do, but I'll look later."

"Ok then, I'll come back in a couple of hours."

"Ok, bye."

After she leaves, he goes to the answering machine and hits the play button. "John this is Ed. I just heard about the accident. I'm so sorry John. Give me a call when you can, take care buddy." That was nice of Ed he thinks. Next message, "How do ya feel MURDERER? Why don't ya have another beer, MURDERER?!" John's blood is boiling now. He wishes he could get his hands on the gutless owner of that voice. It's times like this he wishes he had caller ID. The rest of the messages were from friends expressing to him their heart felt sorrow. He deletes the bad messages so that Kathleen doesn't play them back, and then goes into the bedroom to lay down. He is almost asleep when he hears a load knock on the door.

"Great! I'm never gonna get any rest."

He reaches for his crutches, and before he can even stand up. KNOCK...KNOCK...KNOCK!!!

"John McDuffy! Are you in there?"

John yells, "I'm coming!"

'Who could this obnoxious asshole be,' he wonders. John opens the door to find a uniformed deputy sheriff and the detective from the hospital.

"Mr. McDuffy?" asks the deputy.

"Yes."

"I'm afraid you'll have to come with us sir. I have a warrant here for your arrest."

"ON WHAT CHARGE?!"

"Manslaughter sir. You have the right to remain silent. You have..."

As the detective is reading him his rights, the deputy is reaching for his handcuffs, but notices that John is on crutches, and decides the handcuffs are not needed.

"You guys gotta be kidding! It was that girl's fault! Not mine!"

"I suggest you wait until your attorney is present before you say anything else sir."

"Can I at least leave a note for my mother?"

"I'll call her sir."

John can't believe this is happening. He just lost his boys, and now these bastards are taking him to jail. What next, a public hanging?! The deputy helps John into the back of the patrol car as the neighbors stand outside their homes and watch. John notices their long faces as they drive away.

"This is bullshit! You guys are screwed up!"

"I suggest you remain silent sir until your attorney is pre..."

"I don't have a fucking attorney!"

"Then one will be appointed to you."

"What good will that do?! You guys have already made up your minds that your gonna pin this on me since you can't arrest a corpse!"

They pull up to the county jail and the deputy helps John out of the car. A wheelchair is waiting for him and they wheel him inside. Once inside, they begin the booking process.

"Please place all your personal belongings into this box Mr. McDuffy," says the detective.

John does what they say and they move him to another room for the strip search. They scan the cast on his leg for any metal objects and modify an orange jump suit to fit around his cast. They take him to a jail cell and help him to the lower bunk. After removing the wheelchair from the room, John hears a sound that he's never heard before in his life. SLAM, CLICK! The sound of a jail cell door locking him in. A chill runs up his spine as he looks around the room. It's a cell meant for two, but apparently, he's the only one here, as there is no personal belongings lying around. There is a tiny window on his left that is about six inches wide and six feet tall. No need for bars because it's too small for anyone to fit through. Ahead in the corner on his left is a toilet and a sink. No walls around for privacy. To the right of the sink is a small table and chair. There is another set just like it in front of the window. His leg and ribs are throbbing. That reminds him…

"Hey!" he yells at the detective just before he exits the pod. "I need my pain killers from the house!"

"The county doctor will give you some after he examines you," the detective yells as he goes through the door."

"Ya! I need some too!" yells a voice from another cell.

"Me too!" yells another one.

John lies down on the bed and thinks, 'What the hell am I doing here? I don't belong here with all these scum bags. I wonder who left those messages on my machine? I wonder who put that ribbon around my tree? I wonder why I've been arrested? The blood/alcohol test couldn't have shown past the limit. I could drink a whole six pack and still be sober.'

Then he remembers the two beers he had at the shop Friday before he left. A customer stopped in with a six pack about 4:30, and John drank two beers before locking the place up at 5:00. But that still couldn't have been enough to make him test legally drunk. They are just out to pin this accident on somebody, and since he is the only survivor, he's it. He closes his eyes and tries to rest again. He doesn't have much success though, because his body is throbbing and the inmates are making a terrible racket.

He can hear one of the voices yelling, "Hey bro, check it out, fresh meat!"

"Ya man…I can't wait!"

John thinks, 'Just try it asshole. That'll be the last thing you ever do!'

He's heard about some of the weird things these sick-o's do in prison, but he's not going to be here that long. Hopefully they'll figure it out pretty soon that he didn't cause the accident and let him out of there. If he has to stay here very long, he'll go nuts. John has never been one to be penned up inside. He likes to be outdoors as much as possible.

"Ok John, you've got a visitor."

A huge black prison guard blurts out as he unlocks the door and pushes the wheelchair inside.

"Who is it?"

"I don't know, I'm just supposed to come and get you."

"I hope it's my mother."

"Could be. My name is James, but everybody calls me Bubba."

"Nice to meet you Bubba."

"Whatcha in for?"

"Manslaughter I guess."

"Bummer."

As soon as they enter the visitation area, John sees Kathleen's angry face.

"Hi mom."

"Hi honey. What the devil are you doing in here?"

"That's what I'd like to know! They arrested me for manslaughter!"

"What?! That's a bunch of crap! Can't they see that you're not even healed up yet?!"

"They don't give a shit. Did you go back over to the house?"

"No. I took the groceries home and saw the message on the machine and rushed right down. I can't believe the nerve of these people."

"Will you do me a favor and go by the house and lock the door? I didn't even have time to do that."

"Yes, I will."

"Maybe talk to Bob across the street too and ask him to keep an eye on the place?"

"Yes, I will, and don't you worry! I'm going to get to the bottom of this and I'll have you out of here in no time!"

"I bet you will," smiles John.

If there is anyone he would like to have in his corner, it's her.

"Times up," barks Bubba.

"Just keep your shirt on!" snaps Kathleen. "I'm not finished yet! Do you need anything sweetheart?"

"No. Just get me out of here."

"Should I call a lawyer?"

"No, they said they would appoint me one."

"Oh, dear those public defenders aren't worth beans. Let me get your father's lawyer."

"No mom, we can't afford it. And besides, it's not going to take much of a lawyer to prove that I'm innocent."

"Ok dear."

"Time to go ma'am."

"I'm going, I'm going. You take care dear and I'll be in touch."

"Ok mom, bye."

Kathleen gives Bubba the evil eye as she leaves the room. Bubba pushes John back to his cell.

"Boy! She's quite the fire cracker, yur mom."

"Yes, she is," smiles John. "They're in for a hell of a fight with her, hey Bubba?"

"Yes sir."

Kathleen storms up to the front desk, "Who is in charge here?!"

"May I help you ma'am?" asks a deputy from behind the counter.

"Yes! Who do I talk to about getting my son out of here!?"

"Calm down ma'am. Who is your son?"

"John McDuffy!"

The deputy looks through his manifest of new arrivals.

"Looks like Mr. McDuffy just arrived here."

"But he's innocent! He doesn't belong here!"

The deputy thinks to himself, 'How many times have I heard that before,' but he can see that this woman is fit to be tied, so he better not make any smart comments.

"Ma'am, I'm sorry, but there is nothing we can do today. You have to contact the sheriff's office in the morning."

"You mean he has to spend the night here?"

"Yes ma'am."

Kathleen scowls at the deputy as she turns around and storms out the door. After she gets outside, she starts to cry with the thought, 'Poor Johnny has just lost his two sons, and now he has to spend the night in jail. Those people are going to pay!'

The county physician examines John and gives him some pain killers. He takes them and lies down to rest. It doesn't take long before they take effect and he starts to feel better. As he lays on the bed, all he can think about is the way he has suddenly become hated. He's not used to this. People have always liked him. He can't remember ever having an enemy. Now it appears he is the biggest scum bag in town, thanks to the newspaper.

"Get off me!"

"Settle down Billy."

"Get yur stinkin' paws off me god dammit!"

"C'mon, just a little farther."

John opens his eyes and looks up to see Bubba escorting a drunk, screaming Native American young man to his cell. The same cell that John is in!

'Great!' John thinks, 'things aren't bad enough, now he has to share a cell with a stinking drunk!'

CHAPTER 9

───⊰❈⊱───

"WAIT TILL MY GODDAMN LAWYER hears how you've been treating me! He'll have your nuts on a platter!"

"Ok Billy, whatever you say."

Billy Little Bear is a twenty-four-year-old Blackfoot Native American from Browning, Montana. He lives on the reservation most of the time, but occasionally comes into Great Falls to do some shopping with his family. Inevitably, he gets into trouble when he starts drinking. He is a very proud young man and has a strong sense of the warrior spirit inside him.

John opens one eye to look him over and thinks, 'Well, he's stocky, but he's not THAT big. I could take him if I had to.'

"What the hell are you looking at?" Blurts Billy as he staggers around the cell, kicking and punching things. "You want a piece of me?"

"Listen," says John, "you don't bother me, and I won't bother you, ok?"

Billy notices his cast, "How'd ya bust yur leg?"

"I wrecked my truck."

"So why the hell ya in here?"

"Manslaughter."

Billy suddenly has a newfound respect for his cell-mate, "Who the hell d'ya kill?"

"I don't want to talk about it! I just want to get some sleep, ok?!"

"Ok, ok. Don't get yur nuts in a knot."

Billy sits in a chair for a while before he decides to climb up into the top bunk and lay down. On the first attempt, he almost tipped the bed over, but instead, he tipped over. Second attempt. He decided to take a running leap at it like he would a wild mustang. With one foot hooked on top of the mattress, and the other one kicking John in the back, he cussed and clawed at the mattress trying to pull himself up. After the third kick, John has had enough of this, and decided to roll over and give him a leg up.

"Thanks man."

"Don't mention it."

It wasn't long before Billy was snoring. It also wasn't long before John began to hear the sound that he dreaded.

"Urp...urp...urp...blaaaaa!"

"GREAT! BUBBA! Get in here!"

Bubba came running when he heard John holler, "What's wro...oh, maaan."

Bubba started laughing as he saw vomit all over the floor by Johns bunk and Billy's head hanging over the edge of his bunk.

"Sorry John," said Bubba as he snickered, "we'll get it cleaned up."

Bubba left to round up the maintenance crew as Billy continued to throw his guts up all over the side of John's bunk and the floor. John just held his breath so as not to throw up himself from the smell. If there is anything he can't stand, it's a drunk. He used to tend bar part time, and he's had his fill of drunks.

Back at home, Kathleen is thumbing through the phone book trying to find a phone number for MADD. She finally finds the number of the nearest local office, and calls it.

All she got was an answering machine, so she left a message, "This is Kathleen McDuffy! I want to know who is responsible for tying the red ribbon around the tree in front of my son's house! My son is NOT a drunk driver! You people are in a lot of trouble! Call me back asap, and tell me who is responsible for this!"

Kathleen leaves her number and slams the phone down. As she sinks back in her easy-chair, all she can do is weep. Her grandsons are dead, and her son is in jail. How could things get any worse?

Ring! Ring!

"Hello?"

"Hi."

"Hi, Laura."

"I just heard. Are you ok?"

"Yes, I'll be ok. I just can't help but think, what's next? Did you hear someone tied a red ribbon around the tree in the front yard?"

"Ya, Bob called me. Who do ya think did that?"

"I don't know, but I'm going to find out! I know that it's the trademark of MADD so I have a call in to them. If I find out they're responsible, I'm going to sue them for every dime they have."

"I don't blame you. So why did they arrest him?"

"They charged him with manslaughter."

"No!"

"Yes. I think it's because of all the beer cans they found on the scene. Plus, I think the Wadder's are putting the pressure on to do something too."

"Have you talked to them?"

"No. I wouldn't know what to say. They must be devastated. They were so proud of Amy, and she was their only child. When I was at the funeral home, they told me that they are handling Amy's funeral too.

"By the way, thank you for helping with the funeral arrangements. I don't think I could have done it. Carl offered to help, but it's not really his place. So...does John have insurance to pay for it?"

"I don't know. I forgot to ask him. I'll ask him tomorrow when I see him."

"Ok, well I better let you go. I'll bet you're beat."

"Yes, I am, but every time I close my eyes, all I see are the boys. The holidays are going to be real hard this year."

"Yes, I know. Well, you take care Kathleen, and thanks again."

"You're welcome sweetie, take care."

As Kathleen hangs up the phone, she looks at the clock. It's nine. She decides to go to bed, and at least try to sleep. She's got a big day ahead of her tomorrow. First thing in the morning, she's going down to the courthouse to raise some hell.

The night is another restless one, but Kathleen did manage to get some rest.

Ring...ring...

"Hello?"

"Hello, Mrs. McDuffy?"

"Yes."

"This is Susan Brown with Mothers Against Drunk Drivers."

"Yes!"

"I just got your disturbing message, and frankly, I don't know what you're talking about."

"I'm talking about the red ribbon that someone tied around the tree in my son's front yard."

"Yes, I got that from your message, but I can assure you that it wasn't done by anyone from this organization. We just don't do things like that."

"Well who did then?"

"I don't know, but I assure you, if we find out who did it, they're going to be in a lot of trouble! The red ribbon has always been a trademark of MADD, and if someone is out there using it to harass your son, then we WILL find out who, and prosecute them!"

"Thank you."

"By the way, I read about your son's terrible accident, and I'm very sorry. If you need our support in any way, please feel free to call me."

"Thank you, I will."

"Good day Mrs. McDuffy."

"Goodbye."

Kathleen hangs up the phone and gathers her things as she heads out the door. She thinks to herself, 'That Susan seems like a nice gal. I wonder who IS responsible? If I get my hands on them, they're going to be sorry!'

It's a beautiful Tuesday morning. The birds are singing, the sun is shining, and people are busily on their way to their jobs.

Kathleen thinks, 'It should be raining...that would be more fitting.'

She pulls into the Sheriff's office parking lot and goes inside.

"May I help you ma'am?" asks the receptionist.

"Yes! I want to find out why my son was arrested!"

"Who is your son ma'am?"

"John McDuffy!"

A man from the back of the office heard the commotion and came forward.

"May I help you ma'am?"

"Yes! You can release my son from jail!"

"Why don't we go into my office and I'll see what I can do."

Kathleen follows him into the plush office.

"My name is Detective Cliff Richards, and you are?"

"Kathleen McDuffy. My son John was arrested for manslaughter, and I want to know why!"

"Calm down ma'am. Would you like a cup of coffee?"

"No thank you. Just tell me why my son was arrested!"

"Well, let me go get the file and I'll be right back, ok?"

"Alright, but hurry up!"

Kathleen waits with both barrels loaded, ready to unload on Detective Richards. Soon he returns with some papers in his hands and sits down at his desk. After what seemed like an eternity of silence while the detective thumbed through the papers, Kathleen finally speaks out.

"Well?"

"Ma'am, it seems that the results from Mr. McDuffy's blood/alcohol test were positive."

"Was it past the legal limit?"

"I don't have the exact readings, all I can tell you is that he tested positive. Also, there was an inspection completed at the scene of the accident, and apparently, there were many beer cans found."

"I explained that!"

"Yes ma'am, but the evidence still remains. Results from the investigation of the skid marks also revealed evidence that Mr. McDuffy was possibly in the wrong lane at the time of impact. This, compiled with the blood/alcohol test and the presence of several beer cans found on the scene, produced enough evidence to warrant an arrest. I'm sorry Mrs. McDuffy, but your son will have to remain in the county jail until his hearing. I suggest he hires a lawyer."

Kathleen's emotions have suddenly gone from fire in her soul, to a sick feeling in her stomach.

Her eyes begin to water as she explains to the detective, "He can't afford a lawyer. He just bought a new house and we have the expense of the funeral for the boys, and..." Kathleen can't take it anymore and is reduced to tears.

"Don't worry ma'am, we'll appoint a public defender. I'll get the paperwork started. I'm sorry that this terrible thing had to happen to your family Mrs. McDuffy. I hope everything will come out alright."

"Thank you," cries Kathleen as the detective helps her to the door.

"Are you going to be alright ma'am? Should I arrange a ride for you?"

"No. I'll be fine. I need to see my son and let him know what is going on though."

"Yes ma'am. I'll walk you to the administrator's desk. Kathleen walks down the hall toward the jailer's office trying to rehearse in her head how she is going to tell John that he has to stand trial for the murder of his sons, and Amy Wadder. She just can't believe this is happening. Why is God punishing her so? Isn't the death of her grandsons enough? She couldn't bear to lose her son too.

"Here we are ma'am. I'll leave you here, and I'll get started on the paperwork for the public defender."

"Thank you, detective." Kathleen looks at the jailer with tear-filled eyes, "I need to see my son please."

"Yes ma'am, follow me."

The jailer guides Kathleen to the visiting area, and soon returns with John in a wheelchair. Kathleen looks at him and says, "Didn't you sleep at all dear? You look terrible."

"No. They put a drunken Indian in the cell with me. He puked half the night and snored the other half. What'd ya find out?"

"Well, nothing good. I'm afraid you're going to have to stand trial."

"Why?"

"Well, apparently, your blood/alcohol test came out positive, and they're trying to say that you were in the wrong lane."

"GREAT! First I lose my sons, now I'm gonna rot in jail."

"NO WAY! I WON'T LET THAT HAPPEN! I've got the paperwork started for a public defender. I'm sure that once they take a good hard look at the evidence, they'll see that you're innocent."

John can see that this is upsetting her as much as it is him.

"I suppose you're right. There's no way they can prove me guilty on this. She was in my lane."

"That's right, so you just try to get some rest and get that leg healed up, and I'll take care of everything."

"Ya, right. How am I supposed to get any rest with that drunken Indian in my cell?"

"Well, just dazzle him with your natural charm."

"Right," smiles John, "then he'll probably kiss me."

Kathleen laughs for the first time in days. "Well, just don't kiss him back."

"Time's up you guys," announces Bubba.

Kathleen gives him a scowl.

"Take it easy on him mom, he actually takes pretty good care of me."

"Ok dear, I'll talk to you soon."

"Bye mom." Kathleen turns to leave. "Mom?"

"Yes dear?"

"I love you."

"I love you too, dear."

Kathleen leaves and John goes back to his cell. Each of them is thinking about the long hard road ahead and wonder what the future holds in store.

CHAPTER 10

———— ✦✦✦ ————

"JEANIE, COULD YOU COME IN here please?" announces Jack over the intercom.

Jack Peters is the senior member of Peters-Mathews-and-Campbell Law Offices.

"You called Jack?"

"Yes Jeanie, have a seat."

"Something wrong Jack?"

"No, no, in fact, I want to compliment you on the excellent work you're doing."

"Thanks Jack."

"The reason I called you in here is I just received a call from an old friend, Kathleen McDuffy. She wants to retain our services for her son John who has been arrested for manslaughter."

"What happened?"

"He was in a bad accident up on Rogers Pass. His two sons and the driver of the other vehicle were killed."

"That's terrible!"

"Yes, it is. I want you to take the case Jeanie."

"Really?!"

"Yes. I think you're ready."

"Thank you, Jack! I won't let you down!"

"I know you'll do us proud Jeanie."

"So, why was he arrested for manslaughter?"

"It appears he had been drinking."

Jeanie's happiness and anticipation for getting her first case has turned into anger and contempt for Jack. How could he possibly be so cruel to give her a case like this? Just two years ago, Jeanie lost her husband and little girl in an accident caused by a drunk driver. She still grieves, and Jack knows it.

"Thanks anyway Jack, but you can give this one to someone else."

"I've already decided Jeanie, this one's yours."

"JACK! How can you do this to me? You know damn well Calvin and Britney were killed by a drunk driver!"

"I know Jeanie, and I'm doing this for you own good."

"MY OWN GOOD? What the hell good could come out of me defending the very kind of scum that killed Calvin and Britney?"

"Jeanie, every client is innocent until proven guilty, you know that. This is just the kind of case you need to teach you how to deal with sensitive issues and put your own emotions aside. I know you think I'm being cruel, but I truly believe that this case will help you crawl out of that pit of sorrow you've been living in the past two years. It hurts me to see you mope around the office Jeanie. You need to get on with your life."

"What would you know about it Jack? You still have your family!"

Jeanie's eyes are starting to water now as she thinks about Calvin and Britney.

"I don't claim to know what you're going through Jeanie, but I do know you can't grieve for ever, it's not healthy. Now, I've set up an appointment this afternoon with Kathleen. She's very upset, so I expect you to be the professional that I know you can be."

"Can't I give it some thought first?"

"You'll have plenty of time to think as you work on the case."

"Jack, please!"

"My decision is final Jeanie. You're it."

Jeanie glares at Jack for a moment, then stands up and storms out as she slams the door. She decides to go for a drive to collect her thoughts. As she drives down the river-road, she thinks about the night she received the call. It was New Year's Eve, 1996, about 4:00 pm. Calvin and Britney were on their way home from the ice skating rink. The phone rang.

"Mrs. Philips?"

"Yes?"

"Are you the wife of Calvin Philips?"

"Yes."

"Mrs. Philips, I'm sorry to inform you that your husband has been in an accident. Could you please come to the emergency room at Great Falls Medical Center right away?"

"OH MY GOD! IS HE OK?"

"Well, ma'am I'm not authorized to give you the details over the phone. If you could just please get here as soon as you can."

"I'M ON MY WAY!"

When she got to the hospital, they broke the news to her that both her husband and daughter were killed in a head-on wreck. The other driver was drunk and crossed the center line. He was treated and released with minor injuries and arrested on the spot. He is serving time for manslaughter. Jeanie was destroyed. She felt her life was over. Her husband and daughter meant the world to her. She fell into a state of grief that almost killed her. It was Jack that finally got her back on her feet again. He explained to her that she was needed in the office to help defend victims and their families from criminal drunk drivers like the one who took her family from her. Now he wants her to defend one of these people.

'WHERE IS HIS REASONING?' she thinks as she pulls into the parking lot of the ice skating rink.

She knows Jack is a wise man and respects his opinion, but how can her defending a drunk driver possibly help her get over the grief of losing her family? She sits and stares at the building where she, Calvin, and Britney had so many good times. A tear slowly works its way down her cheek and pauses briefly on her chin before it drops to her breast. Another tear follows, then another. Pretty soon Jeanie is sobbing out of control as the memories of her family flood her heart and mind. Somehow, she must convince Jack that she can't do this. It's almost noon, so Jeanie decides to pull herself together and grab a bite to eat before she heads back to the office. Wadder's Coffee Shop is nearby, so she decides to go there. She walks in and finds a table by the window and sits down. She stares out the window at a man shopping with his baby girl.

"May I help you?"

Jeanie turns to see a young smiling waitress standing by her table.

"Yes. I'd like a diet cola and a menu please."

"Comin right up."

Jeanie looks around the café and notices Judge Murphy sitting at the counter talking to Ron Wadder, the owner. She can't quite make out what they're saying, but Ron is obviously upset the way he's waving his arms around and pounding his fist on the counter.

"Here's your diet cola and your menu."

"Thank you. Excuse me, is that Judge Murphy sitting over there?"

"Oh ya, he's in here every day."

"Really."

"Ya, he's a friend of Ron and Kathy's."

"Oohh, thank you."

"Sure thing, I'll be right back to take your order."

Jeanie remembers back to the time in Judge Murphy's courtroom when the man that took the lives of her husband and daughter stood before him. The man's lawyer explained how his client had just been told by his wife that she wanted a divorce, and he was on pain killers for a back injury he had sustained at work. Therefore, he was out of work pending a workman's compensation claim, and his wife just told him she wants a divorce. The Judge was ruthless. He didn't care about any of the man's hardships. He threw the book at him.

"Ready to order ma'am?"

"Oh, I'm sorry, yes. I'll just take the lunch special."

"Ok, comin right up."

Jeanie finished her lunch and fumbled through her purse for some money as she watched Judge Murphy and Ron Wadder shake hands. The Judge turned to leave, but noticed Jeanie looking at him. He smiled and waved. She waved back and noticed Ron staring at her with a questioning look on his face. She just paid her bill and left. On her way back to the office, she felt nothing inside, just an emptiness like the void between right and wrong. Suddenly, she's not so dead against taking the case, but she can't explain why. Once back in the office, she begins to look up past cases of vehicular manslaughter. Before she knew it, Jack was calling her into his office to meet with Kathleen McDuffy.

"Kathleen," says Jack, "this is Jeanie Philips. I've assigned her to help with John's case."

"Good afternoon," says Jeanie politely.

"Nice to meet you," says Kathleen.

"I'm so sorry about your grandchildren. You must be overwhelmed with grief," says Jeanie.

"Thank you," says Kathleen, "yes I am. It was the most terrible shock I've ever experienced."

"Kathleen," says Jack, "please explain to the best of your knowledge what happened."

"Well, John was taking the boys camping for the weekend like he usually does, except this weekend was special. Not only did they have three days, but the boys just got new mountain bikes and they were going to explore some new trails I guess. John said he had a couple of beers with a customer before he left work, but two beers is nothing to John. It just doesn't affect him like it does some people. Anyway, he went home and packed the camper, stopped for a hamburger on the way out of town, and then hit the road. He said they stopped at the rest area to relieve themselves and grab something to drink. He said he drank another beer there and threw the empty in the back of the truck with the rest that he had been collecting. He estimated that there was probably about twelve cans in the back. Anyway, they went on their way. Then everything was pretty much ordinary, until on the other side of Rogers Pass, he came up to a curve in the road, and suddenly there was a little red car in the middle of his lane. He tried to decide to go in the ditch and total his truck, or take a chance and go around on the left. He said he would have made it, but something hit his trailer. Either it was the little car or the semi behind him. He thinks it was the little car, because the semi was way behind him. Anyway, the trailer was knocked off the edge of the road, and pulled the truck over the edge too. The cops say the skid marks show that HE was in the wrong lane. They also say he tested POSATIVE for alcohol in his blood, but they don't have the details of the blood/alcohol ratio. So, they wouldn't say if he was over the legal limit. And there is NO WAY John could have been over the legal limit! He could drink twelve beers, and you wouldn't even notice it. Besides, Johnny would never, ever drive drunk! ESPECIALLY when he had his boys with him! Johnny loved the boys!"

Kathleen's eyes are starting to show signs of tears again.

"The last vision I have of Brett and Ryan is their excited little faces as they were getting ready to spend the weekend in the mountains with their dad. They loved him sooo much, and loved going camping. That week John had bought them new bikes, and they were so excited about trying them out on the trails. Please!!! You have to prove Johnny innocent. If he has to stay locked up in jail, he'll go crazy! He can't stand to be inside for very long. He loves the outdoors sooo much. Please tell me you can get him out of there!"

"We'll do our best Kathleen. You have my word on it!" says Jack.

Jeanie just stares at Kathleen as Jack gives her a hug. 'What a strong woman,' she is thinking. Having to bare the grief of losing her grandsons, and then having to deal with this. She must be an incredible woman.

"I'll get down there to talk to John as soon as possible," says Jeanie. "Don't you worry Mrs. McDuffy."

"Kathleen."

Jeanie smiles as she says, "Ok, Kathleen. Don't you worry, I'll have him out of there before you know it!"

"Thank you dear! God bless you!"

Kathleen gives Jeanie a big hug. Jack looks on and smiles.

"I'll need to get with you later and ask you some questions," says Jeanie.

"Any time dear."

The void in Jeanie's decision-making has suddenly disappeared. She now knows what she must do. She smiles at Jack as she hugs Kathleen. That sly old fox knew all along. 'The client is innocent until proven guilty,' she thinks. 'I must give this man a chance…for his mother's sake.'

———⟨∞∞∞⟩———

CHAPTER 11

"MAY I HELP YOU?"

"Yes, I'm here to see John McDuffy."

"And you are?"

"Jeanie Philips. I'm his attorney."

"Sign in here please."

Jeanie signs the register and the deputy leads her to the conference room. As she sits waiting for her client to arrive, she can't help but feel eyes on her. There are other prisoners in the room and they are all looking at this foxy little redhead that just came in. Jeanie has had to put up with this all her life, so she's used to it. She's a pretty little lady with a great body, the desire of every man. Sometimes it really bothers her when a man keeps staring at her breasts when she's trying to have an intelligent conversation with him. He doesn't care about what she has to say, he would just like her to take her shirt off.

"Here ya go Johnny. Ya got fifteen minutes."

"Thanks Bubba."

Jeanie smiles as John wheels himself towards the glass.

"Mr. McDuffy I presume?"

"You presume right. And you are?"

"My name is Jeanie Philips. Your mother has hired me to get you out of here."

"I thought she was going to get Jack Peters?"

"She did. I work for Jack."

"Oh. So, you're his secretary or something?"

"No. I'm an attorney. Jack is the senior partner of Peters, Mathews and Campbell. He's tied up with another case right now so I will be handling yours."

"Well, what about one of the other partners?"

"They're tied up with cases also. Don't worry Mr. McDuffy, I can handle this. I graduated at the top of my class, and I passed my bar exam with honors."

"Well, that's all fine and dandy, but if it's all the same to you, I'd still rather have Jack on the case."

Jeanie glares at him and says, "Do you have a problem with female attorney's Mr. McDuffy?"

"No, it's just that…"

"What? Go ahead! Spit it out!"

"Look! Jack has been doing this a long time!"

"I realize that Mr. McDuffy, but he can't take on another case right now. I'm all you've got! Take it or leave it!"

John glares at her and says, "Well, then I guess I'll leave it! Bubba! We're finished here."

"But ya still got ten minutes."

"I don't care. I have nothing more to say to this person."

"Ok, you're da boss."

Bubba wheels John back to his cell as Jeanie just sits there for a moment, wondering what just happened. She can't believe that stubborn asshole is Kathleen McDuffy's son. He is nothing like her.

'What a pig!' she thinks. 'I wouldn't represent him if he was the president's son. He can rot in here for all I care.'

She gets up and signs out. On her way back to the office, you could fry an egg on her head as she thinks about the things John said.

"Jack? Are you busy?"

"No. Come in Jeanie. What's up?"

"Well, I just got back from a lovely visit with John McDuffy."

"Okaaayy."

"He's an asshole!"

Jack chuckles, "What do you mean?"

"I mean he's an asshole! He wants you to represent him. He doesn't trust me."

"Well, why not?"

"I don't know! Probably because I'm a woman and I haven't been doing this as long as you have."

"Did you explain to him that I'm tied up with another case right now?"

"Yes, I did. And as far as I'm concerned, he can hire someone else. The man is a jerk!"

"Now, Jeanie, you just don't understand him."

"Oh, I understand him perfectly! He doesn't think a woman can represent him as well as a man can!"

"That's not it at all. He trusts me because I used to represent his father when he was alive."

"What kind of trouble was his father in?"

"Oh, every now and then he would drink a little too much and try to drive home."

"So, his father was a drunk?"

"No, I didn't say that. There were just a few times when he should have called a cab instead of trying to drive home."

"Like father, like son!"

"Now Jeanie, don't condemn the man just because your first meeting didn't go well. I'll talk to him and explain your credentials. You just try to focus on the evidence. Get the results of the blood/alcohol test, then go out to the scene and take some pictures. He shouldn't even be in jail, but someone is putting the pressure on the DA. By the way, Kathleen called for you this morning. She wants you to call her back asap."

"Can't you put someone else on this case Jack?"

"Jeanie, you need this one. Give John another chance. Try to put yourself in his shoes. Remember! Innocent unt…"

"I know, I know…until proven guilty. Ok, I'll try."

"Thanks Jeanie."

Jeanie goes to her office and tries to collect her thoughts before calling Kathleen. She just can't get over how different those two are.

"Hello?"

"Hello, Kathleen. This is Jeanie Philips."

"Oh, yes. Hi dear. The reason I called is I was wondering if you can do something about the red ribbons that someone keeps putting up around John's house."

"Red ribbons?"

"Yes. They're the symbol of MADD. I called them, but they swear they're not the ones doing it. It's probably someone who was a friend of Amy's. Whoever it is, they better not let me catch them!"

"Gee, I didn't know anything about it. I'll check into it Kathleen."

"Thank you dear. Sooo, have you been up to see John yet?"

"Yes, I have! And I must say, our first meeting didn't go very well at all."

"What happened?"

"Well, he doesn't seem to think a woman can represent him as well as a man can."

"Oh, I should have warned you. He can be kind of a jerk sometimes. Don't you worry dear, I'll straighten HIM out!"

"Ok, Kathleen," chuckles Jeanie. "You do that, and I'll get to the bottom of this red ribbon bandit."

"Thank you, sweetie."

It's almost 11:00, so Jeanie decides to take a trip over to Wadder's Coffee Shop and visit with the Wadder's.

As she walks in the door, the waitress recognizes her and says, "Two days in a row."

Jeanie smiles and takes a seat at the counter. Ron Wadder hurries over.

"Good morning!"

"Good morning," says Jeanie.

"What'll ya have?"

"Oh, let's see, how 'bout an Irish cream latte."

"Comin right up." Ron gives the order to the kitchen and returns to his customer. "Sooo, how do you know Paul?"

"You mean Judge Murphy?"

"Ya, I saw you wave at each other yesterday."

"Oh, I know him from the court room. I'm an attorney."

"Oh really, what's your name?"

"Jeanie Philips."

"Ron Wadder, nice to meet you." Ron reaches out to shake Jeanie's hand.

"Nice to meet you too," says Jeanie. She notices Ron has that kind of puzzling look on his face like 'haven't I seen you somewhere before?' and she knows what's coming.

"That name sounds familiar. Pardon me for asking but, didn't you lose your husband and daughter in an accident a couple of years ago?"

"Yes. Judge Murphy is the one that put the scum bag behind bars."

"I thought I recognized you. I'm so sorry. It made me sick when I read about that."

"Thank you. I'm really sorry to hear about your daughter too. You and Kathy must be heartbroken."

"Well, I don't have to tell YOU how we feel. She was our pride and joy. We're going to make sure Paul throws the book at that son-of-a-bitch that killed her, the same way he did against the drunken bastard that took your husband and daughter from you."

"So, the other driver was drunk?"

"YES! There were beer cans everywhere!" Jeanie can see that Ron's blood pressure is starting to climb, so she tries to re-direct the conversation.

"So, does Judge Murphy come in here every day?"

"Every day. In fact, I expect him any minute."

'Uh oh,' thinks Jeanie.

"How's my latte coming?"

"Should be about done," says Ron as he turns to the kitchen to look.

Too late! Jeanie looks in the mirror above the back counter and sees Judge Murphy coming through the door. Busted!

"Hi Jeanie!"

"Hi Judge, long time no see."

"So…you here on business, or do you have time for lunch?"

"Business?" says Ron.

Jeanie sinks back into her chair.

"Ya. Didn't she tell you?"

"Tell me what?" asks Ron as he looks at Jeanie.

"Peters, Mathews and Campbell are going to be representing McDuffy."

Ron just looks at Judge Murphy with a baffled look on his face.

"Jeanie works for that office."

Ron's face suddenly turns the color of blood as he slowly turns and looks at Jeanie. She sinks further in her chair.

"By the way, I hear congratulations are in order Jeanie. I hear that this will be your first case."

"I haven't decided if I'm going to take it yet."

"Well, congratulations anyway. You deserve it."

"Thank you." Jeanie's thinking to herself, 'you're enjoying this aren't you, you son-of-a-bitch. He must know that this is a delicate situation here, and he is feeding on it like a magpie on a dead carcass. What a cold bastard!'

"Here is your latte," says Ron.

"Thank you, how much do I owe you?"

"It's on the house. Now, please leave!"

Jeanie looks at Ron and feels his eyes pierce her head. She looks over at the Judge and he just smiles and says, "Bye".

It's amazing how one's feelings can change so quickly. Ron's feelings toward Jeanie went from compassionate to 'kill the bitch' in zero-point-three-seconds. And the Judge is just sitting there smiling.

"Thank you, Mr. Wadder. Bye Judge," says Jeanie as she turns and walks out the door with her head held high.

Now she MUST take on this case no matter how much of an asshole John McDuffy is. She heads to the hospital to get the results of the blood/alcohol test. She's going to find out for herself if this man WAS drunk or not. She can't get over the look on Murphy's face. He was actually getting a kick out of that. Just as if to say... 'see you in my court you little bitch!'

CHAPTER 12

"MAY I HELP YOU MISS?" asks the receptionist at the Great Falls Medical Center.

"Yes, I'm Jeanie Philips, Attorney at Law, could you tell me who the physician is that was on duty last Friday evening about 10:00 pm?"

The receptionist looks through her roster and says, "It appears there were more than one on duty."

"The one that worked on my client, John McDuffy."

"Let's see...ok, that would be Dr. Hanson. You can probably catch him at his clinic today."

"Thank you."

On her way to the clinic, Jeanie decided to drive by John's house. Just like Kathleen said, there was a red ribbon tied around the tree in his front yard. She stopped to take a picture of it and then got on the phone to report it to the police. She noticed a man from across the street coming towards her. He had a semi-angry look on his face.

"May I help you?" he said.

"Yes, you may, I'm Jeanie Philips, attorney for John McDuffy."

"Oh! Nice to meet you. I'm Bob Johnson, John's neighbor. Sooo…when is he coming home?"

"Well, I'm working on that," smiles Jeanie. "Have you known Mr. McDuffy long?"

"John? I've known him for about a year now. Couldn't ask for a better neighbor, do anything for ya."

"Really?"

"Ya. Great dad too! You should have seen him wrestling around in the yard with the boys Friday before they left." A tear starts to well up in Bob's eye. "Terrible thing what happened. I feel so sorry for John. He loved those boys SO much."

"Yes. Terrible. So, have you ever known John to drink very much?"

"Oh, every now and then he would go out with the boys from work and have a few, but he was always home early. And he NEVER went out when he had the kids. They were always doing something. Camping, fishing, hunting, or just riding their bikes. And they had just gotten those new bikes too. Never got to use um. What a shame."

"Have you ever seen the person putting up these ribbons?"

"No I haven't, but I'd like to catch the little bastard. He must be a sly one. I look out the window often. Even late at night, and I can never seem to catch him."

"What makes you think it's a him?"

"Well, I s'pose it could be a girl, I don't know."

"Well, I called the police. They'll probably want to ask you some questions."

"No problem."

"Thank you for your time Mr. Johnson."

"You're quite welcome young lady. Oh, and miss?"

"Yes?"

"You tell Johnny that I'll take good care of his place while he's gone, and to hurry home!"

"Ok, I will. Bye, bye."

Jeanie drives down the road and thinks, 'What a nice old guy. Everybody needs a neighbor like him.' Now it's off to the clinic. On her way there, she decides to call the office.

"Jack?"

"Yes Jeanie."

"I'm going to be tied up for a while. Do you think you could call down and get McDuffy on the docket for his hearing?"

"Already done. It's tomorrow at 10:00 am."

"Thanks Jack. You're a pal."

"Don't mention it."

She finally pulls into Dr. Hanson's parking lot.

"Excuse me, I'd like to see Dr. Hanson please."

"I'm sorry, but he is tied up with patients right now. May I help you?"

"Maybe you can. I would like to see the results of the blood work done on my client John McDuffy Friday night. I'm Jeanie Philips, his attorney."

The receptionist has that familiar but unwanted look on her face, like she doesn't have a clue what you're talking about. "Let me see if I can interrupt the doctor. I'll be right back." She soon returns with the doc.

"May I help you?" he asks.

"Yes. I am Jeanie Philips, Attorney at Law. My client is John McDuffy. Apparently, you ordered a blood/alcohol test to be performed on him Friday night?

"Yes, that's true."

"Who authorized this test?"

"Why, the Montana State Highway Patrol did."

"I would like to see the results of that test please."

"I'm sorry miss, but that information is confidential between doctor/patient."

"Then why hasn't my client seen the results?"

The good doctor doesn't know how to answer that one.

"I'm sorry miss, I can't help you. You'll have to contact the MSHP for those results. Good day."

Suddenly Jeanie is smelling fish. People are sure being uncooperative about this blood/alcohol test. She decides to take the doctor's advice and go chat with the good folks at the MSHP office.

"May I help you?"

Yes. I would like to speak to the officer in charge please."

"I can help you," says a young patrolman walking towards her.

"Hello. My name is Jeanie Philips, Attorney at Law. My client is John McDuffy. He was arrested Monday morning on the charge of manslaughter."

"Yes, I'm familiar with that arrest."

"Apparently, someone from this office authorized a blood/alcohol test on my client Friday night. I would like the results of that test please."

"Well, I'm afraid I can't help you with that. But maybe if we go have a cup of coffee somewhere, I can help you in some other ways."

She listens to a couple of officers snickering in the distance, takes one look at the boyish coy grin on this young punk's face, and with a sour stomach, decides to take her chances on the phone.

"No thank you, maybe some other time."

She closes the door behind her and listens to the burst of laughter as she heads toward her car. 'What a bunch of jerks!' she thinks. Once back at the office, she begins to prepare for tomorrow's hearing before going to see John one more time. She calls down to the courthouse to find out which Judge will be hearing the plea, and it doesn't surprise her to discover it's none other than the honorable Judge Murphy. 'What does he have in store for Mr. McDuffy?' she wonders. She looks at her watch. Three o'clock. Better get up to see her client and brief him on the procedures of the hearing.

"LET ME OUTA HERE GOD DAMMIT! I WANNA SEE MY GODDAM LAWYER!" Billy's on the rampage again.

"Shut up Billy! You don't have a lawyer," hollers Bubba.

"WELL THEN SEND THE GODDAM BARTENDER! I NEED A BEER!"

"Shut up Billy."

John just lies on his bunk wishing they would put that punk in another cell. If he has to put up with him much longer, someone's gonna get hurt.

"C'mon Johnny, your lawyer's here to see you," says Bubba.

"Jack?"

"No, the cute one."

"Great!"

Bubba wheels John to the meeting area and up to the glass where Jeanie is waiting.

"What do YOU want?" snarls John.

'Oh boy,' thinks Jeanie, 'this ought to be fun.'

"Let's see…what do I want! Well…I want a million dollars for starters. Then I can retire and won't have to put up with assholes like you. But do you know what I would like most of all? I would like my husband and daughter back! But I can't have that, now can I? NO!

I CAN'T! Why do you ask? I'll tell you why! Because some drunken driver killed them two years ago in a head-on wreck, that's why!"

"OH! So, you've already made up your mind about me then, huh?"

"The only thing I've decided about you already is that you're an asshole!"

"You just said that you lost your husband and daughter in a head-on wreck caused by a drunk driver! You think I'm guilty, don't you?"

"Are you?"

"NO! GOD DAMMIT!" John starts to stand up to lean over the counter so he can get right in the face of this little bitch, when Bubba comes over.

"Calm down Johnny."

"I'll calm down when you get this little bitch out of here!" John reaches for the arm of his wheelchair, and it slips out from under him. He and Bubba both hit the floor. Another guard rushes over.

"We're alright," Yells Bubba.

Jeanie stands to get a better look as she notices a tear running down his cheek.

"LOOK," she says, "all I'm trying to say is I've had to get over the loss of my family and get on with my life. Now you're going to have to do the same. I KNOW how hard it losing your loved ones! BELIEVE ME! I still cry at night!"

John glances at her quickly and sees the pain on her face. The same kind of pain he sees when he looks in the mirror. Maybe he IS being a little hard on her.

"Ok, ok. Now YOU listen," he says in a little softer tone. "I just think Jack would stand a little better chance against the good Judge Murphy. I know he is good friends with the Wadder's."

Jeanie thinks, 'How come everybody knows this but her?'

"Murphy was always hard on my dad, and I know he'll be hard on me. Jack knows how to deal with him."

"Well, we'll just have to appeal to a different court."

"It's not that easy. He's a powerful man in this town."

"Ya, well he's probably never had the pleasure of dealing with a pissed off little redhead either!" John slowly gives her a smile.

"Don't worry Mr. McDuffy..."

"...John."

Jeanie smiles, "Don't worry John, I'll do my homework. We'll win this!"

John sits and stares at Jeanie for a moment, trying to make up his mind about her. Suddenly, he has a different point of view toward this little firecracker. Maybe she CAN do the job.

"Ok you've convinced me. So, what do we do now?"

"Your hearing is tomorrow morning at ten o'clock. They will pick you up and take you to the courthouse about nine. Try to look presentable."

"Yes ma'am!"

"No joking around! This is important. We're going to plead not guilty of course, and we're going to request a trial by jury because you don't stand a chance if it's up to Judge Murphy."

"No shit!" says John. "By the way, have they ever revealed the results of the blood/alcohol test to anyone?"

"No, not that I know of. But believe me, I WILL get the results of that test sooner or later!"

"I don't doubt you will," smiles John.

"Times up!" bellows Bubba.

"I'll see you tomorrow morning."

"Ok. Goodbye Miss Philips."

"It's Jeanie." Suddenly the air is much calmer now. Both feel much better about each other. Jeanie goes back to her office to prepare for tomorrow and John goes back to his cell and Billy only to find him pissing all over the floor. "GREAT!"

CHAPTER 13

"RISE AND SHINE!" ANNOUNCES BUBBA. "C'mon Johnny, big morning ahead of you. Get cleaned up and put your best orange suit on, time to meet the Judge."

'GREAT!' thinks John, 'I'm really looking forward to this.'

Bubba throws him a towel, soap, and a clean orange jumpsuit altered for his cast.

"When are they coming to get me?"

"Between 8 and 8:30."

"Ok, I'll be ready."

John is torn between feelings of excitement and fear. Although he knows he's innocent, he fears Judge Murphy because of the way he treated his father. If it wasn't for Jack Peters, his father would probably still be in jail. John's father was a good man, but he had too much Irish pride. He would never let someone drive him home when he'd had too much to drink. He faced Judge Murphy for three DUI's, and the third one all but destroyed him. He spent the rest of his life working two jobs to pay off the fines. Finally, in his early fifties, his heart gave out on him. John remembers the day vividly when he got the call that his father had collapsed on the job. His name was James McDuffy, and he was an independent excavation contractor. One Friday, he and one of his men were south of town digging a trench with a backhoe when the trench walls collapsed, burying his employee alive. The trench was about twelve feet deep. James McDuffy immediately jumped off the backhoe and grabbed a shovel. He started digging frantically while calling 911 on his cell phone. By the time the paramedics arrived, James had his employee exposed and was administering mouth to mouth resuscitation. After restoring his breathing and letting the paramedics take over, James crawled out of the ditch, staggered for about ten feet, and dropped dead of a massive heart attack. He saved a man's life, but allowed his own life to be taken in his place. The man he saved has never been the same since. He swears that James McDuffy's spirit lives within him because he gave up his life for him. It was a sad day in Great Falls when they buried James McDuffy. He was a huge man with a heart to match. Everyone loved him and knew they could always depend on him. Half of Great Falls turned out for his funeral. Not Judge Murphy though. John learned through the grape vine some days later, that the good Judge was heard saying 'good ridden, another drunk off the streets!' John wanted to go to his home and break his jaw after hearing this, but he didn't. He kept his cool. Now his fate lies within this man's hands. His only hope is a fiery little redhead with an attitude. GREAT!

"Here he is boys," announces Bubba as he leads two officers to John's cell.

"John McDuffy?"

"Yes."

"Let's go, your presence is wanted at the courthouse."

This is it, the moment of truth. The officers wheel John out to their patrol car and help him inside. Once at the courthouse, they take him into the holding room where Jeanie is waiting. She is dressed very distinguished in her navy-blue suit. Her hair is in a bun and her reading glasses are resting neatly on her nose.

"Good morning!" smiles Jeanie.

"Well I hope it is. Are you ready to show this guy what you're made of?"

"No sweat!"

"Good! I just want to go home. If I have to spend another day in that cell with that drunken Indian, I'll go nuts!"

"Well now John, remember, this is just a preliminary hearing to state your plea. All the Judge is going to do today is set bail and a trial date hopefully. Do you have the means to meet bail?"

"Well, I don't know. How much is it going to be?"

"It could be as much as ten thousand dollars."

"TEN THOUSAND DOLLARS! You gotta be shitting me!"

"No. It could be even more."

"What a rip off!"

"I know, but the Judge has the right to set bail at whatever amount he sees fit."

John thinks about the prospect of selling Shelly, his car, and his stomach turns inside out.

"Well, I suppose I could come up with it if I have to. But when this is all over, and you prove my innocence, I'm gonna sue the state and get it all back!"

"Slow down John! Let's take this one step at a time, ok?"

"Ok."

Just then the officers walk in.

"Ok, time to go. The Judge will see you now."

As they wheel him into the courtroom, the butterflies in his stomach are almost overwhelming. He has never had to face a Judge before, not even for a traffic ticket. And now he's facing manslaughter charges. Memories of the accident start flowing into his head and he drifts off into a trance.

"All rise!" announces the bailiff.

John struggles, but finally makes it to his feet about the time Judge Murphy says, "Be seated." Everyone takes their seats as John stares at the Judge. Old feelings of anger start to boil inside him. The Judge has gotten much grayer, and looks tired. Maybe he's developed a heart? After a long silence while the Judge flips through his paperwork, he finally announces.

"Mr. McDuffy, you've been charged with the crime of manslaughter. Do you understand the charges?"

"Yes, we do, your honor," announces Jeanie.

"I assume you are counsel for the defendant?"

"Yes, your honor."

"How do you plea?"

"Not guilty your honor," says Jeanie with complete confidence and authority in her voice.

John just sits and tries to swallow, but he can't. His mouth is too dry. The Judge has not lifted his head once to face Jeanie or John. He just keeps looking down while writing his notes.

"Very well…bail is set at five hundred thousand dollars pending trial."

Jeanie is stunned to say the least. John is speechless. Jeanie finally gathers herself and says, "If it pleases the court your honor, isn't five hundred thousand dollars for bail a little high?"

Now the judge decides to look up from his notes. He glares straight into Jeanie's eyes and says, "No, it does not please the court counselor. Bail is firm at five hundred thousand dollars. Although, I can increase it if you so desire?"

"No, your honor, five hundred thousand is quite sufficient. We would like to request a trial by jury at this time."

The Judge looks back down at his notes and scribbles something down.

"Very well, you will be notified in the near future of the trial date. You may be excused."

Jeanie stands as the officers approach John to take him back to the jail. She bends down and says, "I'm sorry John, there's nothing I can do about it."

"What do you mean there's nothing you can do about it?!" yells John. "There is NO WAY I can come up with that kind of money!"

"There will be no outbursts in my courtroom," announces the good Judge.

"FUCK YOU!" screams John as he tries to stand and walk to the bench. The officers quickly intercept him.

"John please!" says Jeanie. "Don't say another word!"

Too late.

"Bail is now set at one million dollars!" barks the Judge.

"You can't get away with this you bastard!" yells John as the officers wheel him out the door.

"John! Please! Calm down!" cries Jeanie. "I'll take care of it! Don't worry!"

"Ya, it really looks like you took care of it!" yells John. "I knew you couldn't handle this! Now I'm gonna sit in that jail and rot while they jerk me around! Thanks to you!"

"Me?! I wasn't the one who told the Judge to fuck off!"

"No! You were just the one who said NO SWEAT!"

"Alright, alright," says one of the officers, "time to go!"

They wheel John away as Jeanie yells, "Don't worry John! I'll take care of this. I'll get Jack's help, and we'll get you out of there! I promise!"

John doesn't even reply. Jeanie just stands and watches them wheel her client away. There goes her first client, angry and disappointed in her, and for good reason. She has let him down completely. She feels like a complete failure.

'Dammit!' she thinks, 'I should have requested a different Judge. I should have known that crooked old bastard would do this!'

She walks to her car and decides to go for a drive before going back to the office. She drives down to the river, and parks where she usually does when she needs to think. While watching the ducks and geese swim around, she can't help but think about the day she saw Murphy in the coffee shop. How pleasant he was congratulating her on her first case.

'What a phony!' she thinks. "And they talk about lawyers, this guy takes the cake! What are you going to do Jeanie? Are you going to let this crooked old bastard beat you? Are you going to let your client sit in jail while this case gets buried in red tape? Are you going to tell Kathleen McDuffy that you can't get her son out of jail? I DON'T THINK SO!'

She finally snaps out of her feeling of insecurity, and drives back to the office to work on a plan. First plan is to move this trial to a different county, and a different Judge. When she gets back to the office, she goes right into Jack's office and tells him what happened.

"I was afraid of this," says Jack. "Murphy is pretty good friends with the Wadders, and they have a lot of political influence in this town. A million dollars?"

"Yes! And there is no way they can come up with that kind of money!"

"I'm sure Murphy knows that, and I'm sure he'll try to bury this thing so far down in red tape that John will never go to trial. He'll make sure he spends the rest of his life in jail. This is going to be tougher than I thought Jeanie. Do you think you can handle it?"

"You better believe I do! After today, I want Murphy's head on a platter!"

"Atta girl! Go get'em!"

Jeanie smiles and goes back to her office.

"I thought you were goin home?" says Billy as Bubba wheels John back into his cell.

"Not yet!" says John as he stands and limps toward his bunk.

"What happened? Did your pretty little lawyer not do her job?"

"Not exactly!" growls John.

"Maybe she could do a better job on her knees?" says Billy as he grins ear-to-ear and grabs his crotch.

John whirls around and with cast and all, closes the ground between them in the wink of an eye, and grabs Billy by the neck with one hand and picks him up a foot off the floor, then says...

"LOOK! I don't want to talk about it, so shut the fuck up!"

Bubba quickly grabs John as he puts him in a full nelson, and says, "Easy big fella."

John let's go of Billy and sits down on his bunk. Billy coughs and moves to the other end of the cell, and stares at John in a whole new light. "Don't be so goddam touchy. I was just kidding!"

"You alright Johnny?" asks Bubba.

"Yaaa. Everybody just leave me alone, will ya?"

"You got it bro," says Billy, "I'll be a good little Indian."

Bubba leaves as Billy lies down. John rolls over on his bunk and closes his eyes as he tries to calm down. He can't believe what happened today. If he has to stay in jail much longer, he's going to lose his job, his house, everything...all because of Murphy! His blood boils as he thinks about it. He'd like to get his hands around that scrawny little neck! Then he starts to think about the accident again. The memory of Brett and Ryan floods his thoughts as he buries his face in his pillow, and quietly weeps.

CHAPTER 14

——⊗⊗⊗——

JOHN CRIES HIMSELF TO SLEEP for about three hours, right through lunch. About 2:00, Bubba comes in and says, "C'mon John, you have a visitor. It's your mother."

John slowly wipes the sleep out of his eyes and climbs into the wheelchair.

"I hear you're going to be here awhile," says Bubba.

"That's what it sounds like, unless you have a million dollars I can borrow."

Bubba laughs, "I got twenty. Will that help?"

"Well, it's a start. Hey Bubba? What can you do about getting me a private cell? If I'm gonna have to stay here, that little punk is gonna have to go, or I'm gonna hurt him."

"Sorry boss, I have no control over that. But Billy shouldn't be here long. He never is."

"Good! He gets on my nerves."

"He gets on everyone's nerves. Here we are."

"Hi mom," says John.

"Hi honey! Jeanie told me what happened. I can't believe the gall of that Judge. What does he think, we're made of money?!"

"He knows exactly what he's doing. He's going to keep me in here forever."

"Not if I have anything to say about it. I'll bust you out of here if I have to!"

Bubba looks over at Kathleen and smiles, "Now ma'am, we'll not be havin' any talk like that round here."

John smiles and says, "Don't worry Bubba, she's just kidding."

"No, I'm not!" announces Kathleen proudly with her back straight and jaw pushed out.

John and Bubba just smile. But John's smile is a sad one, for even his love for this spunky little woman he fondly calls mom cannot overcome the pain in his heart.

"Is everything set up for the funeral tomorrow?"

"Yes. Jeanie arranged it so you could be there. The deputies will pick you up and take you back."

"Well, what do ya know, she managed to do something right."

"Now Johnny, take it easy on her. I don't think Jack could have done much better with THAT Judge. We'll just have to make sure the trial is held in a different court. That SOB has always had it out for us!"

"I know, but I still think Jack could have gotten the bail reduced to a reasonable amount."

"Well, what's done is done. We'll just have to hope for a speedy trial. Has the doctor been in to look at you lately?"

"No, but I wish I could get this stinkin cast off, it itches like crazy."

"Well, I'll talk to them on my way out about getting you in to see the doctor for a checkup. I'll see you at the church tomorrow. Try to get some rest sweetheart."

"Ya right, in this place?"

"Well, try anyway, I'll see you tomorrow."

"Bye mom."

Bubba takes John back to his cell and Kathleen goes to the front desk to make an appointment for John to see the doctor. John crawls onto his bunk and lies there thinking about the funeral tomorrow. Somehow, he's got to get through this. But the thought of seeing his boys lying in their caskets turns his stomach inside out. 'Why God?' he thinks. 'What did I do to deserve this? Why have you taken my boys from me?'

Meanwhile, back at Jeanie's office, Jack Peters is on the phone with Judge Murphy.

"C'mon Paul, a million dollars!? That's ridiculous! You know the McDuffy's can't afford that!"

"You know Jack, if your client would have kept his mouth shut, it would only be half that much."

"Even five hundred thousand is way too much, and you know it Paul! You're just trying to hurt the McDuffys in any way you can! James McDuffy is dead! Why can't you just let it go?"

"I don't know what you're talking about Jack, I am simply upholding law and order in my community to the best of my abili...

"...Can it Murphy! You know damn well what I'm talking about. You've had it out for James McDuffy ever since he caught you with your pants down. Now you think you can reap your vengeance on his son. Well, you're not going to get away with it! I'll see to that personally!"

"Are you threatening me Jack?"

"No Paul, I'm simply advising you to follow the letter of the law on this one because I'm going to be watching your every step! If you so much as fart in John McDuffy's face, I'll have you thrown off the bench! Do you understand?!"

"Oh, I understand perfectly Jack, and I can promise you that I will follow the letter of the law on this case as I do on every case! And if John McDuffy is found guilty, I will see to it personality that he enjoys the full extent of the law! Good day Mr. Peters!" Jack slams the phone down as Jeanie enters his office.

"Sorry Jack, but I couldn't help but overhear you yelling at Murphy. What's this about catching him with his pants down?"

"Back in 1989, James McDuffy was at his usual watering hole one night, when he noticed Judge Murphy sitting in the corner with a couple of young bar flies. James watched them for a while as the girls were kissing on him, and then he followed them outside. James watched as the honorable Judge Murphy got into the back seat of his car with the two girls, and pretty soon their heads were out of sight."

"You're kidding!"

"No, I'm not!" chuckles Jack. "So, James hurries up and runs inside the bar and announces to everyone that Judge Paul Murphy is getting a blowjob in the parking lot right this minute. Damn near everyone in the bar wanted to see, so they all ran outside and looked as James swung the car door open and yelled, 'ORDER IN THE COURT!' It's too bad somebody didn't have a camera, because Murphy denied everything and was able to keep his place on the bench. But he's had a close eye on him from his peers ever since then, thanks to James McDuffy."

"So, that's the story. I thought it was just because he is a friend of the Madder's."

"That too. So, you better make sure you prove your client innocent Jeanie, or Murphy will hang him."

"Ok boss, are you going to the funeral tomorrow?"

"No, I have to be in court, but I think you should go for Kathleen. She's held pretty strong so far, but I got a feeling seeing those two boys in their caskets is going to be awfully hard on both of them, and John won't be able to be much support for her."

"I was planning on going anyway. I'll stay with her and make sure she's ok."

"Thanks Jeanie."

The next morning John is up and ready to go, when the deputies arrive to take him to the funeral. He doesn't say a word as they wheel him out to the car. He stares silently out the window at the mountains in the distance and Square Butte, an ancient buffalo jump, as they drive to the church. Once there, they wheel him inside where Kathleen is waiting.

"Hi honey," says Kathleen as she bends down to hug him. "Are you ok?"

"I think I'll make it. How 'bout you?"

"Don't you worry about me. I'm getting to be an old pro at these things."

Their eyes meet and both break down. Jeanie watches from a distance. Memories of burring her husband and daughter flood her mind and she too is caught up in the sorrow and begins to cry. John looks at the open caskets in the distance and covers his face with his shaking hands.

"I don't think I can bear to see them like that mom."

"You must honey, it's the only way you'll be able to accept the fact that they're gone. Come on, we'll go together. I'll be right here with you."

The deputies allow Kathleen to push John up to the caskets by herself. Jeanie can see that she's having a hard time pushing the big man, so she takes one handle and

Kathleen takes the other. The three of them slowly approach Brett and Ryan. The closer they get, the more John's hands shake. When they arrive next to Brett, Jeanie holds one of John's arms, and Kathleen holds the other as John slowly stands, and looks down at Brett.

Tears fall on Brett's face as John bends down to kiss him and says, "I love you son. I'm so sorry. Please forgive me." Tears continue to stream down his face as he hobbles over to Ryan and says, "Hey little buddy. You two behave yourselves up there now. I don't want to hear bad reports when I talk to God, ok? You take good care of Bufford, and I'll be with you soon. I love you little buddy."

He then bends down to kiss Ryan on the forehead as Kathleen and Jeanie wipe the tears from their eyes. They help John back into his chair and wheel him into the sanctuary where family and friends are waiting. With trembling hands, he wipes his eyes dry and looks around at all the sad faces. All except Laura's that is. She just looks angry. The funeral lasted about an hour. John stared at the statue of Jesus the whole time wondering 'why?' When the sermon was over, they drove out to the cemetery. When they arrived, they noticed little red ribbons tied to some of the trees. Kathleen and Jeanie immediately became angry. Once out of the car, Jeanie hurried from tree to tree, tearing the ribbons off. She then approached the caretaker and questioned him on who was responsible for this. He pleaded innocent and claimed he didn't even notice them. Jeanie took down his name and promised that she would be talking to him again. John hasn't said a word since they left the church. The deputies wheeled him up to the burial site as everyone gathered around. As the coffins were moved into place, John just stared at the holes in the ground. The only thing he can think of is it should be him instead of the boys. After all, they were wearing seat belts and he wasn't. 'Why?' As he watches the coffins being lowered into the ground, he slips deeper and deeper into a dark silence. People are talking to him, but he can't hear. The only thing he can hear is Brett and Ryan screaming, 'Daaaad, help! I can't get out! Daaaad pleeeease help! I can't breathe! Daaaaaad!' The voices grow softer as the coffins are lowered completely underground.

Suddenly, John jumps to his feet and hobbles towards the graves yelling, "Hang on you guys, I'm coming!"

The deputies quickly intercept him as he fights to get free. It takes everything the deputies have to get him back in the wheelchair.

Kathleen runs to him and says, "John! You can't help them! They are in God's hands now!"

John just stares at her with a blank look and says, "But they were calling for me! They're trapped! I have to set them free!"

"Oh honey," cries Kathleen, "they ARE free! Free to run and play in heaven while God watches over them.

You must accept that Johnny, their souls are in God's hands now. Don't worry! He'll take good care of them!"

John stares at his folded hands as the deputies start wheeling him back to the car. Jeanic holds on to Kathleen as they watch him leave.

"Don't worry Kathleen," says Jeanie, "he'll be ok."

"I hope so. It seems like he's in a trance. I've never seen him like that."

"He's just in shock. Only time can heal such deep wounds. We both know that."

Jeanie and Kathleen hold each other as they rock back and forth crying out their sorrow to each other. As John rides away in the patrol car, all he can see is Brett and Ryan lying in those coffins with their eyes closed... how peaceful they looked.

CHAPTER 15

ONCE BACK AT THE JAIL, John goes straight to his bunk without saying a word to anyone. Bubba tries to console him, but he just stares off into space. Billy is even being halfway civil.

"Hey bro, ya want me ta leave so you can be alone?"

John doesn't answer. It's like he doesn't acknowledge any part of the world around him. Bubba informs him that he has an appointment at the infirmary tomorrow for a checkup. John lets out a grunt as an answer. He drifts off to sleep as his mind is filled with questions, and his heart is filled with pain.

"Jack?"

"Yes Jeanie?"

"Do you have a tape measure I can borrow? I want to take a drive up to Rogers Pass and take some measurements."

"No, I don't have one here. Just take some money out of petty cash and go buy one."

"Ok, I'll see you tomorrow."

"Bye."

On her way to the mountains, Jeanie thinks about the funeral. She can't get over feeling so sad for John, Kathleen and the rest of Brett and Ryan's family. She also can't get over the angry look on Laura's face, and wonders if she is the one behind the red ribbons. She can understand Laura's anger, for she remembers the anger she felt toward the drunk driver that took Calvin and Britney from her. She never thought she would see the day she would be defending a drunk driver in court. Now here she is representing John McDuffy. 'He's innocent!' she reminds herself. She decides to put in some music to try and disperse these thoughts from her head. The first CD she grabs is one of music that Britney used to skate to. She thinks back to an evening at the arena when Britney was skating to this CD. She was so talented. She danced across the ice like she was born with skates on her feet. A ballerina on ice, Calvin used to call her.

'Whoa!' Jeanie thinks as she puts on the brakes. Suddenly, the car in front of her has braked to about thirty miles per hour. She can see the driver talking on a cell phone and looking from side to side as if he's looking for a certain road. Suddenly, he hits the accelerator and speeds up to seventy. Then he hits the brakes again, and swerves all over the road. 'What are you doing you idiot?' thinks Jeanie. He's not even paying attention to the traffic around him. She decides to lay on the horn so he knows she is behind him. She promptly gets the bird in return, as he pulls over and lets her pass. 'What a jerk!' she thinks. 'He's gonna cause an accident one day!' Then it hits her. That's probably why Amy Wadder was in the wrong lane.

"She was talking on the phone!" Jeanie says out loud.

Now she's got a case. All she has to do is prove that she caused the accident because she was talking on the phone, and not paying attention to her driving. With the way everyone is up in arms against cell phones and driving these days, she shouldn't have any problem reaching the sympathy of the jury.

"So, this is where it all happened," says Jeanie to herself as she steps out of the car at the scene of the accident.

The sky is blue, and the birds are singing. The sun is bright and hot, and there is a cool breeze blowing through the pines. It's hard to believe that just a week ago, three young people died in this beautiful part of Montana. The skid marks are pretty faded, but she goes to work taking measurements and pictures anyway. There are still traces of broken glass in the ditch where Amy died. There is also a bouquet of silk flowers arranged around a cross and stuck in the ground alongside the road. This is a tradition in Montana when someone dies in an auto accident on the highway. A white cross, usually decorated with flowers, is placed at the scene to remind us that someone died there. Hopefully it will make people drive carefully. Jeanie walks up close to the cross and notices there is an inscription. 'Our beloved Amy was killed here buy a drunk driver, September 3rd, 1999.' Without giving it another thought, Jeanie goes to her car to get a pen. She crosses out 'buy a drunk driver,' and continues on with her research. Another thing she noticed about the cross is that it had a red ribbon tied around the top. Is it just a coincidence, or are the Wadder's behind the red ribbon capers? 'They would probably be the most likely,' thinks Jeanie. She finishes up her work and heads back to town. Once there, she decides to drop by James McDuffy's old watering hole that Jack described to her. It's a popular working-man's hangout called Dewey's Grill. She's never been in there before, so this will be a new experience for her. The minute she walks through the door, all eyes are on her. She scans the room and spies an empty stool at the bar. Perfect! Now she can chat with the bartender.

"Evenin ma'am. Can I get ya something?"

"Oh, I'll take a glass of white wine if you have it."

"Comin' right up."

'This is a nice place,' she thinks, 'I just hope I don't catch anything.' She would like to turn and look around, but she really doesn't want to make eye contact with any of the guys for fear they might think she's out looking for them.

"That'll be two bucks."

She dig's through her purse, and hands the bartender the money.

"Have you been working here long?" Jeanie asks.

"About fifteen years," replies the bartender.

"Sooo, you must have known James McDuffy then."

A smile comes to the man's face, along with a puzzled look to accompany it. "Why yes, I knew James very well. We miss him around here. And how did you know him?"

"Well, I didn't know him. I'm representing John McDuffy, and I heard that his dad used to hang out here. Is it true he caught Judge Murphy with his pants down in the parking lot?"

The bartender laughs out loud, and so does the man sitting next to her.

"I was here that night!" says the man next to her. "That was great! You should have seen the look on Murphy's face. I'll never forget it as long as I live!"

"So, you're Johnny's attorney?" asks the bartender.

"Yes, I work for Jack Peters."

"Oohh, I know Jack. He did a lot for James."

"Can you tell me a little about James McDuffy? Was he a good man?"

"Was he a good man? Does a bear shit in the woods? James was one of the finest men I've ever known, give you the shirt off his back if you needed it. It just makes me sick what happened to Johnny. It's bad enough his boys got killed, but to be arrested for killin'um. That never would've happened if it was anyone but that Wadder girl that was killed."

"Why do you say that?"

"Well everyone knows…"

"Excuse me ma'am," says the other bartender on duty as he puts a shot glass upside down on the bar in front of her, "the gentleman at the end of the bar would like to buy you a drink."

"Tell him thank you for me."

"Like I was sayin', everyone knows the Madders and Murphy are good friends. He's gonna make sure Johnny hangs for this one."

"Not if I have anything to say about it," announces Jeanie proudly.

The bartender smiles.

"Excuse me ma'am," says the other bartender again… "now the gentleman in the corner would like to buy a drink."

Jeanie smiles, "Tell him thank you also."

"Looks like you're going to be here awhile," says the bartender with a smile.

"No, I don't think so. What can you tell me about John McDuffy?"

"Johnny? He's a chip off the old block. Hard worker, good father. He was a good husband too, if you ask me. He never stayed for more than two beers. She was just too hard on him."

"How's that?"

"Well, she didn't want him to drink at all, thought it was evil."

"Have you ever known him to drink too much?"

"Excuse me ma'am," interrupts the other bartender again as he sets a third shot glass in front of her. "Now the gentleman over there," he says as he points behind her, "would like to buy you a drink."

Jeanie blushes, "Please tell them all thank you very much. I'm flattered, but I only have time for one."

"Yes ma'am."

"I'm sorry," says Jeanie, "I guess not too many single women come in here huh?"

"No," says the bartender, "especially not pretty little gals like you."

"Thank you. Sooo, have you ever known John to drink too much and drive home?"

"Never! In fact, there were many times when he would show up here to take the old man home. He was the only one that James wouldn't argue with. Lots of guys tried to offer James a ride when he'd had too much to drink, but the stubborn old bastard would never listen to anyone except Johnny. I remember one time when he picked James up and threw him over his shoulder like a sack of spuds, and packed him out the door. James was grumbling, kicking and cussin him, but Johnny just held on tight and waved to everybody as he went out the door."

The bartender's expression slowly turns to a serious one.

"Miss, you gotta get Johnny off. If they keep him locked up in jail, he'll go nuts."

"I know, I'll do the best I can."

"Well, if you're anything like Jack, I know you'll do just fine."

Jeanie finishes the last of her wine.

"Well, thank you for your time," she says as she stands and extends her arm to shake his hand.

"My name is Jeanie Philips, and you can reach me at the office if you can think of anything that might be of help."

"Nice to meet you Miss Philips, and I'll call you if I can think of anything."

"Bye."

"Good luck against ol' Judge Hummer," says the man next to her.

Everyone laughs as Jeanie blushes.

"Thanks!" says Jeanie. "Maybe I should hire those two girls to keep him occupied during the trial, huh?"

Now everyone really cracks up.

"Are you sure you can't stay for one more?" says the man sitting next to her.

"No, I have to go, but thanks anyway."

As Jeanie heads out the door, at least six hearts break. She drives home with the windows down. The evening breeze is cool and it feels good. When she arrives home, she notices her answering machine is flashing.

'Jeanie, this is Jack. John McDuffy's trial is set for February seventh. I tried to get it moved up but they claim the docket is full until then. I'll talk to ya in the morning.'

"THOSE BASTARDS!" growls Jeanie.

'The holiday season is going to be hard enough on John and Kathleen,' she thinks, 'now they won't even be able to spend it together.'

After turning on the tap to the bathtub, she goes to the kitchen to pour herself a glass of wine. She places it next to the bathtub and begins to remove her clothes. She puts them in the hamper immediately and closes the lid, for they reek of cigarettes from the bar. She pours her favorite bath oil into the tub and turns on the stereo to some soft music. As she lies in the tub, she remembers her first Christmas without Calvin and Brittany. Even though all her family and friends were close by, there was still a cold emptiness. She remembers crying herself to sleep Christmas Eve. The hot water and the wine begin to work their magic as she lies there with her eyes closed. She thinks about Brett and Ryan's little bodies lying in their coffins. Sorrow fills her soul as she remembers John and Kathleen's tear-filled eyes as John bent down to kiss his boys goodbye. Somehow, she must see to it that those two are reunited as a family...what's left of it. She pictures in her mind the sight of John throwing his dad over his shoulder like a sack of potatoes and waving to everyone as he leaves the bar. A warm, blushing smile comes to her lips as she sinks lower into the tub, and caresses her body with a sponge.

CHAPTER 16

———❦———

"C'MON JOHN, TIME TO GO see the Doc," says Bubba.

John just lies on his bunk and stares at the wall.

"Did ya hear me John? Time to see the Doc. Let's go."

John doesn't move. Billy is already up and showered and in the activity room playing ping pong. Bubba stands patiently holding the wheelchair. John doesn't even acknowledge his presence.

Finally, Bubba kneels down next to his bunk and puts his hand on John's shoulder and says, "I know yesterday was rough on ya buddy, but life goes on. And right now, you got an appointment with the Doc, so let's go. I promise I'll leave ya alone after that."

John blinks his eyes and finally starts to move. He slowly gets into the wheelchair without saying a word.

Meanwhile, Jeanie receives a call from Jack.

"Morning Jack."

"Morning Jeanie, did you get my message?"

"Yes, I did. Can't we get the trial moved up? It won't take me that long to prepare a case. Besides, I'd hate to see Johnny spend the holidays in jail."

"Johnny?"

Jeanie blushes, "I mean my client, Mr. McDuffy."

"That's ok Jeanie, it's pretty hard not to take a liking to that family. I know what you're saying about the holidays, and I argued that point with the DA's office, but it was like talking to a wall. Those people have no hearts."

"Have you told Kathleen yet?"

"No."

"Well I suppose I better get on the phone."

Back at the jail…

"Well Mr. McDuffy, looks like you're healing quite well. We should be able to take the cast off in about a week. Then we need to get you started on some physical therapy."

John doesn't say a word, just stares out the window.

"Are you still taking the pain killers?"

"No."

"Well, alright then. I'll see you in about a week."

The Doc gets up and calls for Bubba to take John back to his cell.

"Is he always this quiet?" asks the Doc to Bubba.

"No, he just buried his two sons yesterday."

"Oh, that explains it. Well, keep an eye on him."

"I will."

Bubba rolls John back to his cell.

"Can I get anything for ya John?" asks Bubba as John climbs on to his bunk.

"No."

"Ok buddy, just holler if ya need anything."

"Hello?" says Kathleen into the phone.

"Kathleen"

"Yes."

"Hi, this is Jeanie."

"Oh, hello dear."

"Are you going up to see John today?"

"Well, yes."

"About what time?"

"Oh, I was thinking about two o'clock."

"Ok, why don't I meet you there at two o'clock. I have some news about the trial that you both need to hear."

"Ok dear, that sounds fine. I'll see you then."

Jeanie hangs up and decides to call John's neighbor, Bob Johnson. After a few rings he answers.

"Mr. Johnson?"

"Yes."

"This is Jeanie Philips. I met you the other day."

"Yes, I remember."

"Hi...I was just wondering if you've noticed any more red ribbon activity going on over at John McDuffy's house?"

"Well, no, but the police never did come by like you said they would."

"They didn't?"

"No, so I finally went over and took the ribbon down. I still have it here if you need it."

"Well I might, so don't throw it away yet."

"I won't. How's Johnny doing?"

"Well, yesterday was pretty rough on him."

"I know, I was there. He looked terrible, and so did his mom. Is he going to get out soon?"

"I'm afraid not. The Judge has set his bail at one million dollars and the trial is set for February."

"You gotta be kidding me!"

"No, I wish I was. So, can you keep taking care of John's house for him?"

"No problem. I'll take care of it as long as it takes. So, this means he'll be spending Christmas in jail, huh?"

"Yes, I'm afraid so. But that might be a blessing in disguise."

"How do you figure?"

"Well, his first Christmas without the boys is going to be rough. There's no doubt about that. But it might be worse if he had to spend it alone in the house where they all lived, ya know what I mean?"

"Ya, I suppose you're right. But still, Christmas in jail? I can't imagine."

"I hear ya. But so far, he can receive visitors, you just have to call ahead of time."

"That's a good idea. I'll get up there to see him soon."

"That would be nice. Well, you take care Mr. Johnson, and please call me if you notice anything going on over there."

"I will, and tell Johnny not to worry about a thing. I've got it handled."

"I will, bye."

"Hey Bro," says Billy as he enters the cell, "how ya feelin?"

John doesn't answer.

"Ya know, your boys are the lucky ones."

John just stares at the wall.

"I mean, look at us. We're stuck here in this stinkin world, havin to live by the man's rules. Your boys are free. Their spirits are flying with the eagles and running with the deer. I wish I was free. The old ones tell me stories of the past when every man was free. Sometimes I think I was born a hundred years too late. I wish I could live in the olden days. Hunt buffalo and chase squaws whenever I want. Now the only thing I hunt for is a job, and the only squaws I can catch are the fat, ugly ones."

A subtle smile comes to John's face. Maybe there's some hope for Billy yet. He still doesn't say anything, just lies there staring at the wall. Just then, Bubba walks in with the wheelchair.

"C'mon Johnny, a couple of pretty ladies are to see you."

"Man!" says Billy. "He always gets pretty girls visit'n him. How come no pretty girls come to see me?"

"You ever consider mouthwash?" asks Bubba.

"Boy, that's so funny I forgot to laugh," says Billy. "If you weren't so goddamn big, I'd kick yur ass."

"Ya, ya. You and what tribe?"

Billy and Bubba's feeble attempt to cheer John up is only in vain, for John is still not speaking. Maybe Kathleen and Jeanie can get him to talk.

"Hi honey," says Kathleen as Bubba wheels John toward her.

"Good luck trying to get him to talk," says Bubba. "He hasn't said two words since yesterday."

Kathleen looks at John, "Honey, you look terrible. Have you slept or eaten anything since yesterday?"

John just stares off into the distance. Kathleen looks at Bubba as he shakes his head from side to side.

"Honey, you have to eat. Even if it's the crap they serve in here."

Everyone smiles except John, just a blank stare. Jeanie figures this is probably as good of a time as any to drop the bomb.

"Well, I wish I had some good news, but I'm afraid I don't."

"What is it dear?" asks Kathleen.

John looks over at her and wonders, 'Now what?'

"We received the trial date yesterday. It isn't until February."

"FUBRUARY?" snaps Kathleen. "Why so late?"

John just stares at Jeanie with an angry look on his face.

"I don't know, apparently, the calendar is full until then. Jack argued with them, but they wouldn't budge. I'm so sorry. I know I promised I'd get you out of here soon John, but it just seems like everything is working against us."

John looks at the floor as Kathleen cries.

"It's that damn Judge Murphy, isn't it?!" cries Kathleen. "He's responsible for this I bet."

"I don't know," says Jeanie, "I looked at the court docket and it does look pretty full. I'm afraid there's nothing I can do."

John looks up from the floor and stares straight at Jeanie and says, "I'm sure getting tired of hearing those words coming out of your mouth."

Any other time, Jeanie would fire right back at him with a quick response, but this time he has a point.

"I know John, I'm sorry." Jeanie looks at the floor and continues, "Maybe you should get another lawyer, I sure don't seem to be making any progress."

"It's not your fault dear, we know that. Don't we John?"

John just stares at Jeanie. He's seeing a side of her he hasn't seen yet. She's actually giving up, throwing in the towel. Something he never expected her to do.

"Don't we John?!" repeats Kathleen.

"That's right!" says John. "If you think you're gonna quit now, you've got another thing coming! We hired Jack and he appointed you to take this case, so stop feeling sorry for yourself, and get your little butt to work to get me the hell out of here! Understand?!"

Jeanie smiles and says, "Yes boss!"

Bubba smiles at the sound of John's voice. Kathleen grins from ear-to-ear. She can see a friendship growing between these two and it pleases her. She had been hoping John would meet someone nice. Who knows, maybe Jeanie's the one. Jeanie is pleased to hear the anger in John's voice, because that tells her he's not ready to give up on her, or himself.

"The first thing I'm going to do is file an appeal to get the bail lowered. Murphy is grossly abusing his right setting bail at a million dollars, so it shouldn't be a problem getting it reduced, although I don't know by how much. We'll just have to fight for the best we can get. Next I'm going to appeal to the State Supreme Court that the trial be moved to a different county."

"How are you going to do that?" asks Kathleen.

"Well, it shouldn't be too difficult because in a community this small, it will be hard to find an impartial jury. It seems like everybody knows everybody and besides, we have to get out of Murphy's jurisdiction. There is no way we'll get a fair trial as long as he's presiding."

"Well, there are other judges in town, aren't there?" says Kathleen.

"Yes, but Murphy still has too much influence over them. We'd be better off in a different county."

"Ok, whatever you think dear."

"John, I need you to think back to the accident and write it down on paper, second by second. Don't leave out anything. Start with Friday morning when you woke up. What you had for breakfast, etc. I want to know how many times you farted in the shower."

"How did you know I fart in the shower?"

"Lucky guess. Anyway, you catch my drift? I want to know every detail right up to the point you were knocked out, understand?"

"Yes boss!"

"Ok, well I guess I've got work to do, so I better get started. I'll talk to you soon. Bye, bye."

"Bye dear," smiles Kathleen.

"Bye counselor," says John.

Jeanie leaves and Kathleen stays a little longer.

"Do you need anything dear?"

"Well, they pretty much give me everything I need. But there is one thing."

"What's that?"

"In my living room, on the bookshelf, there is a book on tai chi and meditation. If I'm going to be stuck in here for a while, I have a feeling I'm going to need it."

"Ok, I'll bring it by tomorrow. I can't believe it's been a week already."

"Don't remind me," sighs John.

"Times up boss," announces Bubba.

"Don't you ever have any GOOD news?" says Kathleen.

Bubba smiles, "No ma'am. Just call me da' grim reaper."

Kathleen smiles and says goodbye as Bubba wheels John back to his cell.

"Sure glad to hear ya talking again boss."

"Thanks Bubba, but don't get too used to it. I'm not much of a talker."

"GOOD! I hear enough yappin from all the other yahoos round here. A little quiet would be nice for a change. So, you gonna be here awhile?"

"At least till February."

"Why so long?"

"Closest trial date they could get I guess."

"Well that sucks! Oh well, you'll like Christmas round here. We do it up right."

"That's alright, I don't think I'll feel much like celebrating anyway."

"I hear ya boss."

CHAPTER 17

⎯⎯ ∞∞∞ ⎯⎯

NOVEMBER 1, 1999. IT'S BEEN almost 2 months since the accident. John's cast is off and he has declined the physical therapy offered to him. Instead, he is doing his own through tai chi. His brother turned him on to tai chi back in the early 90's as a form of self-improvement of both mind and body. At the time, John had just gone through his divorce and needed something to help him climb out of the pit of depression he was in. He loved Laura so much that he didn't think he could go on without her. He spent many weeks moping around feeling sorry for his self in spite of all the love and sympathy conveyed to him by his family and friends. He tried the best he possibly could to save his marriage, but Laura had just fallen out of love with him and there was nothing he could do about it. He even thought of selling everything and hitting the road to try and start a new life somewhere else far away, but anytime that thought entered his head, he quickly remembered Brett, and Ryan and there was no doubt about what he had to do. Somehow, he had to get through this and continue with his life for the sake of his two sons, but how could his family go on without Laura? She was the twinkle in his eyes, the spring in his step. After many weeks of watching him slowly waste away, Pat, John's brother, stepped in and took control. One Saturday morning, Pat stopped by John's house with his pickup loaded with fishing poles and told John and the boys to get their stuff together.

"We're goin fishing," he said.

Brett and Ryan both jumped up and yelled, "YAAAYYY!" and ran to their rooms to get dressed.

John just sat at the kitchen table looking like he hadn't slept all night and said, "You guys go ahead, I'm just gonna stay home."

Pat went to the boy's rooms and told them to stay in there for a little while, that he was going to have a serious talk with their dad. The boys looked at him with surprise and worry, but they agreed to do what he told them. Pat walked into the kitchen and picked John up off his chair and drug him out the sliding glass door into the back yard.

"What the hell are you doing?!" yelled John.

"We're gonna have a little talk bro!"

Pat gave John a mighty shove and sent him rolling across the lawn. Then he grabbed the garden hose and turned it on him.

"TURN THAT OFF YOU ASSHOLE!" yelled John.

"Are you goin fishing with us?"

"NO!"

"Well then, if you're not going to the river with us, then I'm bringin the river to you!"

John finally gets to his feet and charges Pat like a raging bull. He knocks him down and wrestles the hose away from him and sprays him dead in the face.

"HOW DO YOU LIKE IT ASSHOLE?" he hollers as he sits on Pat's chest. Pat manages to roll him off and jerks the hose away from him and tosses it aside. Then he clamps his big hands on each side of John's head as he stares him in the face, both gasping for air.

"SO! You DO have some life left in you!" says Pat.

"GET OFF ME ASSHOLE!"

John pushes Pat aside and sits up with his arms resting on his knees.

"What the hell is YOUR problem?" asks John.

Pat crawls to his hands and knees as he coughs up water and gasps for air. John can see that he might have over did it on the water a little.

"You alright?" asks John.

"Ya. You didn't have to squirt ten gallons down my throat you know."

John smiles, "Well you asked for it."

Pat tries to laugh between coughs as John helps him to his feet.

"Look bro, I'm tired of seeing my brother waste his life away. You got to stop beating yourself up over this divorce! She's gone and life goes on, so stop blaming yourself!"

"What would you know? You've never been married!"

"That doesn't mean I've never experienced love and the heartache that goes along with it! I've felt what you're feeling many times, and each time I felt like I my life was over! But ya know what? Tomorrow always came along no matter how much I tried to avoid it. You can't stop the world from turning, and you can't stop life from kicking you in the gut from time to time. You just have to fight back and not let it beat you. Just like you did just now when I knocked you on your ass. You got up and fought back. Be a fighter bro, that's the only way you'll win."

John's eyes begin to water as he stares at the ground.

"Look bro, those two boys need their dad right now more than anything in the world. It's not their fault all of this happened. What do you think they're learning from you watching you mope around feeling sorry for yourself?"

John looks up and sees the boys peering out their bedroom window at them. They quickly close the curtain when they realize they're busted.

"I'll tell you what they're learning. They're learning how to QUIT!"

John's eyes and fists both clinch in anger, and Pat knows he's finally getting to him.

"I'm NOT a quitter!" barks John.

"GOOD! Then get back in the race! I can help you with that."

"How?"

"Tai chi."

"Tai what?"

"Tai chi. You'll see, I'll teach you, but you have to promise me you'll take it seriously, ok?" John looks down at the ground. Pat slaps him alongside the head and says, "Do I have to kick yur ass again?"

John smiles and says, "What do you mean again?"

Pat laughs and holds his arms open and says, "Come here ya big dope." Pat reaches out and John gives him a big 'ol bear hug and says, "I'm too tired to fight, let's just go fishin."

"Ok," says John, and the two of then walk arm in arm toward the house.

Brett and Ryan come running out the door saying, "Is everything alright now dad?"

John drops to his knees holding his arms open and says, "It will be once I get a hug from you guys." The boys run to him, and he picks them up and squeezes them tight saying, "I'm sorry you guys, I guess I've been a real pain lately huh?"

"Well, no, we were just worried about you," says Brett.

"We thought you didn't love us anymore," says Ryan.

John squeezes them tight and says, "Don't you ever think that! I will always love you guys no matter what happens, understand? I was just real depressed there for a while, and your uncle Pat got me to finally snap out of it, and now we're goin fishin, ok?"

"YAAYYY!" say the boys as John lowers them to the ground.

From that day forward, John was his old self again. He devoted his life to raising his boys to be fine young men. They were healthy and happy and did very well in school. Life was good until that September day when the world stopped turning for him again. Now he must get through each day facing the fact that he'll never see his boys again. Tai chi helped him get through hard times before, so maybe it will help him now. It's difficult for him to practice it in jail because the other prisoners make fun of him, and won't give him a moment's peace. The only one that doesn't make fun of him is Billy. He has become a student of John's. He says that tai chi reminds him of some of the ceremonial dances his ancestors practiced in the old days. John has tried to get Billy to exercise with him, but he's not quite ready to take that step yet. Billy can't take the teasing and jeering as well as John can. One day they were out in the exercise yard and John was practicing tai chi while Billy was sitting on a bench watching him.

About twenty feet away, a group of guys yelled out, "Hey look, our little ballerina is performing again. Should we throw her some flowers?"

They all laughed, and one of the fat ones grabbed his crotch and said, "I got something for ya sweetie."

As they laughed, Billy scowled and said to John, "How can you stand that? I KNOW you could kick all their asses. Why do you take that shit off them?"

John stopped and looked at Billy, "Why do you listen to it?"

"Can't you hear it?" asks Billy.

"All I hear is a bunch of fat asses blowing in the wind. They're opinion doesn't mean shit to me, so why should I let anything they have to say bother me?"

"Because they're saying it about you!"

"That doesn't matter. As long as those fat asses are picking on me, they're not picking on someone else. If it gives them pleasure to make fun of me, then so be it. Better me than someone who might take offence to it, like you."

Billy grumbles as he watches two fat biker-looking dudes dance around like a couple of ballerinas.

John smiles and says, "Watch and learn grasshopper."

He instructs Billy to stay where he's at and keep his mouth shut, and his eye's and ear's open as he walks toward the biker-looking dudes. They stop dancing and stand folding their arms as John nears.

Billy's thinking, 'Alright! He's finally gonna kick some ass!'

Once John is close enough for words, he says, "I couldn't help but noticing your feeble attempt at tai chi.

You know, if you want to learn, I'll be glad to teach you. It's good exercise."

The biggest one, and obviously the leader of the pack, steps forward and says, "If I want to exercise boy, I'll start by doin a little tap dancing on your fuckin head!"

John just smiled and said, "Aren't you a little over weight for tap dancing?"

This obviously pissed the guy off, because he reached back and took a swing at John. John quickly moved out of the way and the guy fell flat on his face. The fat guy scrambled to his feet and ran at John with his hands stretched out in front of him. This time John didn't move. Instead he reached out and met the fat man's hands with his own and stopped him in his tracks. The fat man tried to break free but John squeezed his hands and twisted his wrists backwards causing the fat man to drop to his knees in pain.

John had a blank look on his face as he spoke, "I was just trying to be neighborly. If you guys want to learn the art of tai chi, my offer still stands. I'll be glad to teach you."

John released the fat man and stood back. He looked around at the crowd of men that just witnessed him drop this big man to his knees and said, "That goes for everyone. I'm here every day at this time, so if you want lessons, just let me know."

John walked back to where Billy was sitting and smiled as the fat man stayed on the ground, holding his wrists in pain.

"Classes start tomorrow grasshopper, and you're my first student."

"Do I got'a?"

"Yes! It'll help you get over that anger you have inside you."

"What anger?"

"The anger that keeps landing you in here!"

"Oh, that anger. Well, whatever you say chief. I don't want to piss you off like that guy did."

"That guy didn't piss me off. I think I pissed HIM off. All I did was defend myself. I'll be curious to see how many of those guys want to learn tai chi now. Sometimes you have to use a little force to get your point across."

John and Billy walked back toward the entrance to their pod and none of the guys that were making fun of him said a word as they walked by.

John just smiled and said, "See ya tomorrow boys."

It took a few days, but eventually there was a crowd of guys gathered around John as he and Billy went through their routine. Billy caught on fast, and soon admitted that he felt better both physically and mentally after each session. He even practiced meditation with John in the cell. Bubba was pleased, and so was Billy's family at the change in him. John had become a very good mentor for him.

CHAPTER 18

MONDAY, NOVEMBER 22, 1999. IT's about nine in the morning, and John and Billy are meditating. John is on his bunk and Billy is on the floor facing the window. Billy's grandfather has brought him an old blanket to sit on while doing his meditation. The blanket was hand woven by Billy's great grandmother, and has been in the possession of his grandfather ever since its birth.

"That blanket has brought me comfort and security for many years," he told Billy, "now it is time for the blanket to work its magic for you. Treat it well Little Bear, for it holds many memories, and memories are the playground of the spirits."

Billy has done what his grandfather has asked of him, for he has treated that old blanket like his most prized possession. He has also decided to study up on the old ways of his ancestors, the Blackfoot Nation. John has reminded him that the Blackfoot were a very proud nation, and that HE should be proud to be a part of it.

Now with the help of his grandfather, Billy 'Little Bear' has become quite knowledgeable in the history of the Blackfoot Nation.

"C'mon John," announces Bubba, "your lawyer is here to see you."

John slowly opens his eyes and acknowledges Bubba. He looks down at his student on the floor and smiles. Bubba's entrance didn't even phase Billy. He is still deep in meditation. He is pleased with Billy's progress.

"So, what's she wearing today?"

Bubba smiles and says, "I think you'll be pleased."

The two of them walk to the meeting room where Jeanie is waiting. As John enters the room, his mouth drops to the floor. Jeanie is wearing a short black skirt and a tight sweater. This is the first time that John has seen her legs. In the past, she has always worn pants. He has to force himself not to stare.

"Hi John," she says with her usual pleasant tone.

"Howdy! What's up?"

"Well, I wish I had some good news for you, but I don't."

"What d'ya mean?"

"I haven't had any luck getting your bail reduced. I've tried to schedule a hearing with the appeals court and they're backlogged as bad as the district court. I've got a feeling you're going to be stuck here for a while unless your mom wins the lottery."

"Fat chance of that happening."

"Speaking of your mom, have you seen her lately?"

"She was here a couple of days ago, why?"

"Well, I'm worried about her. She didn't look so good the last time I saw her. How did she look when you saw her?"

"Come to think of it, she did look kinda tired. I figured she just didn't sleep well the night before."

"That's what I thought. She looked kind of depressed and run down, and that's not like her."

"No, it isn't."

"I'll keep checking on her if that's ok, I hate seeing her this way."

"Thanks, I'd appreciate that. She's probably been thinking a lot about the holidays coming up. It's going to be really tough on her being alone."

"No doubt."

"We used to have all the relatives over for Thanksgiving dinner. Now they're either dead or a thousand miles away…or in jail."

Jeanie reaches out and takes John's hand, "Should I invite her to spend Thanksgiving with me and my folks?"

"You can try, but I don't think she'll accept. Stubborn Irish pride you know."

"Well, I'll ask her anyway, and if she says no, I'll still pay her a visit."

John squeezes her hand and says, "Tanks sweetie, it means a lot to me knowing someone is keeping an eye on her, and I know she likes you a lot. I just wish I wasn't stuck in this stinking jail so I could take care of her myself. She has always been there for me, and now when she needs me the most, I can't be there for her."

"Don't worry John, I'll take good care or her."

John looks into Jeanie's sparkling brown eyes, and for a moment, he was back at the senior prom with his sweetheart, Laura. She had the same twinkle in her eyes under the colored lights of the gymnasium when he asked her to be his steady girl as he slipped his class ring on her tiny finger. Even that old familiar sick feeling in his stomach was present again.

"Times up boss," barks Bubba.

The two of them quickly separate their hands and shift their eyes to another part of the room.

"Ok then," says John, "I guess I'll see you after Thanksgiving, huh?"

"Ya, ya. I'll try to come up Monday and fill you in on what's going on, and I'll keep in touch with Kathleen."

"Ok sweetie, you have a nice Thanksgiving and I'll see you Monday."

"You have a happy Thanksgiving also, and try not to get too depressed, ok?"

"Ok."

"Bye, bye."

Jeanie walks away as John watches her shapely hips swing back and forth.

"C'mon boss, time to go."

"Has anyone ever told you that you have rotten timing Bubba?"

"All the time boss, all the time."

Bubba escorts John back to his cell where Billy is sitting at the desk reading. John doesn't say a word, just goes straight to his bunk and lies down. Billy looks up from his book for a moment, then goes back to his reading. John laid there on his back with his hands folded over his waist, staring at the mattress above him, thinking about Jeanie. After a few minutes, Billy looks up and notices John touching himself. The silence is broken by Billy's words.

"Thinking about Miss Jeanie?"

John quickly moves his hand back up to his waste and looks over at Billy to see him grinning and nodding toward John's hands.

"What ya talking about? I had an itch!" says John in a serious tone.

Billy laughs, "White man get itch, him scratch it. Red man get itch, him find squaw."

"Shut up!" laughs John. "I had an itch, ok?"

"Look to me more like a bee sting the way your pants are all swelled up."

John looks down and rolls over and faces the wall. "Go back to yur damn book!"

Billy laughs, "Ya want me to leave and give you and yur 'itch' some privacy?"

"Alright smart ass, that's enough. So, I like her, anything wrong with that?"

"Nothin wrong with that at all chief. In fact, I think ya got pretty good taste."

"Thanks," says John.

Thanksgiving Day arrives, and Bubba announces that both Billy and John have visitors. They go down to the meeting room together to find Kathleen and most of Billy's family there. John smiles as they all cheer when Billy enters the room. Billy's grandfather gives John a nod and a wink because he knows that John is largely responsible for Billy's new attitude towards life. John smiles and nod's back. As he looks over at Kathleen, he can see right away what Jeanie was talking about. She looks like hell.

"Hi mom! Happy Thanksgiving!"

"Hello dear, happy Thanksgiving to you too."

"Are you alright mom?"

"Now you sound like Jeanie. I'm fine dear, just a little tired."

John knows she's not fine. She looks like she's aged ten tears.

"So, when did you see Jeanie?"

"She called me yesterday and asked if I would join her and her folks for Thanksgiving dinner."

"Well, are you going?"

"I told her that I had planned on helping out at the church that day, but that stubborn little brat wouldn't take no for an answer."

"Sounds like someone else I know."

"Well, anyway, I'm going to go over there about two o'clock."

"Good, it should be fun. She's a nice girl. How come you're so tired mom? Haven't you been sleeping well?"

"Oh, I think I've been sleeping alright, I just don't seem to have any ambition these days."

"Have you been to see the doctor?"

"I went for a checkup last week and he says everything looks fine."

"Well, you don't look good so everything is NOT fine. Maybe you should get a second opinion?"

"Oh, I'm fine. Stop worrying. How about you? How are you doing?"

"I'm doing fine. My tai chi class is growing in numbers every week and the guards are pleased with the reduction in violence around here. It seems to be doing some good and it keeps my mind occupied. Maybe that's what you need mom, something to occupy your mind."

"I've got plenty to occupy my mind thank you. The church has been keeping me pretty busy. Maybe that's the problem. Maybe I need to slow down a bit."

"You could be right. Whatever it is, you take care of it, ya hear? I'm worried about you."

"Yes dear," smiles Kathleen, "I will. But right now, I better get home and get the sweet potatoes out of the oven. I told Jeanie that she has to at least let me bring a dish."

"Sweet potatoes! Mmm BOY! That sounds good."

"I'll see if I can sneak some up later with a file inside."

"Ok mom," laughs John, "you do that."

John and Kathleen stand and give each other a long hug before Kathleen says goodbye. John watches as she walks away. The spring in her step has disappeared. John is really worried. He goes back to his cell and stands staring out the window. He sees a truck go by with an elk carcass in the back and he thinks about one Thanksgiving when he and his brother went elk hunting in the Little Belt mountains near Neihart, Mt. John had already bagged is elk earlier in archery season, so they were trying to fill his brother's tag. They left early in the morning and arrived at the hunting spot well before daylight. They had been hunting the same area for weeks and they pretty much knew where the elk were. They sat in the truck drinking coffee and devising their game plan while waiting for daylight to peek its head over the mountains. The plan was that John would hike up the logging trail to the top of the mountain and cut to his left, then come down the steep gulch where they had seen many sets of tracks days before. Pat would start at the bottom of the gulch and work his way up. It seemed like a foolproof plan. The temperature was about ten degrees and there was about four inches of fresh snow on the ground. Things couldn't have been more perfect. John headed up the trail as soon as it was light enough to see, and Pat waited for one hour before starting up the bottom, which is how long they figured it would take John to get to the top. Once it was time, Pat carefully exited the truck as not to make too much noise, and headed toward the bottom of the gulch. He carefully worked his way up the mountain, stopping every few steps to listen for snapping branches or pounding hoofs. The breeze was in his face, so he knew that if there were any elk in the gulch, they would surely smell John and run downhill, right into his crosshairs. About thirty minutes went by and no sign of elk. Finally, Pat was leaning against a tree when he noticed something moving up the hill in front of him. He waited and watched as the object became more clear. It was John. He lowered his rifle and stepped out into the open so John could see him. As soon as John saw him, he started waving his arm for Pat to hurry up the hill. He must have seen some elk. Pat hurried as fast as his old legs could carry him.

When they met, John whispered, "There's some fresh tracks leading over into the next gulch, follow me."

The two of them stalked quietly over the ridge to their left and peered down into the neighboring gulch. They squinted their eyes, searching the bottom for the big animals that made all those tracks when the silence was broken by Pat's whispering voice.

"OH SHIT!"

John looked at him to see his mouth wide open and his eyes bugged straight out at the hillside across the gulch. There, on the hillside, stood five trophy bull elk grazing like majestic kings of the forest, nothing smaller than a six point.

John whispered, "Oh my God!"

Pat slowly raised his 7mm magnum to his shoulder, and scanned the bulls through the scope for the biggest one.

John, being the impatient little brother that he was, kept saying, "SHOOT, SHOOT!" Pat pushed the safety off and moved his finger over the trigger.

"What are ya waiting for? SHOOT!" whispers John.

Suddenly, Pat lowers his rifle and pushes the safety back on.

"What are you doing?" says John.

"I can't," says Pat.

John looks at his brother and notices there is a serious look in his eyes.

"What's wrong?" asks John.

"I just can't kill anymore," says Pat.

John realizes there is no point in arguing, so the two of them just sit and watch the monster bulls walk away in silence. John gained a whole new respect for his brother that day as the two of them walked back to the truck in silence. They never talked about that hunt with anyone else. Some things are better left silent.

CHAPTER 19

———— ✎ ————

"I'M HERE TO SEE JOHN McDuffy," explains Jeanie to the deputy at the front desk.

The date is December 15, 1999. It is a bright morning and the air outside is crisp, but very little snow, doesn't look much like the holiday season. Downtown Great Falls is dressed up in holiday fashion, as it is every year. Garland is strung up on the lampposts, business windows are painted with holiday spirit, and shoppers bustle from store to store hurriedly trying to finish up their Christmas shopping before all the good stuff is gone. All is well and cheerful in Great Falls. You would never know an innocent man is in jail and about to be tried for a crime he didn't commit. Jeanie has been preparing herself all morning for the news she must break to John about his mother.

"C'mon John, your sweetheart is here, I mean your lawyer is here to see you," announces Bubba cheerfully.

John smiles, but doesn't say anything. Billy gives Bubba a wink.

"You guys need to get a life," says John.

"Whatever you say boss, let's go."

As the two of them walk into the meeting room, John notices right away something is wrong. He walks quickly up to Jeanie.

"What's wrong?"

"It's your mom Johnny, she's in the hospital."

"Hospital? Why?"

"They don't know! She has just become so weak and depressed that she's not eating right, and she never remembers to take her medication. It seems like her mind is gone."

"What do you mean?"

"Well, I went up to see her yesterday and talked with her for a while, and, I don't know, it's hard to explain. She's just not her normal self. If I asked her a question, she would answer, but otherwise she would just stare at the ceiling."

"How long has she been in the hospital?"

"Since Monday I guess. She went to see her doctor Monday morning and he admitted her for some tests. I talked to him."

"And what did he say?"

"He said he's afraid to let her go home in this condition."

"What condition?" John is starting to become scared and irritated.

"The condition she's in, forgetful and weak. He's afraid she'll hurt herself."

"Well this is just GREAT! I'm confined to a jail cell and my mother is confined to a hospital bed! What next?"

"I know John. If I could get you out of here, I would do it in a heartbeat and take you up to see her. Is there some family members I should contact?"

"No, everyone is gone. She was the youngest of her family, and they've all passed away. My dad's family has pretty much all passed away too. There are a few still living, but they're back east and we haven't heard from them in years. I'm all she has."

Jeanie looks at John as he covers his face with his big hands and rubs his eyes. She can tell this is upsetting him terribly.

"Oh Johnny, I'm so sorry. I wish there was something I could do."

"You can get me the hell out of here! You're a lawyer, aren't you?"

Jeanie looks at John and her eyes begin to water. John looks at her and realizes that wasn't a fair thing to say.

"I'm sorry sweetie. I know you're doing all you can. Will you do me a favor and pick me up a get-well card so I can send it to her?"

Jeanie opens her briefcase and pulls out a get-well card.

"Already thought of it," she smiles.

She hands it to John and he says, "I should have known."

He smiles and squeezes her hand. She hands him a pen and he writes, 'Hi mom. I heard you were in the hospital. That's a hell-of-a way to get out of doing chores. Mom, you've always been a rock for us, now I need you to continue to be a rock for me. I'm not going to be in here forever, I hope you know that. The road ahead is going to be rough for a while, but we've been down rough roads in the past, we'll make it down this one. There is nothing that can break a McDuffy! And when you feel tired and weak, God is there for you to lean on. Lean on him now mom, and remember, I'll be with you soon! I love you mom, and I'm looking forward to getting all of those projects done that I've been procrastinating on. See you soon! Love, baby Johnny.' John hands the card to Jeanie and she puts it in the envelope and seals it.

"I'll take it up to her right away."

"Thanks, anything new on the trial?"

"Not really. We've requested a change of venue, but all that did is open a can of worms. Now we have to prove that you won't get a fair trial here. That might be a tough road. But don't worry, I'll get it done. How are you doing? Hanging in there?"

"Ya, I'm fine. I'm getting sick of the food around here."

"I'll see what I can do. Well, I better get up to the hospital and back to the office. I've got a lot of work to do." Jeanie stands and squeezes John's hand, "Take care John, and I'll keep you informed about your mom."

"Ok sweetie, thanks."

Jeanie leaves and John goes back to his cell. As he lies on his bunk, he remembers back to a time when he was a little boy. He was about nine or ten, and one day his mother announced that she had to go to the hospital for a few days.

"Why?" he asked.

"I have to have surgery and it's going to take a few days to heal from it. Your dad is going to be real busy at work, so you and your brother are going to stay with the neighbors for a while."

"Well, what's the surgery for?"

"It's nothing serious sweetheart, I just have to get something fixed inside."

That's all she would tell him. Pretty soon, Sunday night came and it was time to go over to the neighbors with their school clothes and toothbrushes packed for a three-day stay. John remembers crying and hugging his mom tightly because he thought he was never going to see her again. She wiped his tears away and told him not to worry, that she would be home before he knew it. As he and his brother walked over to the neighbors, he remembers watching his dad load a small suitcase in the car and then holding the door open for his mom. He couldn't understand why no one would tell him what was wrong. He knew it had to be something bad because his dad was being awfully polite to her. All day Monday in school, he couldn't think of anything else but his mom. He pictured her lying on the operating table with doctors and nurses running around in a panic. Finally, when Tuesday rolled around, he couldn't stand it anymore. He decided to take a detour on his way home from school and walk over to the hospital two miles away and see his mother, just to make sure she was ok. He remembers the surprised look on her face as he walked in to her room.

"Johnny! What are you doing here?"

"I was worried about you," he said as his eyes filled up with tears.

"Oh honey," she said as she held open her arms.

He remembers the warm, comforting feeling he had as she held him tight and kissed his head.

"Children aren't supposed to be on this floor. How did you get in here?"

"I just asked the lady down stairs what room you were in and she told me. Then I just took the elevator."

"My little man," smiled Kathleen as she ran her fingers through his hair. "I told you not to worry. Now you better get out of here before you get caught. I'll call the neighbors so they don't worry about you. You go straight home now, you hear?"

"Ok mom."

"I'll be home tomorrow honey, so you stop worrying!"

John made sure he avoided the hospital staff as he rode the elevator to the first floor. He felt much better now and skipped all the way home. He remembers that feeling, the thought of losing his mother. The same feeling he's experiencing right now.

"Hi Kathleen," says Jeanie as she walks into Kathleen's room. "How are you feeling?"

Kathleen smiles and says, "Oh I'm fine. Do I know you?"

Jeanie sits on the edge of her bed and says, "I'm Jeanie, remember?"

Kathleen looks at her closely and says, "Oh yes, you're that nice girl I had dinner with."

"Yes, that's me. I'm John's attorney, remember?"

"John?"

"Yes, Johnny, your son."

"Oh, Johnny! How is he doing?"

"He's fine. I was just up to see him. He gave me this card to give to you."

Jeanie opens her briefcase and hands the card to Kathleen.

"Oh, that's nice. Was he at work?"

Jeanie looks into Kathleen's eyes. Her heart breaks as she realizes Kathleen is losing her mind. She can't understand how a woman who was so full of life could fade away so quickly.

"Yes, he was at work. Would you like me to read the card to you?"

"Would you dear?"

As Jeanie reads John's words to his mother, her eyes fill up with tears. Kathleen just smiles, as she doesn't have a clue what Jeanie is talking about.

When she finishes, Kathleen just smiles and says, "That's nice. Is Johnny coming up to see me soon?"

"He said he is going to come up to see you just as soon as he can."

"That's nice."

Jeanie wipes the tears from her eyes and says, "Has the doctor been in to see you?"

"I think so. He's a nice man."

"Well, I think I'm going to go now. You take care of yourself Kathleen and I'll be up to see you soon."

"Ok dear," says Kathleen as Jeanie reaches out to give her a hug. Before Jeanie leaves the hospital, she manages to track down Kathleen's doctor.

"Doc, what is wrong with her? She didn't even know who I was!"

"I'm afraid she's suffering from severe depression Miss Philips. We have her on a mild sedative. We're running some tests, trying to find a cure for her, but so far, nothing has worked. Her blood pressure is dropping and she just doesn't seem to have the will to live anymore. I've consulted a Psychotherapist collogue of mine and we're trying desperately to find a cure for her depression."

"Will you keep me informed on her progress?"

"Of course."

"Here's my card with my work number and my home number. Please call me if she needs anything at all."

"I will Miss Philips, and please tell Johnny I'm doing everything I can."

"I will, goodbye doctor."

On her way back to the office, Jeanie stops to pick up a small cuddly white teddy bear to take up to Kathleen tomorrow. As it sits on the car seat beside her, it reminds her of the one that Calvin bought for her when she was in the hospital having Britney.

'Why does life have to be so cruel?' she thinks. She thinks about the words John wrote to Kathleen in the card. He put so much feeling into his words and she didn't even have a clue what he was talking about. She decides not to tell John about the condition that his mom is in. Instead, she'll tell him that she is doing better and should be out of the hospital soon. 'God please make her well soon,' she prays silently.

CHAPTER 20

———❦———

FRIDAY, CHRISTMAS EVE, 1999. A light snow is falling and the temperature is about twenty-five degrees. It's about five o'clock and downtown Great Falls is crazy with last minute shoppers. Charlie Russell stands by his pony and watches the activities as he taps the ashes from is cigarette. The merchants are trying to close early so they can get home to their families and the shoppers just seem to keep coming. Power generators, lanterns, gas cans, canned goods and other such things needed for a long stay without power seem to be the most popular items this year with all the talk of Armageddon when the clocks roll over at midnight, January 31st. No one knows if the computers around the world are going to recognize the year 2000. Therefore, everyone is paranoid that all the computers will shut down, thus shutting down the power plants they control. If this happens, the world could turn into utter chaos, the beginning of Armageddon. But even the gloom of an uncertain future hasn't put a damper on the joy of Christmas and all that it means, for in the hearts of everyone rests the flames of hope, hope for a bright future. The miracle of Christmas shines true for the McDuffy family today, for Kathleen seems to have made a complete recovery. She woke up this morning and informed the nurse that they weren't going to keep her captive any longer.

"I feel fine and I want to go home!" Kathleen declared.

"Well, we'll let the doctor be the judge of that," said the nurse.

"Doctor, schmoctor," barked Kathleen, "he don't know nothing! I feel fine and I'm going home!"

The nursing staff is frantic as they try to track down Kathleen's doctor. They are both happy and angry with her for being so demanding. They can't help but laugh at the change in her. After a while, they finally contact her doctor and he rushes to the hospital to see her.

"Good morning Kathleen," he says as he enters her room.

"Don't you good morning me!" she exclaimed. "You've kept me here long enough! Now I want to go home!"

"Now just hold your horses Kathleen. Just let me give you a quick checkup and then we'll see."

"Well hurry up will you, it's Christmas Eve!"

The doctor checks her vitals and smiles, "Well, you seem to be just fine Kathleen."

"That's what I've been trying to tell everyone around here! Now may I please get dressed?"

"Ok Kathleen, you win. I'll inform the front desk that you're going home and I'll call Miss Philips to come and get you."

"Fine! Now if you don't mind, I'd like to get dressed!"

The doctor can't explain the complete recovery, but it's Christmas Eve, and he has never been one to question the miracle of God. He called Jeanie to tell her about the good news. She was overjoyed and more than happy to pick Kathleen up and take her home.

"I'm not completely convinced with her recovery yet," said the doc, "keep a close eye on her and don't let her drive just yet. I want to see her in my office Monday morning for a complete checkup, ok?"

"Ok," agreed Jeanie. 'This is truly a miracle,' she thought as she drove to the hospital as fast as she could. Kathleen was waiting for her in the lobby with a big smile on her face. She was still pretty weak from lying in bed, but her memory was back and so was the fire.

"HI!" she called out.

"Hi Kathleen! Merry Christmas!" said Jeanie as the two of them embraced. "You look great!" said Jeanie.

"I feel great!" said Kathleen. "Can we go shopping dear?"

Jeanie smiled, "You betcha! But don't you want to go home and get cleaned up first?"

"Oh, I suppose I should, huh? But you pick me up in an hour. I've got lots of shopping to do!"

"You're the boss," said Jeanie and the two of them were off.

They spent the day shopping and laughing like a couple of teenagers. Kathleen talked Jeanie into letting her shop alone for a while so she could find a gift for her. Jeanie expressed her disagreement with the plan, but it was in vain, for Kathleen wouldn't take no for an answer. She bought Jeanie a beautiful leather brief case, as she noticed the one she was using looked old and worn out. After they were done shopping, Kathleen told Jeanie that she wanted to go see Johnny. Then she wanted her to attend the candlelight service with her at nine o'clock. Jeanie agreed as she thought to herself, 'Man, this lady is wearing me out!' When they went up to see John, Bubba was on duty. Jeanie asked him not to tell John that Kathleen was there to see him, only her. She wanted to surprise him. Bubba agreed and went to fetch John.

"C'mon boss, Jeanie's here to see you, and she has a surprise for you," announced Bubba as he grinned from ear to ear.

John bounced up from his bunk.

"What'd she buy me?"

"I can't tell ya, but I'm sure you'll be pleased."

"C'mon Bubba! You can tell me."

"No way! She told me not to tell ya, and the last thing I want to do is piss that little gal off."

"She is a little pistol, isn't she?"

"And a purdy little one at that!"

The moment John walks through the door, he sees the surprise.

"MOM!" he yells as he runs to her.

The two of them embrace and cry for what seems like an hour. Jeanie stands patiently waiting for John to acknowledge her. Finally, he looks at her and reaches out his left arm with his right arm still wrapped tightly around his mother. The three of them embrace in a triangle of love and tears. Even Bubba gets teary eyed as he watches the reunion. When their eyes can finally cry no more, they sit.

"When did you get out?" asks John.

"Just this morning. I told them I wasn't going to stay there one more minute!"

"Well, you look great! How do you feel?"

"A little tired, but then I've been lying on my back for a week. Jeanie and I have been shopping all day and we had a ball! She's going to the candlelight service with me tonight."

"Really?" asks John as he looks at Jeanie.

"Yep! And tomorrow morning we're coming up here to open gifts."

"Good!" says John. "Come up around eight o'clock. They're letting all the non-violent prisoners meet with their families in the cafeteria. They have a tree set up and everything."

"That sounds wonderful!" says Kathleen.

"It's gonna seem a little weird spending Christmas in jail," says John, "but at least you're well again, that's the best present I could ever receive."

"Oh, that's sweet, thank you dear, but I bought something for you anyway," Kathleen confesses.

"I tried to go out and buy something for you, but they caught me trying to climb the fence and sicked the dogs on me," said John with a smile.

"Great!" says Jeanie. "Now I have to explain THAT to the jury."

They all laugh and Kathleen looks at her watch.

"Oh my goodness, look at the time. We better get going dear so we can get ready for church."

"It's only seven o'clock!" says John.

"Johnny, Johnny," says Kathleen, "don't you know it takes a woman at least an hour and a half to get dressed?"

"Oh ya, I forgot."

The three of them stand and embrace again.

"Merry Christmas Johnny," says Jeanie.

"Merry Christmas," says John as he stands and watches his two favorite girls leave, arm in arm. He notices his mom has that spring back in her step.

As John and Bubba walk back to his cell, Bubba says, "Christmas is truly a time for miracles, isn't it boss?"

"You got it Bubba! Merry Christmas!"

"Merry Christmas to you too John. I won't be here tomorrow, so you have yourself a good time and I'll see you Monday."

"Ok Bubba, take care."

John goes in and lays down on his bunk. Billy can't help but notice the big smile on his face.

"Musta been a pretty good surprise."

"It was my mom. She's completely recovered and looks great! She'll be here in the morning for the festivities."

"That's great! My family will be here too, so we'll have to introduce each other."

"Ya."

Jeanie and Kathleen attended the candlelight service and Kathleen introduced her to everyone as John's girlfriend. Jeanie confessed that she didn't mind because she did have feelings for John. After the service, they each went home to their beds and slept sound, for they were both worn out from the busy day. John couldn't sleep from the butterflies in his stomach. The combination of seeing his mom's smiling face and the anticipation of Christmas morning was just too much. He stood at the window and stared at the stars most of the night, thanking God for the miracle.

Christmas morning, and the jail was a buzz with family and friends. John felt sorry for the guards, as it only made their jobs tougher. The cafeteria was decorated nicely and there was much happiness in the air. He waited patiently for his two favorite girls to arrive. Finally, about eight thirty, he saw them walk through the door. He hurried to meet them at the door and help carry the packages.

"Hi mom! Hi Jeanie! Merry Christmas!"

"Hi honey!"

"Hi Johnny!"

"I've got a table for us right over here," says John as he leads them to the middle of the cafeteria. Once they're seated, Billy wastes no time in bringing his family over to introduce them to his cellmate and mentor. John introduces Kathleen and Jeanie and they all shake hands.

After Billy and his family leave, Kathleen announces, "Time to open presents!"

"Ok," says John.

"Oh John, you should see the beautiful new briefcase your mom bought me! It's gorgeous!" says Jeanie.

"Here Johnny, this is for you," says Kathleen as she hands John a package. John opens it and finds a beautiful down ski jacket inside.

"Oh mom! It's great!"

"I thought you might need it if the heat ever goes off around here."

"I love it! Thank you!"

"Here John, open this one next," says Jeanie.

John reads the label. 'To Johnny, Love Jeanie.' He smiles at her as he opens the package. Inside is a beautiful afghan blanket made up of multiple colors.

"Oh Jeanie! It's beautiful!" Jeanie smiles. "Where did you ever find this?" asks John.

Jeanie's smile suddenly turns into a serious look, "I made it for you John."

John's mouth drops open, "You made this?"

"Yes."

John stares at her as his face glows with joy.

"Oh sweetie, you shouldn't have."

"Well, I suppose I could give it to someone else," says Jeanie as she reaches out to take the blanket back.

John pulls it back and says, "Not on your life!"

Jeanie smiles, "So you like it?"

"I love it!"

"I thought it could keep you warm at night."

He stands and leans over the table to give her a hug. As they embrace, they both have the same thought. They would like to perform the duties of that blanket on each other.

"Ok Johnny, time to open this one," announces Kathleen.

She hands John another package and he tears into it like a little child. Kathleen and Jeanie laugh as they watch this grown man tear into his Christmas present. Inside is a bad mitten set.

John stares at it for a moment and then says, "Cool! I've always wanted one of these."

He smiles at Kathleen and then looks over at the confused look on Jeanie's face.

"I saw it in the store and couldn't resist. I thought you and the boys could play bad mitten when you're out camping this summer."

John's face freezes and so does Jeanie's. His breathing stops for a moment as he stares at his mother's unsuspecting face. He looks over at Jeanie and she is just as confused as he is.

He finally swallows hard and says, "What boys, mom?"

"Why, Brett and Ryan silly. Who do you think?"

CHAPTER 21

⸻⚬⚬⚬⸻

JOHN'S HEART HAS JUMPED ALL the way up to his throat now. His face loses its color as he stares at his mother. Jeanie clamps her hands over her mouth and also stares at Kathleen.

"What's the matter?" asks Kathleen. "You two look like you've seen a ghost."

John slowly leans over the table and grabs Kathleen's hands. His mouth has suddenly gone completely dry and he's finding it hard to speak.

"Mom, the boys are gone, remember?"

"Gone? Gone where?" asks Kathleen.

John looks at Jeanie and realizes she isn't going to be any help. She's shaking like a leaf and her eyes are welling up with tears.

He squeezes her hands and says, "They died in the accident, remember?"

Kathleen's smile leaves her face, but her eyes keep the same blank, empty stare.

"They're dead?"

John nods his head.

"Oh...well I guess they won't be going camping then," she says as she stares straight through John.

"Mom? Do you remember the accident?"

"Accident?"

"Yes, the one where Brett and Ryan were killed?"

"Brett and Ryan were killed?"

John puts his hands over his face and tries to hold back the tears. Jeanie finally gets a hold of herself and moves over next to Kathleen and puts her arm around her shoulder and pulls her close. Kathleen begins to shake and the tears begin to flow at the thought of her grandsons being dead. John can't believe this is happening. He thinks, 'How could God be so cruel as to fool him this way. Letting him believe that his mom was alright, and then pulling this shit on him. Why?!' Some of the prisoners and their families are gathering around to sing Christmas carols. John would like to stand up and tell them to be quiet. There is no reason to be happy here.

Kathleen wipes the tears from her eyes and says, "Can you take me home now dear? I think I need to lie down."

Jeanie looks at John for direction.

"Are you going to be ok mom?"

"Yes, I think so. I'm just tired."

John looks at Jeanie and nods. They stand and take Kathleen by the arms and help her up. They slowly walk her to the door.

Once there, John hugs her tightly and says, "You go home and get some rest mom and try not to think about the boys too much. I'll talk to you tomorrow, ok?"

"Ok dear."

John looks at Jeanie and she nods. As the two of them leave, the crowd is singing Joy to the World. John bites his lip as he gathers up the gifts and checks them with the guard. They let him keep the jacket and the blanket, but hold the bad mitten set for safe keeping. Billy watches him from across the room and realizes something is terribly wrong. He walks up to him and sees the despair on his face and knows better than to ask.

Instead, he just puts a hand on his shoulder and says, "Let me know if I can do anything chief."

John tries to smile and taps Billy on the shoulder as he walks past him on his way back to his cell. Once back at the cell, he stands and stares out the window at the snow falling. He can't even cry because he just feels numb. He thinks about the innocent look on his mom's face when he had to break the news to her that Brett and Ryan were dead. He can't help but feel how ironic it is. First, she had to break the news to him, now he had to break the news to her. What a cruel world it is indeed. Memories of the accident flood his mind and he decides to just lay down and try to sleep. Maybe he'll wake up and discover that this has all been a terrible dream.

As Jeanie drives Kathleen home, not a word is said. Jeanie just doesn't know what to say. Kathleen has some serious mental problems, and problems of the mind can be very complicated. She decides that this is better left to the professionals.

"Do you need anything at the store Kathleen?" asks Jeanie.

"No. Thank you anyway dear. I just want to lie down."

Jeanie nods and continues to Kathleen's house. Once there, she helps her inside. She walks her to her bedroom and writes down her parent's phone number and leaves it by her phone.

"Here's my parents number. I'll be there all day. If you need anything at all, you call me, ok?"

"Yes dear, I will. Thank you."

Jeanie helps her on with her nightgown and sees that she's tucked in before she leaves.

"Goodnight Kathleen."

"Goodnight dear."

Before she gets to the front door, she can hear Kathleen snoring already.

'Maybe a day in bed will make a world of difference for her,' she thinks.

She goes to her parent's home and tries from there to get a hold of Kathleen's doctor. The answering service tells her that he is out of town, but they will continue to try and reach him. She passes the time trying to enjoy the holiday with her folks, but it's difficult to be cheerful after what she had just experienced. Her folks do their best to console her as they know how she feels about John and Kathleen.

"She'll be ok pumpkin, try not to worry," whispers her father as he hugs her and pets her long auburn hair.

"But daddy, she seemed so normal! I thought she was completely recovered. I didn't have a clue she was living in a dilemma."

"Sometimes these things happen baby, she could still make a complete recovery. Maybe some sleep will do her good."

"I hope so."

It's A Wonderful Life is on the television when the doctor finally calls.

"Miss Philips?"

"Yes doctor."

"What's wrong?"

"It's Kathleen doc."

"What happened?"

"Well, her and John and I were sitting at a table at the jail cafeteria opening presents this morning, having a great time, when John opened one from Kathleen, a bad mitten set. We looked at Kathleen surprisingly and she said she thought it would be nice for he and the boys to play with when they go camping this summer. Well, after a moment, John and I realized that she had completely forgotten about the accident and thought the boys were still alive."

"Oh no. Where is she now?"

"After John explained that the boys were gone, she became very depressed and said she wanted to go home and lie down, so that's where she is now. What should I do doc?"

"Well, I'm in Calgary right now, so I can't go see her. I'll call a Pharmacist friend of mine and give him this phone number. Will you be at this number all day?"

"Yes, I will."

"Ok, I'll give him a call and have him go down to his office and fill a prescription for Kathleen. I'll tell him to give you a call when he's finished so you can go pick it up."

"What's the prescription for?"

"It's the same anti-depressants I had her on at the hospital. But once she starts taking them, you need to keep an eye on her, because they'll make her a little dizzy."

"No problem, I'll just stay there with her. When are you coming back?"

"Sunday night. I'll be in the office Monday morning. Bring her in to see me then."

"Ok doc."

"You know, my colleague warned me that something like this might happen, but there is no way of detecting it. Depression is a complicated disease. It can really play tricks on the mind."

"You're telling me! You should have seen the look on her face. She was dead serious! She really thought Brett and Ryan were still alive!"

"I believe it. Well, you have a Merry Christmas Miss Philips and I'll see you Monday morning."

"Ok doc, Merry Christmas."

Jeanie hangs up and explains to her folks that as soon as the pharmacist calls, she must pick up a prescription and take it to Kathleen.

"That's ok dear," says her mother.

"The doc says after I give her the medication, I need to keep an eye on her because it will make her dizzy."

"Don't you worry about us dear, Kathleen needs you more than we do right now," says her mom.

Jeanie smiles, "I love you mom."

The Pharmacist didn't call until seven o'clock. Jeanie was just about to call the doctor again and find out what was taking so long. The Pharmacist explained that he lived on the outskirts of town and the roads were bad. Jeanie decided to spare him this time. She said goodbye to her folks and rushed right over to his Pharmacy. After leaving there, she ran home to pack an overnight bag for the short stay at Kathleen's. Once she secured things at home, she drove over to Kathleen's. She arrived about 7:45.

It's nine o'clock pm back at the jail.

"McDuffy?" announced the guard on duty as he walked up to John's cell. John rolled over and wiped the sleep out of his eyes.

"Ya?"

"There's someone to see you, says she's your lawyer."

John stares at the guard for a moment, then stands and follows him to the meeting room. He walked through the door and took one look at Jeanie as she broke down in tears. He ran up to her and hugged her tightly. As soon as he wrapped his arms around her, her knees gave out and he picked her up as she buried her face in his neck. She was crying harder than he had ever seen her cry.

"What's wrong sweetie?"

Jeanie pulled her head back and looked into his eyes and with broken words, said, "I went to take a prescription over to your mom a little while ago, and…"

John knew what was coming and decided to spare her saying those painful words.

"She's dead," said John quietly.

Jeanie buries her face in his neck again and cries hard. Now his knees are feeling weak. The two of them sit and hold each other, rocking back and forth. When Jeanie arrived at Kathleen's, she called out to her, but no answer. She then went to her bedroom to find her still in bed. She bent down to touch her and realized she was cold and stiff. She had been gone for a while. She called 911 first, then her folks. She stayed as long as she had to, then drove to the jail. Her and John sat there and held each other for as long as the guard would let them. Both of their hearts were breaking as Jeanie explained to John how she had planned to spend the rest of the weekend with her and take care of her.

Jeanie kept saying, "I'm sorry! I'm so sorry!"

"It's not your fault!" said John. "There's nothing you could have done. Did they say what she died of?"

"Not really. They're assuming her heart just stopped, but they won't know for sure until they examine her."

"I know what she died of," said John. Jeanie looked into his eyes as he said, "A broken heart."

CHAPTER 22

────⌘────

DECEMBER 29, 1999. NINE O'CLOCK am.

"C'mon John, time to go," says Bubba.

John quietly shifts his eyes from the window to Bubba and nods. It's been four days since Kathleen died and John hasn't spoken two words to anyone. Jeanie has been up several times to talk to him about the funeral arrangements, but not even she can get him to open up. It's like he's forgotten how to talk. Today is Kathleen's funeral and the deputies are waiting to take him to the church. It's a beautiful crisp December morning. The snow on the ground is sparkling like a bunch of diamonds in a bed of cotton and the temperature is low enough to hear a footstep squeak a block away. The smoke from the rooftops billow into the clear blue sky, it's winter in Montana. John shuffles to the patrol car and the deputies help him inside. They don't speak on the way to the church out of respect for John. Even though he is a prisoner, they know what he has been through and the feeling between them is mutual, no man should have to suffer so much pain and loss. At the church, Jeanie is waiting for him, dressed in black. The deputies release him into her custody and the two of them walk up to the front of the church and sit in the front pew. The look on John's face is one of anger. Anger at God for taking his dear, sweet mother from him, anger at the world for continuing to turn while his life is being destroyed, anger at himself for not taking the ditch. Laura is present with her family and they are all weeping at the loss of Kathleen, for they loved her as much as anyone. Many church members are present also to mourn the loss of their dear friend. John just stares at his mother lying in the coffin in front of him, there, right in front of his face as if to punish him, as if to say, 'Look what you've done!' Finally, while the minister is giving his eulogy, John speaks.

He whispers low, "I'm sorry mom," as a tear rolls down his cheek.

Jeanie looks at him and she too begins to cry.

John repeats himself over and over, "I'm sorry, I'm so sorry."

Jeanie squeezes his arm and rests her head on his shoulder. Laura looks over at the two of them and whispers something into her mother's ear.

When the minister is finished with his sermon, John and Jeanie stand and walk down the aisle toward the entrance. As they walk together, John keeps looking forward and tries to avoid the eyes in the room, because he knows if he has contact with anyone, he'll lose it. Jeanie looks around and notices all the sad faces wondering who this young woman is with John. The two of them stop at the entrance to greet the congregation as they leave. Jeanie introduces herself to the people and watches as a look of relief come over their faces as she tells them she is his lawyer. John tries to maintain his composure as he extends his cuffed hands to greet them. All the congregation is sympathetic to his situation and their hearts bleed for his loss. Laura and her folks walk right on by without saying a word to John. They do, however, manage to work up a smile for him as they leave, but Laura just looks straight ahead and ignores him. Once everyone leaves, John and Jeanie watch as they carry his mother outside to the hearse.

John whispers as she goes by, "I'm sorry mom, I'm so sorry."

The deputies gently escort John to the patrol car and drive him to the cemetery. When they arrive, he asks if it would be all right to go over and say hi to Brett and Ryan. The deputies look at each other and agree that that would be ok. John kneels between their graves as Jeanie walks up and kneels beside him.

John stares at the writing in the grave markers and whispers, "I'm sorry you guys, I'm so sorry. I miss you."

Jeanie's finally had enough of the 'I'm sorrys' and says, "John, it wasn't your fault, you have to stop blaming yourself."

"I should have taken the ditch!"

"John, you're only human! We can't make all the right decisions all the time. Please stop beating yourself up. You had a 50/50 chance of making the right choice. There is no way you could have known what the other driver was going to do."

"I should have known! My boys depended on me!"

"John! Stop it!"

Jeanie puts her arms around his neck and pulls his head to her breast and rocks him back and forth, whispering, "Shhh…it'll be all right. It just takes time."

John weeps gently as she rocks him until the minister comes over to inform him that they are ready. They stand and return to Kathleen's burial site and listen as she receives her last rights. The minister makes it short as the temperature is only fifteen degrees and everyone is shivering. John cries hard as they lower his mother into the ground. The tears freeze to his eyelashes and he is shivering out of control, even in the new down jacket Kathleen bought him for Christmas.

After everyone gives John their condolences, Jeanie gives him a big hug and says', "I want you to promise me you'll stop blaming yourself, ok?"

"Ok," says John as the deputies help him into the patrol car.

All the way to the jail, he stares at the mountains in the distance. Anger consumes him as he thinks about the little red car that forced him to make a decision that changed his life forever and took the lives of his sons.

'Why the hell am I in jail?' he thinks. 'If I weren't in jail, mom would still be alive.'

He wishes he were up in the mountains right now, skiing with Brett and Ryan. Once at the jail, the deputies open the door and hold John's head as he steps outside. He stands, staring intensely at the mountains as the deputies try to escort him to the jail. They sense something is wrong because John is just standing there, staring at the mountains. They look at each other and decide to each grab an arm. All at once, John whirls and slings one of the deputies into the patrol car and kicks the other one, knocking him to the ground. He takes off running toward the road. He doesn't know where he's going, but he's going somewhere.

'They aren't going to keep me locked up anymore,' he thinks.

The deputies scramble to their feet and chase after him. It isn't too long before they catch up to him and knock him to the ground. At the jail, sirens are blaring and officers are running to assist. The two deputies have their hands full as John kicks and screams.

"LET ME GO, DAMMIT!"

"Calm down John, you're not going anywhere!"

"You can't keep me here! I'm innocent!"

Two more officers arrive on the scene, and between the four of them, they manage to restrain him and get him inside. John fights them the whole way. Everything he's been through has finally reached a boiling point, and he has snapped. Once inside the jail, he gets another burst of energy at the thought of being locked up again, and manages to get loose and bolt for the door. This time they tackle him and put shackles on his legs so he can't run.

"Throw his ass in confinement!" yells the chief deputy warden.

John kicks and fights as they drag him to solitary confinement.

Bubba comes to the scene and says, "What's going on?"

"Your buddy, John McDuffy, snapped and hurt two of our men!"

"I'll talk to him."

"That's fine, but he's going to solitary until he calms down!"

Bubba goes to the cell to see John pacing like a caged lion.

"What's the matter big guy?" asks Bubba.

"What's the matter?! What'd ya mean what's the matter?! I'm in fucking jail! That's what's the matter! I don't belong here! You know it! I know it! The whole fucking world knows it! But because of one fucked up judge with a hard-on for my dad, I have to spend the rest of my fucking life in jail! What's wrong with this picture Bubba?!"

"I know boss, but you got to have faith. That little lawyer of yurs is gonna get you outta here, I know she will. Throwin a shit-fit and hurtin those deputies isn't gonna help matters at all. You gotta calm down."

"I don't wanna calm down! I want out of here!"

"You can't get outta here till the trial John! That's just the way it is, ain't nothing we can do about it!"

John doesn't say anything, he just continues pacing.

"Yur gonna have ta stay in here fur awhile boss, till ya calm down."

"Why not! I'm a fucking criminal, aren't I?!"

Bubba doesn't say anything, just shakes his head and walks away.

"Do me a favor!" yells John as Bubba walks away. "Bring that fucking Murphy here and put him in this cell with me! THAT will be justice!"

Bubba walks out to the incoming area where four deputies are licking their wounds.

"What's the matter boys? The big guy get the better of ya?"

"Screw you Bubba! You just make sure he stays locked up!" barks one of the deputy's.

Bubba laughs, "Don't worry boys, I won't let him hurt ya."

John continues to pace and yell obscenities through-out the day. All the prisoners are talking about his attempt to escape and it's sparked a small uprising. They're tipping their beds over and busting up their cells and fighting with each other. The commotion became so great that the warden had to order a lock down. Bubba called Jeanie and she came up to do her best to calm him down. She talked to him for about an hour, but it still took him several to cool off. Someone called the local newspaper and the next morning the headlines read… 'PRISONER ATTEMPTS ESCAPE, SPARKS RIOT.' The article went on to say, 'John McDuffy, a local man jailed last September for manslaughter, tried to escape yesterday according to prison officials, injuring four deputies in the process. Once McDuffy was captured and restrained, his rage continued throughout the day, sparking a riot amongst the prisoners.'

Jack walked into Jeanie's office and slammed the newspaper down on her desk saying, "This is just great! I bet the prosecutors are having a hay-day over this!"

"I know, I know" says Jeanie, "but Jack, you know the man was bound to snap sooner or later."

"Yes, but why couldn't he wait till after the trial! Now we have to prove he's NOT a violent man!"

She looks at Jack, rubbing her eyebrows. "I know," she says. "I'm just going to have to convince the jury that anyone can snap under those circumstances."

"Good Luck!" shouts Jack as he slams the door behind him.

Jeanie sits and stares at the briefcase Kathleen bought for her. Memories of their shopping spree come drifting back. 'What a wonderful lady,' she thinks. 'God bless you Kathleen.'

"Jeanie?" inquires the secretary across the intercom.

"Yes?"

"Line one is for you."

"Thank you." Jeanie picks up the phone. "This is Jeanie Philips."

"Hi Jeanie, its Bubba."

"Hi Bubba, what's up?"

"Now he refuses to eat."

CHAPTER 23

―❈―

"Why does he refuse to eat?" asks Jeanie.

"I don't know. I guess he figures he's gonna get outta here one way or the other, whether on his feet or in a box."

"Well, you tell him that as long as he's alive, I can help him, but I can't do anything for a dead man."

"Ok, I'll tell um, but I don't think he'll listen."

"I would tell him myself, but as long as he keeps this tantrum up and remains in solitaire, I can't see him."

"I know, I'll tell um that too."

"Good luck Bubba, and thanks for the call."

"You betcha counselor, I'll keep you informed of what that big dummy does next."

"Thanks," chuckles Jeanie, "bye, bye."

All the pain and heartbreak of losing his sons and his mother and the anger of the injustice that has been done has finally reached a boiling point. John has snapped! Because of his size, the guards are taking no chances.

He will remain in solitary until he proves he has calmed down and will not try to escape again. Suddenly, this mild-mannered man has become a raging bull. The guards have the rest of the prisoners under control and the so-called riot is over, but there is still much protest to keeping John McDuffy locked up in solitary confinement, after all, he has become a mentor to more than just Billy. John has become a symbol of strength and hope to everyone, including the guards. Up until now, he has proven that he can cope with all the terrible things that have happened to him since Labor Day weekend. He has shown his resilience and self-control, and related it to the other prisoners through his teachings of tai chi. The atmosphere had become one of calmness and learning, but now the teacher needs a little teaching. He has given up hope. Hope of ever seeing the mountains again, of ever fishing the Missouri River again.

As for the rest of the country, life goes on. The government is frantically gathering information and transferring data and conferring with experts on the big question on everyone's minds. Will the computers around the world recognize the numeral 'two' in place of 'one' in 1999? After all, nobody knows if the first pioneers of digital electronics and computers thought that far ahead. The prison officials are especially concerned because they really don't need a power outage, and they REALLY don't need the prisoners to be in a point of rage right now. They could certainly use John McDuffy's help, not his hindrance. December 31st is approaching rapidly and the military is on alert, as are all the soldiers of fortune around the country. Citizens are stock-piling food, gasoline, weapons, ammo, kerosene, money, warm clothes, and probably the biggest thing of all, drinking water. If the World-Wide-Web shuts down along with all the other time-sensitive computers around the country, there's no telling what kind of chain reaction this could trigger. President Clinton is doing his best to assure the country that the United States of America is prepared and will handle any crises that might incur. These words from the president are of course like a warm blanket to the citizens of the country.

The whole civilized world is praying for a positive outcome to this potential nightmare. Churches, prayer groups, and consolers everywhere are preparing and training people the best they know how to remain calm and act responsibly in the face of a disaster. Even in the sleepy little town of Great Falls, there is much tension. Firewood is being stacked to the sky, for it is winter in Montana and all the natives know not to trust Mother Nature. The temperature here can change twenty degrees in an hour at any given moment. This has made Montanans tough over the years and born with a sense of survival. The weather has been calm and Mother Nature has been kind so far this winter, but the fear of having no power has put everyone on edge. Visitation rights at the prisons have been suspended until January first has come and gone. Security has increased and extra guards have been hired. All everyone can do now is wait and hope for the best.

"Jeanie?" inquires Jack as he enters her office.

"Yes Jack?"

"Sorry I snapped at you, got plans for lunch?"

"That's ok Jack, and no, I don't have plans."

"Well why don't we go grab a bite and get caught up on this case of yours."

"Ok, that sounds good."

The two of them leave the office and drive to Jack's favorite place to eat, McDonalds. Jeanie chuckles as they pull into the parking lot.

"Oooo, big spender."

"Leave me alone," says Jack, "I like clown food."

After receiving their food, they pick the quietest table they can find in this madhouse of high school students on lunch break.

"So, how's the McDuffy case coming?" asks Jack.

"I don't know Jack, what I need is a miracle."

"Did you get a statement from the truck driver?"

"Yes, but all he remembers seeing is the red car sliding toward him on its top in his lane."

"What does the Highway Patrol's report say?"

"All it says is that the red car must have been struck in the north-bound lane to cause it to flip over and land in the south-bound lane. Therefore, the pickup and camper must have been in the wrong lane at the time of impact."

"So even though he was trying to avoid hitting the red car by switching lanes, he's guilty of being in the wrong lane."

"Exactly!"

"So, they're saying that the pickup must have hit the red car, causing it to flip over, correct?"

"Yes."

"Well then, there should be some red paint on the front of the pickup somewhere that matches the paint of the car, correct?"

"Yes, but the vehicles are in the police impound, and I'm having a hell of a time getting a search warrant to get in there."

"What's the problem?"

"The problem is it has to be signed by a judge."

"Oh, I see. Well, you just let me handle that."

"Thanks Jack. I just don't seem to have much pull in this town."

"Well, I've been around a few more years than you have counselor. Let me take a crack at it."

"Ok."

"So, not to change the subject, but what are you doing New Year's Eve?"

"No plans, why?"

"The wife and I are having a little party and we'd like you to come."

"Oh, I don't know Jack. I don't think I'd be very good company."

"Nonsense! You've been through a lot lately and you need to blow off some steam. Besides, the wife says she hasn't seen you in a long time and I'm not to take no for an answer."

"Well, I wouldn't want to get on Peggy's bad side. Ok, what time?"

"Somewhere around seven will be fine."

"You're right, maybe I do need to take my mind off the McDuffys for a while."

"You're kind of fond of that boy, aren't you?"

Jeanie blushes, "It's just that I sense a good heart, and he's been through so much pain. I know what he's going through."

"He's a good man Jeanie. Did you know he's an eagle scout?"

"No."

"Yep, he and his brother both made eagle. James was so proud of them."

"That probably explains his love for camping."

"They definitely did a lot of camping as a family and with the scouts. James was very active in the troop."

"Maybe I can use that to influence the jury."

"Yes, definitely."

"Speaking of the McDuffy's, have you taken care of Kathleen's estate?"

"Yes, that wasn't too tough. She left everything to John. All her assets are in an escrow account awaiting the outcome of the trial. Is it still set for February?"

"So far, although I wouldn't be surprised if they moved it to a later date."

"Neither would I. Have you heard anything on your request for a change of venue?"

"Not yet, but I've been bugging them every day."

"Good girl, don't let up on them. Well, we better get back. I've got a deposition at two o'clock I need to prepare for."

"Ok, can we drive by my house on the way back? There are some papers I left there this morning."

"Sure thing."

As Jack nears Jeanie's house, they notice a red ribbon tied around some shrubs in her front yard.

"THAT'S IT!" Jeanie shouts. "I'm hiring a private detective!"

"I know a good one," says Jack.

Jeanie jumps out and tears the ribbon off the shrub and takes it in the house. On the way to the office, Jack call's his friend, Angus O'Leary.

"Hello?"

"Angus ol' buddy," says Jack.

Angus snickers, "Sounds like you need a favor Jack."

"Now c'mon, can't I just call and say howdy from time to time?"

"Howdy my foot. I know you too well, Jack."

"Now that's not very nice. Actually, I just called to see what you're doing New Year's Eve?"

"I plan on staying in where it's safe, why?"

"Well, why don't you plan on staying in at my place? We're having a little party and I'd like you to come. Several of my colleagues will be there, you can pass out some business cards."

"Sounds like fun. What time?"

"Oh, about seven would be fine."

"Ok, I'll see you there."

"Good. There's something I want to talk to you about, but it can wait till the party."

"I knew it!"

"See you at seven Angus."

"Bye Jack."

The party starts promptly at seven pm, and there are approximately twenty people there. Everyone is cheerful and awaiting the magic hour. No one in the room seems to be afraid of the impending doom that lies ahead. Jeanie is glad she came to the party, her and Peggy are having a good time talking about old times. Jack introduced her to Angus O'Leary, and he assured her that he would catch the culprit that is harassing her and John McDuffy. That seemed to give her a little piece of mind, but she still can't help feeling a little depressed.

"What's wrong dear?" asks Peggy.

"Oh, I don't know. I guess I just can't get John out of my mind. I feel so bad for him."

"Jack told me you've grown kind of fond of him. Normally I would say you shouldn't get involved with a client, but I think John McDuffy is a good man, and it's just terrible what he's been through. Losing his boys and his mother, and then having to be in jail all this time. I tell you, it's just not right!"

"I know! I just pray that I can convince the jury that he didn't cause that accident and he should be free to go and try to piece his life back together."

"You will dear," assures Peggy gently, "you will."

The two of them hug and Peggy tries to change the subject.

"So, do you think we're all going to die when the clock tolls midnight?"

"I don't think so," smiles Jeanie. "If anything was going to happen, it would have happened by now."

Suddenly a shot rings out! *BANG* Everyone jumps.

"JACK!" yells Peggy. "I thought I told you to warn people before you opened the champagne!"

Jack laughs and says, "Ok everybody, come and fill your glasses, it's almost time!"

Everyone gathers around as Jack hands out the champagne. Peggy turns on the television to watch the ball drop in Time Square. The bewitching moment closes in as everyone begins to sing Auld Lang Sine. Ten, nine, eight, seven, six, five, four, three, two, one!

Happy New Year!

CHAPTER 24

JANUARY 30ᵀᴴ 2000, 6:00 PM. The Super Bowl is over and the St. Louis Rams are champions. John and Billy are just leaving the recreation room after watching the game.

"Looks like Kurt Warner is going to Disney World, aye bro?"

"Ya, looks that way. I still say Tennessee should've won though."

"Ya, but it's over now, and they ain't gonna change it."

"Oh well, Minnesota's gonna win it next year."

"How many years you bee sayin that now?"

"Shut…up," says John as he smiles at Billy. "You just focus on your trial tomorrow and let me worry about the Vikings."

"Whatever you say bro."

Billy's trial date has finally come. Tomorrow he will stand before the judge and face charges for assault and battery, public drunkenness, and indecent exposure. A public defender has been assigned to him and he is pleased with Billy's change in attitude since his arrest back in September. He has collected affidavits from the prison guards and other staff that will support his case. His case, of course, being that Billy has turned over a new leaf and is ready to re-enter society as a new man.

"I'm gonna miss this place, ya know...NOT!"

"Well, I'm gonna miss my assistant, but not my roommate. You're a slob, did you know that?"

"Am not!"

"Are too!"

"I'm not the one that farts all night long."

"Ya, well I'm not the one that rolls over every two minutes. Besides, how am I not supposed to get gas with the crap they serve around here?"

"All tastes like dog to me."

"You're a sick man Little Bear."

John and Billy enter their cell as the guard makes his last rounds before lights out. The two of them have been cellmates for five months, and even though they had a shaky start, they've become pretty good friends. Billy looks up to John, and John is proud of his student, but at the same time, glad he's leaving. They talk through the night like a couple of boy scouts on a campout.

"You remember that time I puked all over your bunk?"

"Yaaa...I can still smell it. You remember the fat guy that needed a little attitude adjustment out in the yard?"

"Ya," laughs Billy, "you sure put him in his place."

"Some people need that now and then. That doesn't mean it's ok for you to go around kicking people's asses all the time though, remember that!"

"Yes, Dances with Spirits."

"Dances with Spirits?"

"Ya, like the movie, Dances with Wolves. I've decided to name you 'Dances with Spirits.'"

"Dances with Spirits huh, has a ring to it, doesn't it? Thanks Billy."

As they drift off to sleep, Billy thinks about his trial tomorrow while John thinks about his trial soon to come. What will he do if the jury finds him guilty? A life in prison is not what he has in mind for his future. But then, there is no way they can find him guilty, after all, he's innocent! And everyone knows that innocent men always go free…He decides to think about Jeanie instead…much better.

"Rise n' shine," announces Bubba Monday morning. "C'mon Billy, time ta git yur rowdy, red ass outta here."

Bubba playfully pounces on Billy and drags him off his bunk.

"Get off me ya big ape!"

"I'm gonna miss pickin on you!"

John watches with a smile as Bubba reminds him of his big brother and the way he used to get him down and sit on him. Pat always used to pick on him when they were little, but if anyone else tried to pick on him, they had Pat McDuffy to face. He remembers one time in high school, he was a sophomore and Pat was a senior. He was walking home from school one day and three guys, all of them seniors, were walking right behind him. It was a warm spring afternoon and the dandelions were in bright color everywhere. John was walking along, minding his own business, when suddenly he heard one of the guys shout, "Hey pussy! Where ya goin?" He looked across the street to find the other sidewalk empty so he knew the slam was directed at him. He began to panic a little as he was still eight blocks from home, so instead of turning around to answer them, he picked up the pace a little.

"Hey pussy! I'm talking to you!" came the voice from behind again. Now he's really going to have to do something, they sound pissed. They leave him no other choice but to...RUN! After about a half of a block, they caught up to him. One of them tackled him while the other two sat on his legs and chest.

"Leave me alone!" yelled John.

"What's the matter pussy? Don't ya want some flowers?"

One of them picked some dandelions and started rubbing them in John's face.

"Get off me, you asshole!" yells John.

They were laughing and having a good ol' time rubbing dandelions in John's face and stuffing dead leaves down his pants, when suddenly there was only one guy sitting on him, then none. John watched as his brother picked one of the guys up and threw him into the other two. After getting to their feet, they stood and faced Pat for a moment, contemplating jumping him all at the same time, but after about five seconds, they decided to be on their way instead.

"You ever mess with my brother again, and I'll be stuffing those dandelions up yur asses!"

They didn't respond, just picked up the pace a little.

"You alright little bro?" asked Pat as he helped John up.

"Ya, but my eyes kinda burn a little."

"Well, let's go home. Mom will know what to put on them."

As they walked home, no words were spoken, but there was a definite brotherly love in the air. To Pat, he was just protecting his family, something that came natural. But to John, he just saw a side of his brother that he didn't know existed. He despised the way that Pat was always pushing him around, but he was impressed with the way he cleaned house on those guys. Maybe he wasn't so bad after all.

"Well, I'm defiantly not gonna miss you, ya big dope!" said Billy

"Oohh, you love me and you know it," laughs Bubba as he picks Billy up. "Ya got all yur stuff ready?"

"Yep."

"Git cleaned up and I'll be back to git ya."

"Ok."

"Well, this is it," says John, "you nervous?"

"A little. What if they throw the book at me?"

"They won't. BUT! If you ever try that shit again, they will, guaranteed!"

"Don't worry teacher, I'm gonna be a good little Indian from now on."

"You'd better!" John gives Billy a big ol bear hug and says, "You take care now Little Bear".

"I will Dances with Spirits, you come up to the reservation and see me sometime and we'll go fishin."

"You got it."

"Ok Baby Bear, let's go," says Bubba as he enters the cell.

"It's LITTLE Bear, you big dummy!"

The two of them walk together down the hall, punching and poking at each other as John waves goodbye. Once Billy's gone, he goes back into his cell and looks out the window. 'Soon it will be my turn,' he thinks. As he stares out the window at the traffic going by, he thinks about Ol' Green and all the time and money he had into it. Now it's just a pile of scrap metal. Memories of the accident began to drift into his head and he decides to go back to sleep for a while. It isn't long before he's asleep.

"DAD!! HELP!!! I can't breathe!"

"Hang on Ryan! I'm coming!"

John pulls and kicks at the truck door, but it won't come open.

"DAAAAD! IT HURTS!"

"I'm coming buddy. Just hang in there!"

John tugs and tugs at the door, but he just can't seem to get any traction with his feet. It seems like he is weightless, and his feet keep floating up. He tries bracing his feet against the truck and pulling on the door, but he has no strength.

"DAD HURRY! BRETT IS BLEEDING!"

"I'm coming buddy, don't worry!"

John decides to move to the other door of the truck. He can see that Brett is unconscious and bleeding badly.

"BRETT! CAN YOU HEAR ME?"

No answer.

"BRETT!!"

John pulls on the door and sees that it will open freely, but it's like he hasn't any strength at all. He can't understand it! Why can't he open the door?! Ryan's cries are fading and he is drifting away.

"Daaaaaaddd…"

"Hold on Ryan! I'm coming!" 'Why can't I open this stupid door?!' thinks John.

He gives it one more tug and the handle comes off in his hand and he floats away like a balloon, completely weightless.

"RYAN!" he yells as he floats away, but there is no answer. "RYAN! RYAAAAAAN! RYAAA…"

"John! Wake up!" yells Bubba.

"RY… huh?"

John looks at Bubba with sheer terror in his eyes, his body soaked through his clothes.

"You had a nightmare boss," John just lies there for a moment, staring at Bubba, his chest heaving.

"I couldn't save um Bubba! I tried, but I couldn't get the door open."

"It's all right boss, it's just a bad dream. It's all over now."

John sits up on the bunk. He's used to this dream, he has it about once a week. He can never seem to save the boys no matter how hard he tries.

"Just got word on Billy's trial. He got one year in jail with seven months suspended, five months already served."

"So, he's a free man?"

"Yep, but he'll be on probation for a loooong time."

"Good, maybe that'll help him to keep his nose clean."

"I think the biggest thing that'll help him is all the tutoring you gave him. You helped him a lot John. I've seen Billy in here many times, and I've never seen him leave in such good mental condition. I really think he'll make it this time."

"I hope so. He's so young. He has his whole life ahead of him."

"Yes he does, and thanks to you, he'll get to live it outside these walls." Bubba gives John a big slap on the back. "I hear ya got a new name?"

"Billy told ya, huh?"

"Dances with Spirits, kinda fits ya, ya know? Specially when yur doin yur Tai Chi."

"Whatever you say Bubba."

"Well anyway, just came in to tell ya it's chow time."

"Noon already?"

"Ya. You slept most the morning."

Bubba and John walk together to the chow line. John can't help but think about the nightmare and wonders how long this is going to go on. After lunch, he goes back to his cell and meditates for a while before he has to teach his class.

About an hour into his meditation, Bubba interrupts him, "John, Jeanie's here to see ya."

Now THERE were some welcome words. He follows Bubba down to the visitation room, and the second he sees Jeanie's face, he knows it's bad news.

"Hi kiddo, what's wrong?"

"Hi John. They've moved your trial out to August twenty-eighth."

CHAPTER 25

—◦◦◦—

"AUGUST 28TH?!" WHY SO FAR OUT?"

"Oh, they say they haven't had enough time to prepare a case."

"How much fucking time do they need?!"

"I don't know John. I warned you they would do this. It seems like this happens in every case, not just yours."

"Why the hell are they dragging it out? You'd think they would want to get it over with."

"On the contrary. The longer they keep you in here, the more chance they have of you doing something stupid again, making their case stronger."

John looks sheepishly at the floor.

"I can't spend another six months in here Jeanie, I'll go nuts."

Jeanie reaches out to holds his hands, "I'm sorry Johnny, there's nothing I can do about it. Jack has been raising hell with the D.A.'s office all morning, but they won't budge, something about needing time to track down all potential witnesses of the accident. They have to run adds in the newspapers asking for people to come forward if they were there."

"What the hell have they been doing for the past five months?"

"I don't know," sighs Jeanie. "I do have some good news though."

"Murphy's been hit by a bus?"

"Nooo," smiles Jeanie. "We have a lead on the red ribbon bandit."

"Really?"

"Yes. Your neighbor, Bob was up late one night and saw a car stopped in front of your house, so he snuck outside to get a closer look."

"Did he get the license number?"

"No, it was too dark."

"What kind of car was it?"

"He said it was an early 90's foreign car, like a Toyota or a Honda, black two-door sedan."

John thinks for a moment.

"I can't think of anyone I know with a car like that."

"Bob said he didn't recognize it either, but there were two people in it from what he could tell, and as soon as they saw him, they took off."

"Sounds suspicious."

"Yes, it does, so I'm checking into anyone and everyone that owns a car like that."

"Any luck yet?"

"No, but I'm working on it."

"Times up," announces the guard.

"Well, I have to go. Try to keep your chin up Johnny. I know six months is a long time, but they can't extend it out much longer than that. Just keep doing what you've been doing with your tai chi classes. That will mean a lot to the jury."

"Ok. When will I see you again?"

"I don't know. I'll surprise you."

Jeanie gives John a sweet smile and says goodbye. John goes back to his cell, rather his home for the next six months. He decides to cancel his tai chi class for this afternoon. He's just too depressed to teach today. The more he stares out the window at freedom, the freedom he once owned, the more he would like to wrap his fingers around Judge Murphy's scrawny little neck. He is really beginning to build a hatred for this man, the man that drove his father to his grave, and is now trying to do the same to him.

'Bubba was right,' he thinks, 'I can't let him beat me. I must do everything in my power to beat this rap and get out of here so I can seek my revenge on that pencil-neck little prick. I owe it to mom and dad and the boys.'

Now that there is more room in the cell and more privacy, John decides to start doing calisthenics to pass the time. He must keep his mind occupied to keep from going crazy.

On her way back to the office, Jeanie makes a detour and stops by Gibson Pond where her and Calvin and Brittany used to skate. As she sits and looks out the window, she sees a little girl working on her spins, and she can picture the three of them skating...

"C'mon mommy, let's go out to the island!"

"Ok baby, I'll race ya."

As Jeanie and Brittany take off, Calvin is still struggling.

"Alright you two, wait for me."

Jeanie skated a lot as a little girl, but this is all new to Calvin. He kind of resembles a weeble-wabble as he steps out on to the ice. Jeanie and Brittany make it to the island and turn and race back. As they near Calvin, he does a little jig just before he falls on his butt.

Brittany giggles, "What's the matter daddy, having a little trouble?"

"Don't you worry about me, I'll be just fine, if I can just get these stupid feet to cooperate."

"Need some help honey?" asks Jeanie.

"No. You two go ahead, I just need to get my ice legs under me."

"Ok, whatever you say."

As Calvin works on his ice legs, Jeanie works with Brittany on her spins. She is a natural, much better than Jeanie was at that age. 'She's going to be a star someday,' thinks Jeanie...

Tears well up in Jeanie's eyes as she watches the little girl spin around and around as memories of Brittany and Calvin flood her mind.

Ring *Ring*

"Hello," says Jeanie as she answers her cell.

"Jeanie, this is Jack."

"Yes Jack."

"You alright? Sounds like you're catching a cold."

"No, I'm alright. What's up?"

"Where are you?"

"Gibson pond."

"Oohh...that explains the sniffle. Are you up to going down to the police impound?"

"Sure. Did you get the warrant?"

"Yep. Do you have a broom in your car to brush the snow off?"

"No, but I'm not too far from home. I can stop and get one."

"Why don't you do that and meet me down there."

"Ok boss, I'm on my way."

"See you there."

Jeanie drives to her house to get the broom. While she's there, she checks the mailbox. Inside is an envelope without a stamp. When she opens it, she finds one letter-size piece of paper. On it is written...MCDUFFY MUST DIE!!! Her heart begins to race as she looks around before getting out of the car. She takes the phone with her as she walks around the house looking for clues. She dials up Angus O'Leary.

"Hello?"

"Angus, this is Jeanie Philips."

"Yes darling, how are ya?"

"TERRIBLE! I just found an unstamped letter in my mailbox with the words McDuffy must die written in bold letters."

"I'll be right there."

"Wait a minute. I have to meet Jack at the police impound so I'll leave it in the mailbox for you."

"Ok, and don't worry, we'll get this guy."

"I hope you get him soon! This is getting kinda creepy."

"It won't be long, I promise Lassie."

"Ok Angus. Call me when you know something."

"Ok, bye."

As Jeanie drives to the impound, a cold chill fills her soul. For the first time during this case, she feels scared. Now this guy is using words like 'die.' Suddenly, he, or she, has made the transition from a prankster to a stalker. She remembers her father telling her once that she should get a concealed weapons permit and carry a small handgun. This idea sounds kind of appealing right now. As she pulls into the parking lot at the police impound, Jack is standing there tapping his watch.

"What did you do, take the scenic route?"

"No, I'll tell ya later. Do you have your camera?"

"Of course."

The two of them enter the impound office and approach the clerk.

"Good afternoon. We're here to look over a vehicle you have in the yard."

"Do you have the proper paperwork?"

"Yes sir."

Jack hands him the warrant.

The attendant looks it over and says, "Right this way."

Jack and Jeanie follow him through the office to the back door leading to the yard when she notices a beautiful German Shepard lying by the heater. He looks friendly with his pink tongue sticking out and his tail wagging.

"Oh, what a pretty dog," she says as she reaches out to pet it.

Before the attendant has a chance to warn her, the dog suddenly lays his ears back and bares his teeth and growls viciously.

Jeanie pulls her hand back quickly as the attendant yells, "Don't touch the dog! He's trained to attack strangers."

"Sorry, he looked so friendly."

"I know. His name is Skitzoid."

Jeanie thinks, 'Fits him. Boy, what a day I'm having!'

Jack turns to look at her, "Did the little doggie scare you?" he says with a smirk on his lips.

"Just keep walking," replies Jeanie.

Once in the yard, the attendant points out Ol' Green and goes back inside. As they sweep the snow off, an eerie feeling comes over them both because two young boys died in this pickup. No conversation is shared. They both know what they need to do and what they are looking for. The temperature is chilling so they waste no time taking pictures and looking for red paint. There is no trace of red paint on the pickup at all, but there is plenty on what is left of the camp trailer. The evidence is clear that the car hit the trailer on the right side.

"Ok. I've used up the roll. Let's get out of here, I'm freezing," says Jack.

"Good idea. This place gives me the creeps."

"Me too. So, what took you so long getting here?"

"Oh, you're going to love this. Now I'm getting threatening letters in my mailbox."

"What?"

"Yes. When I went to get the broom, I checked my mail, and inside was an unstamped letter saying McDuffy must die."

"You think it's the red ribbon bandit?"

"I can only assume."

"Did you call Angus?"

"That's what took me so long, I was talking to him."

"What did you do with the letter?"

"I left it there for Angus to see."

"Make sure he gets it to the police for evidence. I think we need to get you some police protection."

"I don't think that will be necessary yet Jack, although I am going to get a new can of mace."

"Do you carry a gun?"

"No, but my dad has been bugging me to get one."

"We need to get you down to the range one of these days and do some shooting. I've got a little Walther 9mm that would fit your hand perfectly."

"I'm game."

"Once you get comfortable with it, then you need to take a personal protection course and apply for a concealed weapons permit."

"Do you carry a gun?"

Jack opens his coat to reveal a Glock tucked in his pants.

"Do you carry that everywhere?"

"Everywhere but the courtroom."

"Even to bed?"

"Sure. Peg likes the feeling of cold steel against her butt."

"You need help Jack."

As they walk back through the impound office to check out, Jeanie takes a glance at the German Shepard as it lies by the heater, wagging its tail and panting. It makes her think of Judge Murphy as he smiled at her in Wadder's Coffee Shop while he was sticking a knife in her side. How deceiving can he be.

"Peg and I are going out for pizza tonight, care to join us?"

"No thanks Jack, I've had a pretty rough day. I think a TV dinner and a hot bath are in order."

"How did John take the news?"

"About as well as to be expected. I think he'll be alright."

"He's not going to try and escape again, is he?"

"I don't think so. I'll keep checking in on him."

"I'm sure you won't mind that," says Jack with a smile.

Jeanie blushes as she turns to walk to her car.

"Bye Jack."

"Bye kiddo, see you tomorrow."

As she gets into her car, her phone rings.

"Hello?"

"Hi Jeanie, its Angus. I think we got him!"

CHAPTER 26

JEANIE'S MOUTH DROPS OPEN AND a smile comes to her face.

"The Red Ribbon Bandit?"

"Yes. I did some background checking on Amy Wadder and found out she had a boyfriend from high school named Bobby Jackson. She was going to see him that weekend."

"So?"

"So, guess what kind of car he drives?"

"A black, two-door sedan?"

"A 1992, black, two-door Honda Accord."

"What a coincidence."

"Yes, it is, isn't it? I'm going to hire some night owls to watch every move Mr. Jackson makes."

"Sounds like we've got our man."

"It does sound promising, doesn't it? I'll keep you informed."

"Thanks Angus. Oh, Angus?"

"Yes Lassie?"

"Jack wanted me to make sure you gave that letter to the police for evidence."

"I plan on taking it down first thing in the morning. I want to make a copy of it first though, just in case those clowns lose it."

"Good idea."

"Bye, bye Lassie."

'Well that's better,' thinks Jeanie.

She calls Jack.

"Hello?"

"Jack, it's Jeanie."

"Long time no, ah, talk."

"I just got some good news from Angus."

"Really?"

"He thinks the Red Ribbon Bandit might be Amy Wadder's high school sweetheart."

"How's that?"

"He has a black, two-door, 1992 Honda Accord."

"Well now, that sounds promising."

"It sure does. Sooo, is the invitation for pizza still open?"

"Feeling a little better now, are we?"

"Yes, we are," laughs Jeanie.

"We'll pick you up around six thirty."

"I'll be ready."

Jack and Peggy pick Jeanie up promptly at six thirty.

"Hi Peggy," says Jeanie.

"Hello dear, how have you been?"

"I'm fine, and you?"

"Never better."

"Are you keeping that husband of yours in line?"

"You better believe it. Are you keeping an eye on him at the office?"

"Oh, I keep him pretty busy."

"Good. Jack tells me you might be going down to the shooting range with us soon. Is this true?"

"Well, we did talk about it. You mean, you carry a gun too?"

"You better believe it dear. With the kind of creeps we have running around these days, I'm not taking any chances."

"Show her your piece, hun," says Jack. Peggy pulls a nickel-plated Smith and Wesson 38 special snub-nose out of her purse.

"This is what I carry," says Peggy as she hands the gun to Jeanie. "Careful now, it's loaded."

Jeanie holds the weapon and admires the pearl grips. She grips it tightly and points it at the floor.

"This is nice."

"You bet it is, and with those 156 grain, copper-jacketed hollow-points, I can stop any scum bag that ever gets a notion to mess with me."

Jeanie carefully hands the weapon back to Peggy.

"You sound like you really know your stuff."

"Well, Jack's been a good teacher. We enjoy shooting. I can keep a six-inch group at twenty-five yards with that little beauty. But for target shooting, I like my Smith and Wesson 41 mag. I can keep a pretty consistent three-inch group with that one."

"How many guns do you guys own?"

Peggy looks at Jack for assistance, "How many is it now dear?"

"Fifty-two now," says Jack.

"My God," gasps Jeanie, "I'm having dinner with Bonnie and Clyde."

"Oh, no dear," laughs Peggy. "We don't shoot all of them. Most of them are collectors."

"Oohh, I was beginning to wonder if we were going to dinner, or knocking off a bank."

Jack laughs, "We enjoy our hobby. You'll have to come down to our basement sometime and see our collection. We have a reloading bench set up too, so the ammunition doesn't cost as much."

"I'd like that."

Jack pulls the car into Geno's, an Italian restaurant located on the banks of the Missouri River. The building is made of red brick and it used to be the location of the Great Falls Select Brewery in the early 1900's. It has been completely remodeled into a beautiful restaurant and lounge overlooking the river.

"Have you ever been here before?" asks Jack.

"My parents brought me here once, but that was a long time ago."

As they enter the restaurant, Peggy says, "Why don't we sit in the lounge dear? I feel like whopping your but in a game of pool."

"You're on!" says Jack.

"You play pool too?" asks Jeanie.

"Oh, yes dear, we have a table in our basement. I'm surprised you didn't see it when you were over for New Year's Eve."

"I didn't go down to the basement."

"Well, you'll just have to come over after dinner and see it. Jack's got it fixed up real nice with a bar, pool table, fireplace, and of course, our precious gun collection."

"Sounds like a plan."

Jack finds a table located next to the pool table and quickly puts his coat on a chair before someone else takes it. Then he puts some quarters in the table and racks the balls.

"Ok darlin, your break."

Peggy looks for a cue as the waitress approaches the table.

"Jeanie?" she cries out as she nears the table. "Is that you?"

Jeanie turns to see Lisa Andrews, a mother of one of the girls in Brittany's figure skating class, and a friend.

"Oh my God! Lisa!"

Lisa puts her tray on the table and the two hug and wipe the tears from each other's eyes.

"How have you been?" asks Lisa.

"I'm fine. How about you?"

"I'm great!"

"Is Tiffany still skating?"

"No, she quit, the little stinker. Now she wants to be a professional singer."

"Oh no!" laughs Jeanie.

"Oh yes! Boy, when I think about all the money Jim and I put into her figure skating dream, I could just puke!"

"How is Jim?"

"Oh, he's fine, still working at the mill. How have you been? I've been worried about you."

"Oh, I'm hanging in there. You know, one day at a time."

"Are you seeing anyone?"

"Well…not really."

"Jim works with this guy who's really cute, we should all go out sometime."

"I'm not really up to dating yet Lisa, but I'll let you know when I'm ready."

"Ok sweetie, you better!"

"I will."

"Good. What can I get you guys?"

Jack and Peggy order a pitcher of beer and Jeanie orders a glass of wine.

"You need menus?"

"Yes, please," says Jack.

"Comin right up."

Lisa leaves, and Jeanie and Peggy sit down and watch while Jack runs the balls on the pool table.

"Sooo...she has a daughter in skating too," asks Peggy.

"Had. I guess she wants to be a professional singer now."

"Kids!"

"Yes, it's a shame too. Tiffany was really good."

"Is she the same age as Brittany?"

"I think she is a year younger."

"I couldn't help but overhear her talk about a friend of her husband's?"

"Yaaa, she wants me to double-date with them some time."

"You should dear. It wouldn't hurt you to go out and have some fun sometime."

"Oh, I'm not ready yet. Besides, I'm sure the only reason Lisa wants me to double with this guy is so she can check him out herself."

"Really?"

"Oh yes. She is the biggest flirt I've ever known. It pisses me off too, because Jim is a hardworking man and a good father. She doesn't deserve him."

"Funny, it looked like you two were pretty good friends."

"Don't get me wrong, Lisa is a good friend and I love her dearly, but some of the things she does makes me sick. Like the way she spends money. She hasn't got an ounce of financial responsibility. I'm surprised she's actually working. But then, by the looks of her uniform, I bet she has a good time flirting with the customers here."

"She must be new because Jack and I come here all the time and I've never seen her before."

"Well anyway, enough with gossip. What are we going to eat?"

"They make fantastic pizza here."

"Well then, pizza it is."

"Rack um darlin," says Jack.

"I didn't even get a shot!"

"Sure you did, you broke um, didn't you?"

"Alright wise guy, but you better hope you make one on the break."

"Here we are guys," says Lisa as she sets the drinks down. "Are we ready to order?"

Jack orders their favorite pizza while Peggy racks the balls as loose as she can. Jack breaks and the balls barely move.

"That rack was as loose as your mouth!" barks Jack.

"It was not," snaps Peggy, "my mother could have broke better than that!"

"All your mother would have to do is look at them and they would roll in the pockets by themselves."

"That's it! You're dusted now buddy!"

Jeanie is almost choking on her wine as she watches this sideshow in front of her. It makes her heart feel good to watch these two have so much fun together. It's too bad all couples can't be this happy.

They play a few more games of pool and scarf down all the pizza when Peggy looks at her watch and says, "I'm stuffed."

"Me too," says Jeanie.

"You should be," says Jack, "you ate over half the pizza."

"I did not!"

"Did too."

"Did not."

"Alright you two children, break it up," interrupts Peggy. "Jack, pay the bill and let's go."

"That's all you want me for is my money."

"Don't be silly sweetheart. I only want you for your guns!"

They all laugh as Jack pays the bill and they head for the door. Jeanie gives Lisa a hug and promises to keep in touch. Jack brings the car around to the front door and helps the ladies inside. On the way to their house, Jack and Peggy continue to keep Jeanie in stitches. Once there, they escort Jeanie down the stairs to their pride and joy. Jack pulls the cover off to reveal a beautiful full size pool table. It is made of pure walnut and the green is in perfect shape.

"It's beautiful!" exclaims Jeanie.

"Thank you," says Jack. "It was made in England in the early 1900's and brought over on a boat. I bought it at an antique shop in Connecticut when I was there for a convention. It cost almost as much to ship it over here as it did for the table."

"How much did it cost?"

"You don't even want to know."

"Ok, never mind."

"Enough with the pool table," says Peggy, "here's my pride and joy."

She lays on the pool table an oak box. Inside the box is a collector's edition, Model 29 Smith and Wesson 44 magnum. The same model Clint Eastwood used in Dirty Harry.

"Wow," says Jeanie, "that's impressive."

"Just call me Dirty Peggy."

"Ok Dirty Peggy," laughs Jeanie. "I'd love to stay longer, but I hear my dirty body calling for my bathtub, and that wine has gone straight to my head."

"Ok sweetie. I sure had fun tonight. We HAVE to do this again."

"Me too, and I agree. I haven't laughed that hard in years. You two are a crackup!"

"Well, we aim to please. Jack, it's time to take this wino home. Goodnight sweetie."

"Goodnight Peggy."

Jack drives her home and waits till she's inside and the coast is clear before driving away. Jeanie runs a hot bath and slowly slides her naked body into the water. As she lies there soaking, thoughts of John going through his tai chi moves fill her head, and she smiles as she caresses her body under the bubbles.

CHAPTER 27

———— ⊸⊸⊸ ————

FOR WADDERS COFFEE SHOP, BUSINESS has never been better. Citizens from all over Great Falls have made it a point to pop in to get a bite or an espresso and extend their condolences to the Wadders. Folks that have never patronized the establishment before, now have a reason to go there. As for Ron and Kathy Wadder, they couldn't be more pleased with the kind words received and the increase in business, not to mention the increased opportunity to sway public opinion. Since the accident, the main topic of conversation around the coffee shop has been 'That Drunken McDuffy.' You can almost feel the hatred when you listen to the Wadders talk about the 'man that killed their daughter.'

On this cold, cloudy February 1st morning, Judge Murphy stops in the coffee shop about eleven thirty to have lunch. He pulls up a chair at the counter and sits down.

"Morning Ron, morning Kathy."

"Morning Paul. How's tricks at the courthouse?" asks Ron.

"Well, I have some news you might enjoy."

"What's that?" asks Kathy.

"The D.A. has extended McDuffy's trial date to August 28th."

"Really?" asks Ron. "Why's that?"

"Apparently, they haven't had enough time to prepare a good case, so they asked for an extension. Unfortunately, August 28th was the nearest opening I could find."

"You mean poor Mr. McDuffy has to spend another six months in the County Jail? That poor man," smirks Kathy.

"Well, it probably isn't too much different than his future home at Deer Lodge," laughs Ron.

Deer Lodge, Montana is the location of the Montana State Penitentiary. The Wadders are quite sure that John McDuffy will be indicted for negligent homicide and drunken driving, which are both felonies. If found guilty, he could face up to twenty years in prison and a fifty thousand dollar fine. Ron and Kathy, of course, are hoping for the maximum.

"So, what are we going to have today Paul? The special?" asks Ron.

"Oh, I think I'll have a big fat greasy hamburger and some french fries today. I feel like splurging."

"Ya right," chuckles Kathy. "You know we don't serve that kind of garbage here. The special then?"

"Ok," smiles Murphy.

Wadder's Coffee Shop does not serve any fried food at all. Everything on their menu is made of fresh and healthy ingredients. Their motto is printed underneath 'Welcome to Wadder's Coffee Shop' on their menus. It reads, 'Food for people on the go who care about their health.' They serve a wide verity of exotic coffees, including lattes, espressos, cappuccinos, etc., in every flavor imaginable. On the food side, they serve fresh sandwiches, homemade soups, bagels, muffins, etc. Every ingredient is low fat and low cholesterol.

The Wadders originally come from the bay area in San Francisco, California. Ron and Kathy both grew up near there and met each other when they were going to college at UCLA. Both majoring in business, it was clear what their futures held for them once graduated. They would get married and open a health food store. Unfortunately, there was a health food store on every corner in the area where they chose to live, so one day, they saw an ad for a small building for sale on the wharf. After inspecting it from top to bottom and deciding the building was sound, they set the wheels in motion for the grand opening of 'Bagels by the Bay,' their first coffee shop. Business was good, and within two years they were turning a profit. Now it was time to have a child. September 3rd, 1979, Amy Lynn Wadder was introduced to the world. She was a beautiful, healthy baby, and the first grandchild for both sets of grandparents who all lived near bye. That being said, Amy was just a little spoiled. She grew up getting everything she ever wanted. Her bedroom looked like a toy store. As she grew into her teenage years, the spoiling continued. Ron and Kathy were so busy at the coffee shop, they didn't have the time to spend with Amy, so they gave her a car and money and let her do whatever she wanted to do and go wherever she wanted to go. She attended concert after concert and stayed out all night, sometimes not coming home at all. Ron and Kathy finally realized they screwed up by giving her too much freedom when she didn't come home for an entire weekend. She was only fourteen years old. It was summertime and school was out, but Amy was supposed to be helping out at the coffee shop, cleaning up and helping with the books. She was too young for a regular job, but not too young to work. Ron and Kathy were frantic. They didn't have a clue where Amy was, as she didn't leave a note or tell anyone where she was going. The police were contacted and all of the friends they could think of. No one knew where Amy was. Finally, Sunday night about nine o'clock, Amy came dragging her butt through the door, reeking of pot. Ron and Kathy ran up to her, crying tears of joy, for their daughter was ok. Amy didn't understand what the big fuss was about.

"What's wrong with you guys?" asks Amy with blood-shot eyes.

"Amy, where have you been?" asks Kathy. "We were worried sick about you! We have the police out looking for you!"

"What's the big deal? I was just down at the beach crashing with some friends. I didn't think anyone would miss me, so that's why I didn't leave a note or nothing."

"I'll go call the police and tell them she's ok," says Ron. "You go up to your room young lady and we'll deal with you later!"

"Fine. I could use some sleep," says Amy as she drug her tail up the stairs to the pigsty she called her bedroom.

After Ron got off the phone with the police, he sat down on the couch with Kathy. He gently put his arms around her and quieted her tears. They both knew what the other was thinking. They really screwed up with Amy. If they didn't do something pretty soon, she could end up a worthless pot head.

"What are we going to do with her honey?" asks Kathy.

"I don't know. I think we have to get her away from that crowd she's running with, but if we tell her she's not allowed to see them anymore, she'll just rebel and want to see them more. We need to get away from here, start a new life."

"We can't just leave. What about the coffee shop?"

"We could sell it."

Kathy looks at Ron, "You can't be serious! We put our lives into that business! We're turning a profit every year! Why the hell would you want to sell it now?"

"For our daughter's sake," says Ron as he looks Kathy straight in the eye with the look on his face of an early seventeenth century frontiersman seeking a new horizon.

"Honey, a change would do us good. I don't know about you, but I'm getting kind of burned out with San Francisco. "

Kathy realizes Ron is dead serious about this.

"Well, I suppose I could use a change of scenery too, but where are we supposed to go?"

"Do you remember the high school buddy I told you about, Curt Frank?"

"Ya, didn't he go into the Air Force?"

"Exactly. We've been staying in touch, and right now he's stationed at Malmstrum AFB in Great Falls, Montana. He says the mountains are awesome there, and the winters aren't too bad."

"Montana?"

"Yes, Montana."

Both Ron and Kathy like to hike around in the mountains and snow ski, and there is no better place in the country than the Rocky Mountains to enjoy both, so after many more days of discussing the idea, they decided to start a new life in Great Falls. Their plan came as a big shock to Amy and she rebelled terribly. She ran away for several days until the police finally found her hanging out on the beach with a group of modern day hippies. They even received a bonus for finding her by busting a few of her friends for possession of marijuana. When they took her back home, she ran up to her room and locked her door. Ron and Kathy decided to let her stay there until she got hungry enough to come out. Once she did, they sat her down and explained all the good points in moving to a small town, none of which she understood, but eventually she realized they were serious about this and there was nothing she could do about it. She would miss her friends, but she wouldn't miss her school, as there were several teachers she thought were being 'too hard on her.' The coffee shop sold very quickly for close to two million dollars, and their house sold quickly as well for three hundred and seventy thousand dollars, and soon they were Montana bound. They bought a house on the north side of town that was built in the early 1900's and looked forward to fixing it up. After settling in, they began the hunt for a location for their new business, Wadder's Coffee Shop. After several months, they found a vacant building on Central Avenue in downtown Great Falls that would be a perfect location. It wasn't long before it was open for business. At first, the shop did really well, as do all new businesses in Great Falls. For the first year or so, everyone in Great Falls felt compelled to check out the new restaurant. After the curiosities were satisfied, business slacked off a bit until it stabilized with a steady crowd with its usual patrons, like Judge Paul Murphy. Amy attended school at Great Falls High and soon became one of the most popular kids in school. She was active in drama, speech, choir and swimming. Life was good again for the Wadders, even though some of the residents frowned on 'transplants' from California. They felt there was too much land being bought up by rich out-of-staters from the poor hard working people of Montana who just couldn't make a go of it anymore. Many of the big ranches that were homesteaded in the early 1800's were being purchased by groups of rich businessmen to keep and use as their private playground. As for Ron and Kathy though, all they wanted is a good place to raise their daughter. For the most part, the citizens of Great Falls have welcomed them with open arms, and Ron and Kathy couldn't be happier with the town they chose to live in, except for the wind. The wind blows constantly in Great Falls and the residents are used to it, but Kathy swears she hasn't had a good hair day since they moved there. For fun, they go to their cabin on Holter Lake, located about seventy miles south of Great Falls. They purchased it in 1995 from a couple that was from Southern California and decided to move to Arizona after they retired to get away from the winters in Montana. They spend all their weekends there in the summertime and threw lots of barbeques for their friends and Amy's friends. They have a nineteen-foot ski boat that gets used a lot by Amy and her friends, and sometimes Ron and Kathy. When Amy graduated from High School, Ron and Kathy threw a huge party for her at the cabin. All her friends, which totaled about fifty, were invited to spend the weekend. All they were required to bring were pup tents, sleeping bags, and their personal belongings. Ron and Kathy supplied all the food and drinks. Even though they didn't supply any alcohol, it still managed to make it into some of the tents after the sun went down and Ron and Kathy turned in for the night. Most of the kids behaved themselves, but a few couldn't resist the opportunity. Amy and her boyfriend, Bobby Jackson, shared love for the first time that night.

CHAPTER 28

———∞∞∞———

Judge Murphy finished his lunch about twelve fifteen and said his goodbyes. As he was leaving, Bobby Jackson came through the door and gave the good Judge a nod as he pulled up a chair at the counter.

"Hi Bobby!" says Kathy.

"Hi Mrs. Wadder, Mr. Wadder."

"How's life at the lumberyard?" asks Ron.

"Oh, you know, it's a job."

"Are you getting lots of hours in?" asks Kathy.

"Ya. I'm getting in forty a week, but they've laid a lot of guys off this winter."

"Probably because of Y2K, I suppose," says Ron.

"I don't know, it could be. They say it should pick up this summer though, then they'll probably hire the guy's back."

"That's good. So, what are we gonna eat today?"

"Oh, I think I'll just have the special and a coke, thanks."

"Coming right up," says Kathy as she heads toward the kitchen.

"Well, I bought me a new truck this weekend," said Bobby.

"Really," says Ron, "what did ya get?"

"It's a 1998 Toyota 4x4, extended cab."

"Sounds nice, how many miles are on it?"

"It's got quite a few, eighty-thousand, but I guess the guy that owned it drove back and forth to North Dakota a lot."

"Still, that's quite a lot of miles for a two-year-old truck. Did you have a mechanic check it out?"

"No, but I had my dad look at it, and he said it was a good buy. I only paid ten grand for it," replied Bobby.

"Well that's not bad. Has it ever been wrecked?" asked Ron.

"I don't think so. It looks pretty straight. It drives really nice. Everything works, and the stereo sounds awesome."

"Priorities," laughs Ron. "What color is it?"

"Black. Just like my Honda."

"Speaking of the Honda, did you trade it in?"

"No. Josh wants to buy it. I told him five grand, you think that's fair?" asked Bobby.

"That's sounds more than fair! What's blue book on it?"

"I think it's about seven grand, but it needs a lot of work, and he's got a buddy in Billings that's a mechanic."

"Well that works. How's he going to pay for it?" asked Ron.

"He said his folks would loan him the money. Anything to get him out of that death trap he's driving now. I'll just leave it parked at my place for a while until they can drive it down there."

"Well that's great! How's he liking tech school?"

"It's ok he says, he can't wait to get out so he can get a decent job. He's tired of making pizzas. I guess he's gained fifty pounds."

"Holy cow! He must look like a blimp!" laughed Ron.

"Ya, he was looking pretty big the last time I saw him, which was Christmas."

"Gee, I haven't seen him since Amy's funeral."

Just the mention of Amy's name put a frown on Bobby's face. He was very much in love with her, and one of the toughest things he had to do was say goodbye to her when she left for college. Bobby had a good job at the lumberyard. He eventually wanted to be a carpenter, so college wasn't one of the things on his 'to do' list. He and Amy dated all during their senior year, and were even voted king and queen at the senior prom. Everyone thought they would be together forever. Bobby made several trips to Missoula to visit. Amy was living at the dorms, so the back seat of Bobby's Honda saw lots of action. Even with all the boyfriends she had in college, she still saved her heart for Bobby. Ron and Kathy loved Bobby like a son. They couldn't be happier with Amy's choice. He was head and shoulders better than the boys she was hanging out with in California. Bobby was responsible, hardworking, good-hearted, and he treated Amy like a queen. He cried like a baby at Amy's funeral. He shares Ron and Kathy's anger toward John McDuffy for taking is sweetheart from him.

"Here ya go Bobby," says Kathy, as she sets his vegetable soup and turkey sandwich in front of him.

"Thanks," replied Bobby with a sad look on his face.

"Geeze, was it something I said?" inquires Kathy. "You look like you just lost your last friend."

"We were just talking about Amy," says Ron.

"Oh," says Kathy as she touches Bobby's hand. "I'm sorry Bobby. Are you ok?"

"Ya, I'm ok. I was thinking about old times."

"Bobby bought a new truck," interrupts Ron in hopes of changing the subject.

"Really? What kind?" asks Kathy.

"It's a Toyota 4x4," says Bobby.

"Oh, that's great! I've heard good things about them."

Kathy's enthusiasm doesn't have much effect on Bobby. He just sips his soup and stares angrily at the newspaper clippings thumbtacked to the bulletin board behind the counter. The Wadder's have saved every article and headline about John McDuffy, and proudly displayed them in their restaurant. They want everyone to think that McDuffy is guilty of killing their little girl.

"Anything new on that jerk?" asks Bobby as he nods toward the bulletin board.

"Yes!" says Ron proudly. "We just heard that the trial is postponed for six months so the D.A. can put together a better case against him."

"Good!" says Bobby, "I hope they hang his ass!"

"Oh, don't worry, Paul isn't going to let him walk, he's assured us of that."

"Good," says Bobby as he pushes his plate away and reaches for his wallet.

"Bobby, I'm worried about you," says Kathy. "Are you sure you're ok? You seem awfully depressed."

"I'm fine. I just get a little down when I think about Amy, that's all."

"We all do son," says Ron, "but try to keep your chin up. Time is the best healer. Things are bound to get better someday."

"Ya, like the day they hang that son-of-a-bitch McDuffy!" smiles Bobby. "I better get back to work."

"Ok Bobby," says Kathy, "you take care, and keep in touch."

"I will. Bye you guys."

Bobby leaves as Ron and Kathy watch him drive away in his new pickup. Even though they love him like a son, they both wish he would get over Amy's death and get on with his life. He doesn't even go out with the guys anymore, all he does is go to work and then home. He's become quite the loner. Even his buddies are worried about him. He seems to be obsessed with John McDuffy.

"Chuck, will you come and see me when you have a minute?" asks Ed over the intercom back at R&R Equipment.

"Ok, shouldn't be long," answers Chuck. "I wonder what he wants?"

"Who knows," says Kevin. "Probably wants to bitch about sales or something. If he had good news, he would type up a memo," smirks Kevin.

Chuck and Kevin have been running the parts department at R&R by themselves since John's accident. Luckily, it hasn't been very busy, so they've managed to get everything done each day. They both miss John and feel terrible about his accident. They put a donation jar on the counter in John's name, and many customers have contributed graciously, even Bill in Ovando. Everyone agrees that he's been the victim of miss-justice instigated by a phony Judge.

"You wanted to see me?" asks Chuck as he taps on Ed's door.

"Yes sir. Come in, have a seat."

"What's up?"

"I just found out that John's trial has been postponed for another six months."

"Six months!"

"Yes, six months! So, he's going to be in jail all summer."

"That sucks."

"Yes, it does. You two have been doing a great job, but there is no way you can run it by yourselves in the summertime. Chuck, I'm appointing you Parts Manager and I want you to hire someone as soon as possible. Summer is just around the corner."

"Parts Manager? What about John?"

"John isn't here. You are, and you deserve it."

"Well, thanks Ed, but what about when John gets out?"

"We'll cross that bridge when we get there. Meanwhile, we have to take care of business here, and you're the man for the job."

"Gee, I don't know Ed, is there a raise in it for me?"

"Of course."

"Well in that case, I'll take it."

Chuck stands and shakes Ed's hand. He's excited about the raise, but not too excited about the increased responsibility. He remembers all the crap John had to put up with anytime Ed felt like flexing his muscles. If sales were bad, it always seemed to be the fault of the parts department. John always took it with a grain of salt and told the guys they were doing a great job, and keep up the good work.

"So? What was that all about?" asks Kevin.

"You can just call me boss from now on," smiles Chuck.

"You gotta be shitting me!"

"No shit! He just made me Parts Manager."

"What about John?"

"His trial has been postponed for six months, so Ed wants me to hire someone."

"But what about when John gets out?"

"He said we'll cross that bridge when we get there. Don't worry, when John gets back, I'll gladly give him back the position, but I think Ed's right, we do need to get some help hired before summer."

"Amen to that! You got anyone in mind?"

"No, but I'm sure someone will come along. There's a lot of broken down mechanics out there that would love to quit turning wrenches for a steady paycheck, so keep your ears open."

"I will. What about Bill Perkins?" smiles Kevin.

"I wouldn't hire that asshole if he were the last man on earth!"

"Just kidding. Did Ed say why John's trial has been postponed?"

"No. You know Ed, wouldn't want to give me too much information."

"That's true. Man, that means John has to spend another six months in jail. He's got to be going nuts, I know I would."

"I'm sure he is, but what has he got to come home to. He's lost his boys, his dog and his mother. All he has left is an ex-wife. But at least she won't be able to hound him for child support any more. I think that's the only justice that's come out of this whole thing, at least that bitch won't be bugging him for money anymore."

"Oh, I wouldn't count on that. It wouldn't surprise me if she files a suit for wrongful death once he gets out."

"Ya, you're probably right. She is a vengeful bitch."

"Parts line one!" blares Sue.

"Speaking of bitches!"

Kevin answers the phone as Chuck calls his wife to give her the good news. She's pleased with the prospect of a raise for Chuck, but she too feels sad that John won't be back for another six months. After the phone call, Chuck doesn't waste any time moving John's personal things out of the Parts Manager's office, and sits down, putting his feet up on the desk. Thoughts of a new truck enter his head.

CHAPTER 29

‒‒‒‒∞‒‒‒‒

MARCH 18TH, 2000. IT'S JUST another day at the jail, with prisoners going to and from breakfast. John has been up since five o'clock, and has already knocked out a hundred sit-ups, fifty one-armed pushups, thirty minutes of tai chi, and thirty minutes of meditation, the same routine for the last several weeks. Spring has begun to arrive in Great Falls. The robins are starting to drift in from their winter retreats and set up housekeeping in the many elm and cottonwood trees around the city. Snowcapped mountains can still be seen on the horizon and the air is brisk, but not quite 'shorts and t-shirt' weather yet. The St. Patrick's Day parade was held yesterday afternoon on Central Avenue. The traditional bagpipe players marched proudly, squeezing out an Irish tune as bright green floats from various clubs and high schools rolled slowly up the street. It was a day of eating corned beef and cabbage and drinking green beer. Some of the 'one-day-Irishmen' got a little carried away with the green beer. One example is a local man named Scott Lewison. Scott is about five-foot-eight-inches and two-hundred-seventy-five pounds of pure lard. He spends most of his time on a barstool, smoking generic cigarettes and drinking the cheapest beer served. He doesn't work because he pulled a muscle in his shoulder at his last warehouse job, and the doctor told him he shouldn't lift anything more than ten pounds. That's all Scott needed to hear. Now he can lie around the house and dream of a big workman's compensation claim, and how he's going to spend it on a new fishing boat. Scott has had trouble all his adult life holding down a job because he can't seem to make it to work on time. His drinking habit leaves him with a hangover every morning, and getting out of bed is the last thing he wants to do every day. Scott isn't from Great Falls, he's another transplant from the west coast, but he loves to hunt and fish. Because of his love for the sport, he moved to Montana right after high school. He lived in Bozeman for a while where he met his wife Rachael and married her as soon as she graduated from college and landed a job as a Dental Hygienist. Their first child, Amber, was born in Bozeman, and is now eleven years old. Scott had a full-time job at K-Mart making six dollars an hour, but Rachael was always looking for something better, as she was not happy where she was at. She is a native Montanan and all the people she works with in the office are from out of state, and seem to have completely different personalities. Even though she is the native, she feels alienated. In 1994, she applied for a job in Great Falls with a dental office that employed three dentists, three hygienists, and a support crew of six or more. One of the hygienists was leaving, which created an opening in the popular, fast growing office. When she received notice that she was accepted for the position, she was so excited, and went straight home to tell Scott, who was lying on the couch watching TV, since he lost his job at K-Mart, and the two after that. She was hoping the move to a new town would be a positive change for him, and for their marriage. She wanted to get him away from his partying buddies, who, like Scott, did nothing but lie around, drink beer, and watch TV. It was nine am on a Tuesday morning when she walked in the door to find Scott and his buddies watching a smut video and drinking beer already.

"Rachael! What are you doing home?" bellows Scott as he reaches for the remote as his buddies scramble to hide the magazines.

"I came home to tell you some good news, but I can see you're busy."

"Oh no, we were just…um, I mean, Bob's buddy said he had this really sick video, so we just wanted to see what it was all about. So, what's the good news?"

"Bob, Jake, you guys have to go home now. Scott and I have something to talk about."

"Ok, no problem!" says Bob as he quickly jumps up.

"Ya, I gotta get going anyway," says Jake as he gathers up the magazines.

Bob hits the eject button on the VCR, grabs his video, and the two of them rush out the door as they can see that Rachael means business. They don't want to get on her bad side because she is the main source of funding for their beer and cigarettes.

"You know, anything you have to say to me you can say in front of Bob and Jake," announces Scott with authority.

"I don't think they need to be involved in our personal conversations Scott. I know they're your buddies, but they're no friends of mine."

"Personal? Sounds serious. What's up?"

"Do you remember that job in Great Falls I applied for?"

"You got it?"

"Yes!" shouts Rachael as she jumps up and down, smiling and giggling.

Scott stares at the coffee table, emotionless. Then he looks at Rachael.

"Sooo, that means you're moving?"

Rachael's face drops and she tilts her head to one side and stares at this man she calls her husband.

"That means WE are moving Scott! You, me, and Amber. 'US' SCOTT! WE are moving to Great Falls."

"Well...what if I don't want to move? I kinda like it here," announces Scott.

Rachael can't believe what she's hearing. She finally lands a job starting at forty thousand a year, and he's not the least bit excited for her. All he can think about is his own worthless hide. Her eyes well up with tears as her temper flares.

"FINE SCOTT! You stay here with your buddies! Amber and I are moving to Great Falls! With or without YOU! I have to get back to work"

Rachael slams the door of the run down rental house they're living in and cries all the way back to work. Once there, she immediately gives notice and starts making arrangements for the move. Since June is just around the corner, she won't have to worry about taking Amber out of school and starting her at another school in the middle of the year. Scott on the other hand, calls his buddies back over to the house and breaks the news to them. They inform him that he should divorce the bitch, keep Amber and make Rachael pay child support. They assure him that he can get at least five hundred a month for her, and he can probably make her pay alimony too because he isn't working. This all sounds very appealing to Scott, so they all decide to go to the bar and celebrate. Around three o'clock, Scott remembers he has to pick up Amber at Kindergarten, so he and the boys stumble out of the bar and jump in Scott's car, still shouting the revolutionary cry 'SCREW THE BITCH.' On the way to the school, Scott is all over the road, nearly hitting several cars. A policeman spots him, and follows for about six blocks before pulling him over. Scott fails the sobriety test and is arrested for driving under the influence of alcohol. Bob and Jake are given a ride to their homes, and Scott is thrown in jail. Rachael receives the call at work.

"Mrs. Lewison?"

"Yes."

"This is Officer Clark at the Bozeman police department. I need to inform you that your husband, a Mr. Scott Lewison, has been picked for driving under the influence, and he won't be picking up your daughter from school."

"Is he alright?"

"Yes ma'am, he just needs to sleep it off. You may come down and arrange bail if you like, but he will be spending the next twenty-four hours with us. The bail is five hundred dollars."

"Ok, thank you."

Rachael hangs up the phone and cries as she covers her face with her hands. 'What happened to the man I married?' she wonders.

The twenty-four hours in jail made a positive change in Scott's attitude. He didn't like it there, and he certainly didn't want to go back. Rachael went down to the police station after work Wednesday to post bail and take him home. They explained all the charges to her and Scott, and how he must attend substance abuse classes for a while. Scott's car had to be towed twice, once to the impound, and once to their house. The whole thing ended up costing close to a thousand dollars. When they explained the substance abuse classes to Scott, he told them that they were moving to Great Falls, and asked if he could attend the classes there. Rachael looked at him and smiled. He returned the smile. Nothing needed to be said, Scott was ready to start a new life with his wife and daughter.

The following weekend, Scott, Rachael, and Amber drove to Great Falls to look for a house. After many hours of searching, they finally found a small, two-bedroom house on the south side of town with a nice yard, and a quiet neighborhood. They paid the deposit and spent the rest of the day touring the town. They decided to get a motel room instead of driving back to Bozeman in the dark. After securing a room, Scott came up with the idea to go out for pizza. Amber was all for it, but Rachael was a little reserved, because she knew that Scott would what to drink beer with the pizza. She didn't want to disappoint Amber though, so she went along with the plan, and was shocked when Scott ordered a pitcher of pop instead of beer. It was a perfect day. Scott and Amber had a pillow fight in the motel room that night, and even though there were two beds, they all slept together in one. The next morning, Scott suggested they check out some churches in their new neighborhood, and Rachael about fell over.

"CHURCH?" cried Rachael.

"Ya, church. I think it's about time for Amber to start Sunday School," announces Scott.

"School on Sunday?" complains Amber.

"It's not like regular school sweetheart," says Rachael, "it's where you go to learn about Jesus Christ."

"Who's Jesus Christ?"

"See what I mean?" says Scott.

After agreeing on the plan, they set off to find a church. It didn't take long to find a Lutheran Church just three blocks away from their new home. They went in and attended the service, and the congregation welcomed them with open arms. Rachael was amazed at the change in Scott. Life couldn't be better.

The move went smoothly. They rented moving trucks, and did all the moving themselves. Bob and Jake were nowhere to be found when Scott tried to commandeer their help. Members of the church happily volunteered to help them move in. Amber already has a new best friend from Sunday School, and Rachael is quickly making friends with many of the ladies from Church. Life was like a storybook for the Lewisons, they even decided it was time to expand their family. Rachael stopped taking birth control, and before they knew it, a family of three turned into a family of five. Cole was born in 1995, and Nathan came along in 1997. Scott found a job at a wholesale food supply warehouse, and quickly moved up the ladder to foreman. Even though his job paid fairly well, he still didn't make as much as Rachael, and he didn't like the guys he worked with. They were always teasing him about his wife making more money than him. His boss put more and more responsibility on his shoulders every day, and the stress became too much for him. Scott started drinking again, and going to the bar after work. Many nights he closed it down at two am. He started showing up to work late, reeking of booze. His boss warned him that it would have to stop after sending him home to sleep it off several times. Rachael was stressed also because she had to take care of the kids by herself, taking them to school and daycare, and picking them up in the afternoon. Scott was turning into the man he used to be right before her eyes, and the more she lectured him, the worse he got. They had just bought a house in the same neighborhood, and the payments were double the rent they were paying. Scott's drinking became worse and worse, and his weight had increased by a hundred pounds. Rachael was just about to the end of her rope when she receiver a familiar phone-call at two am.

"Mrs. Lewison?"

"Yes."

"This is Officer Payne of the Great Falls Police Department. Is your husband Scott Lewison?"

"Yes, is he alright?'

"Yes ma'am, he's just had a little too much to drink. He's been picked up for driving under the influence."

"Oh no."

CHAPTER 30

———— ✦ ————

THE DATE IS JULY 30TH, 1999. Saturday morning. Rachael drove down to the police station to post bail and take Scott home. This time the bail was a thousand dollars, and Scott had to hire a lawyer and go before a Judge. Rachael lectured him all the way home and begged him to seek help. He just ignored her and rubbed his head.

"You can't keep doing this Scott," she cried. "By the time we pay the lawyer and the fines, this will cost us a fortune. Besides that, you're going to have to start helping out with the kids, I can't keep doing everything by myself. It wouldn't hurt you to get up a little earlier and help me get them ready. They're your kids too."

"I have to be to work earlier than you," complains Scott.

"Big deal! One hour! You could still help feed the baby and dress Cole and fix their cereal. Why should I have to do everything?"

"Well excuse me, but you were the one that wanted more kids."

"Don't try and change the subject Scott! The problem is your drinking! You have to stop, it's killing our marriage and our family!"

"Are you trying to say you want a divorce?"

"That's not what I said Scott! I love you, and I want you to get help!"

"I don't need help! I can quit anytime I want to!"

Famous last words. Scott didn't quit drinking, in fact, he started drinking more. Judge Murphy slapped a five thousand dollar fine on him, and took away his license. That didn't stop him from driving though. He still drove, although he kept a wary eye on the road, and watched for cops like they were his worst enemy. Rachael took a second job on the weekends at Target to help pay for his fines. She also applied for public assistance, but was turned down. Scott became a complete slob. Often times, he wouldn't shower for days, and he stopped shaving. He wasn't liked by any of his co-workers, and there were rumors of sending him packing. His kids didn't even want to be around him because he stunk. Rachael begged him and begged him to get help, but the more she bothered him about it, the more he rebelled. Her friends helped out a lot by taking the kids for the weekend sometimes so she and Scott could be alone, but it didn't do any good. The only thing Scott wanted to do was lie on the couch and drink beer. When hunting season came, he spent every weekend hunting, draining their bank account. He would fill the truck up with gas and beer early in the morning, and not return until after dark. Rachael started sleeping on the couch because she just couldn't stand to smell him anymore. Her friends at work tried to convince her to divorce him, while her friends at church encouraged her to stick with him and remember the man he used to be. It was tearing her apart inside, but she stuck with him, hoping that someday, something would happen to make him turn his life around, just like in 1994.

When Christmas came, Scott didn't buy any gifts for the children or Rachael. He didn't even stay home on Christmas Eve. He found an open bar and stayed there until they closed at midnight. Rachael did her best to keep the Christmas spirit alive. She bought a tree, and her and the children trimmed it without Scott. Working at Target on the weekends turned out to be a plus, as she received an employee discount on everything she purchased. Therefore, she was able to stack a fair number of gifts under the tree, despite their hardships. On Christmas morning, when Rachael and the kids gathered around the tree to open gifts, Scott stayed in bed with a hangover. Rachael just informed the kids that daddy was sick, and maybe if they all prayed together, God would help him get better. So, she and the children bowed their heads and prayed, thanking Jesus for his blessings, and asked him to please take care of Daddy.

On New Year's Eve, Rachael and the kids celebrated with homemade pizza and ice cream, while Scott spent the night at the bar. About one o'clock in the morning, Scott stumbled through the door, his face covered in blood. The kids were just getting ready for bed, and Amber screamed when she saw him walk through the door. Cole cried because it scared him too. Instead of assuring them that he was ok, he threw his arms in the air and roared, sending them running scared and crying to their mother. He laughed and staggered over to the couch and sat down.

"Scott! What happened?" screamed Rachael.

"Oh, some asshole decided he didn't like me kissing his wife at midnight, so he broke my nose. Kind of appealing, don't you think?"

"Well you didn't have to scare the kids!"

"Oohh...what's the matter kids? Haven't ya ever seen blood before?"

Scott raised his arms and growled again as Cole screamed and shook like a leaf. Rachael picked him up and rushed him and Amber to their rooms and rocked them until they fell asleep. Afterwards, she went to the kitchen and poured cold water into a bucket and took it out to the living room where Scott was passed out on the couch. She stood for a moment in front of him, shaking with anger. Then she raised the bucket and poured it over his head, dousing the couch and carpet with bloody water. Scott's eyes flew open as he gasped for air.

"GET OUT!" screamed Rachael. "GET OUT OF MY HOUSE!"

Scott jumped up and punched her in the face, knocking her across the room and into the Christmas tree, sending it crashing it to the floor.

"This is MY house you fucking bitch, and don't you ever forget it! If anyone's gonna leave, it's you!"

He then stumbled to the bathroom and threw up in the toilet, passing out on the floor afterwards. Rachael crawled over to a chair and pulled herself up. She sat there for a while, crying and holding her face. She could feel a trickle of blood coming from her left eyebrow. When she stopped shaking, she stood and walked to the mirror to survey the damage. She was going to have a hell of a shiner in the morning. She went to the bathroom, stepped over the whale that was sleeping on the floor, and found a bandage in the cabinet above the sink. She put it on her brow and fetched some ice from the freezer to place on the swelling. After a while, she picked up the tree and attempted to clean up the blood. Luckily, she didn't have to work in the morning, so she had a couple of days to get the swelling down. She started thinking of excuses for her shiner. She decided to tell everyone that she was starting to take the trimming off the tree and lost her balance, falling into the coffee table. Everyone at work pretended to believe her out of kindness, but they all knew the truth, that her scumbag husband smacked her. In the days, weeks, and months that followed, the violence continued. Scott injured himself at work in February, just before he was about to be fired, and filed a workman's compensation claim. The doctor told him not to lift anything over ten pounds, so he did exactly that. Lucky for him, a glass of beer was less than ten pounds. He spent most of his time at the bar, and when he was home, he became more and more abusive, and Rachael seemed to suddenly become accident prone, falling into a lot of things. Everyone begged her to seek help, and she was just about ready to, when she received another familiar phone call at two o'clock in the morning on March 18th.

"Mrs. Lewison?"

"Yes?"

"This is deputy Johnson calling from Great Falls Medical Center. Is your husband Scott Lewison?"

"Yes."

"Mrs. Lewison, I'm afraid your husband has been in an accident."

"Is he alright?"

"Yes, he's got some cuts and bruises, but I'm sure he'll be released."

"Do I need to come and get him?"

"Well, Mrs. Lewison, I'm afraid that won't be necessary. You see, your husband has been drinking heavily, and he's been involved in a hit and run."

"Hit and Run?"

"Yes. He hit a pedestrian and fled the scene."

"Oh my God! Is the person ok?"

"She is in intensive care with several broken bones, but she is alive. Since she's a senior citizen, only time will tell. I'm afraid your husband is going to be spending some time at the Cascade County Corrections Center until he can be arraigned."

"Why don't you just keep him there?"

"Well ma'am, that's exactly what our intentions are. I'm sorry to have wakened you. You can receive more information on Monday morning at the Sheriff's office. Goodnight Mrs. Lewison."

"Goodnight."

Rachael hangs up the phone and lies in bed staring at the ceiling, emotionless. She decides to say a prayer for the old woman. A feeling of relief spreads over her like an enormous burden has been lifted from her shoulders. Suddenly she feels safe and unafraid. She clasps her hands together and continues to pray for the old woman until she drifts off to sleep.

"Hey Johnny," says Bubba as he taps John's door.

"Hey Bubba. What's up?"

"Well, it looks like yur gonna get a roommate for a while."

"Oh maaan! Who? How long? I was just getting used to this."

"They just brought a guy in last night on his third DUI, and this time he hit a pedestrian, so he might be here awhile."

"Can't you put him somewhere else?"

"Can't. Yours is the only available cell."

"GREAT! What's this guy like?"

"Well," laughs Bubba, "he ain't no Billy."

"What that supposed to mean?"

"He weighs more than twice as much as Billy."

"GREAT! Now I'm going to have to give up the bottom bunk too! Any more good news?"

"No," laughs Bubba, "that's about it. I'll bring him up to introduce you two after we hose him off."

"Make sure he uses soap, will ya?"

"Ok boss, oh and by the way, if you can teach this guy to do tai chi, I'll kiss yur ass."

Bubba laughs all the way out of the block as John wonders what that could be all about. 'Anyone can learn tai chi,' he thinks, 'what's this guy's problem?' Once he sees Bubba escorting Scott into the block, he realizes what Bubba was laughing about. 'Oh my God,' thinks John.

"John McDuffy, meet Scott Lewison. Your new roommate," chuckles Bubba.

"Howdy," says John, "you can have the bottom bunk."

Scott doesn't say a word. He just lies down on the bunk and goes to sleep. John follows Bubba outside and punches him on the arm.

"You think this is funny, don't you?"

Bubba laughs and slaps John on the back.

"Good luck boss. Just keep your hands away from his mouth."

"I'll get you for this Bubba!" shouts John as Bubba leaves the block.

He can already hear the whale snoring as he stands outside the cell. Other prisoners gather around to see the new resident. Everyone snickers as they marvel at the rolls of fat on this man. John stands in the doorway watching him sleep, when suddenly, his nostrils are stung by a foul smell. Scott farted.

"GREAT!"

CHAPTER 31

———∞∞∞———

"LOOKS LIKE BABY BEAR HAS been replaced by Papa Bear," says one of the inmates.

"Wanna trade cells?" inquires John.

"No way! I would rather sleep next to the oil refinery!"

"It's a good thing they don't let us bring matches in here. We could have a hell of an explosion."

In the last few weeks, prison life has been almost bearable for John. He has his days down to a routine, and that helps pass the time. In the morning, before breakfast, he does his calisthenics and his meditation, then he showers and goes to breakfast. After breakfast, he reads every book he can get his hands on, and sometimes watches a little TV with the other inmates. Jeanie brings him an occasional novel to read, but they are usually romance novels, and he hasn't the heart to tell her he can't stand romance novels. She also brings him magazines like Outdoor Sportsman, Sports Illustrated, and Car and Driver. Those get opened.

Just before lunch, he says a prayer for his mother in remembrance of the days when he would pick her up at noon, and take her to lunch. She always enjoyed those little lunch dates, for it gave her a reason to dress up. One beautiful spring day in 1994, John picked her up for lunch, and she said she wanted to try out a new coffee shop she'd heard about on Central Avenue, Wadder's Coffee Shop.

"I hear they serve all natural, fresh food," said Kathleen.

"Ok. Whatever you say mom, you're the boss."

The two of them sat down at a table by the window as the waitress brought their water and menus to them. The water was served with a slice of lemon, and the menus were one page and the size of a newspaper. Everywhere you looked, there were plants. They had everything from ferns to ivies, umbrella trees to palm trees. It was a regular greenhouse.

"My goodness," said Kathleen, "I'll bet it's a job to water all these."

"No doubt," said John. "Miss!" he said as he waved the waitress over.

"Yes sir. Are you ready to order?"

"No, actually I was wondering if there was another page to the menu. I don't see any hamburgers on here."

"We don't serve any fried food sir. The only hot dish we serve is homemade soup."

"Oh, I'm sorry. We'll be ready to order in a minute."

"I could have told you that Johnny," said Kathleen, "everything here is healthy and good for you. It wouldn't kill you to eat a fresh sandwich for a change."

"Well, I'm going to have a bowl of soup to go with it then."

John grumbled a little, but he managed to choke down a turkey sandwich and a bowl of vegetable soup. It didn't matter though, because mom was enjoying herself as she filled John in on all the gossip from the church. On their way back to Kathleen's house, John expressed his thoughts on the high prices in comparison to the small portions.

"That's just another reason why it's good for you Johnny, you don't eat as much, so it's easier to burn it off."

"Ok mom, whatever you say."

Once dropping Kathleen off, John went straight to Burger King and bought a whopper to take back to work with him.

After John says his prayer and chokes down the bland prison food, he walks around the block gathering recruits for his tai chi classes. The newcomers are always hard to convince because they are still pissed off at the world, and really don't feel like socializing with a bunch of prisoners. If they are there for very long though, they eventually show some interest. Once they do that, it's easy for John to convince them to try a few moves. Once they realize they can do it, they soon look forward to class each day. Class usually starts around two o'clock, but sometimes doesn't start until three, depending on delays in lunch or delays due to fights or other disturbances. It usually takes about an hour to go through the entire routine. Afterwards, everyone goes to their cells to relax, some of them to meditate. The guards are amazed with the calmness in the atmosphere. They all agree it will be a sad day when they have to say goodbye to John McDuffy.

After dinner, John will read a little or watch some TV, or just stare out the window. Bedtime comes around nine o'clock for him, as he likes to get up at five. He hopes his new roommate will keep a similar schedule.

"Time for lunch Scott," says John as he taps Scott on the shoulder at eleven forty-five. Scott doesn't answer.

"Ok, whatever. Looks like you could stand to miss a few meals anyway."

Scott still doesn't answer, instead he replies with another eye burning purge.

"My God man! What did you eat? It smells like something crawled up that big ass of yours a week ago, and died!"

Scott lets out a slight snicker.

"So, it does speak. That's good to know. Why don't you go speak to the guards about getting a cork for yur ass! You stink man!"

Scott laughs louder this time.

"I had a rough night, ok?" he bellows.

"So? Does that give you the right to stink up my area? If you're sick, go to the hospital!"

"I'm sorry, I can't help it. I ate a bunch of corned beef and cabbage yesterday."

"Corned beef and cabbage never did that to me."

"Well, maybe it was the pickled eggs."

"What did you do, eat the whole jar?"

"Just about."

"Well, I hope you get it out of your system before ten o'clock, because if I have to be locked in this room with you when you drop another one of those, I'll stuff a pillow up yur ass."

"Ok, ok. You go to lunch and I'll take a shit. Maybe that will help."

"At least go to the shower room to shit. You'll probably plug this one up."

Scott agrees to do what he says, and John leaves for lunch. Everyone watches while Scott waddles to the shower room, his belly bouncing with every step. After he relieved himself and thoroughly quarantined the shower room, he went back to his bunk to sleep. Prison life suits him fine for now because he's used to lying around doing nothing, that is until he realizes beer isn't on the menu here. Once his head is healed and his body starts craving beer again, he is going to be very hard to live with. John is going to have his hands full.

"Angus here."

"Angus? This is Jeanie Philips."

"Yes lassie, top of the morning to ya."

"Top of the morning to you too," laughs Jeanie. "How have you been?"

"I've been just fine darling. How about yur self?"

"I'm fine Angus. I haven't heard from you in a while so I thought I would call and see if there is anything new in the red ribbon situation."

"Nothing new here. Mr. Jackson has been pretty quiet. His car hasn't moved in weeks. I think it must be broken down or something. He's been driving a newer Toyota pickup lately. Have you had any trouble at your place?"

"No, everything's fine. I talked to John's neighbor the other day, and it's been pretty quiet there too."

"He must know we're on to him. We better lay low for a while. Wouldn't want to scare him off now when we're this close."

"Right, well you let me know if anything comes up, ok?"

"You got is lass."

"Bye Angus."

Jeanie sits and ponders the possibility that Bobby knows he's being watched. Maybe that's why he stopped driving his car. She doesn't ponder the question too long for she has an appointment to meet Jack and Peggy down at the pistol range at two o'clock. Jack has been bugging her for weeks to go shooting with them, so today she's finally going to try it. Since she found the note in her mailbox, she's been looking over her shoulder a lot. She's asked herself often what she would do if suddenly a big man jumped out of the bushes and attacked her. She's too small to put up much of a fight, but the odds would be a little more even if she slowed him down with a few well-placed pieces of led. Besides, what harm is there in giving it a try.

"Hi Jack. Hi Peggy."

"Hi kiddo," says Jack, "glad you could make it."

"Are you ready to blow away some scum bags?" asks Peggy.

"You bet! Let's get started."

Millers shooting range is a private club that is made up exclusively of police officers, deputies, and citizens with concealed weapon permits. Jack and Peggy have belonged to the club for years. It is an indoor range, and is strictly meant for handguns. The police department also uses it to train their new applicants for concealed weapon permits. Before you are issued a permit, you must prove you can handle a gun and shoot straight.

Jack hands Jeanie a set of earmuffs and shooting glasses, and instructs her to stand aside and observe for a while as he and Peggy touch off a few rounds. Jack starts with his Glock and empties the clip in a six-inch group on a human shaped target twenty-five yards away. Jeanie feels a slight rush come over her as the smell of burned powder fills the room. Next, Peggy steps up to the bench with her forth-one mag and takes aim at the same target. Jeanie jumps when the first round is fired and jack laughs.

"That one's got quite a bark to it, doesn't it?"

"My God, she could kill a moose with that thing!"

Peggy continues to shoot away while Jack pulls out the pistol he wanted to show Jeanie. It's a beautiful Walther PPK 9mm, with acorns engraved into the breech. He hands it to Jeanie and her small hands wrap around the custom grips perfectly.

"Oh Jack, it's beautiful."

"I thought you'd like it. I picked up a couple of holsters for you also. One for your purse and one that straps around your leg."

"Jack, that's awfully nice of you, but I can't afford this."

"If you win your first case, consider it a bonus."

"Jack, I can't accept this."

"You have too. That's an order young lady! But first, we better see if you can shoot straight."

Jack guides Jeanie through the basics of handgun safety and shows her how to grip it as she aims at her target. Once she is confident that she is ready, he pushes the button controlling the target retriever and places a new target at about fifteen yards. After loading the clip full, Jack engages the safety and hands the Walther to Jeanie. She takes the weapon and grips it tightly with her right hand, cupping her left hand under her grip. She places her left foot forward and leans into her target like

Jack instructed her too. Jack and Peggy stand back and smile at their new student. After lining up the sights in the middle of the target, Jeanie pushes the safety to the off position and pulls the trigger. BANG! The first shot misses the target completely. She lowers the weapon and turns to look at Jack and Peggy, her heart pounding.

"What a rush! Did I hit it?"

"I think so," says Jack, "keep shooting until the clip is empty."

"Ok."

The next shot hits the target in the upper right hand corner. Since it moved this time, she realizes the first one missed completely. Now she is over the initial shock and takes aim again. The next shot is closer to the center, and each shot after that is better than the last. Once the clip is empty, she lays the Walther down gently on the bench and turns to give Jack a hug, then Peggy.

"That was so much fun!" she shouts. "I love it!"

"I think you're a natural dear!" gasps Peggy.

Jeanie's first shooting experience was a success. She's hooked!

CHAPTER 32

——⊗⊗⊗——

APRIL 1ST, 2000, SATURDAY. SCOTT is completely healed from his hangover and ready to drink again. One problem though, he's in jail. John has been up for hours by the time Scott decides to roll out of bed. He's finally realized that if he wants to eat breakfast, he's going to have to get up before nine o'clock. For some reason, the kitchen won't hold his breakfast for him, even though he's voiced his complaint to the guards.

After inhaling his food in all the elegant fashion of a Kansas hog, he waddled back to his cell and laid down on his bunk to suck his teeth and belch. John has just finished with his shower and walks through the door when his nostrils are stung by one of Scott's prize-winning farts.

"Good God man! Put a cork in that thing!"

"Fuck you! You aren't exactly a rose yourself, you know!"

"Well, at least I leave the room if I have to shit my pants!"

"So? What'd ya want, a medal?"

"No, just a little respect."

"Who the fuck died and put you in charge?"

John's face turns red as he thinks about teaching fat boy a little respect but he remembers what happened the last time he got a little rowdy, and decides instead to just let it go. The last thing he wants is more time in jail, especially with a cellmate like Scott Lewison. Not only does he release gas every ten minutes, he has the body odor of a transient. The man is so lazy he won't even shower unless the guards force him to, which is about once a week. Scott rolls over and faces the wall to take his mid-morning nap as John leaves to get some fresh air. On the way to the outdoor area he runs into Bubba.

"Bubba?"

"Ya boss?"

"Isn't there something you can do about that pig in my cell?"

"Fraid not boss. The jail is full. You're just going to have to put up with him for a while."

"What's he in for anyway?"

"His third DUI. Plus, he hit an old street woman who is still in critical condition. He might be here for a while."

"GREAT! Can't you at least have a fart fan installed? A three horsepower outta do it."

Bubba laughs, "Sorry boss, no fart fan. Ya know, maybe you can help this guy the way you helped Billy. I guess he used to be an alright guy according to his wife's report."

"He has a wife?"

"Ya, and three kids!"

"Why hasn't she been up to see him?"

"I guess he knocked her around a bit too."

"Real nice guy."

"Ya, so she's hoping he'll stay here awhile. Looks like she might get her wish since the courts are backed up till Christmas."

"Well, I guess if I have to put up with him, I might as well see if I can straighten his ass out."

"That's what I wanted to hear," smiles Bubba.

Bubba leaves and John stands outside for a while and takes in the fresh air. He stares up at the sky and dreams about freedom. The freedom he took for granted…the freedom that seems so far away. Four more months of hell and he'll be able to go wherever he wants to go, and do whatever he wants to do…sweet freedom.

"Where the hell is my lawyer?! I wanna see my God Dammed lawyer?!"

John wonders, 'Who the hell is that,' as he heads back to the block to see what all the commotion is. As he gets within sight, he realizes its Scott. He's pounding on the window at the guard's station and shouting for his lawyer. The guards rush in immediately to restrain him. Scott tries to fight them, but is soon out of breath. He decides to go to his cell and pout as he catches his breath. The guards look at John and shake their heads. John smiles and shrugs his shoulders as if to imply, 'What am I supposed to do?' After the guards leave and things quiet down, he decides to talk to fat boy and try to find out what made him turn into such a wonderful human being.

After pulling up a chair in front of Scott, who is sweating and huffing and puffing on his bunk, he says, "What's eatin you?"

"What do ya mean, what's eatin me! That's about the stupidest fuckin question. What do ya think? I want outta here! A DUI! A measly fuckin DUI! I should of been outta here weeks ago."

"Was it your first?" asks John, giving Scott the chance to tell the truth.

"Third. But they can't keep me here for that. I'm supposed to be getting a public defender and I haven't seen anybody. Them fuckin cops are jerkin me around."

"I know the courts are backed up. I've been here since September."

"September?! You mean I could be here for months?"

"Probably."

"That's fuckin bullshit! They aren't keeping ME here that long. I'll go to the supreme court!"

John smiles, "And how do you propose to do that?"

"I don't know, but I'll think of something."

Scott stares at the floor for a while. He knows he hasn't a snowballs chance in hell of taking his case to the Supreme Court.

After a moment, keeping his eyes focused on the floor, he asks John, "So what are you in here for?"

"Negligent homicide and drunken driving."

"Homicide? You killed someone?" asks Scott as he looks up at John.

"My kids."

"Oh. Sorry man, I didn't know."

"There's a lot you don't know Scott, but that's my problem and I'll deal with it. What you need to concern yourself with is how to turn your life around so you can get out of here and not come back."

"Oh great! I suppose you're going to lecture me too!"

"That's right, and there ain't a damn thing you can do about it," smiles John. "I'm going to follow you like a shadow and harp on you until you listen to me."

Scott smiles, "I'll just drop a greasy fart. That'll get rid of you."

"That's true," laughs John, "but I'll be back when the air clears."

John and Scott finally start to get along after that moment, and Scott actually begins to listen to John. After weeks of eating nothing but prison food and no alcohol, Scott loses some weight and starts feeling a lot better about himself. Instead of John being his shadow, Scott has taken to following John everywhere. He's discovered there is something about the way John explains things that just makes sense. He has even considered trying tai chi, but he wants to lose some more weight first. One day, Scott opened up to John and told him his entire life history. After hearing about Scott's wife and children, John feels he must help this guy get his life together for their sake.

"It sounds like you have a great family there Scott," says John.

"I do," says Scott, "and the best part is, they're still alive and well. I just wish I could go back in time and erase the last year and start over. I really screwed up this time."

"It's never too late to change. Like you said, they're still alive and well, and waiting for you to get your shit together. It's up to you. It's your choice. Do you want to be Scott Lewison, loving husband and father, or do you want to be Scott Lewison the drunk. You have the power to be whatever you choose."

"I choose husband and father."

"Well that's it then, the rest is downhill."

"Ya right. How do ya figure?"

"Well, the hard part is making the decision which road to take. Now that you've made that decision, all you have to do is stay on the road. If you slip off, you just remember the reward at the end of the journey, back up, and get back on the road."

"And that reward would be?" asks Scott as he tries to understand.

"A loving and loyal wife, and three beautiful children. Children that miss their daddy, children that will grow up to bring you grandchildren Scott, something I'll never have."

John looks out the window and Scott realizes he's hit a sore spot. John hasn't talked much about his accident, but it's obvious he misses his children terribly. He still gets chocked up when he sees a group of students taking a tour of the jail as he remembers Brett and Ryan.

"So, you don't plan on having more kids when you get out?" asks Scott.

"No, I'm too old to start over. I would be an old man when they became teenagers, and teenagers don't relate well to old people."

"What are your plans when you get out?"

"I don't know. Just gonna take it one day at a time. The question is, what are you gonna do when you get out?"

"I'm gonna try and get my family back for starters."

"Good man. Then what? Do you think you'll have a job waiting for you when you get out?"

"I doubt it, I pretty much screwed that up too. I don't care though, I hated that job. I think I'll go back to school and learn a trade. My wife makes twice as much as me and that's always bugged me. She's always been the breadwinner and I've always had shit jobs. The guys at work teased me about that all the time, and I starter resenting her for it, like it was her fault I'm such a looser.

I can't believe the way I've treated her. She should have left me a long time ago."

"You're a lucky man to have her Scott, hang on to her."

"Oh, I plan on it. I called her the other day, and she's coming up to see me on Sunday."

"Really?! That's cool!"

"Ya. She's still a bit skeptical on taking me back, but at least it's a start."

"Were you two separating before you got thrown in here?"

"No, but she hasn't even tried to post bail, and she told the cops to just keep me here, she didn't want to see me again."

"So, what are you going to tell her when you see her?"

"I'm sorry, for starters. Then I'm going to tell her I've changed, and pray she believes me. I guess the old woman I hit is out of the hospital and recovering, so hopefully I won't have to spend any time in Deer Lodge."

"That's good."

"Ya, but this is still gonna cost me a fortune."

"Everything worthwhile takes time Scott. You just have to keep focusing on what matters in your life, and use it to keep you on track. Like I said, if you slip off the road, just remember the reason you took that road in the first place, and back up and try again. You have a wife that supports you, and children that want nothing more than to make their daddy proud of them. With tools like those, you can rebuild anything. You have to be strong, and don't let fast food and beer take control of you. You are bigger than that. Don't let those material things kick your ass. Feed off the important things in life, things that matter to you, like your family. You must start working out and eating right so when your kids want to roughhouse or play some hoop, you can join them without having a heart attack. Do you want to live long enough to dance at your grandchildren's wedding?"

"You bet!"

"Then you better lose that gut and stay away from the booze, or you'll never see your grandchildren. It'll be tough, but you can do it! I know you can! I can help you with that."

"How?"

"Tai chi."

"Well, I know tai chi is supposed to be good exercise, but how is it supposed to help me stay off the booze?"

"Because it cleanses the spirit as well as the body. Tai chi is a form of meditation and exercise all in one. While your body goes through the motions, your mind relaxes and clears itself of all stress and pressures of the outside world. It gives you inner peace, which is the element you need to fight all the bad influences the world tries to shove down your throat."

"Ok, so when do we start?"

"We can start this afternoon."

"I'm game."

Scott joins John's tai chi class that afternoon, and everyone laughs at him at first as he stumbles and falls several times. They laugh, but they still support him in his struggle to straighten out his life. John smiles as he watches everyone pitch in to help Scott. There has been an enormous change in Scott since he first arrived, and everyone is pleased, including the guards. Bubba watches in amazement as John guides Scott through the moves.

"I don't believe it," he says to another guard, "he really did it."

CHAPTER 33

JULY 4TH, 2000. TUESDAY, 12:30AM.

"Hello, Angus here."

"Hello, Angus? This is Bob Johnson."

"Yes Bob."

"I'm sorry to bother you, but you told me to call you anytime."

"Yes, that's not a problem Bob. What's up?"

"Well, I heard a door slam outside, so I got up to look, and a black car took off down the street. It looks like there's a red ribbon tied to the tree in John's yard, should I go look?"

"No Bob. You stay right where you are. How long ago did this happen?"

"Just about five minutes ago."

"Thanks for the call Bob, I'll be in touch."

Angus wipes the sleep from his eyes and jumps out of bed. He throws on his pants and slippers and rushes out the door to his car. Instead of going over to John's house, he decides to go straight to Bobby Jackson's to try and confront him when he gets home. Angus makes pretty good time, as there is not much traffic on the roads, but it looks like Bobby made better time. His Honda is already parked on the street in front of his place, and his pickup is in the apartment complex parking lot. Angus turns off his headlights about a half a block away and quietly pulls up and parks across the street from Bobby's. After watching his apartment window for a while for movement, Angus gets out of his car and walks up to Bobby's Honda to feel the hood. The engine is cold, and the front driver's side tire is quite low, too low for safe travel. It's apparent this car hasn't moved in quite some time. Could it be possible he's been chasing the wrong man? Angus is confused now, if Bobby Jackson isn't the red ribbon bandit, then who is? He goes back to his car to sit and contemplate when he sees headlights coming toward him. The car pulls up behind Bobby's pickup and stops. After idling for a while, the engine and lights are turned off and two men get out, the passenger being Bobby Jackson. The two men go up to Bobby's apartment and turn on the music. Angus knows this because he can hear it from where he is sitting. Looking at the car they drove up in, Angus notices it's an early model Toyota, dark in color. After writing down the license number, he walks over to investigate. The engine is gurgling as the fluids settle to the bottom, and there is a fair amount of heat rising from the hood. It seems that this little car has been driven hard. Maybe Angus has his man after all. He decides not to go up to the apartment to confront them now, as they have obviously been partying, and he isn't exactly dressed for battle. Instead, he decides to come back bright and early in the morning to have a little talk with Mr. Jackson.

"A look at your forecast on this beautiful fourth of July morning, looks like it going to be a warm one this afternoon with the highs in the mid-nineties, and very little wind. The skies should remain clear throughout the day and into the evening, with the temperatures cooling off to the mid-fifties. Should be a nice evening for the fireworks display down at riverfront park. The time now is six fifty-nine here at AM570, time for a look at national news…"

Angus looks at his clock radio and sits up to wipe the sleep from his eyes just as the phone rings.

"Hello, Angus here."

"Angus, this is Jeanie. You better get over here and have a look at this!"

"What's the matter darlin?"

"There is a hunting knife stuck to my door with a note attached saying, 'If McDuffy walks, you die!' Angus, I want this psycho caught and put behind bars! He's beginning to scare me!"

"I'll be right there darlin!"

Angus quickly showers and shaves, then rushes over to Jeanie's. He arrives at the same time her folks do, and they all investigate the note together. The handwriting looks like that of a fourth grader, and there is blood on the paper and the knife blade.

"Honey, go in and call the cops!" instructs Jeanie's father to his wife.

"Don't bother lassie, I already called them," says Angus, "they're on their way."

After Jeanie and her folks go inside, Angus looks around for clues. He finds a few drops of blood on the sidewalk leading to Jeanie's door. He pulls out his camera and takes pictures of them, as well as the knife and note, then he goes door to door to talk to the neighbors. One neighbor remembers hearing a car door slam about midnight, but didn't get up to investigate. After taking notes, Angus goes back over to Jeanie's about the same time the police arrive. Two officers, a man and a woman, greet Angus as they enter the house. Jeanie explains to the female officer that she didn't hear anything all night as Angus describes the other events of the evening to the male officer. After hearing everyone's statements about the events of the evening, the officers decide to join Angus in his visit with Bobby Jackson. They too believe he is a strong suspect, and there would be no harm in asking him a few questions. Angus takes the back seat of the patrol car, and the three of them leave. Before going to Bobby's though, they make a trip over to John's house to investigate the red ribbon in his front yard. When they arrive, Bob

Johnson exits his home and introduces himself to the officers as he says hi to Angus.

"Hi Bob, top of the morning to ya," says Angus

"Hi Angus. Well, did ya catch him?"

"No, but we're on our way to talk to him now. Describe the car you saw Bob, was it the same as before?"

"I'm sure it was the same car. I still couldn't get the license number though. I think I need to invest in a spotlight."

"That won't be necessary Bob, I think we've got our man."

The officers finish taking pictures, and the three leave John's house. On their way to Bobby's, Angus fills the officers in on all the shenanigans that have been going on. They're main concern is the threatening notes, and now, the bloody hunting knife. These are not just pranks anymore...this man is making serious threats to Jeanie's life.

After arriving at Bobby's, the female officer walks around the complex to watch the balcony, just in case he tries to make a run for it. The car from last night is still parked behind Bobby's pickup, so his friend must have spent the night. Angus and the male officer walk up the stairs and knock on Bobby's door. No answer. They knock harder. No sound of movement. This time the officer pounds hard on the door and yells, "Police! Open up." Now they hear some movement! The sound of running footsteps and voices are muffled, but the occupants are obviously in a rush. The female officer sees something being thrown off the balcony, and she walks over to retrieve it. The door finally opens, but the safety chain is still attached.

"Can I help you?" asks Bobby.

"Are you Bobby Jackson?"

"Yes."

"Open up. We'd like to ask you some questions."

Bobby opens the door all the way, and Angus and the officer immediately smells pot. Bobby's friend Chad is sitting at the kitchen table, his hands shaking. Angus waits by the door while the officer walks to the balcony and motions his partner to come up. The apartment is a mess as though there was a party there last night, and the two boy's eyes are bloodshot.

"Is there a problem officer?" asks Bobby.

"Is that your Toyota parked outside with license number 2P27895?"

"That's my car," says Chad. "Is there something wrong with it?"

"Can you two explain your whereabouts last night between eleven o'clock and two o'clock?"

Chad and Bobby look at each other and agree.

"Well," says Bobby, "we were cruising around till about midnight, then we came here. Why?"

Angus and the officer look at each other, both concluding they have their man.

"Where were you cruising?" asks the officer.

"Nowhere special, just cruising. Chad's got a killer stereo, and we just like to cruise around and listen to tunes. Anything wrong with that?" says Bobby in a smart-alecky tone.

"No, but there might be a problem with this," says the female officer as she enters the room and hands a sandwich bag to the other officer. In the bag is a pipe and approximately a quarter-ounce of pot.

"I saw them pitch this off the balcony after you pounded on the door."

"That isn't mine!" says Bobby.

"I think you boys better take a ride with us downtown."

The officers read the boys their rights as they handcuff them and escort them to the car. The female officer calls for another patrol car to come take Angus to his car as they proceed to the station to book Bobby and Chad on position of illegal drugs. Once booked, they can be questioned about the red ribbon capers and the threatening notes.

The dispatched officer arrives and takes Angus to his car. Thanking him, Angus goes in to tell Jeanie and her folks everything that happened.

"Thank God!" says Jeanie's mother. "Now we can all rest easier!"

"They won't be able to keep them for long though," says Jeanie, "I'm sure they'll make bail and be out before the end of the day."

"Well, at least they know we're on to them," says Angus. "Maybe this will convince them to put a stop to this nonsense."

"I hope so," says Jeanie.

"Well, I'd better get my but down to the station and see if we can get them to confess. I'll be in touch."

"Bye Angus, and thank you," smiles Jeanie.

Angus goes to the police station and listens in as the police officers question the boys, but they aren't saying a word until they have a lawyer present. Seeing this, Angus decides to leave and go visit Bob Johnson. Since the boys will probably make bail soon, Angus decides Bob's idea makes sense. After pulling into Bob's driveway, Bob comes out to greet him.

"Hello again Angus, long time no see."

"Hello Bob. I've been thinking about what you said, and I have something for you."

Angus opens his trunk and pulls out a battery-operated spotlight.

"You should be able to read a license number with this little beauty."

Bob holds the spotlight and smiles, "Thanks Angus, but isn't this powered by your car battery?"

"Yes, it is. I've got an extra battery at home. I'll bring it by and we can rig it up in your bedroom so you can jump out of bed and nail him with five hundred thousand candle-watt power the next time he decides to decorate John's yard."

"That's a good idea," says Bob, "and I'll keep a pen and paper close by so I can write the number down."

"Sounds like we have a plan."

"I think I'll put film in my camera too, just in case."

"Couldn't hurt."

Angus shakes Bob's hand and leaves with the confidence in knowing that if Bobby and Chad continue their little game, they'll have solid proof this time, enough to send their asses to jail.

CHAPTER 34

———✺———

IT'S ELEVEN-THIRTY AM. BOBBY'S PARENTS and Chad's parents have just made bail for the boys. Now they're in for a royal butt chewing. Both of their parents are good, hard working people. The fact their son's now have a record for possession of marijuana is too much for them to stomach, even though they are both over eighteen. All four of them let the boys have it on the way to their vehicles.

"Maybe we should just leave you two in jail for a while!" says Bobby's father. "Then you'll know what it feels like to be a criminal."

"Ya!" says Chad's father. "You can be like John McDuffy."

"Dad, I'm sorry," says Bobby. "I told you, that's the first time we ever tried the stuff. It'll never happen again."

"It had better not!"

"It won't! And speaking of McDuffy, did I tell you they were accusing us of harassing him and his lawyer?"

"No. What's that all about?"

"They think we've been putting red ribbons in his front yard and stuff," said Bobby.

"You mean, like the MADD symbol?"

"Ya! And they accused us of putting notes on his lawyer's door saying crap like, 'McDuffy must die,' or something."

"You're kidding," says Bobby's mother.

"No! That's why they knocked on my door in the first place. They had a private dick with them that McDuffy hired to catch the guy."

"The term is detective," says Bobby's mother.

"Sorry mom, but anyways, that's what they think we were doing last night."

"Were you?" asks Bobby's father.

"No! We were just cruising around. I hate McDuffy, but I wouldn't do anything stupid like that."

"I can vouch for that Mr. Jackson," says Chad, "we weren't doing anything wrong."

"Except for smoking pot!" barks Chad's mother.

"Well, you guys just make sure you keep your noses clean, understand?" announces Bobby's father.

"Yes sir," says Bobby.

"Yes sir, we will," adds Chad.

The air is finally a little calmer. The parents are satisfied they've gotten their point across. Bobby and Chad slump their shoulders and push their hands deep into their pockets as their parents say goodbye to each other.

"We'll have to get together sometime on a little more pleasant note," says Bobby's mother.

"Yes, we should," agrees Chad's mother.

"Are you two going to the fireworks tonight?" asks Bobby's father.

"Well, we were planning on it," says Chad's father, "are you two going?"

"Ya, why don't we meet you down there in front of the amphitheater?"

"Ok, sounds like fun. Are you guy's coming too?" asks Chad's father of the boys.

"No, we were planning on going up to Holter Lake. The Wadders usually set off some fireworks up there, and besides, we want to get in some skiing," says Bobby.

"Ok well, STAY OUT OF TROUBLE!" says Chad's father.

"Yes sir."

"Yes dad."

"Chad can ride with us to Bobby's" announces Bobby's mother, "we'll see you two at the park tonight."

"Ok, sounds like a plan," says Chad's mother.

They all leave to their destinations as the temperature climbs into the nineties. It looks like the weatherman is right for a change.

"Hello?"

"Hi, Peggy? This is Jeanie."

"Oh, hi dear. What are you doing?"

"Well, I was just wondering if you and Jack were going to watch the fireworks at the park tonight?"

"Well, I don't think we planned on it, but let me ask the old man. JACK!" bellows Peggy. "Jeanie wants to know if we're going to watch the fireworks tonight." There is a pause as Jeanie can hear Jack yelling in the background. "No, we hadn't planned to, are you going?"

"Yes, my parents and I usually go every year. It's so much fun. Have you guy's ever gone?"

"Yes, we went once when they first started doing it down by the river, but we haven't gone since. There's just getting to be too many people there, and you know how impatient Jack is in crowds."

"Well, tell the old stick-in-the-mud he has to come this year. We have a spot up on the river's edge trail where we sit every year. It's not crowded there."

"Ok dear, I'll talk him into it, it sounds like fun."

"Good! We usually park on Fourth Avenue and Park Drive, but you have to get there early, around seven."

"Ok, we'll meet you there. What should we bring?"

"Oh, just lawn chairs and a cooler with whatever you want to drink."

"Sounds good dear, see you at seven."

Jeanie hangs up and calls her mother to inform her of their change in plans. Afterwards, she slips on her bikini and lays out in the back yard for a couple of hours to improve her tan. Before she knows it, it's time to head over to her folks for dinner. Her dad is barbequing steak, and she doesn't want to miss that! On her way over there, she remembers how Brittany used to get so excited when she found out they were going to Grandpa's for barbequed hamburgers. She loved her Grandpa and his burgers.

The dinner was fantastic as usual, and after a long rest, they all pitched in and packed the car for the evening's festivities. At seven o'clock exactly, they arrive at their usual parking area just in time to meet Jack and Peggy as they park their BMW. After parking the cars and greeting each other, the five of them walk to their favorite spot on the trail to set up housekeeping for the long evening. The main fireworks don't start until after dark, which is usually about ten o'clock this time of year, but there is always a crowd of people lighting off their own fireworks before the main event, and a jazz band plays in the park to the delight of many. Children and dogs are running here and there, laughing and playing as their parents and owners sit on the grass and enjoy the entertainment.

"Oh, this is a perfect spot Jeanie," says Peggy.

"Isn't it though? We've been coming to this spot for years. It's kind of like having season tickets."

"So, where's the cheerleaders?" asks Jack

"In your dreams!" smirks Peggy.

Jeanie's father laughs and changes the subject to a more serious tone.

"Did Jeanie tell you guys about the note on her door this morning?"

"Yes!" says Jack. "I'm glad they finally got off their asses and did something about it. I guess they busted him and his buddy on possession of marijuana. Now they HAVE to keep their noses clean, or they'll be spending some time in jail, and I'm sure John McDuffy would really enjoy that!"

"Yes, he would!" says Jeanie. "I think what angered John the most about the whole thing is the way it upset Kathleen, God rest her soul."

"She was a wonderful woman indeed," says Jack. "I miss that little pistol."

"So do I," says Jeanie, "I'll never forget our shopping spree at Christmas. I can't remember when I've had so much fun."

"She was a sweetheart," says Jeanie's mom. "How is John doing?"

"The last time I saw him was a couple of weeks ago. He's making some progress with that slob he has for a cellmate. He's even got him doing tai chi."

"You're kidding..."

"No, I'm not. He said the guy is actually working out and trying to better himself. It's amazing what John has done for Billy Little Bear, and now this guy. The guys just seem to follow him naturally like Gandhi or something. I really admire him."

"We can tell," smiles Peggy.

Jeanie blushes as she hands a soft drink to her father.

"What about John?" asks her father. "I suppose he's getting anxious for the trial to get here."

"Yes, he is. I just hope I can prove his innocence. The cards are staked pretty high against him."

"Alright, that's enough shop talk," announces Peggy, "we came here to have fun!"

"Ok Dirty Peggy," smiles Jeanie.

"Dirty Peggy?" asks her father.

"Long story," says Jeanie.

The fireworks start promptly at ten o'clock, and as usual, the show is spectacular. The grand finally lasts for about twenty minutes, and the whole show went off without a flaw. The only bad part is fighting the crowd on the way to the vehicles. Small children are cranky and tired, and parents are short tempered. Laughing and joking, Jack and Peggy reach their BMW first, and are in the process of saying goodbye when Jeanie is shocked by what she sees. Looking across the street at her car, she notices a red ribbon tied to her antenna.

"JACK! LOOK!" yells Jeanie.

Jack looks at her car, and Jeanie's father puts his arm around her. Suddenly, a black compact car squeals its tires a block away and speeds down river drive.

"C'mon!" yells Jack as he grabs Jeanie's arm. "We'll take my car!"

"Jack, be careful!" yells Peggy.

Jack and Jeanie jump in, and Jack pours the coals to the Beamer. After laying rubber for ten feet, the tires finally grip and they are in hot pursuit. Jeanie calls the police while Jack maneuvers the Beamer in and out of traffic. Most people respect his blaring horn, but a few think it's their road, and they're not moving for anyone. Eventually, they make it past the congested area and out into the open.

Jack spots a set of fast moving taillights several blocks ahead and says, "There he is!"

Jeanie informs the police of their location as Jack closes the distance between them. The black car is no match for the Beamer. They chase the car west on Central Avenue West until it turns right onto Interstate fifteen…big mistake. The interstate is where the Beamer really shines. It doesn't take Jack anytime at all to catch up to the car. As they get close to it doing a hundred and ten mph, Jack reads the license number off as Jeanie writes it down.

"4P3215! Got it?" says Jack.

"Got it!" says Jeanie. "That car is from Missoula!"

They can tell this by the '4' as the first number. The next letter stands for 'passenger car.' The first number on the license designates each town or county in Montana.

Jack looks in his mirror and sees flashing lights coming up behind him. He maintains his speed until the Highway Patrol car catches up to them. Jeanie has been on the phone with the dispatcher the whole time. The patrol car passes Jack and pulls in behind the black car. Instead of pulling over, the black car continues its speed until it reaches the exit to Highway 200, the road to Missoula, where it slows down only slightly. The exit is marked 25 mph, but the car is doing at least a hundred. The patrol car and Jack slow down to a safe speed as they watch the black car skid sideways and roll over, landing right side up in the ditch. The patrolman jumps out and rushes up to the car as Jeanie informs the dispatcher what happened, and that an ambulance is needed. Jack starts to run up to the vehicle, but the patrolman yells at him to get back in his vehicle. Upon investigation of the black car, the patrolman discovers the driver is bleeding and unconscious. In the back seat is a large roll of red ribbon material.

CHAPTER 35

———⊗⊗⊗———

FLOYD BILLARD SUSTAINED A BROKEN left arm and multiple lacerations from the accident. He was treated at the hospital and taken to the Cascade County Corrections Center for booking. He made a full confession to the detectives for harassing John McDuffy and Jeanie Philips with the red ribbons and threatening letters as he cried for forgiveness. He claimed the reason for the harassment was because he was in love with Amy Wadder, and he was angry with McDuffy for killing her. Billard used to frequent the restaurant where Amy worked. He's a dirty man, thirty-two years old, and works nights at the college as a janitor. He lives with his mother close to the college, and spends most of his money on girly magazines and exotic knives, which he collects. Amy didn't care for him much, but she tolerated him as a customer. He asked her out several times, but she always declined, claiming she had a boyfriend in Great Falls she planned on marrying someday. Floyd was persistent though, as he thought he could wear her down in time with his dirty jokes and two-dollar tips. All the waitresses were disgusted with him and begged Amy to tell him off once and for all so he would stop coming in, because his odor was foul and his dirty jokes were offensive. Amy just didn't have the heart to crush him. He reminded her of the Hunchback of Notre Dame as he sat in the counter and shoveled food into his mouth.

Jeanie pressed charges, and Floyd was transported to the Missoula County Jail Wednesday morning, where he is to await arraignment. Finally, she can rest assured knowing the culprit is behind bars. Now she can put her full concentration on the upcoming trial. The prosecution has had plenty of time to prepare their case, and so far, there's been no rumors of them asking for another extension. Jack's request for a different Judge has been granted due to his relationship with the Wadders, and things are actually looking better than they did a few months ago. Jeanie has statements from the guards on what a model prisoner John has been, and what an asset he's been to the moral of the other prisoners. She has subpoenas in order for John's co-workers, friends, neighbors, and customers. She's even prepared one for Billy Little Bear. She has her line of questioning laid out for the truck driver that was involved in the accident and the other witnesses the prosecution will probably subpoena. She's found out that the deputy prosecuting attorney assigned to the case is Richard Collingsworth III, a pretty boy who has tried to hit on her several times. His favorite pastime is looking in the mirror. He's about five feet, six inches tall, brown hair and eyes, and truly believes he has been put on this earth as a gift to all women. He keeps his hair as short as possible, as it would be devastating to him to have it messed up by the notorious southern winds of Great Falls. The very sight of him primping in front of the mirror turns Jeanie's stomach. She's looking forward to facing him in court.

After leaving the police station Wednesday morning, she drove up to the jail to tell John the good news. It's been a couple of weeks since she's visited, and she's anxious to see him. It's about ten am when she enters the conference room.

"Hi counselor!" says John as he enters the room smiling.

"Hi! My, my, you're in a good mood," says Jeanie.

"Ya, well, you know, no sense in being negative. It just makes things worse. How are you?"

"Great! I've got good news."

"Murphy got hit by a bus?" smiles John.

"No, no, he's still avoiding the busses. We caught the red ribbon bandit."

"Really?"

"Yes. Turns out he was a customer of Amy's at the restaurant where she worked. He had a real crush on her."

"So, it wasn't her boyfriend?"

"No, but the police and Angus went to have a chat with him yesterday morning because your neighbor saw a black car drive off late Monday night after leaving another ribbon around your tree. Bobby denied everything, but he and his buddy were arrested for possession of marijuana."

"No kidding?"

"No kidding. They were here yesterday morning. Too bad you didn't get to say hello."

"Riiiight. That would have been interesting."

"Well anyway, we thought our troubles were over. Then, after leaving the fireworks show last night down at the park with Jack and Peggy and my parents, I noticed a red ribbon tied around the side mirror of my car. Then we saw a black car take off down the street, so Jack and I went after him. We chased him for about ten miles till the highway patrol caught up with us and tried to pull him over. He ended up rolling his car at the Vaughn exit."

"Woah, was anybody hurt?"

"He got a broken arm out of it, but no one else was hurt."

"That's good. I'd hate to see you end up in the hospital just before the trial. That would be just my luck."

Jeanie looks at him with a smirk, "So that's all you care about me, huh?

John looks at her puzzling, "What do you mean? Of course I care about you!"

"Sure you do, as long as I get your butt out of jail," smiles Jeanie.

John smiles and places his right hand on the glass. After she joins it with her left hand, he says, "Just get me out of here and I'll show you how much I care."

Jeanie's heart beats heavily as she stares into his eyes.

"It won't be long now Johnny, I promise."

"Is everything still set for the twenty-eighth?"

"Yup, and we won't have to worry about Murphy either. Jack was able to get a different Judge assigned because of Murphy's friendship with the Wadders."

"That's awesome!"

"Yes, it is, but we've still got a battle ahead of us. The prosecuting attorney is a real sleaze ball. I know him, and he'll use every trick in the book to win, even if means breaking the law."

"Great! Just what we need."

"Don't worry, I've got his number."

"How's that?"

"He's asked me out several times. Maybe I'll promise to go out with him if he throws the case," says Jeanie as she gives John a coy smile.

"Well, is he good looking?"

"Sure he is. If you don't believe me, just ask him."

"Oh, real pretty boy huh?"

"Yup, so all I have to do is flash him a wink now and then, and he'll mess himself and forget what he was saying."

"You shameless hussy," smiles John.

Jeanie laughs as the guard informs them that their time is up. She throws John a wink and says goodbye. He watches her little fanny sway as she leaves the room.

"You lucky dog," comments the guard as he escorts John back to the block. John just smiles and agrees. He's grown quite fond of his lawyer, and everyone knows it. As he walks back to his cell, he thinks about the prosecuting attorney and Jeanie in bed together, and jealously fills his mind. The thought of her with someone else is not pleasing to him. Seven more weeks and he'll be able to actually touch her and hold her in his arms as they sit on the couch and watch a good movie over pizza and popcorn.

Seven more weeks and this will all be behind him. In the past ten months, John has suffered through malnutrition, anxiety, depression, and just about every other emotional disorder you can think of, and still managed to keep his sanity. The road has been tough, but the reward at the end of the journey is within sight now, and the butterflies are starting to set up housekeeping is his stomach. What if Jeanie loses the case? Then what? Will he be able to maintain his sanity with any more time in jail? Just the thought of that depresses him. As he enters his cell, he sees Scott on the floor pumping out some push-ups, and it makes him smile. Scott has lost about a hundred pounds, and his muscles are actually noticeable. He showers every day and works out with John, and then some. He is a completely different man than the one that waddled in here about four months ago. John decides to drop to the floor and join him. Bubba watches from a distance as the two of them compete, and smiles. He's going to miss his new friend John, and the peacefulness he's brought to the jail. The violence level has been cut by eighty percent, and the rate of return of released prisoners has been reduced drastically, all thanks to John McDuffy. Things will be quite different around there after John leaves, and the guards know it. The ones that have been subpoenaed for the trial are looking forward to testifying in John's behalf, Bubba especially.

As the days and weeks wear on, John spends most of his time working out with Scott. The two of them have actually become pretty good friends, and have promised to stay in touch on the outside. When they team up on the basketball court, they can't be beat. They seem to know what the other is thinking all the time. Scott still has a little fat around his mid-section, but John is about as lean as they get. His abs ripple under the shadow of his pecks, and his shoulders and arms are budging with lean muscle. This is the best shape he has ever been in. He's promised himself that he is going to stay in shape when he gets out, as has Scott. They've talked about the days when they can get together and do some mountain biking and backpacking. Those days that once seemed like an impossible dream are now within reach. Rachael has been up to see Scott on a regular basis, and she can't wait to get her 'new man' back. John's ex-wife hasn't been up to see him once, and neither has his boss or co-workers. The only visitor he's received since Kathleen died is Jeanie and Bob Johnson. Jeanie has been a good friend through it all, and he looks forward to building a relationship with her. After all, she's lost her family too. Maybe they can start a new life together and put the past behind them, but first they have to get through the trial, and John must be found innocent before any hopes of a new life can become a reality.

CHAPTER 36

AUGUST 28ᵀᴴ, 2000, MONDAY, 6:00 am. John has been up for about an hour, but he's been awake all night. Like a kid on Christmas Eve, the butterflies just wouldn't let him sleep. Today is the day of the trial, the day that will change his life, like the one almost a year ago. He's ready to leave this jail for good. As he sits on his bunk and meditates, the cell doors are just beginning to open. One by one the other prisoners work their way to John's cell and tap on the door jam and say, 'good luck.' John decides to cut his meditation short and thank everyone for their support. Scott finally wakes up from all the commotion and joins everyone else in their thanks and good luck wishes.

"Well ol' buddy, this is it," says Scott.

"Yep," says John.

"Nervous?"

"Does a bear shit in the woods?" says John.

"Don't be Johnny, I'm sure everything will be just fine. You'll leave here this morning and never return, unless of course you come to visit," smiles Scott.

"Fat chance of that. I'll see you when you get out."

As John and Scott head off to the showers, across town Jeanie is frantically running around getting ready. She's laid out her light blue suit for today's ensemble with a salmon top, soft colors to reflect a soft heart. The trial is scheduled to start at nine am sharp, but she needs to be at the courthouse by eight for briefing with Jack. John is scheduled to show up at eight also. This morning she is feeling the same butterflies as John. Not only is this her first trial, in which she needs to ace, but also John's future depends on the outcome, and she wants his future to be part of hers. The clock seems to be moving faster than usual this morning and the coffee pot is taking its sweet time. The skies are cloudy and rain is starting to fall. Even though the rain is much welcomed by the farmers and the Forest Service, a gloomy day is not what she needs today.

Eight forty-five am. Everyone is present and waiting for the arrival of Judge Santos. Jeanie and Jack are briefing John on this morning's plan of battle, and Rich is straightening his tie and cuffs.

John notices that Laura is in the audience and asks Jeanie, "Did you subpoena her?"

"No, but the prosecution probably did," answers Jeanie.

"All rise for the Honorable Judge Santos," announces the bailiff.

It's nine o'clock sharp, and the good Judge enters the room.

"Here we go," whispers Jeanie into John's ear.

John reaches for her hand and squeezes it.

The jury is made up of six men and six women. They have been briefed on the accident and its location, and are poised and ready for the process to begin. After the Judge goes through his usual opening announcements and introductions, the prosecution stands to address the jury.

"Good morning ladies and gentleman," announces Rich, "thank you for coming."

As he paces up and down the jury box, he rubs his eyes hard so they look red and watery when he takes his hand away. There is a long silence as the jury watches this man, who seems to be breaking down, struggling to find words.

Finally, he clears his throat and says, "Three young people are dead. Three young people were torn from their families and from this earth by this man!"

Rich spins around and thrusts his arm toward John McDuffy. After wiping his eyes, he continues.

"Today ladies and gentlemen, you will be asked to make a decision. A decision that won't bring back the lives of Amy Wadder, Brett McDuffy and Ryan McDuffy, but a decision that will bring justice to the man that caused their tragic deaths. After seeing the evidence and listening to the testimonies, I am confident you will see your way fit to punish this man for what he has done."

Rich went on for another fifteen minutes, slamming John and preaching patriotic duty as the jury watched with intensity. John sat and watched him with a blank stare. Memories of the accident and Brett and Ryan filled his head. His eyes swelled up and he began to shake and sweat as Rich spewed fire and brimstone and death to John McDuffy. Jeanie took his hand and squeezed it hard.

After looking into his eyes and whispering, "It's ok," he felt a little better. After Rich was finished with his performance, Jeanie stood and walked over to the jury box and smiled.

"Good morning ladies and gentlemen," she said in a bubbly tone. "First off, I'd like to congratulate counsel on that commanding performance!" She turns to look at Rich and applauds. "What a show! The ol' high school drama club training is really paying off today! There is just one problem with his performance ladies and gentlemen, it's just a performance. There are no facts supporting it. There is no proof supporting it. There is no evidence supporting it. John McDuffy is a good, decent man, and you will know this without a doubt by the end of this trial. No one misses those two boys more than he does. His whole life revolved around them.

John McDuffy did not cause that accident. A cell phone caused it."

The jury looks at her with interest.

"Amy Wadder was notorious for talking on the phone while driving, and that is just what she was doing September 3rd, 1999. Today, I will prove to this court, without a doubt, that Amy Wadder caused that accident. John McDuffy has suffered enough! Not only has he been jailed for a year for a crime he didn't commit, but he has lost his two sons AND his mother, who died of a broken heart last Christmas. Today ladies and gentlemen, you will have the privilege of righting a terrible wrong. You will be allowed to set an innocent man free to start his life over again."

Jeanie walks back to the table and resumes her position next to John. Jack smiles and gives her a wink. The first witness called by the prosecution is the truck driver, Jim Haskell. After being sworn in, Rich greets him and asks him to explain to the jury who he is, and what he does for a living. Jim explains that he is an independent trucker. Rich goes on to ask him where he was bound on September 3rd, 1999.

"I was headed to Missoula after dropping a load of produce in Great Falls," he explained.

"When did you first encounter the green pickup and camp trailer that was involved in the accident?" asks Rich.

"Well, I was about five miles this side of where the road starts to get narrow and steep goin up Rogers Pass when he passed me like I was standing still."

"How fast were you traveling Mr. Haskell?"

"I was goin the speed limit, sixty-five."

"So, Mr. McDuffy must have been going pretty fast to, as you put it, pass you like you were standing still."

"I'm sure he was going at least ninety."

Rich walks over to the jury and says loudly, "Ninety miles per hour in a 1972 pickup, pulling an old camp trailer, on a steep and narrow road with two young children in the cab with him. Didn't this seem a little dangerous to you Mr. Haskell?"

"Well, we hadn't quite gotten to the steep and narrow part yet."

"Just answer yes or no Mr. Haskell."

"Well, yes."

"And after Mr. McDuffy passed you like you were 'standing still,' when was the next time you saw him?"

"Well, I didn't see him again until the other side of Rogers Pass when I came around the curve to see him tipping over the edge of the road."

"Which side of the road was that, Mr. Haskell?"

"The left side."

Rich walks over to the jury again and says, "The left side of the road. Isn't that the wrong side to be on Mr. Haskell?"

"I guess so."

"What did you see next?"

"Well, the next thing I know, this little red car is sliding toward me on its top, so I hit the breaks. I couldn't stop in time though, so my tractor ended up rolling over the car, coming to rest on top of it."

"What part of the road was the car on when you saw it, Mr. Haskell?"

"Well, if I remember right, it was on the left side and sliding across the road to the right side."

Rich faces the jury once again and shouts, "So Amy's car was on the left side of the road?"

"Well, I think it was…"

"That will do Mr. Haskell, no further questions."

Judge Santos asks Jeanie if she wishes to cross-examine, and she acknowledges yes. She squeezes John's hand and approaches the witness box.

"Good morning Mr. Haskins," she says. "How long have you been driving truck for a living?"

"About twenty years."

"So, would you call yourself somewhat of an authority on trucks?"

"Well, I aint no expert," smiles Jim, "but I do know a good rig when I see one."

"So, in your professional opinion, did the green pickup that passed you look like it was beat up and run down, unfit for road travel?"

"No, actually I remember commenting to myself on what a fine looking rig it was, reminded of my own pickup back home." Jim looks at John and smiles, saying, "Must have had a 454 the way you passed me."

John nods and smiles.

"So, Mr. Haskins, at the location Mr. McDuffy passed you, how were the road conditions there?"

"Oh, it was no problem. The shoulders were still pretty wide there. I figured he was just passing me so he didn't have to follow me up the pass, happens all the time."

"In your professional opinion, was Mr. McDuffy driving erratically or in an unsafe manner?"

"No, I don't think so."

"Thank you, Mr. Haskell, that will be all. No further questions Your Honor."

Jim Haskell steps down from the witness stand and takes his seat.

Jeanie sits down and leans over to Jack and says, "This is going to be a long day."

CHAPTER 37

———⊶⊷———

THE NEXT WITNESS CALLED BY the prosecution is the Montana State Highway Patrol officer on duty at the time of the accident. The officer is sworn in and Rich goes right to his line of questioning.

"Good morning officer. Would you please describe to the court the events that took place on the evening of September 3rd, 1999?"

"Yes sir. I was on my regular patrol on Montana Highway 200, just south of Simms, when dispatch called to inform me of an accident that was called in from the south side of Rogers Pass. I immediately responded to the call."

"And what did you find when you arrived on the scene?"

"May I?" asked the officer as he pointed to the easel containing a grease board.

Rich looks at the Judge for permission to let the officer proceed. He nods, and the officer illustrates the scene on the grease board for the court.

"When I arrived on the scene, Mr. Haskell's tractor-trailer was jackknifed in the middle of the road, and Miss Wadder's car was upside down under the tractor."

"Was Miss Wadder still inside the car?"

"Yes sir."

Ron and Kathy are in the courtroom. Kathy buries her head in Ron's shoulder and weeps. Rich notices the jury look her way, and decides to play on the emotions.

"Was she alive officer?"

"No sir."

"Isn't it true officer that her body was completely crushed under the weight of the tractor?"

"OBJECTION!" shouts Jeanie. "Your honor, the cause of death has already been determined. There is no need for the witness to describe the graphic details!"

"Sustained. The prosecution will withdraw the question."

"My apologies to the court and to the Wadder's, your honor. Please continue officer."

"After inspecting the body, Mr. Haskell informed me of another vehicle involved that rolled down the cliff here." He points to his drawing on the board. "At that point I called in for a couple of wreckers and ambulances, after which I began to direct traffic through the wreckage."

"After the wreckage was cleared, did you inspect the scene for evidence for what caused the accident?"

"By the time the wreckage was completely cleared, it was dark, so I came back first thing in the morning about six am to make my report."

"In your report officer, you talk about empty beer cans found on the scene. Could you explain this to the court please?"

"As I worked my way down the cliff to where the defendant's pickup rolled down, there were beer cans scattered everywhere. Since there were no signs of weathering or age on the cans, I assumed they came from the defendant's pickup because of the way they followed the same path as it rolled down the cliff."

"So, one would assume that Mr. McDuffy had been drinking?"

"Yes sir. That is why I called in to have a blood/alcohol test performed on Mr. McDuffy."

"And the results of that test?"

"The result was 0.05 blood/alcohol, which is under the legal limit, but it proved that he had been drinking."

"No further questions your Honor."

Jeanie doesn't wait for Rich to take his seat. She quickly approaches the officer for cross-examination.

"Tell me officer. You 'assumed' those beer cans found on the scene belonged to my client, correct?"

"That's correct."

"So, if a passing motorist drives by your house and throws a sack if beer cans in your yard, can we 'assume' that you are an alcoholic?"

"Well, no, but that..."

"And if you have a couple of beers with the boys after work, bringing your blood/alcohol level to 0.05, can we 'assume' you are too drunk to operate a vehicle?"

"No but..."

"Then how can you legally 'assume' all these things about Mr. McDuffy?"

"There was due cause!" snaps the officer.

"Was Miss Wadder tested?"

"No."

Jeanie walks toward the jury and angrily announces, "There were three drivers involved in the accident, but only one was tested for his blood/alcohol, and or drug level. Please tell the court, why is that officer?"

"Because I didn't smell alcohol on Miss Wadder."

"Do narcotics have an odor to them officer? How did you know Miss Wadder hadn't been doing drugs that day? Why didn't you 'assume' that?"

"There was no cause."

"Isn't it true that Amy's boyfriend was just recently arrested for possession of marijuana?"

"OBJECTION!" yells Rich. "Miss Wadder's boyfriend is not on trial here!"

"Sustained. Counsel will withdraw the question."

"No further questions your Honor."

The prosecution went on the rest of the day, calling Ron and Kathy Wadder to the stand, Amy's friends and coworkers, and a professor from one of her classes at U of M. Rich played on the jury's emotions, trying to make them fall in love with Amy Wadder, the deceased pretty and young promising student whose life was ended by a drunken driver. Jeanie cross-examined each witness and did her best to neutralize the feeling of pity in the air for Amy Wadder, and instead, repeated the fact over and over that John's boys were killed too, and he has to live with that the rest of his life. The prosecution couldn't supply any hard evidence proving that John caused the accident. There were no incriminating skid marks because no one hit the brakes accept for the semi. The day was filled with circumstantial evidence and high emotions. John looked like he had aged ten years by the end of the day. When the Judge announced at the end of the day that they would reconvene at nine am the next morning, Jeanie gave John a big hug and told him to sleep well, as he would be the first one on the stand in the morning. Jack told the two of them that he thought the trial was going quite well, and that John's testimony was crucial. He is the only survivor of the accident and the only eyewitness, so he must convince the jury that Amy Wadder was in the wrong lane, causing him to switch lanes to avoid the accident.

John was taken back to the jail and everyone was sad to see him until they found out the trial wasn't over yet. Jack and Jeanie spent several hours at the office going over her list of witnesses and her line of questioning. Peggy picked up some Chinese food and brought it down to them. As the three of them ate their dinner, Peggy tried to lighten the air with a few jokes, but Jack and Jeanie were strictly business. They knew the trial was far from won, and tomorrow's testimonies would determine the jury's decision. They finished up around ten o'clock.

"Well kiddo, I guess I'll see you in the morning," says Jack.

"Ok boss, sleep well," answers Jeanie.

Jeanie goes home and takes a long bath, and Jack and Peggy decide to have a nightcap at Geno's before going home. As they sit at the bar, a friend of Jack's approaches.

"Hi Jack."

Jack turns around to see Nancy Black standing there, smiling.

"Hi Nancy," answers Jack as he puts one arm around Peggy. "Honey, this is a friend of mine, Nancy Black. She's the receptionist at the DA's office."

Peggy smiles and shakes her hand.

"How have you been Nance?"

"Oh, I've been fine. I was at the trial today."

"Really? Where were you?"

"In the back row. I was going to talk to you afterwards, but you looked pretty busy."

"You should have. I'm never too busy for my favorite bureaucrat. So, what did you think of Rich's performance?"

"He makes me sick. If he would have straightened his tie one more time, I think I would have puked."

Jack and Peggy laugh.

"One thing I didn't understand though, is where the guy from Missoula was?"

"What guy?" asks Jack.

"The photographer that supposedly saw the whole thing."

Jack's mouth drops open as he looks at Nancy and smiles.

"What are you talking about?" asks Jack.

"Didn't you know? About a week ago, a man called our office and said he was an eyewitness to the McDuffy accident, and he even had a video of it. I thought for sure he would be on the stand today."

"Do you know his name and phone number?"

"I've got it at the office, you want it?"

"You bet I do! I'll even drive you there to get it right now."

"Oh, that's ok Jack, I was just leaving anyway, so I'll swing by and get it and give you a call. It was nice meeting you Peggy, take care."

"Nice meeting you too dear, have a nice night."

"Thanks Nance, I'll talk to ya soon," says Jack as he grins from ear to ear, and orders another round of drinks for himself and Peggy.

"Why do you suppose this man wasn't in court today?" asks Peggy.

"Because this video of his probably proves McDuffy's innocence," says Jack as he dials a number on his cell phone.

"Hello?" answers Jeanie as she towel's herself off.

"Hi kiddo, it's Jack."

"Hi. What's up?"

"We've got an eyewitness!"

CHAPTER 38

AUGUST 29TH, 2000, SIX AM. Jeanie's alarm goes off, and she jumps out of bed ready to face the day. The first thing she does is goes to the window. The rain has stopped and the sky is bright blue. The robins are singing their good morning song as she picks up the phone to call Jack. After a few rings, Jack picks up.

"Good morning counselor."

"I hate caller id," says Jeanie, "good morning! Did you get a hold of our star witness?"

"He'll be here by seven o'clock. I called Santos last night and informed him of the new evidence, and we have to meet him in chambers at eight o'clock along with Rich. It'll be interesting to see the look on the Judge's face when he discovers this man came to the DA's office over a week ago."

"I hope he nails Rich for concealing evidence."

"He just might. I'll meet you there at eight."

"Ok boss," says Jeanie. "Hey Jack?"

"Ya?"

"Have I ever told you how much I appreciate your help?"

"I'll send you the bill."

Jeanie hangs up and jumps in the shower with the stereo blasting. It seems like every song that is played on the radio this morning is one of her favorites. It's going to be a great day in Great Falls.

Nine o'clock am. Judge Santos enters the courtroom, and the bailiff makes his usual announcement. The video was reviewed in chambers and allowed as evidence. The Judge made it known to the prosecutor that he was not happy about the evidence being ignored. Once everyone settled down, Jeanie called her first witness, John McDuffy. After being sworn in, he bowed his head and murmured a quick prayer before the questioning started.

"Good morning Mr. McDuffy. I know this is going to be hard for you, but please explain to the best of your ability exactly what happened on September 3rd, 1999, beginning at five o'clock that afternoon."

John cleared his throat and began.

"Well, the day had been kind of a busy one because I let my two guys have the day off, so I ran the parts department by myself. When five o'clock came, I was ready to relax. A customer and friend of mine stopped by with a six pack, so I stuck around for about a half hour and had a beer with him."

"How many beers did you drink?"

"Two. Then I rushed home because Brett had called and said he found a puddle of oil under the pickup. That worried me because we needed it to go camping that weekend. Once I got home, I saw that it was only a drop the size of a quarter. So, me and the boys loaded the camper and headed out of town. We stopped for a burger on the way instead of waiting till we set up camp because it was a pretty long drive, and the boys were hungry. I think we finally got out of town about seven."

"Did you and the boys go camping a lot?"

"Every weekend we could. I had just gotten new mountain bikes for the boys, and they were anxious to try them out."

"Go on."

"Well, I remember seeing a semi ahead of me just before we got to Rogers Pass, so I decided to pass him so I didn't have to follow him up the pass. Everything was fine until I got just about to the top, then the truck started bucking."

"Bucking?"

"Ya, it was running out of gas. I reached down to switch the tanks and everything was fine."

"Go on."

"Well, I geared down because I knew the other side of the pass was steep and I didn't want to rely completely on my brakes. Brett had his eyes closed, listening to his CDs, and Ryan was asleep. The next thing I knew as I approached a hairpin curve, there was a little red car in my lane. There was no time to hit the brakes, and my first reaction was to go around it on the left because there was no room on the right. So, I jerked the wheel to the left, and I remember seeing the driver pop her head up and see she was in the wrong lane. She must have tried to get back into the right lane because she hit my trailer and knocked it over the edge of the road. That caused my truck to slide off the edge and roll down the cliff. Everything went blank after that. The only thing I remember is the boys screaming and Bufford yelping."

John stares at the floor as he tries hard to hold back the tears. Jeanie swallows hard and continues.

"Do you think you could have avoided the accident by going around the car on the right instead of the left?"

"There wasn't enough room. She was completely in my lane and there wasn't any shoulder to speak of. I would have hit her head on."

"So, do you think you made the right decision?"

"If she wouldn't have hit my trailer, I think I could have made it back into the right lane before another car came, because if I remember right, there weren't any cars right behind her."

"No further questions your Honor."

Jeanie takes her seat and Rich approaches the witness stand. John glares at him as he clears his throat and begins.

"Do you have a beer with the boys after work often Mr. McDuffy?"

"Not really."

"Really? Then how do you explain the fact that you've been seen many times at Dewey's Bar and Grill after five o'clock?"

"I have a lot of friends that go there. I stop by now and then to shoot the breeze, but not during the summer when I have…" John stops and swallows hard, "had the boys."

"Wasn't that your father's hangout too?"

"OBJECTION!" shouts Jeanie. "The defendant's father is not on trial here!"

"Your Honor, it's a known fact that Mr. McDuffy's father was a heavy drinker, and many studies have shown that children of alcoholics often turn out to be alcoholics themselves."

"Overruled. The defendant will answer the question."

"My father used to go there when he was alive, yes. In fact, that's where he caught Judge Murphy engaging in oral sex with a couple of young girls."

Much laughter arises from the courtroom and Judge Santos smacks his gabble and yells, "ORDER! I suggest you keep your comments to yourself about my colleagues Mr. McDuffy if you don't want to add to the charges."

"Sorry your Honor."

"How many beers total did you have on the day of the accident?"

"Three. Two at work and one at the rest area on the way."

"Three beers total. Then how do you explain all the empty cans at the scene of the accident?"

"I collect aluminum cans. I throw them in the back of my truck until I have enough for a full bag, then I bag them up. Some of those cans were probably about a month old."

"So, you admit to those beer cans belonged to you."

"Sure, there's nothing wrong with collecting aluminum."

"When you allegedly saw Miss Wadder's car in your lane, you claim there wasn't time to hit the brakes. How do you explain the fact that Mr. Haskell found time to hit his breaks?"

"I don't know."

"Isn't it true that your reactions weren't quick enough to react properly due to the alcohol in your blood?"

"No! I just made…"

"Isn't it true that if you had honked your horn and hit the breaks that Miss Wadder would have realized she was in the wrong lane and corrected?"

"My horn didn't work."

Jeanie puts her face in her hands and Jack rubs his forehead.

"Your horn didn't work? Are you saying, Mr. McDuffy, that you chanced a trip on a treacherous road with your children with faulty equipment?"

John doesn't answer right away. He pauses, then looks over at the jury and says, "I was gonna get it fixed."

"No further questions your honor."

Judge Santos looks at Jeanie and she shakes her head.

"The witness may step down," he announces.

The next several witnesses Jeanie calls are John's neighbors, friends, and coworkers. Everyone confirms the fact that he was a good father and a good man, not a drunk. She saves her star witness for last, who she calls to the stand right after lunch break.

"Your Honor, I would now like to call Ian Stewart to the stand."

Ian Stewart is a professor from the University of Montana. He teaches in the fine arts department, mostly photography. He is originally from Scotland, but has lived in the United States most of his life. He spends a lot of his time traveling and taking pictures and videos of wildlife. After being sworn in, he has a seat while Jeanie approaches him.

"Good afternoon Mr. Stewart," starts Jeanie.

"Good afternoon."

"Mr. Stewart, would you please explain to the court where you were on the evening of September 3rd, 1999?"

"Certainly. I was near the Continental Divide trail on the south side of Rogers Pass shooting a video of a bald eagle I'd been following."

The members of the jury murmur amongst themselves and Judge Santos is forced to ask for order in the courtroom.

"Isn't it true, Mr. Stewart, that in this video you captured, not only did you film the flight of a bald eagle, but also the vehicle accident between Mr. McDuffy and Miss Wadder?"

"This is true."

The jury is really getting restless now as Jeanie walks to the evidence table and picks up the videocassette and plugs it into the monitor placed in front of the jury.

"Ladies and gentlemen of the jury. You are about to witness inconclusive evidence proving my client's innocence. This video shows Amy Wadder's car jerking from one lane to the other as it climbs up the south side of Rogers Pass. Not only this, but if you look closely, you will see a road sign. This is the yellow sharp left curve sign that is located just before the hairpin curve where the accident took place. Notice the position of Miss Wadder's car at this point."

Jeanie runs the video and the jury watches with intense interest. Afterwards, she addresses the witness again.

"Mr. Stewart, what did you do after you witnessed the accident?"

"Well, my first thought was to run down the cliff and see if I could help because I heard a lot of crashing, but it was a sheer drop off in front of me, and I would have had to go south about a mile, and then down to the road. I watched for a while and I saw several cars stop, so I didn't think I was needed."

"Why didn't you report to the authorities later that you were witness to an accident?"

"I didn't think it mattered that much since there were several other people on the scene. Besides, I was leaving the following Tuesday for Scotland for six months to visit my homeland, and I didn't want my trip canceled because of a subpoena to appear in court. Had I'd known it was such a terrible accident and I was the only witness, I certainly would have stayed to testify." Ian looks directly at John and says, "I'm sorry Mr. McDuffy, I didn't know."

CHAPTER 39

THE COURTROOM BUZZES WITH CHATTER, and Judge Santos is once again forced to use his gabble.

"I have no further questions your Honor," announces Jeanie as she takes her seat.

The Judge looks at Rich and he shakes his head.

"The witness may step down. Does the defense have any more witnesses?"

"No, your Honor," says Jeanie.

"Has the prosecution prepared a closing statement?"

"Yes, your Honor," exclaims Rich.

As he stands to address the jury, he checks his tie one more time.

"Ladies and gentlemen of the jury. Three young people have died in a terrible accident, and one man has survived, a man who has admitted to this court to drinking prior to AND during the journey. A man who felt it was ok to put his young children in an unsafe vehicle with him after he had been drinking, and drive on a treacherous mountain road. You need to make an example of this man, ladies and gentlemen, an example to the good citizens of Great Falls that we will not tolerate drinking and driving, an example to citizens everywhere. I implore you to do the right thing and deliver to this court a verdict of guilty...of all charges."

Rich goes on for another fifteen minutes reminding the jury of the beer cans in the back of John's truck, the faulty horn, and the poor decision to pass Amy on the left instead of hitting the brakes and slamming into the rocks on the right. The jury listens patiently and give a sigh of relief when he is finished, after which Jeanie takes the floor.

"Ladies and gentlemen, Mr. Collingsworth is right. You need to make an example of this case, an example to the world that we the people will not stand for injustice. The evidence is crystal clear. John McDuffy's blood/alcohol level was well under the legal limit, and the video proves who caused the accident. John McDuffy has spent the last year in hell. Not only has he lost his two little boys AND his dear mother, but he's spent a year in jail awaiting trial, arrested for a crime he didn't commit. Ladies and gentlemen, Mr. McDuffy has been waiting a long time for this day. For the past year, he has devoted his life to helping people, people that were on a collision course with trouble. You've heard testimonies from fellow prisoners and guards alike, and they have told you what an inspiration John McDuffy has been to them.

You've also heard testimonies from friends and neighbors on what a good father he was to his boys, whom he will never see again thanks to an irresponsible driver." Jeanie pauses for a moment, then walks up close to the jury box, and softly says, "It's time to let him go home. He has suffered enough. I'm confident that you will return with the right decision, a verdict of not guilty. Thank you, and God bless you for making the right decision."

Jeanie takes her seat and holds John's hand as the Judge asks the prosecution for a rebuttal. Rich denies the opportunity, and Judge Santos reminds the jury of their duties as he dismisses them to deliberation, after which he dismisses the rest of the court to be reconvened upon the arrival of the verdict. John and Jeanie look into each other's eyes as they clasp their hands together.

"Pray with me?" says John.

The two of them bow their heads to pray as the bailiff stands patiently waiting to take John to the holding cell. After a few moments, they stand and hug.

"Don't worry Johnny," whispers Jeanie, "it'll be ok."

"I hope so," answers John.

As the bailiff escorts John out of the room, Jack puts his arm around Jeanie and says, "Nice job counselor. I've got a good feeling about this one."

"Thanks boss. I hope you're right."

"C'mon, I'll buy you a cup of coffee."

It's three o'clock when Jack and Jeanie reach the courthouse cafeteria. Ian Stewart joins them for coffee, along with Peggy. At four o'clock, the bailiff enters the cafeteria to inform them the jury has reached a decision. Jack smiles at Jeanie because he feels confident that a short deliberation means the right decision was made. As they enter the courtroom, John is escorted in and placed at the table next to Jeanie and Jack. He has a worried look on his face.

"Shouldn't it have taken longer than that?" he asks.

"Not necessarily," replies Jeanie as she grabs his hand and squeezes.

Everyone stands as the bailiff announces the arrival of Judge Santos.

"Please be seated," he announces. "Bailiff, you may bring in the jury."

As the jury enters the room, John begins to shake and sweat. The moment of truth has come. The past year is flashing before his eyes as he watches the jury shuffle into the room, one by one. He turns to look around the courtroom. Laura's eyes meet his and she smiles. John smiles back and shifts his eyes to Ron and Kathy Wadder. They are both staring directly at the jury, awaiting their decision. As his eyes continue to move around the room, he notices Billy and Bubba smiling and he returns the smile.

"Has the jury reached a decision?" asks Judge Santos.

"Yes, we have, your Honor," answers the foreman.

"The defendant will rise and face the bench."

Jack and Jeanie stand and help John to his feet. John is shaking and can barely stand. Jack holds tightly to his arm as the foreman hands the verdict to the Judge. Judge Santos stares at the paper for an eternity before handing it back to the bailiff. Jeanie squeezes John's hand hard as the foreman reads the verdict.

"We the jury find the defendant, John McDuffy, NOT GUILTY on all charges!"

John's knees give out, and he drops to his chair. Jeanie bends down to hug his neck as the courtroom bursts with cheers and laughter. Everyone in the room is cheering except for Ron and Kathy Wadder, who are pushing and shoving their way out the door. Jack joins John and Jeanie in a group hug as Judge Santos beats away with his gabble.

"Quiet!" he yells. "Order, order in the courtroom!"

Finally, after a few moments, everyone settles down and John rises back to his feet with Jeanie holding tightly to his arm. They smile as tears run down their cheeks, awaiting the Judges final announcement.

"John McDuffy, you have been found not guilty by a jury of your peers. All charges are hereby dropped. You are free to go."

Cheers once again fill the courtroom, and Jeanie throws her arms around John's neck and says, "Welcome home Johnny!"

The bailiff comes up to John and removes his hand-cuffs, and the first thing he does is put his arms around Jeanie, picks her up, and squeezes her tight. Next, he turns to give Jack a big hug, then Peggy, then Bubba, then Billy, then Bob, then Kevin, then Chuck, then he turned to find Laura waiting in line to congratulate him. She smiled as he reached out to hold her.

"Can you ever forgive me?" he whispers.

"It wasn't your fault Johnny," whispers Laura, "that was proven today. You have to stop blaming yourself and get on with your life now, that's an order!"

"Ok boss."

Laura leaves and the courtroom slowly starts to clear out.

Jeanie says, "C'mon Johnny, I'll give you a ride up to the jail to get your belongings."

"Whatever you say counselor."

John and Jeanie leave the courthouse, and the first thing John does is roll in the grass. Jeanie laughs as she watches this grown man rolling around like a child on recess.

"You better not get grass stains on my car seats," she yells.

John stops and looks at her standing over him with her hands on her hips. He slowly gets to his feet and creeps toward her like a stalking lion.

"Don't even think about it," she says as she backs up.

Suddenly, he leaps toward her and picks her up and gently lowers her to the grass. She tries to fight him as he plucks grass from the ground and puts it in her hair. Jack and Peggy watch from a courthouse window at these two kids and laugh. John finally lets her up and brushes the grass from her hair as they walk to her car. Once inside, he goes right for the radio. After scrolling through station after station, Sharp Dressed Man by ZZ Top comes on. John cranks it up and the two of them jam as they drive to the jail. John sticks his head out the window like a dog and lets the air flow through his long black hair. Jeanie looks over at him and smiles. She has never seen anyone so happy before. Once they arrive at the jail, the news of his freedom has preceded them, and the guards have a going away cake ready for him. Everyone cheers as they enter the jail, guards and prisoners alike. John takes his time to say goodbye to everyone while Jeanie takes care of the paperwork. After changing his clothes, they wave goodbye and head for home.

"I can't believe I'm actually going home," says John.

"Believe it. We'll be there in about ten minutes."

"Has Bob been watering the grass? Who's been paying the bills?"

"I've taken care of that for you. I've been using the money in the escrow account from the sale of your mom's house."

"Oh ya, I forgot," says John as the smile disappears from his face.

Jeanie sees the troubled look and reaches over to take his hand.

"It's going to be hard starting over John, but I want you to know I'll be right by your side if you need me."

"Thanks sweetie, I appreciate that. Have I even thanked you for setting me free yet?"

"No, but don't worry, you'll have plenty of time for that tomorrow night."

"What's up with tomorrow night?"

"I'm taking you out to dinner with Jack and Peggy."

"Cool! Where?"

"Geno's."

"PIZZAAAAAA!" yells John as he stomps his feet like a teenager.

"Calm down boy," laughs Jeanie. "We're here."

After pulling into John's driveway, they sit and stare at the house.

"Do you want me to come in?" asks Jeanie.

"No, I'll be fine. You go on home and I'll talk to you tomorrow."

He reaches over and gives her a peck on the cheek before getting out of the car. She waits till he's inside before leaving. Once inside, the first thing he notices is his answering machine blinking. Memories of the day he was arrested come haunting back. He decides not to listen to the message just yet. Instead, he walks around the house surveying it for damage. The next thing he sees is photos on the bedroom wall. He stands and stares at the ones of Brett and Ryan.

CHAPTER 40

‗⸺⸻⸺‗

'ELEVEN MONTHS AND TWENTY-SIX DAYS ago, we were packing the camper for a fun weekend,' John thinks as he stares at the photos of Brett and Ryan. He takes the photos off the wall and sits on the bed, holding them in his lap. "I miss you guys," he whispers quietly.

"Mail call," comes a voice from the front door. Bob has walked across the street with a sack of mail and dropped it on John's living room floor.

"Good grief," says John, "that's all mine?"

"Yep, mostly junk mail. I gave everything that looked like a bill to Jeanie. Welcome home big guy!"

"Gee, thanks. It's gonna take me hours to sort through all this."

"Well, I know what you're doing tonight. By the way, I've been watering your lawn for ya. I hope that's ok."

"I see that Bob. Thank you. I put a lot of time into that lawn."

"No problem. Well, I'm sure you've got a lot to do, so I'll talk to ya later Johnny. Take care, and keep in touch."

"I will! Thanks for everything Bob!"

John sorts through his mail, and Bob was right, it's mostly junk mail. One letter did stand out though. It resembled the writing of a third grader and there was no return address. It was postmarked from Missoula. Inside was one piece of notebook paper with the words 'DIE DRUNK' scribbled in what looked like crayon.

'What a moron,' thinks John. 'I'm glad I don't have to worry about that psycho anymore.'

After checking the rest of the mail, he decides to listen to the answering machine. It was maxed out at twenty messages, and all of them were soliciting calls. After letting out a sigh of relief, he continues his survey of the house for any damage from winter. Once satisfied the place is secure, he moves out to the garage to greet Chelly.

"Hi beautiful," he says as he enters the garage and opens the big door.

He climbs in and pumps the throttle a couple of times and turns the key. She starts just like a dream. While she idles, he gathers up the things he needs to wash her, and then goes in the house to put on his shorts. The afternoon sun is warm, a perfect night for a car wash. Before leaving the house, he cranks up the stereo and opens the doors and windows so he can hear it outside, then he backs Chelly out for her bath, chirping the tires in the process. Just as he turns the engine off, he hears the phone ring inside. He runs in the house and gets to it just before the answering machine does.

"Hello?"

"Hi! It's me," says Jeanie.

"Hi! What are you doing?"

"Well, I was just about to make dinner and it hit me, you don't have any food in the house, do you?"

"Well, no."

"Are you hungry?"

"Ya, kinda."

"Whatcha hungry for?"

"A Whopper and fries!"

Jeanie laughs, "Comin right up. I'll be there in a few."

She hangs up the phone and grabs her purse. She paused and thinks, 'I better change my clothes,' so she puts on a pair of tight shorts and a tank top. After looking in the mirror, she decides her hair could use a comb also. After further surveying, maybe some eye shadow too, and some rouge, and some perfume. After the makeover is finished, she stands in front of the mirror and rubs the cheek that John kissed. A smile comes to her lips as she pictures him rolling around in the grass. She shakes her head and snaps out of her daydream and heads out the door to Burger King.

John has just about finished Chelly's bath when Jeanie pulls up. He is wearing nothing but shorts. As he wipes off the last of the water from the hood, Jeanie looks at him, sweat shimmering in the sun and thinks, 'oh my God.' She feels a slight itch between her legs and her lips become moist as she watches his muscles flex.

"Chow time," she hollers as she gets out of her car.

John looks up and replies, "Cool, I'm starved."

"I hope you like chocolate shakes."

"They're my favorite, how'd ya know?"

"Lucky guess," says Jeanie as they sit on the lawn to enjoy their food.

"You look nice," says John, "I've never seen you in anything but business clothes before."

"Thanks, so do you."

"I'm not wearing anything," smiles John.

Jeanie blushes, "I know."

John devours his Whopper as Jeanie nibbles on her food and watches this over grown kid smacking his lips and licking his fingers.

"John?"

"Ya?"

"Can you teach me how to do tai chi?"

"Sure! If I can teach Scott Lewison, I can teach anyone," laughs John. "C'mon, we'll start now," he says as he stands and helps Jeanie to her feet.

They walk to the center of the lawn and stand, facing the street.

"The first step is to distribute your weight evenly on both feet and relax. Let your mind be free of all thought. Close your eyes and imagine you are standing in a field of wild flowers on the top of a mountain, and you haven't a care in the world. The temperature is just right, and the sky is bright blue. The birds are singing and the bumblebees are buzzing from flower to flower. Are you there yet?"

"Yes, I'm there," replies Jeanie as she stands next to John with her eye's closed, smiling.

"Now, lift your arms up over your head, evenly and slowly as you take in a deep breath. Then, let your arms down slowly as you exhale."

Jeanie follows his instructions and repeats the exercise several times.

"Do you feel relaxed?"

"Yes, I do. That's amazing."

"We haven't even started the exercise yet. It will feel awkward at first, but after you have the moves down, it will come naturally."

"I'm ready to start."

"Ok, just watch me at first as I go through the moves, then it will be your turn so take notes."

"Ok boss."

John glides through the motions with grace and beauty as Jeanie watches and smiles. She wonders how such a big, powerful man can move so gracefully. Once he finishes, he informs her that it's her turn.

The two of them stand and face the street and begin moving in unison. Jeanie struggles a bit, but catches on after a while, and John compliments her on her progress.

As cars go by on the street, they slow down to view the spectacle. Teenagers laugh at them because they don't understand what these two people are doing. They just assume some pretty good drugs are involved.

After about an hour, Jeanie announces she's tired.

"Ok," replies John, "that's enough for the first lesson. You did very well, I'm proud of you!"

"Thanks! Boy, I can feel it already. I bet I'm going to be sore in the morning."

"If you are, just do some stretches. That'll help."

"Ok boss. Do you have any soap left in the bucket?"

"Ya, why?"

"Well, I just thought you could pay me back for dinner by helping me wash my car."

"Sure, I'll put Chelly back in the garage."

"Chelly?"

"Ya, that's her name, short for Chevelle."

"Men and their cars!"

John laughs as he puts Chelly back in the garage. For the next hour, they wash Jeanie's car, and themselves in the process. John pays close attention to every detail as he cleans the interior. Jeanie towels down the outside and waits for John's approval. After he inspects it and touches up a few spots they missed, he gives it his final approval, and they empty the bucket and put everything away as it is starting to get dark.

"Can you come in for a while?" asks John.

"Ok," answers Jeanie.

They go inside and John closes the windows, shuts doors, and turns down the stereo. The house is pretty, hot so he turns on the central air conditioning.

"I'd offer you something to drink, but I don't have anything," says John.

"That's ok, I'm fine," replies Jeanie as she sits on the couch.

John goes into the bedroom and puts on a t-shirt and has a seat next to her.

"This is nice John, I love the way you've decorated it."

"Well, I had some help from mom in that department."

"I thought I sensed a woman's touch. Speaking of Kathleen, I need you to come by the office one of these days so we can get started on all the paperwork. There's a ton of it, and it's going to take a while, so why don't we wait till you're all settled in."

"That's ok by me, I hate paperwork. Ed is always try- ing to bury me in it. Speaking of Ed, I guess I better get over there tomorrow and see if I still have a job. Do you know that prick never came to visit me once?"

"Really?"

"Ya. Kevin and Chuck did, but never a sign of Ed. But that's ok, I can't stand that asshole anyway."

"So, why did you stay there all those years?"

"Well, he did pay me well, I'll admit that, and the thought of starting over with a new company really didn't appeal to me. Besides, I would lose all my vacation pay, health insurance, and everything else for at least a year, and Laura would have thrown a fit if I didn't have insurance coverage for the boys."

"You had to supply the insurance?"

"Of course, they couldn't afford it."

"Oh, I see."

"But I don't have to worry about that now," says John as he stares at the floor. A cold silence is in the air as a soft song comes on the stereo. Jeanie reaches over and pulls John to her and holds his head to her chest and strokes his long black hair. He slips his arms around her waist and holds her tight as she rocks him back and forth. Thoughts of Brett and Ryan enter his mind and tears fill his eyes.

Jeanie whispers, "Shhh…It'll be ok Johnny. It just takes time."

She rocks him until almost eleven o'clock when he finally sits up and pulls himself together.

"I have to get going Johnny, are you going to be ok?'

"Ya, I'll be fine. I'm sure you have to get up pretty early."

They stand and walk out to Jeanie's car. John puts his hands around her waist and pulls her close as she puts her hands on his chest.

"I don't know if I could have survived this past year without you," says John as he rubs his hands up and down her back.

Jeanie just smiles a sweet smile and wraps her arms around his neck. John hugs her tight for a moment, then moves her back and cups her tiny face in his hands as he bends down to kiss her. He hasn't kissed a woman in a long time, so he feels a little awkward. At first, he brushes her lips lightly with his to see what her reaction would be. He opened his eyes to see her smiling up at him, so he closed his eyes again and kissed her with meaning this time. He moved his arms back around her waist and pressed himself hard against her body as they kissed passionately for what seemed like a lifetime.

When the finally decided to take a breath, Jeanie whispered, "I've been dreaming about that kiss for a long time."

"Me too!" answered John as he moved his hands up and down her back, drifting lower and lower on each down stroke.

They hold each other in the moonlight for a few more moments, when Jeanie finally says, "I better go before I decide to stay."

After one more passionate kiss, she gets in her car and drives away. All the way home she smiles and thinks about the kiss, as does John too while he stands in the shower and dreams of her standing in front of him.

CHAPTER 41

—∞∞∞—

AUGUST 30TH, 2000. IT'S EIGHT am, and John feels like he has a hangover. Thoughts of Jeanie kept him occupied all night. His sheets are on the floor and the pillows look like they've been through sixteen rounds. The smell of her perfume is still in the air, and he really doesn't want to get out of bed, but there are things he needs to do today. After all, it's the first day of his new life, and there is much freedom to be had out there. After taking in a sizable dose of perfume from the sofa pillow where Jeanie was sitting, he stumbles to the shower for another hot dream. Thoughts of her full breasts and long auburn hair fill his mind as he washes off the nights sweat. Just as he steps out of the shower, he hears the phone ringing.

"Hello?"

"Good morning!" says Jeanie.

"Hey you! Whatcha doin?"

"Working. What are you doin?"

"Just got up! I had kind of a rough night."

"Why?" asks Jeanie with a worried tone in her voice.

She hopes he wasn't having nightmares about the accident.

"Well I couldn't sleep cause a certain little redhead kept popping into my head and squirting me with the hose."

"Hey, you squirted me first!" laughs Jeanie.

"I know," laughs John. "So, how did you feel this morning?"

"Like I had a hangover, but I don't know why, I didn't drink a thing."

"Me too! Must have been the Whopper."

"Ya, I suppose. Anyway, the reason I called is I wanted to tell you we're picking you up at about six o'clock, is that ok?"

"Sure, that sounds fine. What should I wear?"

"Nothing. I…mean, nothing special," stutters Jeanie. "I'm just going to wear jeans."

"Ok, I think I can find some jeans too. I'll see you at six. Bye sweetie."

"Bye, bye."

Jeanie hangs up the phone and sits, daydreaming for a while before getting back to work. John puts the phone down and glances in the mirror on the wall above the bed. Jeanie has obviously aroused him as he notices his bath towel protruding about eight inches more than it should. He smiles and adjusts himself as he walks to the living room to crank up the stereo. So many little things in his life he took for granted like hot showers without an audience, and being able to listen to the stereo anytime he wants. After getting dressed, he steps out into the back yard, and the first thing he sees is Bufford's doghouse and dish. He's forgotten all about his faithful yellow lab. Sadness overcomes him as he remembers the wrestling matches that he, the dog, and the boys used to get in to. He can hear the boys giggling and Bufford growling as he pulls on their pant legs. After a few moments, he snaps out of it and heads to the garage to greet Chelly. The day is a beautiful one, a great day for a drive. First on the list is R&R Equipment. Butterflies of anticipation flutter around in his stomach as he drives to R&R. Chelly is running good, she seems to be happy to get out of that garage. The temptation to jump on the throttle is almost too great, but he knows he needs to behave himself for a while, a speeding ticket would not be a good thing to receive. As he pulls into the parking lot of R&R equipment, he sees Kevin loading some parts into a customer's pickup, and the temptation becomes too great. He drops Chelly into second gear and smokes the tires. Kevin looks up and smiles, as he would recognize the sound of Chelly's 454 anywhere.

He yells inside, "John's back," and waits patiently for him to park and come inside.

"It's about time," hollers Kevin. "Your late!"

"Ya, about a year late," replies John.

"Good to have ya back buddy. I see Chelly's runnin good."

"Yes, she is. If she had a tail, I think she'd be wagging it. Is Ed in?"

"Ya, he's in his office."

When John walks in, the first thing he sees is a new face behind the counter as he talks on the phone.

"That's the new guy Jason," says Kevin. "Chuck hired him last March."

"How's he working out?"

"Real good. We stole him from the John Deer boys. He was with them for about a year."

As John walks toward the warehouse, he notices Chuck in the parts manager's office with his feet on the desk and talking on the phone.

"Looks like the position has kinda gone to his head," says John.

"Big time," says Kevin, "I'm glad you're back. Maybe now things will get back to normal and Chuck will get off his ass and do something."

John notices his personal things piled up in the warehouse as he makes his way to Ed's office. Ed is on the phone and smiles as he motions for John to come in and have a seat. Memories of a year ago drift into John's head as he thinks about the last time he sat in the hot seat.

"Johnny my boy," says Ed as he hangs up the phone, "congratulations on your acquittal."

"Thanks. How have ya been Ed?"

"Oh, I've been just fine. Question is, how have you been? I suppose it was pretty rough in there huh?"

"Well, I can think of better places to spend a year of my life. But I'm out now, and I just have to put it all behind me somehow."

"Johnny, I'm so sorry about your boys and your mom. When I heard about the accident, I was just sick. Then when I heard about your mom, I thought to myself, how much pain does one man have to suffer? No one deserves to go through that much sorrow."

"I appreciate that Ed. I'll get through it somehow. I just need to get my life back again and put this behind me," says John, hinting around about his job.

"Well, you're right John. When life knocks you down, you just have to get back in there and fight. Don't let the bad times get the better of ya."

John can see that he's going to have to come right out and ask.

"Well, speaking of getting back in the fight, do I still have a job here Ed?"

John looks Ed right in the eye, and Ed leans back and rubs his forehead and doesn't answer right away. John can tell the answer isn't going to be good.

"Well, John," Ed pauses, "we've got a full crew back there now, and business hasn't been all that good this year."

"Here it comes," thinks John.

"I just don't think we have room for one more man in the part's department. I might be able to put you on in the warehouse."

"Why can't you let the new guy go and put things back the way they were, with me running the show? I hear Chuck spends most of his time sitting on his ass, and by the looks of the weight he's gained, I'm inclined to believe it."

"Chuck's doing a fine job as parts manager," scowls Ed.

"I thought you just said business was bad this year?"

"Well, yes, but it wasn't Chuck's fault. I think customers are just afraid to spend any money right now."

"Funny, that's what I said a year ago and you thought I was full of shit. Now all of a sudden it's true?"

"A year ago it WAS bullshit John! You had some problems in the parts department, but now the problems seem to have gone away."

"Don't you mean the 'problem' has gone away Ed?"

"Whatever! Chuck is the parts manager and that's not going to change. Like I said, I might be able to put you in the warehouse for minimum wage until things get hopping again."

John stands up and kick's the chair back.

"You know what you can do with your warehouse position Ed?!"

John storms out of Ed's office and walks to the part's department to gather his personal belongings. As he enters the parts manager's office and shakes Chucks hand, he hears Ed's voice on the intercom.

"Chuck, John is on his way back there to clear out his things. Make sure he doesn't take anything that belongs to the company."

John and Chuck just smile at each other.

Chuck answers, "Ok Ed."

"Good luck Chuckie boy, you're gonna need it."

"Where are you going?" asks Kevin.

"Apparently, there isn't room for one more guy. I'm outta here. You guys take care."

Chuck and Kevin both look at John with puzzled faces as he turns to leave. Kevin walks to the window to watch him burn rubber all the way out of the parking lot. John feels both angry and relieved. He thinks about how many times the competitor has tried to get him to go to work for them, and how he always turned them down, his loyalty staying with R&R.

'Up yours Ed,' he thinks as he grabs third on the way out of the parking lot, 'I'm gonna run you into the ground!'

Next stop, the police impound.

As John nears the impound, he can see Ol' Green behind the fence, and his stomach ties up in knots. After signing the papers inside, he walks out with the attendant to have a look at the damage. The closer he gets, the more anxiety he feels. There isn't much salvageable from Ol' Green or the trailer, except for maybe the drive train. He walks up to the cab and peers in through the roof where the rescue crew cut into it, and the first thing he sees are bloodstains on the seats. He turns around right then and there and informs the attendant that he'll be having a wrecker haul it to the dump along with the trailer. Seeing the boys blood on the seat was just too much. The attendant nods and shows him out.

After stopping at Wendy's for lunch, John decides to pay the John Deer dealership a visit. The second he walks in the door the branch manager welcomes him with open arms and takes him right into his office. After about fifteen minutes, John emerges shaking hands with his new boss. Feeling a little better, he decides to go grocery shopping. Two hundred dollars later, he returns home. With the cupboards and the refrigerator and his belly full, it's time to take a nap. He hasn't had a day this busy and stressful in quite some time. He sleeps until five o'clock when the phone rings. It's Jeanie.

CHAPTER 42

---∞∞∞---

JOHN KNOCKS THE PHONE TO the floor, then reaches to pick it up.

"Hello?"

"Hi," says Jeanie, "what were you doing, sleeping?"

"Ya, I laid down to take a short nap about three hours ago."

"Wow, you must have had a rough night. Well, you better jump in the shower because we'll be there in about an hour."

"Yes counselor."

"And quit that 'counselor' crap, I like sweetie better."

"Yes dear," laughs John, "I'll be ready."

"That's better, bye."

John rushes around the house getting ready, with so many thoughts going through his head. What if he doesn't get along with the guys at John Deer? What if they don't get along with him? He hasn't started a new job in over fifteen years, what if things just don't work out? Who's going to hire a man who's pushing forty? The feeling reminds him of when he started at R&R Equipment, the anxiety and anticipation was the same then, as he was determined to do well. Thoughts of the blood-stained seats in Ol' Green invade his mind and try to bring him down, but after looking at the picture of Jesus on his kitchen wall, he feels a little better knowing the boys are in safe hands.

"Hey!" comes a voice from the living room.

John looks at the clock, six o'clock sharp.

"Hi," says John, "boy, you're prompt."

"Prompt is my middle name," says Jeanie as she throws her arms around John's neck.

Today's kiss doesn't include any hesitation at all. John picks her up and they join lips in a full, wet French kiss.

"I've been thinking about you all day," says Jeanie.

"Likewise," says John as he squeezes her tight.

"Are ya ready Freddy?"

"Yep, let's go!"

Jack and Peggy are waiting in the Beamer. Peggy stands to let the two lovebirds in the back seat. John's knees are up to his chin as he tries to get comfortable.

"Damn foreign cars," he says.

"Hey, don't knock the Limo service," barks Jack. "So, how was your first day out?"

"Interesting to say the least," says John, "I lost a job and gained a job all in one day."

"You mean they wouldn't hire you back?" asks Jeanie.

"Nope. But, that's ok though. I hated that son-of-a-bitch Ed. He's been trying to get rid of me for a long time, now he's got his wish."

"How has he been trying to get rid of you?" asks Peggy.

"Oh, he's always blamed poor business on the parts department, claiming we never stocked the parts the customers need, but the truth is the parts department was the only thing that kept that business alive, and what the customers were really complaining about is the fact that the equipment Ed sold them was always breaking down."

"So where are you going to work now?" asks Jack.

"John Deer," replies John, "they've been bugging me for years to work for them, hired me at the same pay and benefits I was getting at Cat."

"Good, because you're going to need all the money you can get your hands on to when you see my bill," spouts Jeanie.

"GREAT! So, I guess I'm still in prison except this time the warden is a redhead, huh?" jeers John as he puts his arm around Jeanie.

The two couples laugh as they drive to the restaurant. Jack smiles and Peggy beams as they watch the two lovebirds in the back seat snuggled closely to each other. The evening is a pleasant one with the temperature in the mid-eighties. When they arrive at the restaurant, they are pleased to see there is plenty of vacancy and the pool table in the bar is un-occupied. Jack immediately puts two quarters in the slot and more on the green neatly tucked under the side rail. The rest of the crew seat themselves at the closest table.

"PIZZA!" exclaims John. "I know what I want."

Jeanie laughs, "You act like you haven't eaten in a year."

"I haven't eaten anything decent in a year. The food in there tastes like cardboard."

"Well," says Jack, "I'm sure you'll like the pizza here. Even the dough is hand made."

"Cool!"

"Do you play pool John?"

"A little. Laura and I used to go out a lot when we were dating. I, being the big spender that I am, would always take her to the bar where my buddies hung out. That way if she got on my nerves I would have someone to talk to."

"No wonder she divorced yur ass," smirks Peggy as she turns to Jeanie. "If he ever does that to you sweetie you just find the biggest, best lookin stud in the place, and snuggle up to him. That'll get things fired up!"

"Sounds like a good idea," smiles Jeanie as she throws John a wink.

"Oh, that's all he needs," spouts Jack, "to get busted for bar fighting."

"Don't worry Jack," says John, "I'm a lover, not a fighter."

"OOOOO BABY," shouts Peggy, "girl you better get him home now before he loses interest!"

Jeanie blushes with no response as the waitress approaches. It's her friend Lisa.

"Jeanie?" smiles Lisa. "Oh my God, you're back."

"Hiiiii," says Jeanie as she stands and hugs Lisa, "how have ya been?"

"I'm great! You're looking good," says Lisa, keeping her eyes on John the whole time.

"You remember my boss and his wife, don't you?"

"Sure, they were with you the last time you were here in the winter, weren't they?" answers Lisa as she says hi to Jack and Peggy, keeping one eye on John.

"And this is John," says Jeanie as she sits next to him and curls her arms around his.

"Hi," smiles John, "nice to meet you."

"Hi," beams Lisa. "Dang Jeanie, where ya been hiding this one?"

"In jail," answers Jeanie.

Lisa's mouth drops, speechless.

Jeanie joins Jack, Peggy and John in laughter as she explains, "John has been in jail for the past year on a phony charge awaiting trial. You probably read about it in the paper. The trial was Monday and Tuesday, and he was acquitted."

"John McDuffy?" asks Lisa as her coy smile merges into a serious inquiry.

"In the flesh," smiles John.

"Oh, yes, I did read about it. Well, what can I get you guys?" she inquires as her focus moves to her order pad, her disapproval obvious.

Jack orders a pitcher of beer for him and Peggy, Jeanie orders wine, and John a diet coke.

"Do you need menus?" asks Lisa in a somber voice.

"Yes please," says John.

"I'll be right back," says Lisa as she turns to walk back to the bar.

Jeanie is stunned by her sudden coldness.

"I wonder what the hell her problem is?" she asks.

"You two are going to have to get used to that," answers Jack. "Even though you were acquitted, some narrow-minded people will still frown down upon you John because you spent some time in jail. It's just a cold hard fact of human nature. Try to ignore it."

"Well, I'm not going to ignore it!" snaps Jeanie as she stands to walk over to the bar and confront her friend.

John tries to stop her, but she pulls her arm away from his hand and storms over to Lisa.

"What the hell was that all about?" asks Jeanie, sharply but quietly.

"What was what all about?" reply's Lisa innocently.

"You know damn well what! As soon as you found out who John was, iceberg city! What's the matter? Don't you approve?"

"What are you doing with an ex-con Jeanie? You're a lawyer for Christ's sake, you can do better than that!"

Jeanie's face glows red as she replies, "He's NOT an ex-con. Can't you read? He was acquitted! Maybe I should explain that to your feeble brain! That's means he's innocent you moron! He has spent the last year in pure hell. Not only has he lost his children, his mother, AND his job, but now he has to put up with ignorant assholes like you while you look down your nose at him! You make me sick!"

Jeanie turns and stomps back to the table, her face still red with anger.

"People like that just piss me off!" she says as she takes her seat next to John.

"Geeze," smiles John, "remind me never to piss you off."

Jeanie doesn't answer as Lisa walks over and slaps the menu's down on the table.

"Well, this proves to be a pleasant dining experience," says Jack as he stands and says, "c'mon John, rack'um up. Straight eight, no slop."

"You got it," reply's John.

Jack and John play pool while Peggy does her best to cool Jeanie off. Lisa eventually pulls Jeanie aside and apologizes. Jeanie accepts her apology, but the anger still remains. She's realizes she's going to have a tough time coping with the ignorance and prejudice of narrow minded people as she dates John, but it's a battle she's willing to fight. Once the food arrives, they all sit down to eat. Jack, Peggy, and Jeanie laugh as they watch John devour the pizza. In between bites they talk about the trial, and this helps take Jeanie's mind off her anger toward Lisa. Jack compliments Jeanie on her performance in the courtroom and informs her she is well on her way to becoming a full partner. Jeanie basks in the glow and orders more drinks from Lisa. Before they know it, the eleven o'clock hour is upon them, and Jeanie announces her weariness as she covers her mouth to hide a yawn. Everyone else agrees accept John. He had a long nap and doesn't have to get up early, so he's ready to party.

Jack laughs and convinces him there will be plenty of other times to party, and reaches for the bill on the table. Jeanie quickly snatches it from under his hand and takes it up to Lisa, along with her credit card. Jack tries to argue, but Jeanie wins out. After signing the receipt and leaving a nice tip, the four leave. They drive to John's house first.

"You wanna come in for a while?" John asks of Jeanie. "I can give you a ride home."

"Ok," replies Jeanie.

Jack and Peggy say goodnight, and the two lovebirds enter the house. John turns on the stereo while Jeanie has a seat on the couch.

"Want something to drink?" asks John.

"No thanks," replies Jeanie as she yawns, "I've had enough."

John retrieves a beer from the refrigerator and sits next to her on the couch. After taking a drink from his beer, he sits back and puts his arm around her. She kicks off her shoes and snuggles her head into his chest. They sit there for a moment quietly when John leans down to kiss her and sees her eyes are closed and she's almost asleep.

"Hey sleepy head," he whispers.

Jeanie slowly opens her eyes and gently kisses him until it is rudely interrupted by a yawn.

"My goodness, excuse me," she says, "I can't keep my eyes open."

"I better take you home," says John, "you're tired, and you have to work tomorrow."

"I suppose you're right, I'm sorry."

"Don't be sweetie. Tell you what, dinner is on me tomorrow night. I bought some steaks and corn on the cob and garlic bread. Why don't you come over about six and I'll fire up the barbecue."

"Sounds good to me," reply's Jeanie with another yawn.

John grabs her shoes from under the coffee table and slips one arm under her knees, the other under her waist. As he picks her up, she sighs sleepily as she rests her head on his shoulder. He kisses her gently on the forehead as he walks through the house turning off the stereo and lights, and finally out to the garage where he places her in the passenger seat of Chelly. On the drive to her house, the conversation is light as Jeanie dozes, her head resting on John's shoulder. When they reach her house, he carries her to the door and waits while she fumbles for her keys.

"This is kinda nice," she says, "I can save money on shoes."

John smiles and kisses her as he unlocks the door. Once inside, he puts her down and they stand in the dark and kiss passionately. John moves his hands all over her body, from her bottom to her breasts. Her nipples are hard as he gently caresses them with his fingertips. Her breathing becomes fast and hot as he slips his hands inside her top and unsnaps her bra. She lowers her arms from his shoulders and gently places her hands on his chest.

"You better go," she whispers. "We can pick up where we left off tomorrow night."

"Ok," sighs John, "if I must. Goodnight baby."

They kiss long and hard one more time and John turns to leave. All the way home he thinks about the feel of her breasts and her hot breath. He notices a car has been following him for the several blocks. Three blocks from home, he realizes who is following him when he sees the lights.

Red, blue, red, blue.

CHAPTER 43

—⊷⊶—

"Is there a problem officer?" asks John as the patrol officer shines his flashlight in John's face.

"I was just about to ask you the same question. You were driving fifteen mph in a thirty-five mph zone. Is there a problem?"

"No sir, I guess I just have a lot on my mind."

Next, the officer asks for John's license and registration, and instructs him to sit tight while he calls in. He sits in his patrol car for fifteen minutes with his lights flashing. John hopes that everyone in the neighborhood is asleep and not watching out their windows, as Chelly is pretty well known in town, and everyone knows who owns her.

'Ten years without so much as a parking ticket, and now they pull me over for going too slow!' thinks John as he waits for the officer to get back with his license and registration, 'I wish Jeanie were here.'

Finally, after twenty minutes, the officer approaches his window again.

"Mr. McDuffy, due to the fact that you were driving well under the speed limit, and you have alcohol on your breath, would you object to a breathalyzer test?"

"Breathalyzer test? You gotta be shittin me. I had half a beer."

"Yes sir, does this mean you are refusing the test?"

John agrees to take the test, and, of course, it turns out negative. The officer gives him back his license and registration and sends him on his way. When he gets home, he decides to finish the beer, and a few more with the stereo cranked up to Jethro Tull. At about two am, he goes to bed. Another restless night filled with thoughts of Jeanie.

The next day, he decides to clean the house from top to bottom. After all, it hasn't been cleaned in over a year. Every room gets an overhaul, except the boy's rooms. He still can't muster up the nerve to go in there. After the house is cleaned to his satisfaction, he tackles the yard. Bob has taken pretty good care of the watering and mowing, but the trimming needs some attention, and a coating of fertilizer wouldn't hurt either. Before he knows it, it's five o'clock, time to jump in the shower.

Just before he gets in the shower, the phone rings. It's Jeanie.

"Hello?"

"Hi baby. Whatcha doin?"

"Hi! I was just about to take a shower. I've been cleaning house and working in the yard all day. What're you doin?"

"I'm still at work. I was just wondering if you wanted me to bring anything tonight."

"Just yourself."

"What should I wear?"

"Hmmm," thinks John, "do you have any leather?"

"No," laughs Jeanie, "you're just going to have to settle for cotton."

"Ok, if you say so. See you at six."

"I'll be there. Bye sweetie."

John showers and puts on his best cologne. He decides to wear a tank top and shorts as the temperature is in the nineties. Afterwards, he lights the charcoal in the barbeque and gets the steaks out. Jeanie arrives exactly at six. She's wearing tight, cut-off jeans with all of her tanned legs exposed, and a sheer top with a blue lace bra underneath.

"Hi baby," says John as he picks her up, "boy it's a good thing you weren't with me last night on my way home."

"Why's that?"

"I got pulled over for driving too slow, can you believe that?"

"You're kidding!"

"No! And the worst part is, I had to take a breathalyzer. He thought I was drunk because of how slow I was going, and the fact that I had beer on my breath. Of course, this was after he called in and found out who I was. He made me sit there for twenty minutes with his lights flashing."

"Why were you going so slow?"

"I don't know, I guess I was just preoccupied with a certain little redhead."

Jeanie smiles and kisses him as she compliments him on his cologne.

"Well, you better watch yourself," says Jeanie, "the cops are going to be watching you real close from now on. If you so much as belch, they're going to stick a breathalyzer in your mouth."

"GREAT! Now I can't have any fun."

"Don't worry, if they start harassing you too much, I'll file a complaint."

"I'm sure lucky to have you," smiles John as he kisses her. "C'mon, let's go out in the back yard."

The two of them sit in lawn chairs across from each other sipping wine and beer as John tends to the steaks. Jeanie slips off her sandals and rubs her foot up and down the inside of John's thigh, inching dangerously close to his crotch. After about the fifth stroke, John feels himself getting aroused, so he takes her foot and holds it up to his lips. With the other hand, he takes the marinating brush and dips it in the barbeque sauce and brushes it on her ankle. Jeanie squeals as he slowly licks it off.

"Better than a T-bone," he grins.

"Now it's my turn," she says as she stands and straddles him.

She dips two fingers in the sauce and spreads it across his lips. As she licks and sucks the sauce from his lips, he cups the cheeks of her butt in his hands and squeezes them like melons. She moves her waist back and forth, rubbing herself against his lap and he becomes fully aroused. John opens one eye and notices a lot of smoke coming from the barbeque.

"Shit! The steaks!"

Jeanie dismounts, laughing as John quickly tends to the steaks.

"Looks like someone's happy to see me," smiles Jeanie as she nods to his manhood bulging under his shorts. John blushes and adjusts himself.

"You need to keep your distance, or we're going to have burnt steak for dinner."

"Oohh, party pooper," smiles Jeanie.

She reluctantly grants his wish and the steaks turn out perfect. They sit down to eat about seven o'clock. John lights two candles on the table and pours each of them a glass of Merlot. Jeanie comments on the fine meal as she resumes her foot games under the table. They finish eating about eight o'clock and move to the living room with their wine. John closes the curtains and thumbs through the CDs for some mood music. He decides to put in Kenny G's Breathless CD, track two,

Forever in Love. As the music starts, he walks over to Jeanie and holds out his hand.

"May I have this dance my lady?"

"Why certainly kind sir," she replies.

She rises and puts her arms around his neck, her feet barely touching the floor. John moves his hands around her waist and stares into her eyes. The moment he's dreamed of has finally arrived, alone, with Jeanie in his house. Her body is soft and hot as he holds it tight against his. They dance slowly in tight circles as they exchange kisses. Jeanie straddles John's right thigh and rubs up and down as they dance. After the song is over and the next one starts, John bends at the waist and slips one arm under her knees, picking her up. They're eyes meet and no words need be spoken. They both know what they want as he carries her to the bedroom. He gently places her on the bed and hovers over her, kissing her neck. His lips move up and down her delicate neck as she squirms under him. Her breath becomes hot and fast and her entire body displays goose bumps as she spreads her legs to allow him to lie on top of her. Slowly, his lips move south to the waiting, supple breasts. John gently removes her top as she clutches at his shirt, pulling it over his head. She shakes as his chin moves down her cleavage as his long raven hair tickles her. His hand moves up her back and finds the hook of her bra. As he releases it, it snaps open like a rubber band under the pressure of her swelled breasts. She pulls the bra over her arms and feels his tongue on her nipples. Left to right, he caresses her nipples with his tongue as she moans and gasps.

"Oh Johnny," whispers Jeanie, "I've dreamed of this moment."

"Me too baby. You don't know how many times."

John moves up to find her lips, wet and searching for him. As he kisses her, his tongue explores the inside of her mouth as his hand works the snap of her cut offs. Once the snap is undone and the zipper is down, he glides his hand inside to find her patch, wet and waiting for him. Gently, he searches for the hot spot and rotates his fingers around and around, making her hips lunge up at him.

"Oh Johnny, I want you! I want you now!" gasps Jeanie as she reaches for his crotch to find his manhood, fully erect and ready for her.

John gradually moves his tongue south as he pulls her shorts and panties down over her feet. His tongue finds her patch and she squeals with ecstasy as he works it up and down, side to side. After a few moments, she lifts her hips, pushing her vagina into his face while clutching the sheets.

"Oh Johnny," she yells as an orgasm consumes her body and causes her to shake uncontrollably.

Just then, John begins to work his way north, peeling off his shorts on the way. Gently, he kisses her navel and continues his way north as her body lunges underneath him. He pauses briefly at her breasts to taste her nipples one more time before finding her lips. As he presses his lips against hers, he reaches down to guide his manhood to its destination. Gently, he moves its head up and down her vagina till he finds the door. After the head is securely in place, he moves his hand under her butt and begins rotating his hips until he's halfway in. Jeanie gasps and opens her mouth fully as his tongue reaches in. All at once, he pushes his manhood all the way in until it bottoms out. Then he pulls it back and plunges it forward again.

"Oh Jeanie," he gasps as he thrusts his manhood in and out of her until he explodes his load in her as she shakes from her second orgasm.

They kiss passionately and embrace each other like there is no tomorrow as their breathing returns to normal. John rolls over on his back and Jeanie clings to him, their bodies dripping with sweat. As they lay on the bed, neither one speaks, but both are smiling with a feeling that overwhelms them...a feeling that can only be described as love.

CHAPTER 44

———— ∞∞ ————

"You asleep?" whispers John.

"No, just dozing," replies Jeanie.

"I can't believe you're actually here in my arms. So many nights I dreamed of holding you. I think I squeezed the stuffing out of my pillow."

Jeanie slides her leg all the way over John and lays on top of him with her hands and chin resting on his chest. She twirls his chest hair around her fingers as she gazes into his eyes and smiles sweetly.

"I must admit I had a few hot dreams of you too. Especially when I filmed you doing tai chi. That night I dreamed we were doing tai chi in a grassy field, and you took me in your arms and made love to me right there. Then, I remember we were suddenly in a park with people walking all around us, but nobody knew we were there. It's like we were invisible. Then I woke up. That sucked."

"I think I know just the field," says John as he pulls Jeanie up to kiss her.

They laid there and exchange kisses while Jeanie moved her body up and down, back and forth. She reaches down to find John's manhood, and softly strokes it. Soon, it becomes hard and he kisses her more passionately as she holds his manhood under her, and moves her hips into position to accept it. Slowly, she works it inside her and sighs with pleasure as she lifts her body and sits straight up, moving her hips in a circle. John moans as his hands explore her nipples. Jeanie rides him like a mighty steed, her breaths coming faster and faster. John sits up and holds her hot, sweaty body close to his and kisses every square inch of her face, then he softly bites her neck. Jeanie squeaks as she runs her hands through his long black hair. She feels him swell up even bigger inside her and knows the time is near. She moves her hips faster and faster, and John explodes his load deep inside her as she shakes in ecstasy, she too experiencing an orgasm. After sitting there exchanging kisses for a while, they laid on the bed, holding tight as though a strong force might come along and try to separate them. No words are spoken as they drift off to sleep.

"DAAAAAAAAD...HEEEEEELP! I can't move! DAAAAAD please! I'm stuck and it hurts!"

"I'm coming Brett! Hang on buddy!"

John tries to move, but it seems like gravity is holding him down. It feels like he weighs a thousand pounds.

No matter how hard he tries, all he can do is watch Brett's despairing face calling for him from the twisted pile of metal he used to call Ol' Green. He can hear Ryan's crying as thousands of flies buzz around him. He looks to his left to see Bufford's carcass about ten feet away, bloated and covered in flies as well. He looks back at Ol' Green and sees the skeleton of a young boys arm waving at him as the earth folds around him.

"NOOOOOOOOOOOOOOOO!!!"

"Johnny wake up!" cries Jeanie as she shakes her lover until his eyes open. "Johnny, it's me! It's ok!"

John's eye snap open with fear written all over them, his chest heaving and body drenched from sweat. It's three am.

"You were having a nightmare baby," whispers Jeanie, "what were you dreaming about?"

"Oh man! It was horrible, worse than before, and grosser."

"The accident?"

"Ya, but this time it was different...scarier."

John gets up and sits on the edge of the bed as he reaches for his shorts. After finding them and pulling them up in place, he walks over to the window to peer out into the back yard where more enjoyable times were had. Jeanie pulls a sheet around her and joins him.

"You know, I know someone who can help you with your nightmares. His name is Dr. Youngman. He helped me a lot when I lost Calvin and Brittany.

His office is on the west side, in his home. I think you should talk to him."

"Oh, I'll be alright. It just takes time. I don't need no shrink poking around in my head."

"That's what I thought at first too sweetie, but the dreams just got worse to the point where I was afraid to go to sleep. Then I lost my appetite and became borderline anorexic. Jack was ready to fire me because all I did at work was sleep with my head on my desk."

"Don't worry baby. If it gets worse, I'll go see your friend. But I think I just need a little more time. After all, I've only been out for three days."

"Promise?"

"I promise," says John as he holds her close to his side and kisses her gently on the lips.

The two of them stare together out the window at the moist grass gleaming in the moonlight until Jeanie breaks the silence.

"Did I tell about how Ian Stewart decided to testify?"

"No."

"It was really weird. He was hiking on the same trail where he was a year ago, taking videos when he noticed two teenage boys sitting by the side of the trail. He walked up and started talking to them, and somehow they got on the conversation of the accident."

"Really?"

"Ya. Ian told them that he had a video of it, so the boys said that he should take it to the police, because the man in the camper was arrested for causing it, and his trial was coming up."

"Two teenage boys huh?" says John as stares out the window.

"Ya. And here's the weird part. He said he thanked the boys and assured them he would do just that, and said goodbye as they walked down the trail the same way he had just come, but after just a few steps, he turned around to ask them they're names, and they were gone!"

"Gone?"

"Ya, disappeared! Ian said he only took three steps and they just vanished. He said he looked up and down the hill and even called for them, but it's like they just vanished into thin air. Weird, huh?"

John's face suddenly turns white, his forehead clammy.

"Did he say what they looked like?"

"No, but he did say they had a nice looking yellow lab with them, kinda like the one you had. But when he turned around, even the dog was gone."

John stares blankly out the window at Bufford's dog-house and holds Jeanie close to his side as he begins to shake.

"Baby you're shaking. Let's go back to bed."

"Ok," whispers John and they both laid on the bed as Jeanie tucks the blanked around them.

"Goodnight sweetie," she says.

"Goodnight," says John as he laid on his back and stared at the ceiling, his head pounding and his ears ringing.

Jeanie drifts off to sleep and softly snores, her breath caressing the hair on John's chest. No sleep is enjoyed by him as the faces and voices of his sons haunt him through the night. Thoughts of the accident intertwine with thoughts of camping trips of past, Bufford's tail wagging as Ryan hugs him. He finally drifts off to sleep about five-thirty, just as the sun began to peek through the window. Jeanie wakes up about six-thirty and sees her sweet lover sleeping peacefully, and decides not to wake him. Instead, she gently kisses him on the cheek and carefully lifts his arm over her and lays it across his chest while she slips out of bed. Quietly, she puts on her clothes and walks to the kitchen to leave him a note before she goes home to get ready for work. It read...

'Good morning baby! Xoxoxoxo. You were sleeping and I didn't want to wake you. Call me when you get up. I should be at work by eight. I was thinking we could have dinner at my house tonight and rent some movies. Do you like lasagna? Hope so. Talk to you soon sweetie. Love, Jeanie. P.S. Last night was incredible!'

CHAPTER 45

—◦◦◦◦◦—

"Mornin Jack," announces Jeanie as she bounces through the office.

"Boy, you're in a good mood. Good night last night?" inquires Jack.

"Oh, nothing special," blushes Jeanie. "Just had dinner at John's, that's all."

"That's all?" smiles Jack.

"Well, we would have had breakfast too, but he was still sleeping."

Jeanie is really blushing now as she moves to her office. Jack and everyone else in the office applaud and whistle as she closes her door and picks up the phone. John's phone rings four times, then the answering machine picks up. It's still early, so she decides not to leave a message, as he's probably still asleep. Work is piled up on her desk and waiting for her, so, reluctantly, she takes on the task of sorting through it, her whole face smiling with the memories of last night.

John finally rolls out of bed about ten am, his head pounding. He stumbles into the kitchen, right past Jeanie's note on the table, and steps through the slider and into the back yard. As he sits on the edge of the redwood deck holding his head in his hands, he can't help but notice a small green arm protruding from the dirt, surrounded by grass. He stares at it for a few moments before reaching down to see what it is.

'Ryan,' he thinks and smiles as he holds the dismemberer Ninja Turtle in his hand.

Memories of Halloweens past fill his mind. Brett was Leonardo and Ryan was Michelangelo as they went from house to house chanting 'Trick or Treat.' John decides to look for more body parts, and crawls through the grass on his hands and knees, when the phone rings. He lets the machine answer it because he's on a mission.

"Johnny if you're there, pick up," say's Jeanie, "are you up yet baby?"

After a pause, Jeanie hangs up the phone and stares sadly at it sitting on her desk. It's nearly ten-thirty, he must be up by now. Maybe he's in the shower.

"Jeanie?" blares the intercom.

"Yes Jack?"

"Don't forget, we have lunch today with that reporter."

'Shit!' thinks Jeanie, 'I forgot.'

"Ok Jack, I'll be ready."

She was just thinking about running by John's house on her lunch hour, looks like that's out. What is he doing?

John searches through the grass for an hour, finding no more body parts. Once he's satisfied the Turtle's arm is the only one to be found, he takes it to Ryan's room. He stands in front of his closed door for a few moments before opening it. The hinges squeak as it opens. The smell of dirty laundry stings his nose as he stands and surveys the room.

Sitting on his bed is his bike helmet. He'd forgotten to pack it. John sits on the floor in the middle of the room and quietly looks around. Pressure begins to build up in his head, so he lies down, hoping that will relieve it. In the corner, under the bed, he spy's the Vikings coffee cup he thought he'd lost. It's eleven forty-five. The phone rings again and again, but he doesn't answer it.

"Johnny? Honey, are you there? If you are, please pick up baby. I need to talk to you. Well, anyway, call me at work, ok? Did you get my note? Call me and let me know if that sounds like a plan or not. I miss you baby. Call me. Bye, bye."

John lies on the floor for a few more minutes before getting up to go to Brett's room. When he opens the door, a feeling of overwhelming anxiety hits him, and he drops to his knees. He looks up at the picture of Jesus on the wall above Brett's bed and remembers the day he received it from Grandma McDuffy. It was Easter Sunday, 1990. Kathleen bought one for Brett's room, one for Ryan's room, and one for John to hang wherever he wanted.

"Now you can always feel safe, knowing He's watching over you," she told them.

John remembers the pride they took in hanging the pictures up as Kathleen supervised. Brett and Ryan's laughter fills the room, and his head begins to spin. He can almost feel Bufford tugging on his pant leg as he lies down on the floor. As he stares up at the ceiling, the room spins around him and his breathing quickens.

'What is wrong with me,' he thinks.

"Did you know about the secret witness Miss Philips?" asks the reporter from the local news channel.

"No, he didn't come forward until the trial was already in process," answers Jeanie.

Even though she's being interviewed for the TV news, her mind is not there. She can't wait to get back to the office and call John again. He must be up by now.

John gets up and moves to the kitchen to find something to drink. In the refrigerator, he sees an open twelve-pack of beer. After a few moments, he takes one and opens it. The bitter taste makes him shutter, but he forces it down anyway. Maybe it will make the ringing in his ears go away. Sitting at the table, drinking beer, and staring at the pocket knife in his hand that he had given Brett a couple of years ago to take camping, he jumps when the phone rings again, it's one-fifteen.

"Johnny, it's me. Are you there? Baby, where are you? Please, call me at work. I need to know you're ok."

After a few beers, John decides to go check on Chelly. The beer didn't help the ringing in his ears at all, in fact, it's worse now. He opens the driver's door and sits inside. A CD of hits from the seventies is sitting on the seat next to him. He pushes it into the slot and turns the key to accessory. American Pie is the first tune. The ringing in his ears stops as he remembers driving up to the mountains with the boys to go skiing and listening to American Pie as they all sang along.

'They loved that song,' he thinks as a tear rolls down his face.

Suddenly, it's clear what he must do!

Running into the house, he stops briefly to look at the note on the table, but doesn't bother to read it. After throwing on some pants and a shirt, he grabs the rest of the beer from the refrigerator and lays it on the floorboard in front of the passenger seat. After opening the garage door, he turns the key and fires up the 454. He doesn't wait for Chelly to warm up. He lays rubber as he backs out the door and onto the street. He doesn't even acknowledge Bob Johnson watering his lawn and waving at him. He just steps on the gas and burns rubber for a half a block as if he's late for an appointment.

Four o'clock. Jeanie can't stand it any longer. She's left six messages for John, and still no word. She grabs her purse and briefcase, and informs Jack she's leaving early. Jack bids her good afternoon, and she drives over to John's house to find the garage door wide open. Looking around inside, she sees the note, un-touched. As she surveys the rest of the house, she notices the empty beer cans.

'Why is he drinking so early?' she thinks.

As she backs her car out of the driveway to leave, Bob Johnson exits his house and waves her down.

"Hi," he says, "is Johnny ok?"

"I think so, why do you ask?"

"Well, I was just wondering, because he took off out of here about three o'clock like a bat out of hell. I waved at him, but he looked like he was in a big hurry to get somewhere."

"That's odd. I wonder where he was going?"

"I don't know, but he was sure in a hurry."

"Well, I'm sure everything is alright, I'll let you know if I find out anything Bob."

"Thanks, you do that. I worry about him you know."

"I know Bob, I'll be in touch."

Jeanie drives away wondering what has become of her lover. Did he get called in to work suddenly? Why didn't he call her? Is he mad at her? She decides her worries are all in vain, and stops at the grocery store to get supplies for dinner anyway. After stopping at the video store to rent a couple of movies, she enters her house to see her answering machine flashing. She drops the bags and rushes to it and pushes play.

"Hi honey, it's mom. Give me a call when you get home, ok? Bye, bye."

No more messages. Sadness overcomes her as she puts the groceries away.

"Born to be Wiiild!" sings John as he flies up Highway 200 at about 110 mph.

Chelly is running good, and the stereo is blasting out Steppenwolf. There are two beers left from the twelve pack, and John opens one of them up and takes a gulp as Chelly's tires squeal around a curve. Rogers Pass is about 20 miles ahead.

Jeanie looks at the clock. Six o'clock. She picks up the phone and dials John, just to get his machine again. This time she doesn't leave a message. The lasagna is in the oven and will be done in a few minutes. She puts down the phone and stares out the window.

'Where is he?' she thinks.

John slowly pulls over to the edge of the road where his life ended a year ago. After turning off the engine, he steps out and looks down the cliff. Memories bombard his mind as the ringing in his ears resumes. Voices call to him as he sits by the edge of the road. At approximately seven pm, a silence surrounds him. The wind dies and the ringing in his ears stops. It's almost like a huge weight is lifted from his shoulders. Suddenly, he feels like everything is clear. After staring up at the sky for a while, he gets back into Chelly and fires her up.

The table is set, and the candles are lit. Jeanie has her favorite top on, her breasts bare underneath it. Her jeans are pressed and tight. Soft music is playing as she sits at the table and softly weeps. She decides to pick up the phone and try calling her lover again. After four rings, the machine picks up, 'Hi, this is John, leave your number and I'll call you back. Thanks, bye.'

"John, where are you?" Jeanie sniffles. "Call me, please!"

She hangs up the phone and glances at the calendar on the vanity. Friday, September 1st, 2000. Her heart begins to pound and her hands shake as she can't take her eyes off the calendar. Pain fills her chest as a vice clamps around her heart, crushing it in its jaws. A flood of tears the size of pearls drip from her eyes as she realizes… John isn't coming to dinner.

John reaches the top of Rogers Pass and slams the brakes on and drops Chelly into second and hits the gas, spinning her around to face the other direction. He sits and looks at the steep canyon below as he laughs and cries at the same time. There's one more beer left, so he cracks it open and cranks the stereo up as loud as it will go, engine still running. Drivers gaze at him as they seem to pass by in slow motion. John stares at the canyon, laughing and crying uncontrollably while drinking his beer, engine still running.

CHAPTER 46

———⚬⚬⚬⚬———

A STEADY FLOW OF BLACK smoke reaches for the sky from the canyon bottom as John sits and watches. It's a beautiful evening. The sun is slowly saying goodnight from behind the Rocky Mountains and a cool breeze is making itself known, cooling the rocks where John is sitting. The breeze becomes stronger. He can hear the grass moving and the distant sound of sirens. Suddenly, a hand touches his shoulder.

"Hey dad," says Brett as he takes a seat next to John.

"Hey dude!" says John, putting his arm around Brett.

The two sit and watch the smoke, saying nothing for a while. Then Brett speaks up.

"Chelly?"

"Yep."

"Bummer, I loved that car."

"So did I bud. But, she's only a car."

They sit quietly while each remembers the good times they had with Chelly. Then it's John's turn to break the silence.

"Where's your brother?"

A voice from behind him calls, "Right here."

John puts his other arm around Ryan as he sits next to him. The three sit and stare at the canyon.

"Chelly?" asks Ryan.

"Yep," answers John.

"That sucks. She was a nice car."

"Oh well," replies John, pulling the boys close to him.

Sadness dominates the air until John feels an obnoxious licking of his ear.

"Shithead!" he shouts as Bufford jumps all over him, tail wagging.

The boys laugh as they watch Bufford lick John's face, whining and swinging his hips back and forth to keep up with his tail. John leans back, laughing, trying to get away from the savage tongue. Pretty soon, he calms down after John's face is thoroughly washed and curls up in his lap for a long overdue scratching behind the ears.

The sirens move in closer and the sun dips farther behind the mountains. The land is cooled off nicely as the moment couldn't be more perfect. John, with his arms around his boys and his faithful Lab in his lap, looks off into space in the direction of the canyon, and contemplates his life. He thinks about Jeanie. A lump grows in his throat and almost blocks his breathing. His eyes start to water. Suddenly, a voice breaks the silence.

"Dad?" asks Brett.

"Ya, Bud?"

"Can we go camping now?"

The lump subsides and his eyes clear up. The smell of pine burning touches his nose, and for a moment, he hears the sound of chopping wood, children's laughter, and splashing water. Camping! What a wonderful idea. He places his hands on the boys' shoulders and leans on them, using them to push himself up.

As he stands, he replies, "I s'pose." Brett and Ryan shout, "YES!" and Bufford jumps up and down as John finishes his statement, "BUT!" he says seriously, looking down at the boys.

They look up at him, holding their breath, waiting for him to say something.

Finally, he speaks, "Ya gotta catch me first," he says smiling as he cuffs each of them gently on the side of the head, then bolts to the side and takes off running across the grassy field, laughing like a madman.

Brett yells, "GET HIM!" and he, Ryan, and Bufford begin the chase.

"I got the top!" yells Brett as he and Ryan close the ground between them quickly, with Bufford already there.

"I got the bottom!" shouts Ryan.

With Brett on his back and Ryan and Bufford tying up his legs, John does his best to imitate Goliath, roaring and stomping as the young Davids pull him to the ground with the help of their trusty pet lion. First, one kneels, then another falls to the ground, and the mighty John McDuffy is soon overcome. The three laugh and poke and tickle as they roll around in the tall grass, Bufford growling as he tries to dominate the enemy pant leg. The wrestling goes on for about fifteen minutes until John finally concedes and they lie on their backs in the grass, panting and smiling while looking up at the stars beginning to show themselves against the turquoise sky.

John holds his boys to his chest and bear hugs them, whispering, "I love you guys."

"I love you too, dad," they each reply.

"C'mon," announces John as he tries to stand, "we're burning daylight."

They all rise to their feet and walk arm in arm toward the waiting tree line. The increasing wind and the sound of their feet shuffling through the grass dominates the air with the occasional cry of a bald eagle circling above. John is reunited with his boys, and Brett and Ryan have their Dad back. They have finally made it to 'The Last Campout.'

As they close in on the trees, Brett speaks, "Dad?"

"Ya, Bud?"

"Can we go see Grandma Sunday?"

"Sure."

"Will Grandpa and Uncle Pat be there?" asks Ryan.

"Everyone will be there," answers John, pulling Ryan close to him.

"Cool!" shouts Ryan as he reaches around his dad to give Brett a high five.

"Dad?" asks Brett.

"Ya, Bud?"

"Can we build a lean-to to sleep in tonight?"

"I don't care," answers John.

"No!" objects Ryan. "I wanna sleep in the camper Brett! After all, dad put a lot of work into it so we wouldn't have to sleep outside."

"So!" argues Brett. "It's not going to rain. You never want to do anything I want to do!"

"Bull crap! You're the one that never wants to do anything I want to do!" replies Ryan.

"Do you guys ever agree on anything?" interrupts John.

"Ya," smiles Brett, looking up at his dad.

"What?" inquires John.

Brett grins and winks at Ryan as he answers John, "We agree that you're a big dough head!"

And the chase is on!

The End

Is it the end, or is it the beginning…
For as one door closes, and I open another…
Some dreams are left behind…
As new ones are yet to discover.

I tried to be true to 'The Word…'
I tried to endure the pain…
But the heartache became too great…
When I heard the angels calling my name.

Be still my angels…
Please don't cry…
I will be with you soon…
At the last campout in the sky.

I've always been a fighter…
I didn't know how to quit…
When life's Bronc bucked me off…
I simply got back on it.

But when life took away…
Everything I loved…
And every reason for living…
What's a man to do?
But look for a new beginning.

Be still my angels…
Please don't cry…
I will be with you soon…
At the last campout in the sky.

I hope that when I reach…
My final destination…
My Father will forgive me…
For my last act of desperation.

For without my loved ones…
There is no point in living…
I would rather spend eternity with them…
Fishing, and hunting, and camping.

Be still my angles…
Please don't cry…
I'll be with you soon…
At the last campout in the sky.